Fergal s                                   ard, head
down, sho                                  chievous,
the wind pulled a long strand of hair free from her ponytail. It
blew behind her like a pennant, catching the faint rays of the
sun and reflecting auburn lights. He was struck, as on previous
occasions, by the air of fragility about her.

Fergal turned back towards the stables, his mind still occupied
     thoughts of Anya. He remembered her arrival at Lismore
sev     years before, Sister Martha playing the role of Mother Hen,
       g her chick before her and casting a warning eye in his
     on. She needn't have worried for Macdara had already made
     plain that Anya was out of bounds.

    u're to think of her like a sister,' he instructed. 'That girl has
    hrough more in her short life than you could dream of. What
    eds now is a family, people she can depend on. Do you read
    ergal?'

One of six children, Tara Moore was born in Kildare, Ireland, but spent her formative years in the Middle East. Tara always harboured a passion for writing but that was initially eclipsed by her passion for music, dancing and unsuitable boyfriends. She now lives in the beautiful town of Ramsgate with her husband and two sons.

*By Tara Moore*

RSVP
Blue-Eyed Girl

# *Blue-Eyed Girl*

## TARA MOORE

An Orion paperback

First published in Great Britain in 2012
by Orion
This paperback edition published in 2013
by Orion Books Ltd,
Orion House, 5 Upper St Martin's Lane,
London WC2H 9EA

An Hachette UK company

1 3 5 7 9 10 8 6 4 2

A CIP catalogue record for this book
is available from the British Library.

ISBN 978-1-4091-0278-6

Typeset by Input Data Services Ltd, Bridgwater, Somerset

Printed and bound by CPI Group (UK) Ltd, Croydon, CRO 4YY

The Orion Publishing Group's policy is to use papers
that are natural, renewable and recyclable products and
made from wood grown in sustainable forests. The logging
and manufacturing processes are expected to conform to
the environmental regulations of the country of origin.

www.orionbooks.co.uk

*For, my husband, Dr David Moore. You raise me up!*

# *Acknowledgements*

I always dreamed of being a writer, but that dream would never have come true, were it not for the wonderful family and friends supporting me every step of the way. This is particularly true of *Blue-Eyed Girl*, during the writing of which my mother passed away.

David Moore, my husband – what can I say? 'You *are* me. I *am* you. Apart, we are nothing.' I stole that quote from Javier, but it says it all.

Kevin Moore, my brother-in-law, and possibly Number One fan, perennially interested, full of suggestions (of variable quality), always in good humour, even when I'm not which can be irritating. Love you, Kev!

My two sons, Tarek and Emmet – for whom I sacrificed my flat tummy and peace of mind, and whose little dramas help take me out of my own. Adore you both.

The Manning family – my father, Colonel Gerard Manning, sisters, Angela and Sharon, brothers, Niall and Mark. So glad you're on my team. Love you all. A special mention for my sister-in-law, Ann Manning, whose sense of humour is legendary and who never fails to leave me laughing.

Best friend, since God was in nappies – Susan Cummins. Can't imagine not having you in my life.

Ramsgate writers: Denise Bareham, Carol Salter and Eric C. Bartholomew, brainstorming buddies and purveyors of good conversation. And, their long-suffering other halves, Josef, Michael and Mary. Marry a writer and you marry three people: the person, their ego and their mind-blowing mood swings.

Professionals: Sara O'Keeffe, ex Orion, Kate Mills, Julia Silk, Laura Gerrard, all at Orion Publishers, and all of whom have had a hand in shaping *Blue-Eyed Girl*. To that list, I must add Jenny Parrott, freelance editor and gently guiding hand. Sincere thanks to all of you.

Thanks must also go to Diane Banks, my agent, and a true professional.

Not forgetting the lovely readers who buy my books, even in this less than buoyant economy. You are my motivation. Thank you.

Finally, I must mention two very special people who, though no longer here, are with me always in spirit, and always on my mind: My lovely mother, Emily Manning, and my brother, Gerard. I think of you both, and I smile. *Ar dheis Dé go raibh siad.*

# Prologue

The young woman grasped the telephone to her ear, long after speech had given way to the eerie hiss of white noise. In the mirror opposite, her face showed disbelief, before slowly relaxing into a blinding smile of gratitude. The fates had finally relented and thrown her a lifeline and, by God, she was going to grab hold of it and hang on for dear life.

A sudden explosion turned her head to the Sydney skyline outside and the New Year fireworks lighting up the magnificent Harbour Bridge below. Another night, another party. And now, at last, she felt like partying too.

Thoughtful, she went and stood on the balcony where the air was balmy and char-grilled, and the fabric of the sky was tie-dyed with white whorls of spent gunpowder. Snatches of conversation drifted up from the street, the words losing form on their ascent. A karaoke bar on the corner opposite thrust its doors open on 'Get the Party Started'. Horns blared. Tonight each sound seemed magnified, imbued with portent, resonating in her brain with utmost clarity. A firework climaxed in a burst of colour over the Opera House, lending it the wavering air of a Monet.

She went inside and returned with a bottle of champagne and a crystal glass, the better to mull over the get-out-of-prison card that had quite unexpectedly come her way. Prison! The idea was preposterous, given the luxury of her lifestyle. But luxury has its price, in this case her self-respect, her independence and her beautiful young body.

Yet such was her need for money, more money than she could ever hope to make dancing in a dingy nightclub, that she had readily succumbed to the monetary charms of a sugar daddy, choking back her disgust at his sour breath and covetous old-man fingers. Lately, though, his ardour had cooled. His visits to the penthouse apartment had grown less frequent, his charm less evident, his handouts fewer and far less generous. Her financier was obviously growing bored and it would be foolish not to suspect his sights were already firmly fixed on a newer, younger model. She shrugged and took a sip of the ice-cold champagne, savouring the zing of bubbles bursting on her tongue. Karma! She herself had usurped his former mistress without so much as a qualm as to what would become of the other woman. But now that the tables had turned, this evening's phone call seemed more fortuitous than ever.

She topped up her glass from the pretty green floral bottle. Perrier-Jouet! Might as well enjoy it whilst she could, as well as the spectacular antipodean view, for soon the view would be very different. Lusher. Greener. Wetter. So much wetter. And more than ten thousand miles away. Her eyes grew dreamy, almost as if she were looking inward to her new home nestled comfortably in its verdant surroundings. Picture-postcard perfect, all blemishes and eyesores carefully blended away and the dirty underbelly of reality concealed from view.

At this thought, the champagne went suddenly flat in her mouth, its sweetness tainted by the bitterness of bad memories. Sad memories. Memories that had helped shape her into the thing she had become. Yes, thing! Angry at this insight, she dashed the glass, still three-quarters full, against the wall, shattering it into a million crystal tears. Her lips curved in a non-smile. Tears were something she knew all about. Over the last seventeen years she had cried a river of them. No, an ocean!

High above, a spectacular roman candle collided with the firmament, releasing a piñata of shooting stars over the penthouse. She shivered suddenly, assailed by a long-repressed image from the past, a summer's night, sitting in the garden on her mother's lap. Above, a purple sky. Around, the heady scent of sweet peas, stocks and Mexican orange blossom.

'Look, darling, a shooting star. Make a wish. Quickly. Before it disappears.'

And she had made a wish, following her mother's pointing finger as she sketched the path of fire blazing across the sky. She had made a wish that nothing would change, just before everything did.

But now, Macdara's granddaughter was going home. Back to Ireland. Back to Lismore. Back to where it all went wrong.

*Estancia Del Fin Del Mundo – near Buenos Aires, Argentina*

Like a magician saving the best of his act for last, the sun prepared to exit the sky in a glorious finale of scarlet, orange and stippled gold. The tourists milling round the traditional barbecue at the 'Ranch at the End of the World', regarded it with great delight, as though the spectacle was part of the scheduled entertainment, and then gazed further enraptured at the two riders who appeared silhouetted on the brow of Colina De Diablos, almost as if they had been choreographed.

'*Gaucheros*,' they whispered excitedly, '*real* Argentinian cowboys.'

The taller of the two riders looked contemptuously upon the little group.

'*Parásitos!*' he snarled. 'Pigs! I didn't want to believe it was true, but how can I doubt the evidence of my own eyes? My father would turn in his grave if he knew how Rodriguez has turned his beloved ranch into a two-bit theme park.'

'It was his own doing,' Javier reminded him unnecessarily. 'One does not like to dishonour the dead, JC, but his bigotry did you a grave injustice. There is talk that your uncle's gambling debts grow heavier by the day.' He shrugged expressively.

'If this venture fails my ranch will be lost forever.' JC's brows drew together in a thunderous scowl. 'I know it! And, goddamn him, my uncle has no sense of family honour. He would sell it to the devil himself. But I swear, Javier, I will get it back. Whatever it takes, I will get it back. My father would have forgiven me. In time. Despite … despite …'

Anguished, his thoughts turned inevitably to that last bitter argument that had turned his life upside down, and deprived him of his birthright. The old man's final words resounded still in his head like echoes in an empty room. *'Get out of my sight, Juan Carlos. You are not fit to bear the proud and glorious name of Fernandez de Rosas. I am ashamed of you and you are dead to me. Do you hear? Dead!'*

And that was the image he carried with him still, his father's face that of a stranger contorted with disgust, his hands clenched, as if he would beat his only child to death.

'I dream of him still,' JC said softly. 'And in my dreams we are as before. I am his beloved son, and he is my hero. But enough!' Wheeling his horse about, he glanced back over his shoulder. 'There is nothing I can do for the moment, but return to live with my grandmother in Ireland. She, at least, has never deserted me.' His brow furrowed. 'You will come back with me, this time? To Castle Mac Tíre?'

Javier gave a slight nod. 'You have only to ask. This, you know.'

'And you know I was busy with other things. But now the Hell Fire Club is rebuilt and finally ready to throw its doors open.' JC grinned suddenly. 'Does it not frighten you to throw in your lot with the devil?'

Javier looked serious for a moment. 'Yes,' he said, then he grinned too. 'But I did that a long time ago.' Swinging his horse round, he gave a sudden whoop and spurred it to a gallop.

By the time the tourists looked again, breaking off from their feast of barbecued meats and ruby-red Malbec wine, the only evidence to show the riders had ever been there at all were the horseshoe motifs stencilled into the sand and a skirl of dust winking in the mandarin-coloured light of the ailing sun.

Back in his room, JC replaced the telephone on its rest. Lamplight illuminated the planes of his beautiful face, accentuating the sharp cheekbones, the aquiline nose, the determined, almost sculpted lips carved now into a triumphant smile. He had made the opening gambit. And now the first pawn was already moving inexorably into position.

# Chapter 1

Shocked, Anya Keating stared at her employer, then dropped her head into her hands. Dizzy, she tried to focus on the leafy pattern of the carpet, but it swam before her eyes, each colour bleeding into the next in an abstract haze of colours. The radiators were on full-blast, yet she felt freezing cold but was only dimly aware that her teeth were chattering like the wind-up sets sold in joke shops. Thoughts jumbled crazily in her head. Emotions spun out of control. Time seemed first to stop, and then to fragment into a thousand pieces.

'What?' she asked disbelievingly, her voice sounding odd even to herself. The feeling of disorientation grew, as though she had been lifted up and spun round and round in a vortex. 'You're not seriously asking me to marry you, Mac? This is … this is a joke, right?' A fat tear plopped down on the very ground she wished would open up and swallow her, even as the realisation dawned that this was not the reaction most people might have had to a proposal of marriage. And especially to a proposal of marriage from a man such as Macdara Fitzgerald. A man both decent *and* wealthy. Fairytale stuff, really, marrying the boss, were it not for the fact that he was seventy-four to her twenty-four, as well as on his way to going blind.

'Is it really so unbelievable?' Anxiously, Macdara regarded her from across his desk, loathing the desperation that had forced him down this route in the first place. 'Do you really find me so repulsive?'

Tears running down her face, Anya shook her head. 'No. No, of course not. It's just that I don't think of you in that way, Mac.' Her eyes rose in mute appeal to his face, then skittered away from the hurt in his own. 'It's not as if you've ever given me the slightest hint that you felt any more for me than ... well, you're my employer. And ... and friend, of course,' she added hastily. A father-figure too. That particular thought was left unsaid, but it hung between them nevertheless; formless, invisible, an accusation. A betrayal.

'I know,' Macdara flinched. 'And if things were different I would never have ... Oh God dammit!' Angry all of a sudden, he slammed the flat of his hand against the desk top, making Anya jump nervously. 'I'm sorry. I'm sorry,' his voice cracked. 'It's just that with my eyesight failing, I need you to be more than just my PA. I need you to be my eyes.' Christ, he loathed himself for even starting down this path of emotional blackmail, for putting her through the wringer like this. But now that he had, it was inconceivable not to give it his best shot. 'Please,' he pleaded. 'Don't dismiss the idea out of hand. Think about it. Put on your business head and really think about it. I've already outlived my three score and ten, and the clock's ticking. I'd leave you well-provided for, and chances are you'd still be young enough to marry again and start a family, if that's what you wanted.' His stomach turning at sinking so low, he ratcheted the thumb screws up a level, tugging at her soft heart. 'Seriously, Anya. I don't know what I'd do if I lost you. How would I manage? No one else knows me like you do. And we get on well, don't we? There's never been a cross word between us.'

Despairing, Anya begged him not to pursue the matter. 'Oh, please, Mac. Please don't say any more. I'll be here for you as long as you need me. I don't need to marry you to promise you that. We can go on just as before. Why does anything need to change?'

Macdara's face mirrored her despair, then crumpled in bitter resignation. 'Because everything is about to,' he told her softly. 'Don't you understand, Anya? Don't you realise? Everything is about to change.'

But the imminent changes were not of Anya's making. Neither were they her fault. And Macdara knew it was not right to expect her to sacrifice herself to him, to put her own youthful hopes and dreams on hold. It was not right to expect her to be the crutch he leaned on. 'I'm so sorry, my dear.' He dipped his head, capitulating suddenly. 'I mean it. I'm truly sorry for putting you in such a terrible position. I'm just a silly old fool. Please forgive me.' He gave a brave pretence at a smile. 'Tell you what, let's make-believe this morning never happened.'

Shaky, her heart breaking for him, Anya got up, walked round the desk and placed her lightly trembling hands on his shoulders. 'There's nothing to forgive, Mac. Really. And I meant what I said. I *will* be here for you, for as long as you need me.' Just as he had been there for her these past years.

He smiled up at her, though at some cost, and patted her hand. 'Thank you. You're very kind. Far kinder than I have any right to expect.' Clearing his throat, he tried manfully to inject a bit of normality into the situation. 'Now, run along why don't you, or you'll be late for lunch and Bridie will have my guts for garters. Tell her that I'll be along shortly.'

When the door clicked closed, gently but with finality, Macdara picked up a leather-framed photograph of his late wife from the desk and scrutinised it, tracing his fingertips over her pretty glass-encased features, as though the answer to all his problems might be written there. Nancy, the other half of himself, his childhood sweetheart. If only she were here with him now.

But Nancy was dead, killed through the careless actions of their own granddaughter. After all these years he should have had time to get used to it. But no, the pain still gripped him, picked him up and shook him till he wanted to scream and bang his head against the wall. Only his own death would erase the appalling memory of the woman who was his soulmate lying on a stretcher, burnt beyond all recognition.

A child, everyone said. Sinéad was just a child. She didn't know what she was doing. It was an accident. Accident or not, the end result was the same. Nancy was dead. And Macdara felt often that he might as well be too.

\*

Anya bypassed the kitchen and, risking Bridie's wrath, went straight to her room where, still in turmoil, she sat on the bed and cried as though her heart would break. Damn Macdara! Damn him to hell! She meant what she said. She would be there for him every step of the way. She would be his eyes, his hands, his guide-dog, whatever he needed. But his wife? Never! Her 'business head' didn't come into it. When she married, *if* she married, it would be for love, pure and simple. Love, the Holy Grail that had eluded her all her life. Snatching up a pillow, Anya punched it clear across the room. Despite what Macdara said, things would never be, *could* never be quite the same again. His proposal would always be between them, the elephant in the room, unacknowledged maybe, but there still large as life.

Anya's eyes wandered round her room, as if seeing it for the very first time, alighting on the homely possessions she had accumulated over the years, the small touches, that made her feel safe and rooted. Indeed just as Macdara had made her feel safe from the first day Sister Martha had escorted her to his door, with stern instructions to look after her little flower. And he had looked after her, carefully, as though she was a fragile flower, patiently nurturing her to full bloom. He'd imbued in her a sense of belonging, a sense of family, such as she had never experienced before. He took on, in effect, the role of a kindly father, the sort she'd dreamed of as a child.

Furious suddenly at the abrupt death of this fairytale, Anya batted her tears away. It seemed her happy ending was just an illusion. Like the long line of 'fathers' and 'uncles' preceding him, Macdara had begun to cast a long shadow. What was it about her, she wondered, that made men always want far more from her than she was prepared to give?

Miserable, Anya wandered over to the window overlooking the stable yard below. As usual, it was bustling with a mixture of people, horses and vehicles. The latest boarder, a magnificent mare owned by an Arab prince, was being unloaded from a horse transporter. Skittish after her long journey from Dubai, the horse shied and sidestepped, and Anya watched absently as Lismore's vet, Liam

O'Hanlon, expertly brought her under control, before leading her off to a holding stable. After a few days of acclimatisation, the mare would be allowed out to train with the other horses.

Although the yard appeared to be in a state of utter bedlam, the reality was that everyone and everything was in the right place and doing exactly whatever was required to keep Lismore running with military precision. Set in one thousand acres of prime Tipperary farmland, the estate was bracketed on one side by Slievenamon, the Mountain of the Women, and on the other by a densely packed pine forest. When Macdara had inherited the place forty years before it had been only moderately successful, barely ticking over. Now, it was renowned far and wide. 'Say it with Winners' was not just a clever slogan on the website. Lismore not only talked the talk, but walked it as well. Or, more accurately, galloped it.

Lismore House, like the rest of the estate, was similarly stunning, an excellent example of eighteenth-century Palladian architecture. It had been designed by the eminent Irish architect, Sir Edward Lovett Pearce, for one of the younger Ormond sons, who had managed to lose it in a game of cards to a Fitzgerald ancestor. And, as Macdara often boasted with a wink, it had been in the hands of the cannier Fitzgeralds ever since.

The front was dominated by a grand portico entrance with two splendid Doric columns, and semicircular arched windows, and the walls were heavily cloaked in Virginia creeper that turned the most glorious shade of carnelian in the autumn. Stately on the outside, dramatic on the inside with enormous high ceilings and intricate cornicing, it was still small enough to be a real family home. And Anya loved it.

A sudden flash drew her gaze to the lower slopes of the mountain where a string of horses were returning from the gallops. In their red and emerald fleece jackets, the Lismore stable lads and lasses struck a jaunty note against their surroundings, and the clip clop of the horses' hooves was audible, even through the glass of the bedroom window. For a split second, Anya forgot her distress in the enjoyment of watching them. She was totally unsurprised to see Cashel Queen prancing along in front; there was a diva who knew her own worth and rightly so considering how she had swept all before her at the Curragh racecourse recently, and prior to that at Fairyhouse in County Meath. Limerick Leader, a magnificent grey stallion, was next, followed in turn by Shandon Bell, Bandon Boy and Cavan Cate. It was a long-standing tradition at Lismore to name all the horses after Irish placenames.

The only exceptions to this were the horses at livery that came to be trained at Lismore, and VIP, an elderly black mare that had once belonged to Macdara's granddaughter, Orla. 'Because she was a very important person, Macdara used to kid her,' Bridie O'Regan, garrulous after one too many Babychams, had confided in Anya one Christmas. 'The most important person in the world. And, for sure, he genuinely worshipped that child. It broke his heart when his daughter took her girls away after the two of them had a big bust-up.'

'Over what?' Anya had asked.

Torn between loyalty to Macdara and the chance to indulge in a bit of gossip, Bridie looked slightly uncomfortable. But then the Babycham overcame her conscience. 'On the face of it,' she told Anya, 'over the state of Nessa's marriage, which was going down the pan. She wanted a divorce, but Mac wasn't having any of it. Catholics married for life, he said. There was no get-out clause. She went anyway, sneaked out like a thief in the night, taking the youngsters with her. He never clapped eyes on her again.'

'What? She never came back? Ever?' Wide-eyed, Anya had topped up Bridie's glass, as she held it out for a refill.

'Never set foot in the place again. Never called. Never wrote so much as a line. And she never will now either because she died of breast cancer in Australia several years ago. The ex husband phoned Mac to tell him, though he hadn't been aware of it himself before the Australian social services rang him. Anyway, he took the grand-kiddies back to Paris to live with him and his new French wife. By which time Nessa was long buried.'

'How old were they, do you know?'

'Fourteen, fifteen, something like that. Too young to be alone, anyway.'

'What were they like as children?'

Bridie gazed into the distance. 'Chalk and cheese, in one sense. Thick as thieves in another. Where one was, the other was never far behind.' She smiled. 'Orla was the extrovert, though, a real live-wire, who thought nothing of jumping on the biggest horse in the yard and careering round like a loony. There was a wildness about her, but also a sweetness and generosity. And it didn't hurt that she looked like an angel with a great cloud of gilt hair and eyes the same blue as cornflowers. But Sinéad—' Bridie paused and took a sip of her drink, 'she was Orla's opposite in almost every sense. Dark hair. Dark eyes. There was a bit of a side to her. She was difficult. Wilful. Always up to mischief. Macdara has always blamed her for setting the fire in the barn that killed her grandmother.' Bridie finished her drink and gazed into the bottom of the empty glass. 'And that, I suspect, is the *real* reason Nessa took off. After all, no mother wants to hear her child branded a murderer. And though Macdara didn't exactly use that terminology, he might just as well have.'

A pebble rattling against the window not only made Anya jump, but also recalled her to the present. Directly below Fergal Fitzgerald stood gazing up at her, flashing his trademark wide grin. He mimed the sign for tea, jerking his head towards the kitchen door directly below her bedroom window.

Anya sent him a weak smile, her heart suddenly racing, which was the effect he had on her and seemingly every other woman on the planet, irrelevant of age. Even the usually caustic Bridie waxed flirtatious in his presence. 'There in five,' Anya mouthed, holding her hand up palm out, before turning away to repair her tear-streaked face and slick on a bit of make-up. Not that he would notice if she came down with a sack over her head, for Fergal Fitzgerald was the embodiment of the black-haired, blue-eyed Irish hero, a man way above her punching weight. Tall, strong, gorgeous and fit, he ticked all the most-eligible bachelor boxes and was the fantasy and prey of every red-blooded huntress for miles around. But so far he had managed to evade capture. 'Too busy with Lismore,'

Macdara maintained with a certain amount of satisfaction. 'Those girls would have more luck if they'd long faces, buck teeth and were called Shergar.' But there had been someone once, Anya recalled. When first she'd come to Lismore, she'd seen her hanging on his arm, a striking raven-haired, model type, who seemed suddenly to fall off the radar.

Bridie's views accorded with Macdara's. 'More chance of taming a tiger,' she remarked more than once in Anya's hearing. 'There's some men that simply aren't the marrying type. Confirmed bachelors. Sadly, for the female population, I'm beginning to suspect Fergal is one of them.'

Since both Macdara and Bridie knew him far better than she, Anya was resigned to the fact that all she could ever hope for from Fergal was his friendship. And they were friends. Good friends, she liked to think. Nevertheless, she checked out her reflection one last time and imagined how different she would feel had the proposal of marriage come from Fergal, instead of from his grandfather.

Still in his office and still castigating himself, Macdara put down his wife's photograph and pushed his chair back. He rose to his feet and began to pace the room. Backwards and forwards. Backwards and forwards, his mind torturing him with images of Anya's tearful face. Selfish bastard! Imminent blindness or no, there was no excuse for importuning her like that. Not only was he more than twice her age, but this was very much in dereliction of his duties as a father-figure. Finding it difficult to breathe suddenly, Macdara struggled to open the top button of his shirt. He took a deep breath as the button popped. *In loco parentis.* Latin. *Retinitis pigmentosa.* Also Latin, and the grand name given to his eye condition.

With a sigh, Macdara paused by the rosewood credenza, one of Nancy's cherished pieces, and picked up a bottle of Jack Daniel's and a tumbler from the tray on top. He poured a couple of generous fingers. As a rule, he was not much given to drink but something was required now to take the edge off his shame. The bitter liquid burned the back of his throat and made him cough. Truly, he must have been mad to blot out the voice of reason and convince himself that it all made perfect sense. 'Put on your business head.' He squirmed at the memory. The crassness of trying to tempt her with money. As if she could be bought. Lovely, honest Anya, who, if she found a penny piece, would go in search of the owner.

Macdara smashed the glass back down on the tray. Lismore was his life-blood, his oxygen. He lived and breathed the stables. Nothing moved him like the sight of the horses; the smell of them, the feel of them, the raw power, the glory as they showed a clean pair of heels on the racecourse. Jesus, it might be wrong to say it, but if darkness was to be his fate, then he might as well be dead.

By the time Anya appeared, Fergal was already at the kitchen table, helping himself from the large brown teapot Bridie kept permanently on the hob.

'Gannets!' she frequently complained. 'That's what the lot of you are like. Mouths always open. Never satisfied.' Not that anyone paid attention, knowing full well that the housekeeper loved nothing better than to fuss and cluck round them like a mother hen.

'Ah, there you are, Anya,' Fergal smiled, taking another mug from the tray in the middle of the table and filling it for her. 'Sit down. Take the weight off your feet. Mac not joining us?'

'In a while, I think,' Anya stuttered, taking the chair he pulled out for her and feeling a blush creep up her face. 'I left him in his office.'

'Counting his money, I suppose.' She jumped as Liam came in behind her, his rubber wellingtons making little noise on the quarry tiled floor. The vet winked as Anya swung round, his eyes lingering on the soft swell of creamy bosom just visible over the sweetheart neckline of her cotton blouse. 'Well, aren't you looking gorgeous today, Anya, if a bit peaky around the eyes.'

Anya looked down and busied herself, adding both milk and sugar to her tea, though normally she drank it black. She always felt uncomfortable in the vet's presence, and yet she couldn't say why. It wasn't as if he was rude to her. If anything, he went overboard on the compliments. The stable girls thought he was gorgeous, a real Harrison Ford, with his thatch of thick, bleach-blond hair and deeply-tanned outdoorsy skin. Persistent rumours abounded that more than one had willingly succumbed to a roll in the hay, despite the wedding ring on his left hand. Anya suppressed a sigh of relief as he turned his attention to the teapot.

'I hope you've left some of that tea. Any sandwiches going, Fergal? Honest to God, my stomach thinks my throat's been cut. Bridie!' Liam yelled into the scullery where the housekeeper could be heard rattling pots and pans about. 'There's a man out here who'd kill for a slice or two of your famous soda bread.'

'How is Glengarriff?' Fergal said, tipping three heaped spoonfuls of sugar into his cup and adding a fourth for luck. 'I heard you were up with him half the night.'

Quarter of the night, certainly! The vet gave an inward smirk. The remaining three-quarters he had spent putting Kitty Brennan, one of Lismore's pretty stable lasses, through her paces. 'He'll live,' Liam answered Fergal's question. 'But he won't be bringing home prizes any time soon. That's a nasty sprain, no doubt about it.'

'Macdara will be disappointed.' Fergal stirred the liquid in his cup, slopping some over the edge. 'He had a mind to race him at Ascot in June.'

'No, it won't improve his mood any.' Liam took the seat beside Anya, spreading his legs wide. She edged away as his lips twitched. 'What the hell has got into him lately, anyway?' Liam addressed the question to her. 'Talk about a bear with a sore head. I only wish I had his troubles instead of my own.' He nodded out the window. 'Lord of all he surveys, but with a face like a permanent wet week.'

*He's going blind!* Anya wanted to snap. But whatever her confusion about Macdara and his excruciating proposal of marriage, she was unquestioningly loyal. And Macdara had chosen to conceal his condition from everyone else. Still, Liam was looking at her expectantly, so she mustered up a nonchalant shrug. 'I haven't noticed anything wrong.'

The vet gave a snort of laughter. 'Well, of course he's all right with *you.*'

Anya flushed at the pointed innuendo.

'You're out of order, O'Hanlon,' Fergal cut in, an edge to his voice.

Liam blew on his tea to cool it, whilst steadily regarding the younger man over the rim of his mug. 'Hit a raw nerve, have I, Fergal lad?'

A muscle pulsed in Fergal's cheek. He took a deep breath. With a contemptuous look at the other man, he picked up his mug, drained it in one gulp and strode quickly towards the door. He paused with his hand on the handle. 'Talk out of turn again and, make no mistake, I might make something of it.'

Anya hurried out too, her virtually non-existent appetite completely gone. A moment later, Bridie, a large tray of sandwiches in her hands, emerged from the scullery.

She looked round the near-empty kitchen, her glance lighting on Liam accusingly. 'Well, a nice how-do-you-do this is, I must say. Cooking and slaving morning, noon and night, and what thanks do I get? I might as well be working on board the *Marie Celeste*, so I might.'

'Ah, don't take on Bridie, me darlin'.' The vet winked and reached for a sandwich, sex with pretty Kitty having whetted his appetite in more ways than one. 'You know you're one in a million! Besides, there's all the more for me.' More was good, Liam reflected, as the housekeeper retreated back to her eyrie in the scullery, clattering and banging with renewed gusto. More money. More sex. More of all the good things in life. And if he played his cards right, he'd have more. Much more!

Anya went after Fergal, who was heading towards the stables. The sun was a pale yolk in the January sky and any heat it produced was promptly cancelled out by a stiff easterly breeze that raised goosebumps on her skin.

'Fergal!' she panted, her breath puffing cloudy rosettes in the air. 'Wait! I need to talk to you.'

At first he appeared not to hear her, but then he slowed and turned to face her, tension evident in the set of his shoulders and the obdurate line of his mouth.

'Yes, Anya, what is it?'

She caught up and placed a hand on his sleeve, then removed it just as quickly, suddenly at a loss. It had been her intention to tell him about Macdara's proposal, to share it with someone but, suddenly, Fergal did not seem like the right person.

Anya knew that Fergal was proud and very much his own man, hugely principled and independent. Like Macdara, Lismore was his life, and it had been since he was a child. His father, Bridie the fount of all knowledge had told Anya, was completely the opposite. At eighteen, Macdara's son Connor had shaken the dust off his feet and never looked back. It amazed him that Fergal would choose to spend all his free time and school holidays at Lismore, up to his neck in straw and horse shit. But Fergal and Macdara had always been practically joined at the hip, which some could have thought odd, considering that Fergal was Connor's adopted son and not a blood relative at all. But that made not one ounce of difference to Macdara, who could see how much Fergal shared his love of Lismore. As far as Macdara was concerned, Fergal was his grandson, and heir to Lismore. End of!

And yet it occurred to Anya, as she stood shivering in the January wind, that perhaps it did make a difference to Fergal that he was only an adopted heir. She decided to say nothing about Macdara's proposal. There was nothing to be gained by the disclosure, but she could lose his friendship if Fergal thought there was any suggestion that Macdara had been thinking of marrying her and producing a blood heir.

'Well?' Fergal prompted, slightly impatiently. Anya forced a smile. 'Oh, it's nothing. Nothing at all really. Just don't let Liam get to you. He's not worth the aggravation.' She headed back to the house, with a growing realisation that her lovely life at Lismore might not be as safe as she would like. And there wasn't a damn thing she could do about it.

Fergal stood and watched her slight figure cross the yard, head down, shoulders slightly hunched against the cold. Mischievous, the wind pulled a long strand of hair free from her ponytail. It blew behind her like a pennant, catching the faint rays of the sun and reflecting auburn lights. He was struck, as on previous occasions, by the air of fragility about her.

Fergal turned back towards the stables, his mind still occupied with thoughts of Anya. He remembered her arrival at Lismore several years before, Sister Martha playing the role of Mother Hen, ushering her chick before her and casting a warning eye in his direction. She needn't have worried for Macdara had already made it very plain that Anya was out of bounds.

'You're to think of her like a sister,' he instructed. 'That girl has been through more in her short life than you could dream of. What she needs now is a family, people she can depend on. Do you read me, Fergal?'

'Do I look like Don Juan?' Fergal recalled asking him drily, amused at Macdara's transition into guard dog. 'Besides, it may have escaped your notice, but I'm already seeing somebody.' He found it difficult to remember her name now. Miriam, he thought. He also thought she had dark hair and was tall, but he couldn't be sure after all this time.

Fergal reached the stables and paused in front of Glengarriff's stall. The horse put his head over the half-door and snorted a greeting. Fergal reached out and patted the side of his long neck, loving the silky feel of the animal beneath his hand. He didn't need to die to find out what Paradise was like, he thought passionately. Paradise was Lismore.

# Chapter 2

'Come on now, be a good girl and let me help you get dressed. Your sister will be along any minute. She'll go mad if she sees the state of you.'

'Get off me!' Weak hands reached out and pushed ineffectually at the nurse's uniform. There were track-marks running up the inside of the young woman's arms and her eyes were glassy from her most recent fix, the pupils constricted to the extent that they looked like two tiny but very deep black holes. 'Fuck my sister and fuck you too! Why can't everyone just sod off and leave me alone?'

The nurse gripped her firmly. 'You ungrateful little madam! If it wasn't for your sister you'd probably be lying dead right now in the corner of some filthy squat or other, like many another useless druggie! It's a credit to her how much she cares. A perfect angel is what she is.'

The young woman gave a laugh tinged with hysteria. 'Lucifer was an angel once,' she said.

## Castle Mac Tíre – Co. Tipperary, Ireland

Macdara slowly urged his horse up the gentle incline that led to Castle Mac Tíre, Castle of the Wolf, home for almost six hundred years to the Ormond family, a distant branch of the illustrious Butlers of Kilkenny. What had once been a fairly modest Norman castle was now, thanks to successive generations adding their own stamp, a sprawling fairytale structure of towers, turrets and arches, more suited to the Brothers Grimm and the Black Forest than the languorous landscape of County Tipperary.

'Easy, girl,' he whispered, reining in VIP who, disturbed by the whine of machinery working on the old church nearby, pranced restlessly to one side despite her advanced age. As she settled down beneath the soothing tones of her rider, Macdara drew her to a stand and let his eyes drink in the glory of it all, committing the memory against a time when he would no longer have the power of sight. Today, kissed by opalescent sunlight, all he saw looked particularly beautiful, while the woods, embracing the old church like a pair of protective arms, were every bit as lush as back in those halcyon days spent playing tag amongst the copper beeches and great horse chestnuts with his best friends, Kathleen Ormond and Nancy Devine. Or the Divine Nancy, as he had come to think of her when they grew up and fell in love. And it was in these same woods that he had first taken her in his arms and kissed her in the midst of the carpet of bluebells that seemed to blossom suddenly at their feet. The bluebells would flower again in April, but he would not go to see them. Some memories were best left frozen in time.

Macdara gathered up the reins and the horse walked towards the castle which, as they drew nearer, revealed many flaws unseen at a distance. The stark truth was that Castle Mac Tíre was crumbling away. Of the Ormonds, only his childhood friend Lady Kathleen, and her grandson JC, remained. And Macdara was in no doubt that upon Kathleen's death, JC would sell in a heartbeat without any thought for the castle's history. But despite numerous summer visits as a child, the boy had never made any secret of his determination to return to Buenos Aires soon and reclaim his ranch, a determination that Macdara admired against his own inclination. Why, after all, should JC not make his own history? It was sad, but hardly a tragedy. New brushes swept clean. And that's just how it was.

VIP made her way under the East Arch that led to the cobble-stoned courtyard and the stables where once there had been enough boxes for upwards of fifty horses. But that was in the days when the Ormonds were still wealthy landed gentry, who entertained on a lavish scale, riding to hounds, hunting, fishing and shooting with others of their class. But the star of the Ormonds had long since tipped off-kilter, and although they retained the castle and much of the land, their coffers were resoundingly empty. As with many a great Anglo-Irish family, the death knell had sounded and soon it would toll for the last time.

Macdara carefully dismounted – he did everything carefully these days – and tethered the horse to a hitching post in the yard.

'I won't be long,' he promised, patting the long nose gently, before covering the short distance to a flight of steps leading up to the back door. As he reached the top, it swung open and Liam came out. Startled, Macdara stepped back.

'Liam?' he said, surprised. 'What on earth brings you here? I thought you were back at Lismore with Glengarriff.'

Surprise flashed across Liam's face too, but he recovered quickly. 'Mac. Hello. I'm just on my way back there now. Don't worry, though, Fergal's been keeping an eye on things. Besides, Glengarriff, I'm pleased to say, is all but out of the woods.'

Behind him, JC nodded a greeting to Macdara and looked contrite. 'Oh, hi, Mac. Blame me. I asked Liam to pop in to take a look at Tango Lass. She was unwell during the night. I hope you don't mind.'

'Not at all,' Macdara said, immediately concerned for the young mare, the first foal out of Dublin Road and Cavan Cate, and for whom he predicted a great future. It had cost him a pang to part with her, but Kathleen had wanted to buy the horse for her grandson and, as one of his oldest and dearest friends, he could refuse her nothing. 'Nothing serious, I hope?'

'Just a touch of colic,' Liam informed him. 'We caught it in time.' He tapped the flat cap he'd been clutching against his leg. 'Anyway, I'd better be getting back. I'm giving the new mare a final check today before Fergal puts her in training. We'll be down at the north paddock, if you fancy taking a look.' Liam replaced his cap as Macdara stepped back to allow him past.

'I'll walk you to your car, Liam,' JC offered, following behind. He jerked his head towards the open doorway. 'You go on up, Mac, you know the way.'

'If I don't by now, I never will,' Macdara smiled, turning away diplomatically. He guessed that JC wanted to slip Liam a few bob without the embarrassment of his legitimate employer looking on. It wasn't that he minded Liam doing a bit of moonlighting, just so long as it didn't impinge on his duties at Lismore.

With a backward wave of his hand, he disappeared into the dim hallway beyond.

'Jesus Christ!' Liam wiped his brow. 'You should be paying me twice as much for that fucking heart attack.'

'We have a deal.' JC's voice cracked with sudden menace. 'Don't go playing games with me, my friend.'

'It was a joke, JC.' Quickly Liam lifted the rear door of the Land Rover and extracted a small box from beneath an old blanket covered in dog hairs. 'Here you go, a sample of the goods.'

JC snatched it from him, examined it briefly before stowing it away in the inside pocket of his jacket. 'And now, I am laughing,' he said, his white teeth flashing in his dark face. 'And you, Liam, will make sure that I keep on laughing, no? *Adiós*.'

Liam watched the younger man turn and walk abruptly away, his bearing regal, supremely sure of his privileged little place in the world. Fucking little dago! But it was too late for regrets. Liam knew he had shaken hands with the devil and, in doing so, inadvertently palmed away his soul.

Macdara stood for a moment letting his eyes grow accustomed to the murk, his vision still sharp enough to see that the decay so obvious on the outside was also reflected on the inside of Castle Mac Tíre. No longer majestic and grand, it couldn't even masquerade under the kindly epithet of shabby chic. Everywhere were the signs of ruin. The wonderful gilded cornicing, so much a feature of the stately rooms, was crumbling away and in places large pieces had actually broken off altogether, never to be replaced. The lofty ceilings were cracked, and in the great hall the *trompe l'oeil* created by the eminent eighteenth-century painter, Francis Bindon, was faded and peeling. The silk-covered walls had mushrooming patches of damp, and the Old Masters that had once hung upon them had long since been sold. As with all houses of its size, the castle was a money pit, a cavernous maw continually demanding sustenance. But now the cupboard was bare. Castle Mac Tíre, like the wolves after which it was called, was almost extinct.

Depressed by the thought, but determined to look cheerful for Kathleen's sake, Macdara made his way up along the sweeping oak staircase that led to her suite of rooms in the east wing. She liked the east wing, she'd told him once, because the sun always rises in the east, bringing renewed hope for a better day. Javier, the Castle Mac Tíre butler-cum-caretaker-cum-jack-of-all trades was emerging from her suite with a tea tray in his hands and an anxious expression on his face. His arrival in the area, Macdara recalled with amusement, had caused a great deal of excitement amongst the female population, who were thrilled to find such a handsome, exotic creature had landed in their midst. And handsome Javier undoubtedly was, with flashing dark eyes and hair worn just a little too long, and strong white teeth made whiter against the bronzed glow of his skin.

'Ah, Señor Fitzgerald!' The white teeth glimmered in a smile. 'How nice to see you. Lady Kathleen will be so pleased.'

'Hello, Javier.' Macdara glanced at the tray. 'Were you giving Lady Kathleen her lunch?'

'Just a little zoop,' Javier said in his heavily accented English, with a disappointed look at the still half-full bowl on the tray. 'My lady, she eat like a little bird. But please to go in. Today, she is feeling a little *doloroso*.' His mouth turned down in empathy. 'A little sad.'

And why wouldn't she be feeling sad, Macdara thought, hoisting a smile on his face before raising his hand to tap on the door. The poor woman's life read like a Shakespearean tragedy.

'Mac!' Kathleen's face brightened as he peered round the door. 'I was rather hoping you would pop by.' She gestured to a chair by her bed. 'Well, don't stand on ceremony. Come in, won't you?'

Striding over, Macdara leaned across and kissed her lightly on the forehead before sitting down.

'Javier said you didn't eat much. Bad day?'

Kathleen chuckled. 'I wasn't hungry. Javier fusses too much. He spoils me quite alarmingly, you know.' A dimple played in and out at the side of Kathleen's mouth, and Macdara was reminded what a very pretty woman she still was, despite the lines of pain etched into her forehead and the silvering of her once jet-black hair. Unlike many of her Hollywood peers, Kay had chosen not to go down the route of plastic surgery and nips and tucks. 'Because,' as she pointed out frequently, 'it is the job of an actor to show expression, and how can one express oneself without moving one's face?' Not that there was much chance of her ever acting again, as there had been an accident on set in which she had broken her back, thus putting paid to any likelihood of that.

'Enjoy it,' Macdara advised. 'He's a handsome lad. There's more than one round here envies you his attention.' He reached for his friend's hand and cradled it between his own. 'I'd give a lot to be as young and strong as that young man again. Whoever said old age is not for sissies knew what they were talking about.'

'Bette Davis.' Kathleen's eyes lit up, as they always did, when given the chance to talk about her glory days on the silver screen. 'I met her once or twice at various red-carpet functions. She really was rather formidable even as a little old lady, with those compelling hooded eyes and rather clipped way of speaking, though she was kind to me.' Kathleen gave a wry twist of her lips. 'And now I'm a little old lady myself, and I don't quite know at what point I crossed the line from simply mature, to old.' She held out a hand, scrutinised the freckled, vein-mapped skin as if she didn't quite believe it belonged to her. 'I used to have such beautiful hands, Mac. Once, when Liz was a bit squiffy at a premiere, I even got to try on the Burton-Taylor diamond. Oh, what a pretty bauble!' She gave a little deprecating shrug. 'Sorry, I really don't mean to name-drop. I find myself retreating more and more into the past these days. Life seemed so much kinder then. Or maybe distance has blurred the reality. Why is that, Mac? Why is the past always summer? Why were emotions more intense back then, love affairs more passionate?'

Macdara dropped a light kiss on the back of the hand he was holding. 'Simple. We were young and our hopes and dreams were all before us. Anyway, you're still beautiful. And seventy-four is hardly old these days. More like the new fifty, isn't that what they say?' He caught himself suddenly. He and Kathleen were of an age, and it was ancient as far as Anya was concerned.

'Dear Mac.' Kathleen brushed her fingers gently down his cheek. 'So gallant and such a dreadful liar. But don't worry as I don't spend all my time hankering after my lost youth. I'm just feeling a little low today. I don't sleep so well some nights. Never mind, I'll sleep long enough in the grave.' She shrugged, dismissing her own problems. 'Anyway, let's hear what's on your mind. I know you well enough to know that something is up.'

'Anya,' Macdara confessed at once and proceeded to tell her, somewhat haltingly, about his clumsy proposal. 'And from across the desk, what's more. Can you imagine it? Take a letter, Anya. Fix a meeting, Anya. Oh, and by the way, will you marry me, Anya? Pathetic! Needless to say, she turned me down flat. No, more than that, she looked horrified.' He gave a disparaging laugh. 'What possessed me, Kay? What made me think that a beautiful young slip of a girl like Anya would seriously consider hooking up with me?'

'Don't be so hard on yourself,' Kathleen told her old friend gently. 'Desperation makes us all do things we'd never normally even consider. There's no shame in that. It quite simply means you're human. And, okay, so it might have come as a bit of a shock to Anya, but it's not like you've done anything terribly wrong. You haven't held a gun to her head or committed a crime. Anya's a sensible girl. She'll understand when she has a chance to stand back a bit and consider matters. She thinks the world of you.'

Macdara looked hopelessly back at her. 'I hope you're right, Kay. I really hope you're right. Because, if I've driven her away, I'll never forgive myself. I'll be just as bad as everyone who let her down before. And she doesn't deserve that.'

'Nonsense!' Kathleen made her voice deliberately brusque. 'You've been like a father to that girl. Like her own flesh and blood. No one could have done more.'

Macdara's visit had, as usual, stirred up memories and Kathleen lay thinking for a long time after he left, letting her mind drift back through the years to when they were all as strong, vigorous and good-looking as Javier. The Three Musketeers – Macdara, Nancy and herself – one for all and all for one! Until, that is, Nancy and Macdara had grown up and fallen in love, and suddenly three was a crowd. Not that they had ever meant to exclude her; it was natural that they wanted to spend as much time as possible together. That's what courting couples did. The courting led to engagement and then marriage and Kathleen had been the happy, smiling, heartbroken chief bridesmaid. For Kathleen had been in love with Macdara for years. But neither he nor Nancy had ever known. And never would. The time for that, if ever there was a time, was long past. The hands of the clock moved inevitably forward. Wounds healed and scarred over, only aching a little now and then, when prodded by a careless finger. Besides, thought Kathleen, her own life hadn't turned out so bad. Opportunities had come her way that would never have arisen had she settled down with Macdara. Within a year of his marriage to Nancy, she met her first husband, a successful film producer, and moved with him to the States. At his suggestion, she took acting lessons and, two years on, obtained her first starring role.

The weak New Year light gave way as long dark shadows oozed over the ledge, slicked like oil across the floor. Suddenly weary, Lady Kathleen reached for the buzzer on her bedside table.

'Javier,' she requested, when the door opened a short time later, 'come sit by me and tell me of Argentina. My thoughts grow so gloomy, I am in need of some South American sunshine.'

His face lighting up, Javier strode over and plonked himself on the side of her bed, his hand taking possession of hers, stroking it gently.

'Oh no, my lady, please to tell me about Hollywood. I always wanted to be an actor. Like James Bond. Like Terminator.'

'Dear Javier,' Lady Kathleen smiled indulgently. 'You are as handsome as any actor. I can see you in the role of Casanova. Yes, definitely, Casanova.'

'I don't think so,' Javier shook his head rather definitely.

Lady Kathleen laughed. 'Okay, back to the drawing board.'

# *Chapter 3*

'So,' Sister Martha patted the seat beside her, 'sit down here beside me and tell me why it is you put me in mind of Atlas with the troubles of the world on his shoulders.'

With a tremulous smile, Anya sat, obedient as when she had been the nun's star pupil at school. Faltering, and with many pauses, the story of Macdara's proposal came out, her confusion and embarrassment, her attraction to Fergal, and the growing feeling that she might have to leave Lismore.

'Leave Lismore? Sure, why would you want to do that?' Sister Martha's eyebrows rose. 'Ah, don't be so impulsive, Anya. You're making mountains out of molehills. So, you received a proposal of marriage – *marriage*, mind you, nothing underhanded or immoral – from a perfectly nice, decent man? That's hardly a tragedy. And, okay, whilst he might be a bit long in the tooth to play the part of Romeo, there's more than one girl would give her eye-teeth for the chance to play Juliet.' The elderly nun grinned naughtily. 'Many a good tune played on an old fiddle, isn't that what they say? Hush!' She held up a hand as Anya's mouth opened indignantly. 'I think you were right, as it happens. Macdara deserves someone who will love him for himself and not for his bank balance. The man has enough on his plate without some gold-digger getting her claws into him.' She patted Anya on the knee. 'Not saying you're a gold digger, far from it! But there's some out there would marry a three-legged stool if it came with a fat wallet and a big house.' She beamed widely. 'You know, I'm so proud of you, Anya, and the lovely young woman you've turned into. You're honest and principled and, believe me, your prince will come along one day. Fergal's got the black charger, but whether he's the one remains to be seen. That's in the hands of the Good Lord.' She bent a little closer, conspiratorial. 'Now, for what it's worth, my advice would be to sit tight at Lismore. Act in haste, repent at leisure. This whole business with Macdara will blow over, although it might be a bit awkward between the pair of you for a day or two. Besides, the poor man was desperate.' She nodded at Anya's look of surprise. 'Oh, yes, I know all about his eye condition. He's frightened, God love him, and clutching at straws. And you're the obvious straw, Anya. Rightly or wrongly, he's come to depend on you so much. But there's too much affection on both sides to let this one hiccup ruin your relationship. He's a proud man, Macdara. It must have been torture for him building up the courage to speak out.'

She broke off as a young novice nun came in pushing a beautifully laid tea trolley. 'Thank you, Benedicta.' Sister Martha waited till she had left the room, then lifted the primary-coloured red and blue teapot and poured for them both.

Beginning to feel better, Anya helped herself to a biscuit and dunked it in her tea, despite Sister Martha wrinkling her nose disapprovingly.

'Ginger nuts – you must have known, I'd be calling.' Anya smiled gratefully at the nun who, since she had arrived in her class as a dirty, neglected, fearful ten-year-old, had stepped not only into the official role of teacher, but also the additional roles of saviour and substitute mother. Without Sister Martha's kindly intervention, her life could – *would* – have turned out so differently.

The moment she finished, Sister Martha pressed another biscuit on her, having 'no truck with that Size Zero thing, while people are going hungry around the world'. She topped up both their cups and they talked of incidentals for a while, although Anya gained the impression that Sister Martha was leading up to something more important. So, it didn't come as any surprise when she cleared her throat and leaned hesitantly forward.

'Now, I've got something to tell you, Anya, and I don't want you to be alarmed. Your mother has shown up again.'

'Clare? Clare's back?' Anya never called her 'mother', could never dignify the woman with so precious a title. Her cup almost fell from her suddenly nerveless fingers, her naturally pale complexion blanched to the point where the scattering of marmalade freckles across the bridge of her nose and upper cheekbones stood out like dots of paint.

Sister Martha nodded. 'I'm afraid so. Turned up large as life at the convent door last night.' *Reeking to high heaven of booze and sweat*, she might have added, but there was no point in piling on the agony. Anya already knew more than enough about her mother to be in any doubt of the whole picture.

'Dumped again, no doubt, and on the cadge?' Anya's mouth took on a bitter twist.

'Something like that all right,' Sister Martha agreed, unwilling to insult her intelligence by trying to put a gloss on things. Clare Keating had put her little daughter through hell. And, unlike some who could plead ignorance and poverty, she had no such excuse. Quite the opposite. She had been privileged, born with a silver spoon in her mouth, cherished from the outset by parents determined to give her the best of everything, including all the tools required to make her way in the world. But intent on pursuing a path of selfish depravity, she had turned her back on decency, and poor little Anya had been the collateral damage. A cat, Sister Martha often thought, would have made a better mother. 'Needless to say, she wants to see you.'

'Oh, does she now?' Anya's face contorted in a mixture of rage and fear. Her eyes took on the sheen of hard green glass, but there was a distinct tremble in her voice.

'It's all right,' Sister Martha said, her own voice soft with understanding. 'I staved her off.'

'Bought her off probably, you mean. How much did it cost this time?' Anya reached for her handbag, but Sister Martha caught her by the wrist.

'Please, Anya, don't insult me. Don't deny me the pleasure of helping out. You know I had an inheritance from my parents and although I donated most to the convent, I still have a small competency left over. Let me do some good with it, eh?'

Anya bowed her head, knowing better than to press the matter, but tears pricked her eyes. It was difficult to imagine two such different women as her mother and Sister Martha. They might have been from different planets, different species, one a walking saint and the other nothing less than pure evil. Sister Martha, now in her seventies, could have chosen to retire years earlier. She could simply have whiled the rest of her life away with her feet up and her head buried in a book. She could have; but she didn't. Instead, she spent her time helping out drug addicts, putting herself in line for all kinds of abuse, not to mention danger, at the local drug clinic. But, as she pointed out, she had taken the name Martha for a reason, and whilst she still had the use of two good hands and two good feet, she had no intention of lazing about.

Now, she clapped those good hands together, as though to disperse bad karma. 'Enough of all that! Tell me more about Fergal. I remember him as being very good-looking. Nice too. Always polite and with a ready smile. Macdara never stops singing his praises.' Macdara and Martha were not only second cousins, but firm friends too and it was this connection that had prompted Macdara to take Anya on as his PA at Lismore. Delighted to change the subject to one so close to her heart, Anya obliged, unaware that all the hardness had left her face and that her eyes were lit up like twin stars. When she voiced the fears planted in her head by Liam, Sister Martha waved a biscuit like a baton.

'Now, Anya Margaret Mary Keating, don't go putting the cart before the horse. You have no way of knowing what's going on in Fergal's head, no more than that Liam O'Hanlon does. If there's a change in his manner, you'll sense it soon enough. Until then, keep calm and carry on.'

Anya placed her empty cup back on the tray and stood up. 'Sister Martha,' she smiled. 'You should be running the country. What would I do without you?'

'You'd survive,' the nun said drily. 'You're too strong a woman not to.' She offered her cheek for a kiss and Anya left, little realising the prophesy of those words. Sister Martha went to the window and watched Anya walking down the street, as proud as if she really was the girl's mother and as fiercely protective, which is why she'd refrained from telling her everything about Clare's nocturnal visit and how the woman had broken down and begged her assistance in getting on a methadone programme.

'I know you think I'm scum,' she'd wailed, practically wringing her hands, 'but I really want to turn my life around. I know I did wrong by Anya, and that guilt is something I have to live with every day. It tortures me. Really, it does.' Scarecrow-like, she stood shivering on the doorstep, her emaciated arms hugging herself for warmth, her face seamed with dirt, eyes and nose running, a half-scabbed sore by the side of her mouth. 'I just want the chance to make things right or, at least, the chance to tell her I'm sorry. There's no one else I can turn to. Nowhere else I can go. Please help me, Sister Martha. Please.'

As Anya disappeared round a corner, the nun turned back into the room, her gaze settling on a picture of the Sacred Heart over the mantelpiece, a small red lamp burning in front. Sad eyes met sad eyes. What could she do? Turn her back and walk away? When asked by Saint Peter how many times someone ought to be forgiven, Jesus had answered seventy times seven. A lesser being like herself could surely do no less. And yet, deep inside in a part she kept hidden even from her own view, Sister Martha felt there were certain things for which Clare Keating should never be forgiven. Never, in a million years.

# Chapter 4

'Will she be all right here?' Orla looked round dubiously, as her sister, half-drugged still from the sedative she'd been given to knock her out on the private plane JC had arranged, shambled over and threw herself on the narrow but, thankfully, clean bed. Immediately, she held her arm out, beseeching.

'Please. Please. Give me my stuff. I need my stuff.'

'Not yet,' Orla was firm. 'I'll take care of you later. Okay?'

JC grinned nastily. 'Yeah, later, if you're a very, very good girl.'

'Bastard!' the girl sobbed, holding her arm out again, the most recent set of track-marks now fading to dots. 'Please. I'll do anything.' Pathetically, she fumbled at her top, pulling it open to expose a scrawny breast.

'*Ay, dios mio!*' JC turned away in disgust. 'I don't know why you bother.'

'You know exactly why I bother,' Orla snapped, rushing over to readjust her sister's clothing. 'Stop it!' She gripped her wrists, as Sinéad struggled and lashed out. 'I don't want to have to tie you up, okay? If you behave yourself, I'll be back soon to take care of you. But if not ...' She let her eyes stray tellingly round the bare, grey cell-like room, with the tiny, dirty window and air of being miles from anywhere. Sobbing, her sister quietened and Orla strode for the door. 'Come on, JC,' she said impatiently. 'Let's get the party started.'

'Sure you're ready?'

'As ready as I ever will be.' Orla waited as he produced an enormous key and locked the door firmly behind them. 'You know, I've been waiting for this practically all my life.' She smiled brilliantly, filling her lungs with a deep breath of air. 'Mm, can't you just smell it, the sweet scent of revenge?'

'My favourite perfume,' JC laughed, following her down the steps, content in the knowledge that he was already leading her by the nose.

Red-faced, Macdara was in the middle of a stumbling and excruciating apology to an equally embarrassed Anya when a sudden commotion outside the door of his office thankfully brought it to a swift conclusion. Puzzled, they exchanged glances, just as the door burst open and Bridie O'Regan practically fell in.

'Mac! Mac! You'll never guess.' Out of breath from the unaccustomed exertion of running upstairs, she held her hand to her heart as if it might burst. 'Something amazing.' She grabbed his arm. 'Oh, but you'd better come see for yourself!'

Exchanging yet another puzzled glance with Anya, Macdara found himself hustled over to the window, below which stood VIP, a young blond-haired woman perched on her back.

'Who the hell?' Furiously angry, he raised his hand to rap sharply on the window. 'How dare she! Bridie! You know nobody is supposed to ride VIP but me, and ...' His hand fell back slowly, his anger dissipating as the young woman turned her gaze upward, and smiled brilliantly. 'Orla?' His granddaughter's name fell slowly, disbelievingly, from his mouth. It felt odd, unfamiliar on his tongue, sweet, like a fruit once tasted in a foreign land and recalled with pleasure. 'Orla? he said again. Greedily, his eyes roamed over her face, searching for familiar points of reference. 'Sweet Jesus, could it be possible? Is it really my little Orla come back to Lismore?'

'Yes, yes it is! Oh, Mac.' Tears were flowing freely down Bridie's face. 'It's her all right. Can you doubt that beautiful smile?' She joshed him gently. 'Well, what are you waiting for, man, get down those stairs quick before she vanishes. Go on.'

Needing no further encouragement, and regardless of his failing eyesight, Macdara took the steps two at a time like a man half his age.

'Grandy! Grandy!' Orla slid down from the horse's back and ran straight into his arms as he appeared at the door. 'Oh, Grandy, I've missed you so much!'

Grandy! His heart overflowed with joy. If there was ever a doubt in his mind, that one word dispelled it completely. Grandy was Orla's special name for him, used only by her. Overwhelmed, he enveloped her in his arms, holding her tight as if Bridie's warning would come true and she would, indeed, disappear in a puff of smoke. 'And I've missed you, my little one, more than you'll ever know. Here, let me look at you.' Still maintaining a tight grip, he held her away from him slightly, his eyes devouring her well-remembered features, recognising the promise of the child come to fruition in the fine-boned face of the woman. 'Orla! Orla! Orla!' He repeated her name foolishly, like a mantra, or a genie conjuring her up. 'I can hardly believe it.' He reached out and stroked her blond hair, soft as corn silk, just as he remembered. Nessa used to wash it for her in rainwater. He flicked it gently and his lips quirked. 'No pigtails?'

'Not for a while now.' Cheekily, she ran her hand over his balding head. 'Not much hair?' And they both laughed, the banter still there between them, the loving easy patter of a grandfather and his granddaughter.

'Oh, welcome home, love! Welcome home!'

'Home! Oh, Grandy,' Orla's voice caught, 'you've no idea how wonderful that sounds.'

'Lismore was always your home,' Macdara said softly. 'It always will be.' Emotional, he cleared his throat, finally remembering they were not alone and that Bridie and Anya were standing observing them. He turned to the housekeeper. 'Orla, you remember Bridie?'

'Of course I do. Bridie was the first person I saw today. You used to make me pink scrambled egg, didn't you, Bridie?'

Bridie flushed delightedly. 'That's right, darling, with a bit of beetroot juice. And I used to paint funny faces on the boiled eggs at Easter, do you remember?'

'Indeed I do. You always saved the biggest one for me.'

'And this is Anya, my PA and right-hand woman.' Macdara flushed a little, unable to quite meet Anya's eyes, both unhappily aware that the introduction he was performing could have been entirely different. 'Anya, meet Orla, my little VIP!'

With her thoughts carefully concealed, Anya smiled and held out her hand. 'Welcome back to Lismore, Orla. It's so lovely to meet you.'

'And you.' Orla pumped her hand enthusiastically. 'And how fantastic to have someone my own age to talk to. I do hope we can be friends, Anya.'

'Of course you will,' Macdara said, beaming with certainty. 'Why wouldn't you?'

'And who's this?' Orla asked, as Fergal walked towards them, his midnight-blue eyes crinkled in a smile. 'That's Fergal, your cousin,' Macdara laughed at the slow recognition dawning on his grand-daughter's face. 'Hard to believe that the filthy urchin of your youth could grow into such a handsome brute, isn't it?'

'It certainly is. But are you sure it's Fergal and not a changeling?' Orla chuckled, as he enveloped her in an easy hug and kissed her on both cheeks. He scrutinised her admiringly.

'Well, well, well. Look what the cat's dragged in. As ugly as ever, Orla, I see.'

'Oh, you!' She gave him a playful punch, before linking her arm through first his and then Macdara's. 'Well, come on the pair of you, I'm gasping for a cup of tea and a sit down. No wait!' She pulled away suddenly and went over to where VIP stood patiently waiting. She wrapped her arms around the horse's neck. 'I'll be back soon,' she crooned, dropping small kisses on the tip of the elderly mare's nose. And then we can go for a nice ride, just you and me.' She paused, turned to Macdara hesitantly. 'If that's all right with you, Grandy, of course?'

'It's more than all right,' Macdara nodded delightedly, feeling time roll back some seventeen years. 'In fact, I insist on it. But first, young lady, I want to hear chapter and verse about where you've been all this time and I hope you know where to start, because I certainly don't.'

Bridie wiped a final tear away from her eye as she watched Orla leave, protectively sandwiched between her two male relatives.

'Now, that's a right turn up for the books, I must say. I never thought I'd live to see the day. And what a beauty she's turned out to be. A real stunner.' She gave herself a little shake. 'Listen to me standing around jawing, when I should be off preparing a room for her. Oh, Lord, what a happy day this is for Macdara. And Fergal seems quite smitten too,' Bridie added, giving voice to the very thought that was already troubling Anya. 'And, of course, they're not really cousins, not blood cousins anyway. What a great thing if Orla turned out to be the One.'

Anya smiled, just a quick twitch of her lips. 'Y-yes, indeed. Anyway, I ... I'd better take VIP back to her stable. I'll see you later, Bridie.' Unaware of the dejected figure she cut and with Bridie eyeing her speculatively, Anya led the horse away.

# Chapter 5

Macdara and Orla were alone in the kitchen, everyone else having diplomatically found chores to occupy them elsewhere. Macdara still couldn't quite get his head around the fact that Orla was there, *there* sitting side by side with him at the kitchen table, *there*, large as life, and twice as lovely, her limpid blue eyes glistening as she filled him in on the lost years in a voice that trembled and sometimes broke with emotion.

'You know, Grandy, I couldn't believe it when JC got in touch – right out of the wide blue yonder!' She drew in a ragged breath. 'It was like a miracle. I thought of you so often, but Mum said you'd cut us off completely and that you didn't love us any more.' Her eyes dropped, as though fearful of the answer in his. 'Is that true, Grandy? *Did* you just cut us off?'

'Jesus no! It wasn't like that at all.' Macdara's heart turned over in his chest, assailed once more by painful memories and regrets. A shaft of light beaming through the window came to rest on Orla's golden hair, little dust motes flickering in it like fireflies. It didn't take a large stretch of the imagination to look beneath the sophisticated veneer of this young woman and see the innocent, hurt little child beneath. He reached for her hand, tanned with long slim fingers, the female version of his own, and his heart flipped again as he caught sight of the gold charm bracelet encircling her wrist. One charm only, a tiny galloping horse inscribed with the word VIP. He'd given it to her for her sixth birthday and she had kept it all this time, adding more links as her wrist grew bigger. Macdara swallowed down a sudden lump in his throat.

'You must understand, there was so much pain back then. I was like a mad man. I couldn't think straight. Losing your grandmother sent me right over the edge. To be honest, I don't think I ever will get over it. She was my whole world.' He bent his head almost as if he was looking inwards. 'I still have nightmares about that evening. No one should have to die like that and no one, who loved them, should have to stand so uselessly by.'

'Mum said you blamed Sinéad,' Orla said, 'for the accident.'

'For the fire. I did,' Macdara said simply.

'Even though she was just a little girl?' Orla let her hand lie in his, but he felt it tense to iron and her nails dig slightly into his flesh.

'I know it sounds harsh,' he said. 'And, of course, it's upsetting for you to hear this about your sister, but Sinéad was a difficult child. No, more than difficult. There were depths to her that made us suspect that she might not be, well, quite normal.' Deep lines corrugated his brow as he struggled to explain. To be open. To be honest. To conceal nothing from her. He owed her that. 'You set the benchmark, you see, and when your sister came along we expected she'd be just like you, a bundle of pure joy.' He nodded, bringing to mind the picture of baby Sinéad, cradled in Nessa's arms in a pink cellular blanket, her chubby little hands grabbing fistfuls of empty air. 'And she was. But, almost from the moment she took her first step, she was into everything and anything. Nothing was safe. If she wasn't smashing up everything she could lay her hands on, she was pulling the tails of the dogs and the cats and pitching stones at the horses. And the more we tried to discipline her, the more defiant she became.'

'But isn't that just what kiddies do?' Pulling her hand free, Orla caught a lock of hair and twisted it round her finger. It stirred a memory. Orla sitting on his lap when she was five years old, breaking her little heart over Loppy-Lou, her pet rabbit, drowned by Sinéad in the water butt.

'Yes,' he answered her. 'All toddlers are wilful. That's their way of finding out about the world. Testing the barriers. But it seemed like Sinéad was more than wilful or naughty. She was destructive. She appeared to take pleasure in destroying things, ripping the heads off flowers, tearing up little drawings you had made, pouring vinegar into the milk and salt into the sugar. And whilst on the face of it most of those things just seem like pranks, a bit of high jinks, cumulatively they rang a warning bell that perhaps something was not quite right.'

Most little girls loved bunnies and kittens, remembered Macdara, but clearly Sinéad wasn't like most little girls. JC, who was visiting his grandmother for the summer, caught her red-handed but sadly when it was already too late to save the poor animal. Loppy-Lou had bitten her, Sinéad said. It was stupid and ugly and she hated it. She didn't cry when Nessa spanked her, just glared at JC as though it was all his fault.

Macdara got up and strolled over to the window, his hands linked thoughtfully behind his back. Outside, he could see Fergal leading a prize-winning mare down to the north paddock. Even to the untutored eye, hundreds of years of aristocratic lineage were apparent in every line of the horse's powerful yet graceful body. Her perfect form gleamed, so clearly delineated that it looked almost as if she had been clumsily Photoshopped out of some wonderful golden habitat and plonked down into the muddy surroundings of Lismore. Amirah, she was called; it meant princess, in Arabic.

'Perhaps we should have sought some sort of psychiatric help for Sinéad then,' Macdara said thoughtfully. 'But your mother and grandmother were dead set against the idea. And then Sinéad set fire to the barn.'

A sound from behind brought him spinning round. Orla, her back ramrod straight, was making for the door. He ran after her, caught her by the arm, and cradled her to his chest.

'I'm sorry, love. So sorry. I didn't mean to upset you. You always were a tender-hearted little thing.' He led her gently back to her chair, sat down himself, half-twisted towards her. 'It broke my heart when your mother took you away, you know. But what could I do? Nessa was your mother and I had no rights over you. Looking back, I realise that neither one of us was thinking clearly. We were both desperately unhappy, me because I had lost your grandmother and, hands up, I was bloody difficult to live with and could hardly bear to be in the same room as Sinéad. I was too grief-stricken or, perhaps, too selfish to think about the effect of my behaviour on Nessa. She, after all, had to live with the knowledge that the fire, in which she lost her mother, was lit by her own daughter. And as if that weren't punishment enough, her marriage was falling apart, and I harangued her every time she brought up the subject of divorce. No wonder she ran.'

Idly, Macdara flicked at the little VIP charm on Orla's wrist. 'If I'm honest, I suppose I thought that putting a little distance between us all wasn't such a bad thing, but I always expected she'd come back one day, when things had settled down. And then … And then we ran out of time.' Despite his best efforts to stay calm, Macdara's voice broke. 'I didn't even know my daughter was ill, let alone that she had died. Now that, my dear, is payback of the worst kind.'

'But you didn't come looking for us,' Orla accused, unwilling to let him off the hook. 'After Mum died, you didn't try to find us.'

'I only learned about Nessa when your father phoned me from France,' Macdara told her, grief pleating his face at the memory. 'He also told me you and Sinéad were living with him. As you can imagine it was all a bit of a shock, and by the time I'd got my head together and asked if I could visit, Sinéad had fallen out with his new wife, and the pair of you had gone walkabout again. I hired a private investigator, but the trail had gone stone cold. I never stopped hoping, and wishing, that when you grew up, you'd find your way back.'

'But you never hated us?' Orla insisted, battling back tears.

Macdara shook his head. 'Never you. Nor your mother.'

'Just Sinéad, then?' Orla gave a hopeless little shrug.

'I'm sorry.' Macdara caught her chin, tipped her tearful face up so that their eyes were on a level. 'I shouldn't have implied that. I don't hate Sinéad. I hate what she did. But somehow I can't seem to disassociate one from the other.'

Orla set her mouth in a stubborn line. 'Whatever she did or didn't do, we're sisters.'

'Where is she now?' Macdara asked. 'Are you still in contact?'

'No,' Orla said. 'For all I know, she could be dead and buried. So don't look so worried, Grandy, she's not going to show up on your doorstep, like me.'

Macdara was ashamed both at Orla's perspicacity and at the relief he felt. Relief mixed with equal parts guilt. Of course, he didn't wish his granddaughter dead, but he'd be a liar if he pretended he ever wanted to see her again. He blamed her for Nancy's death. And he always would.

He gave a little shrug. 'I'm sorry, love,' he said. 'I wish things were different and I genuinely hope your sister is safe and well. But you have your own life to live and we've got a lot of making up for lost time to do.' Bringing the conversation to an end, he pulled her to her feet and dropped a light kiss on her forehead.

Dinner that evening was a joyous affair. Bridie produced a wonderful roast lamb with all the trimmings, followed by deep-filled apple tart with home-made cinnamon ice cream. After the intensity of earlier, Macdara deliberately kept the conversation light. Right now, he wanted nothing more than to enjoy the spectacle of his granddaughter sitting at his table once more.

Macdara wasn't the only one enjoying the spectacle. Liam had managed to wangle an invitation to dinner too and it was almost comical to watch him vie with Fergal and Macdara for her attention. And who could blame them, Anya thought, glancing at the other girl, who was looking sublime in a sleeveless white fitted dress that showcased her Australian tan to perfection. Blessed with near-perfect skin, she had kept her make-up artfully light, with no more than a slick of bronze on her eyelids and sinfully high cheekbones, and a dab of clear lip gloss to emphasise her natural pout.

Anya's own dress was pretty enough but slightly girly by comparison, with a full skirt and sweetheart neckline. In shades of green, it echoed the colour of her eyes, and contrasted well with her fiery hair. With hindsight though, Anya wished she had worn something a little more glamorous, a little more sexy. She also wished she had spent more time on her hair, instead of the few seconds it had taken to pile it atop her head in an untidy bird's nest.

And Orla not only looked sensational, she sparkled. There was no other word for it. She was confident in company too, effervescent as a bottle of vintage champagne when the cork is popped. Anya, on the other hand, felt slightly gauche as she worried about saying something stupid or using the wrong knife or fork. A story she'd once heard about someone who had unwittingly drunk the finger bowl had left her transfixed with horror for months. Thankfully there were no finger bowls tonight, although even if there were and she had drunk the lot, Anya doubted anyone would notice, given how smitten they all were with Orla, herself included. The idea of having a confidante her own age and sex was exciting, especially since she had never before had a close friend. On the rare occasions somebody at school had made overtures, somebody else was always bound to mention her mother Clare, with the result that she would find herself dropped like a hot cake. Shyly, Anya hoped that was all about to change.

'More wine?' Orla leaned across and topped up her wine glass, treating Fergal, sitting directly opposite, to a view of the curve of her breasts. Anya smiled as Orla sat back down and raised her glass to her. 'Here's to you and me, Anya, the prettiest girls in the room,' she giggled charmingly and fluttered her eyelashes. 'The *only* girls in the room. May we buy many pairs of shoes together! Cheers!'

'Cheers!' Anya raised her own glass, oblivious to how very pretty she herself looked with her wine-flushed cheeks and gleaming peridot eyes. Liam noticed, though. And so did Fergal. Anya was more than a little squiffy when she went to bed that night, but felt happy, not only at the prospect of a new friend but also because Macdara need no longer worry about being on his own. Anya felt that the pressure was off herself, now that Orla was back to look after him. As usual, Sister Martha was proved right. Things were already sorting themselves out.

Back in her old room, minus the Peter Rabbit wallpaper and Barbie quilt, but with an old one-eyed teddy bear Bridie had dredged up from somewhere guarding the bed, Orla lay assessing the day. She felt tired, but triumphant. All had gone just as smoothly as JC predicted. The proverbial walk in the park, really. Macdara was so pleased to see her. As was cousin Fergal. Now, he really had come as something of a surprise. The charming, blue-eyed, black-haired Paddy of mythology, made flesh and blood. She'd forgotten how rich the local accent was, how utterly seductive it could sound, especially when spoken by Fergal. Double cream on the top of a glass of Irish coffee. Would she go there?! Cousin or not, she would most definitely consider it, were it not for the fact that her heart lay elsewhere, and had done for many years. Not that that would have stopped her normally, but only because of distance and biological needs. And now that the distance was closing between herself and her true love, Orla could see that Fergal was a complication she just did not need. That left the field clear for Anya, clearly head-over-heels in love with him. Not, Orla suspected, that it would do her much good. Anya was nice. And, if there was one thing life had taught her, it was that nice didn't cut it. Nice girls finished last. In her experience, most men liked a challenge, notches on their bedposts, scalps swinging from their belt, women of fire and steel with a working knowledge of every position in the Kama Sutra. *Not* frigid Brigids, too frightened to say boo to a goose or hello to a penis! Orla chuckled at her own choice of phrase. Anya needed a lesson in self-assertion. She needed to learn how to reach out and grab whatever she needed. Just as she, Orla, intended to do.

Shivering – she'd forgotten how cold January could be in Ireland – she climbed into her pyjamas and jumped into bed as quickly as possible. Her mobile phone vibrated beside her on the bedside cabinet. She picked it up and clicked the answer button, without bothering to check the caller ID.

'Hi, JC.' Her voice sent a smile down the phone line.

'So, how did it go?' Straight to the point. The no-frills Argentinian.

'Good! Great! It's good to be back, actually. If I'd known the red carpet was waiting, I'd have come back years ago, instead of busting my ass dancing for perverts.'

'*Si?*' JC chuckled. 'Well, don't get too comfortable, honey. Remember the game-plan.'

'Don't worry, I'm on the ball.' Suddenly weary, she stifled a yawn behind her hand. 'Anyway, how … You know? Is everything okay?'

'Come tomorrow and see for yourself.'

'If Macdara lets me out of his sight.' Orla yawned. 'He's petrified I might disappear again.'

'Good. Then all is well.' JC blew a kiss down the telephone. '*Buenos noches, chiquita*. Sweet dreams, eh?'

'A *mañana*, JC.' Orla smacked her lips in return, then, strangely unsettled after the conversation, got back out of bed and padded over to the window, grabbing her dressing gown en route for warmth.

Outside, Liam was getting into his Land Rover, clearly intending to drive, despite having put away more than his fair share of wine at dinner. Interesting. Dangerous. In her days as a nightclub dancer, Orla had met enough men of his ilk to recognise the nature of the beast. God help any woman who got involved with him, like the one who was just slinking round the side of the house trying to make herself invisible. She grinned, as the female in question made a sudden mad dash for the car. For her sake, she hoped he was worth it. Instinct told her quite the opposite. But then it was ever thus, women making fools of themselves for men. And, when it came to JC, she was no different. He had her exactly where he wanted her. Always had. And always would have.

## Chapter 6

Fergal was leading Glengarriff back to his stable when Orla emerged from the house and made her way across the yard.

'Good morning, Orla.' He brought the horse to a stand. 'I didn't expect to see you up this early. Did you sleep well?'

'Not too bad,' she said, surprised at how good he looked in his low-cost, high-street checked shirt, jeans and muddy wellies. Carter, her ex, had worn designer this and that, but when you came right down to it, he still resembled a pig in fancy dress. A wealthy but elderly pig. 'It took me a while to nod off, but I suppose that's only to be expected. Too many ghosts, if you know what I mean.'

Smiling straight into those gorgeous speedwell-blue eyes, the sort you wanted to skinny-dip in, Orla had the wicked thought that she would like him to take her into one of the loose boxes, rip her clothes off and make passionate love. The thought gave birth to a pleasurable kick at the base of her stomach. It had been a while since she'd really lusted after someone, and it would be no hardship whatsoever to break the deadlock with Fergal. What a shame she had already decided it was just too complicated. And a shame for Fergal too. She was good. Very good. Fergal nodded understandingly. 'I can imagine. It must feel very strange to you being back at Lismore. After all, when you went away you were no more than two hands over a duck. And now look at you. All grown up.'

'All grown up, indeed,' Orla grinned, inferring from the admiring sweep of his eyes that the growing-up process was one of which he thoroughly approved. The fact that she was wearing sprayed on Sass & Bide jeans didn't hurt. Neither did leaving her blouse unbuttoned beneath her leather jacket, all the way to the tanned hollow between her breasts, despite the chill air. She raised her hand, stroked Glengarriff's neck, her long fingers gliding up and down hypnotically. 'Anyway, the past is past and I'm sure I'll acclimatise soon. In the meantime, tell me about this poor guy. Glengarriff, right? I hear he's been in the wars. Is he better?'

'Much,' Fergal said, his eyes glued to the rhythmic stroking of her fingers. 'A few more days of rest and then I'll take him out for a gentle trot.'

'Perhaps I'll come with you? Remember how I always loved *riding*.' Suggestive, Orla drew out the last word, though her face remained as open and innocent as that of the Virgin Mary. What the hell, it was only a bit of harmless flirtation.

Fergal grinned. 'Sounds like a plan. Just say the word and I'll be happy to saddle you up.'

'Oh, I will,' Orla assured him, 'I most definitely will.' Turning away, she waved an airy hand. 'See you later, alligator!'

'In a while,' he responded *sotto voce*, his eyes locked appreciatively on to her denim-wrapped backside as she sashayed saucily away. He pursed his lips in a soundless whistle. Back in the day, he had never paid much attention to his young cousins, but time had waved a magic wand and turned Orla into the quintessential Australian beach babe. He looked up and saw Anya watching him from her bedroom window. He raised his hand to wave but she had already disappeared. Fergal stood gazing at the window for a moment longer, then clicked his tongue and led Glengarriff back to his stable.

Mortified, Anya sprang quickly back, her heart beating so wildly it felt as though it might jump straight out of her chest. What she had just witnessed disturbed her, though it had come as no real surprise. That Fergal would fancy his beautiful cousin was inevitable. How could he not? Orla was irresistible, everything she wasn't – confident, beautiful, tanned, blonde, blue-eyed, almost a centre-fold from *Playboy*. In short, every man's fantasy. And though it hurt to admit it, Orla and Fergal really did look good together; a perfectly matched pair of thoroughbreds, as Macdara might have put it.

Her glance went briefly to the suitcase on top of her wardrobe. Despite the rosy glow of last night's wine goggles, when it seemed like everything might work out after all, now Anya felt her position at Lismore was becoming more untenable than ever. Whether she liked it or not, she needed to make a decision about her future. But even thinking about it hurt. Lismore was her home, the only real home she had ever known, and Macdara and Fergal were her substitute family. She couldn't bear to think about leaving them all behind, but neither could she bear to think about the alternative, staying to watch Fergal and Orla fall in love and live out the happily-ever-after for which she herself longed.

Her gaze swept around the room that had become her haven, starting slightly as her face loomed wanly back at her, a triptych of misery in the mirrors of her Louis-style dressing table, which along with the matching stool and wardrobe had been a birthday present many years ago from Macdara. Almost everything in the room had similar sentimental value: the little watercolour of Wishbone Lake, a gift from Lady Kathleen; the small, chipped statue of the Child of Prague, donated by Sister Martha to 'watch over her' when she was a child; the now faded straw-coloured St Brigid's Cross that she had fashioned out of reeds; and perhaps most precious of all, the photograph of Fergal and herself taken last year at the Galway races. How ridiculous she looked in the wide-brimmed picture hat Lady Kathleen insisted she wore, but how radiantly happy.

Anya met her own gaze again, searching for signs of life in the ghost-like image looking back at her. And slowly it dawned that there was a third option. Instead of just rolling over and playing the martyr, she could stand her ground and bloody well fight. After all, it wasn't as if she was a child any more, powerless to defend herself. Surely happiness was worth fighting for? Certainly Fergal was worth fighting for. But could she do it? Did she have the courage to go up against somebody so assured as Orla, so much a woman of the world?

Anya sighed. Only time would tell.

# Chapter 7

'It's lovely having Orla back,' Bridie announced for the umpteenth time, a few weeks after Orla's return. 'That girl has singlehandedly managed to breathe new life into the old place. And as for Macdara, he's as happy as a dog with two tails.'

Anya laughed at the picture that conjured up. She looked up from the trug of peas she and Bridie were shelling in the kitchen. 'Has she changed much, do you think? I don't mean in the obvious ways, but personality?'

The housekeeper tipped her head slightly to one side. 'Not really. She's still a real live-wire. We were always close. For years, she called me Bridie Boo. But that was Orla, a pet name for everyone.'

Anya giggled. 'Bridie Boo! She doesn't call you that now, surely?'

'Sometimes,' Bridie admitted, looking slightly embarrassed, but pleased too. 'When she's trying to get round me in some way or other. That's why we're having roast lamb again tonight, the little minx. Still, you'd have to have a heart of stone to resist her.'

Anya cracked a pod and rattled the peas into the basin. 'She doesn't talk much about the past, though, does she? I mean, she never mentions Sinéad. Do you not think that's strange?'

'Not really.' Bridie popped a pea into her mouth and bit down. 'It would be too painful for Macdara. Don't forget that everything changed when her grandmother died in that fire. Mac, as you know, rightly or wrongly blamed Sinéad. Those two things, combined with the breakdown of Nessa's marriage, changed the fabric of life at Lismore forever.' Bridie took another pod from the trug on the table, waved it absently. 'Poor Nessa. Small wonder she went on to develop cancer. That kind of stress is enough to kill anyone.'

She sniffed. 'And to die out in Australia estranged from her family, with only her two young daughters by her side ... I know for a fact Mac still tortures himself over it. But that's life for you, full of regrets and mistakes. Sure, if we had the benefit of hindsight, we'd all still be living in paradise.'

'Yes, it's very sad,' Anya agreed. 'Poor Nessa, and poor Orla. Life has certainly knocked the corners off her.' And Anya knew all about having your corners knocked off. She felt for the other girl and admired the way she managed to stay so bright and bubbly.

'Enough misery!' With an air of finality, Bridie cracked open the last pod, threw the peas in the bowl in the centre of the table and the empty pod into the bucket on the floor between them. 'What cannot be cured must be endured, as my own mother, God rest her, used to say. Let's cheer ourselves up by seeing who's blowing who up today.' She glanced at the clock on the wall, reached for the remote control and clicked on the television. Her timing was perfect as the opening news credits were just flashing across the screen.

They both sat back to watch, pleasantly surprised to find the housekeeper's pessimism unwarranted as news of a royal wedding was announced. But soon Anya's thoughts went back to Orla, with whom she was beginning to identify more and more, despite their disparate backgrounds. It was true that because of Orla, she and Macdara were gradually beginning to lose the self-conscious awkwardness around each other following the abortive proposal of marriage. Bridie was right: having Orla back was doing Macdara the power of good, and despite him protesting frequently that she was fussing around him like an old mother hen, it was plain to all that he was relishing every minute of having her back in his life. And Mac wasn't alone in appreciating his granddaughter's charms. Naturally friendly, Orla was one of those people who effortlessly drew others into their aura. Her laugh was infectious, her smile warm and inclusive, making the recipient feel special and as if they been singled out for special treatment. Everyone, from the most junior employee at Lismore to the big old tomcats patrolling the stables, seemed to adore her.

All except one, that is. Sister Martha observed that Orla sounded too good to be wholesome when Anya phoned her to relate the goings on at Lismore. But since the elderly nun's arthritis was playing her up, Anya blamed the uncharitable remark on that.

Meanwhile Orla continued to hold everybody in thrall at Lismore, including Fergal, with whom she flirted mercilessly, and Liam, who followed her about while slavering like an old dog. Even JC from Castle Mac Tíre seemed to find increased business at Lismore every other day, much to the stable lasses' delight, not that he so much as glanced their way, which seemed only to inflame their passions further. JC didn't look Anya's way either, although she didn't expect him to, other than in brief acknowledgement of her friendship with his grandmother. Drop-dead gorgeous to look at he might be, but there was something about him that put her teeth on edge – a calculating look in his eye and a proprietary manner, as if he was master of all he surveyed.

Fergal shared Anya's unease about the Argentinian. In fact, he disliked him intensely, and had done since they were boys together. It was his fervent belief that the increased frequency of JC's visits weren't totally related to Orla's return. That was just a convenient excuse. Fergal thought he knew the real reason, although he couldn't prove it. Yet.

'He wants Lismore,' he raged to Anya once, after he and JC traded harsh words over JC's unnecessary rudeness to a junior member of staff at Lismore, which had resulted in the poor girl dissolving into tears. 'He thinks he has a claim because it was part of the Castle Mac Tíre estate a couple of hundred years ago, before some gambling ancestor lost it to the Fitzgeralds in a game of cards. And now that he's lost his ranch in Argentina and Lady Kathleen is on her uppers and desperate for money, he's snooping round and plotting to get his hands on Lismore. But why is it only me that can see that? Why does everyone else think he's some sort of plaster saint?'

'A plaster saint? Oh, surely not,' Anya giggled. 'A sex symbol, maybe. But, seriously, JC couldn't possibly think he has any rights to Lismore, at all, after all this time. That's just too bizarre.'

'No, legally he knows he hasn't got a leg to stand on, but some people like to think they are above the law. You wait, Anya. Something is in the wind,' Fergal warned. 'Call it gut instinct. Call it nonsense. Call it whatever you like. But I'm right. I know I am.'

Secretly, Anya suspected Fergal was making mountains out of molehills and, though the thought hurt, she couldn't help but wonder if his concerns weren't linked more to present-day jealousy over Orla's undoubted affection for the Argentinian, than to ancient history.

In any case, whatever her reservations regarding JC, Anya had a great deal of affection for his grandmother. She had first made her acquaintance through running errands up to the castle for Macdara. Now Anya visited often on her own account and spent many happy hours listening to Lady Kathleen's often embellished tales of her heady days in Hollywood, as well as rummaging through her Aladdin's cave of a wardrobe.

Suppressing a sigh, Anya got up to take the bucket of empty pea pods out to the compost bin at the back of the house. Much as she loved Lismore, it was all a long way from Hollywood. Worse still, her own prince appeared to be sizing Orla up for the crystal slipper.

Outside, the air was close and grass-scented, the sky violet, shot through with candy floss strands of pink that promised shepherd's delight on the morrow. But first, there would be a spring storm. Camouflaged in a thicket nearby, a jay chattered crossly and scolded its mate while, super-sensitive to changes in atmospheric pressure, the horses moved restlessly in their stables. It was all so beautiful. Painfully beautiful.

Anya went and sat on a bench encircling an old oak tree, her face upturned waiting for the first drops of rain. Benediction, Sister Martha called it, a blessing on the earth, and the rainbow, she said, was God's promise never to drown the world again, which put the likes of Noah out of a job.

There was a sudden flash of light on the horizon. Anya started to count. At fifteen, there was a muted clap of thunder. She closed her eyes and smiled, waiting for the blessing as the first drops of rain fell. Going by the old lore, the eye of the storm was still fifteen miles away.

# Chapter 8

Not bad. Not bad at all for an opening night, JC congratulated himself, looking round at the crowd thronging the dance floor of the newly restored Lismore Hell Fire Club. It had taken two years of his life and a lot of begging to raise the money but, like the mythical phoenix rising from the ashes, the club's doors were once more open for business. The idea behind the club was nothing new, of course. In the eighteenth century there were Hell Fire Clubs the length and breadth of the UK and Ireland, dens of iniquity, where debauched gentry indulged their taste for all things immoral amongst like-minded peers. And, following in the infamous foot-steps of the Ormond ancestor who had established the Lismore branch in a disused church in the grounds of Castle Mac Tíre, JC was hell-bent on reviving it all – everything! The drunken drug-fuelled orgies, the gambling, séances, even Satanism if that's what the punters demanded. There were as many spoilt rich kids now as back then, searching for ever more inventive and expensive ways of spending their daddies' hard-earned money. And there wasn't one good reason JC could think of why they shouldn't spend it in his club. Assuming his calculations were accurate, he would soon have the money to repay the huge loans taken out for the restoration of the club. Any remaining profits would go towards renovating Castle Mac Tíre for his grandmother, the only woman he had ever really loved. And that included his bitch mother, who had simply stood by as his father had thrown him off the ranch, never so much as lifting a finger in his defence. He wondered if his grandmother knew the reason behind his banishment. If she did, she never said so, but had simply lowered the drawbridge, hung out the welcome home bunting and hugged him senseless. Castle Mac Tíre, he knew, was as important to her as the ranch in Buenos Aires was to him. It was not only his intention, but his raison d'être, to ensure that both were secured for their rightful owners.

'Hey there, JC!' Orla called, dancing up to him. 'The club is amazing, everything you promised, and more.' Provocatively dressed in a near transparent muslin mini-dress, her breasts strained against the material, nipples erect, the darker areoles visible beneath. Somehow Orla managed to look more naked than if she actually was. Her eyes glittered in the dim light of the club, which was decorated to resemble a torture chamber. The ceilings were purple and the walls black and hung with an array of porno-satanic art. One entire wall was given over to a huge upside-down wooden crucifix, which had been fitted with leather hand and foot holds. Sconces threw down a dull orange light on the revellers while skulls, roped into service as candle and joss stick holders, gazed hollow-eyed from various niches and table tops, teeth eternally bared in gappy, rictus grins. Suspended above the dance floor, cages rotated slowly, showcasing ghoulishly made-up creatures that cavorted to the mindless thump of grime music. The theme was dark, decadent and downright dangerous – something for everyone, no matter how bizarre the palate.

'Hello, *querida*.' JC's eyes slid over her, an unreadable expression in their depths. 'So you managed to escape Macdara, after all? And dressed like that? However did you manage?'

'Oh, he doesn't mind, although I was careful to keep my coat on when I said goodbye. Besides, he thinks that because it's a private members' club, it must be a cut above your regular lager and lout shit-hole.' Orla giggled, looking round. 'Poor old Grandy, he'd have a fit if he could see what it's really like.' She pirouetted, the muslin flying out to reveal her long brown legs all the way up to her lacy thong. 'As for this, never in a hundred years would he believe me capable of making such a public exhibition of myself.' She pouted. 'Not his precious little blue-eyed girl.' She twirled again. 'Which means I can pretty much get away with anything. Anyway, what do you think, JC? Do I look sexy?'

'Heartbreakingly so,' JC said, clearly amused at the idea of such unworldliness in a man of Macdara's advanced years. 'And I'm not the only man to think so. Given the opportunity, that lot over there look as if they'd like to eat you from the feet up.' Drily, he jerked his head towards a small group of people who were watching her, women as well as men, faces avid, emanating an almost primeval lust, showing just how thin the veneer of civilisation really was. Orla pouted prettily. 'Who cares about them? You're all that counts.'

'I care about them.' JC turned her around swiftly and patted her on the backside. 'Now run along, honey, and charm them with your dancing,' his expression changed from pleasant to calculating, 'while I charm the money from their pockets.'

'Bastard!' Orla groaned playfully. 'Do you never think about anything else?'

'You know I do,' JC said, his voice suddenly so passionate and warm it sent a rosy flush across the bare skin of her back. Turning back, she reached out and drew a tender finger down along his cheek. Her expression changed from flirtatious to earnest. 'We will make it work, JC, won't we? Soon, we'll both have our heart's desire. And nothing and nobody can stop us.'

Amused, JC spent a few moments watching her dance, revelling in her ability to enslave with her beauty and feminine wiles. Women! They were too easy. He caught her eye as, now draped around a pole, she hung upside-down by one leg, the other gracefully extended, her foot flexed *en pointe*, like a ballerina. Stupid girl! Stupid for trusting him. Stupid for loving him. Stupid for believing he would ever love her back. Stupid for being his ever-adoring slave, despite everything he had done to her. And he wasn't finished yet.

JC turned away and scanned the room, his eyes hardening as he spotted Liam pawing some half-naked woman in a corner. He hurried over and pulled him off, leaving the woman to collapse in a near-senseless heap on the floor.

'For God's sake, Liam,' he spat. 'You're not here to enjoy yourself. Remember that, eh?'

Aggrieved, Liam straightened his clothing. 'Jesus, JC, must you always be so fucking po-faced? Don't you ever let your hair down?'

'Never.' JC glared at him. 'Never ever!' He lowered his tone. 'Now, did you manage to get the refreshments?'

'The refreshments?' Liam snorted, earning another glare from JC. Hurriedly, he lowered his tone. 'Yeah. Yeah. I got it all.' And he reeled off a list of drugs like a shopping list.

Satisfied, JC nodded. 'Good, that should keep the punters happy. But remember, Liam, be discreet. The private rooms only, eh? No one gets in without a password. Keep the doors locked. Always. We don't want anything that will bring the *gardaí* snooping round.'

Liam nodded. 'I'll be careful.' A sudden tug on his trouser leg reminded him of his drunken paramour, who had now struggled into a half-sitting position. He leaned down and helped her to her feet. Her long auburn hair fell back revealing her face and JC, recognising her as one of the young stable girls from Lismore, jumped back in shock.

'*Ay, dios mio*! What did I warn you about outsiders? Members only, that's the rule. Keep it small. Keep it contained. You fucking idiot!'

Liam held up his hands. 'Cool it. Cool it. Kitty's not a problem.'

'You'd better pray she isn't.' Furious, JC pushed Liam hard in the chest, sending both him and Kitty, who was hanging on to him, staggering backwards. 'Because, I warn you, if your stable lass turns out to be a fucking unstable lass, I will have your balls for *empanadas*. Understand?'

'She won't!' Liam promised JC's retreating back, righting himself first and then Kitty, who was rocking precariously on her too-high heels.

'I heard you.' With a sly kind of triumph, she gazed blearily up into his face. 'You and JC. You said Special K. That's horse tranquilliser.' Her eyes grew round, as even through her drunken confusion, the import hit her. Her hand flew to her mouth in a schoolgirl gesture of disbelief. 'Liam! You took that from Lismore, didn't you? What if Mac finds out? You'll lose your job.'

'Shut the fuck up, Kitty,' Liam ordered. 'You know nothing. Sweet fuck all. Isn't that right?'

Kitty hesitated, then unnerved by the fury in his eyes, nodded.

'You're right, Liam. I don't know anything,'

'And again!' Liam ordered. 'And this time, say it like you mean it.' He flexed his fingers.

'I do mean it. I swear,' Kitty panicked at the strange note in his voice, tears gathering in her eyes. 'I … I don't know anything.'

'Good. That's very good. And that's also why ignorance is bliss. Remember that, Kitty.' Liam pulled her deeper into the shadows. Out of view, he pushed her roughly up against the wall, his hand searching beneath her dress, working its way up along her slender thighs.

'Please, Liam, no,' she begged, as he spun her about and spread her legs.

But Liam didn't stop. In fact it was debatable as to whether he even heard her because, in his own mind, the pain he was inflicting was not just on Kitty, but on JC, and every other blue-blooded, over-privileged, up-their-own-arse, hoity-toity little fucker that had ever lived.

Dawn was breaking by the time the last clubber left, a Russian oligarch's son, who was so out of his skull on drugs and alcohol that he had to be half-dragged, half-carried to his limousine by his muscle-bound bodyguard.

Amused, JC and Liam watched as he was bundled none too gently into the back seat, the bodyguard presumably taking full advantage of the chance to get a bit of his own back for past grievances.

'Better hope he doesn't run into any drug barons,' JC said. 'Considering how he's personally responsible for swallowing almost all of Columbia's stock of cocaine. They'd disembowel him for just half of it.'

Liam guffawed, perhaps a little too loudly, his ill humour of earlier miraculously replaced by a sense of well-being that owed nothing to drugs – filthy things, he didn't touch them himself – and everything to do with the large wad of notes nestling in his breast pocket. JC was a tosser, that was for sure, but he was a tosser who paid well.

Liam held out his hand. 'Nice doing business with you, JC. Tip me the word, when you want some more refreshments, eh?'

After a momentary hesitation, JC shook it, just a little too firmly to pass for a cordial handshake. There was no camaraderie in his eyes. 'Remember what I said about the girl, Liam. Make sure she keeps her mouth closed.'

'She will. She knows I'll fucking kill her if she doesn't.' Annoyed, Liam yanked his hand free, his fingers tingling painfully, although he was damned if he was going to rub them before JC was out of sight.

JC watched disdainfully as the other man swaggered away, shoulders swinging from side to side, tough-guy style. Liam was a bully and a nasty piece of work, he thought, attributes that went ill with his undoubted skill as a vet. Regrettably, he needed him. But not for long.

Back in the club, JC flicked on the electric lights and looked around. The place had been well and truly trashed, with debris and the occasional pool of vomit scattered about.

A slow smile spread across his face. Clearly the night had been an unqualified success, better even than he had hoped for. And the next would exceed this.

There was a sound behind him. A woman had come in and stood just inside the door. She was middle-aged, hollow-eyed, her face unmistakeably ravaged by drugs or alcohol, and probably both. She was dressed in a velour tracksuit that had once been pink, but which was now varying shades of grubby grey. It hung on her gaunt frame as if moulded in the shape of someone several sizes larger. Her trainers were filthy, and her hair was part-tucked behind her ears in a straggly grey mess that hadn't seen a hairbrush in some time.

'Hey! You JC?'

JC's mouth curled with distaste. He raised an inquiring eyebrow.

'Clare Keating. I was told you were expecting me?' She held out a hand, so filthy it might have belonged to a coal miner. 'Liam O'Hanlon sent me. To clean up?'

JC ignored her outstretched hand. 'Ah, yes. The cleaner.' It struck him that she might have looked more convincing had she been cleaner herself. Still, beggars couldn't be choosers and the most important thing was that she was discreet, which was vital after a night like this, as who knew what she might find? She looked around almost as if she could read his mind.

'Hey. Don't sweat it.' She bared her yellow teeth in a grin. 'This little monkey sees nothing, hears nothing, says nothing. Besides, I've seen it all before, and then some.'

This JC could believe. Ignoring her attempted chumminess, he pointed to a door at the back of the club marked 'Private'.

'Everything you need is in there. Do what's expected and you'll be paid well.'

'For you, darlin', I might even consider payment in kind.'

'Just do your job,' JC snapped. Hastily he walked away, feeling as though he had been dipped in the sewer.

JC cut through the bluebell wood on his way back to the castle, stepping over a sea of blue. Bone-tired and weary, he longed for his bath and his bed, and the blissful sleep of the just-made-a-packet. But the smell of the club clung to him, and he imagined it seeping from his pores in a noxious miasma, and shuddered. A blackbird, foraging for worms on the forest floor, flew up startled at his footfall and berated him noisily from a nearby tree.

'Sorry, my friend,' JC said aloud, waving an apologetic hand towards it, feeling a sudden overwhelming urge to laugh. Yes, he was weary and yes, he was dirty, but his plans were beginning to come together very nicely.

As he broke cover from the trees and Castle Mac Tíre loomed above him, magical in the vaporous morning light, he thought he must know how God felt when he made the world. Power. It was such an aphrodisiac.

# Chapter 9

Javier was outside snipping stems of rosemary from a large terra-cotta planter when Anya pulled up beside him in her car. His eyes widened as she turned off the ignition and climbed out.

'*Ola*, Anya,' he underscored the words appreciatively. 'Hey, you look so pretty today. Like a film star.'

'Thank you, Javier,' Anya dipped a small curtsey. 'I'm glad you approve.' Taking a leaf out of Orla's book, she had made a real effort getting dressed that morning and so it was nice to know it had been worthwhile, even though her shoes were pinching. She pointed at the stems in his hand and grinned. 'Um, let me guess, chicken and rosemary soup?'

Javier shrugged good-naturedly. 'But, of course, it is my lady's favourite. I try her with tomato and basil too, but she don't like that so good.'

'I quite like it, myself,' Anya said. 'How is she today, anyway?' Anya gazed up at the castle, as though she could see through the walls into Lady Kathleen's bedroom.

Javier made a so-so gesture. 'A bit tired. She is not sleeping so good.' He tapped his forehead and looked knowing. 'Too many ghosts, in here.'

'Oh, dear,' Anya looked concerned. 'Poor Lady Kay. I'll try not to tire her out too much, I promise.'

Javier gave a small phut of annoyance. 'Macdara. That man is always making her tired.' He made a mouth with his hand. 'Talking. Talking. Always talking.'

'I'm sure he doesn't mean to,' Anya said, soothingly. 'They've been friends an awfully long time. There's probably a lot to talk about.' She waved a casual hand. 'I'd better get going, before she falls back to sleep. See you later, Javier.'

'Yes, later,' Javier nodded, and went back to snipping. 'Anya,' he called as she reached the back door. 'You really do look good today. Hot. Very hot!'

Hot! Anya looked pleased. Hot would do nicely. She opened the door and let herself in. Hopefully Fergal would think so too when they all met over dinner that evening. She suspected Liam already did, judging by the way he'd gawped as she passed him on her way to the car that morning. Even as she drove away, she could feel the burn of his eyes on her back. But, as usual, the vet's admiration was unlooked for. He made her feel uncomfortable, grubby almost. There was something unsavoury about him. Something she couldn't quite put her finger on. Sister Martha would have said, 'Always trust your instincts, Anya. Your inner voice is there for a reason. It's your primeval warning system, the equivalent of the hair rising on the back of a dog's neck, or a horse suddenly shying. It's a flock of birds taking off in a flap for no apparent reason. Listen, always listen, and it will never let you down.'

'Anya!' Lady Kathleen's face lit up as Anya tapped lightly and peered round the bedroom door. She gave a little start of surprise. 'My goodness, don't you look a picture! Come in, come in, so I can see you properly.'

A little self-consciously as Lady Kathleen was, after all, Hollywood royalty, Anya stood awkwardly as the older woman's eyes travelled over her. But her worries were unfounded as Lady Kathleen clapped her hands with delight.

Anya blushed modestly. 'It's nothing special. Everything's from the high street.' She smoothed her hand down the skirt of her retro-style tea-dress. 'And I've had the shoes for ages. They were on sale somewhere.'

Lady Kathleen threw up her hands with a mock groan. 'Anya, Anya, Anya. What am I always telling you? Some people could get away with wearing a bin bag and look like a million dollars, whilst others can throw all the money in the world at designer clothes and still look like a dog's dinner. You, my dear, very luckily, fall into the first category.' She tilted her head to one side. 'In fact, you remind me of a young Maureen O'Hara, with that glorious Celtic colouring. I met her once and was quite dreadfully star-struck. I believe she thought me an idiot.' She gave a throaty giggle and smacked the back of her hand. 'Oh dear, naughty, naughty. There I go again. Living in the past. You must think me such a bore.'

'No, no, not at all,' Anya hastened to reassure her. She sat beside the bed and took the hand Lady Kathleen had slapped, gently rubbing the slight red mark left. Though showing signs of age, Lady Kathleen's hands were soft, with long manicured nails and a whopper of a diamond ring given to her by one of her leading men, whose identity she kept secret, 'Because, if his wife were to find out, my dear, she'd kill him. Or, worse, divorce him and take half his worldly goods. Californian law, you see. Fifty-fifty. Straight down the middle.'

'Shall I open the drapes?' Anya looked round the dimly lit though luxurious room. 'It seems such a shame to block out the daylight, especially today when the sun has got his hat on.'

Lady Kathleen looked pensive. 'Oh yes, please do. You know, sometimes I forget there's a whole other world out there. And to think I travelled across most of it at one time or another.' A wicked grin and a wink. 'By private jet or yacht, usually, wined and dined by gorgeous and wealthy men. But now, alas, my world has shrunk to these four walls, and the gorgeous, wealthy men are either dead, dead fat, dead bald or dead broke.'

'I'll take you out for a walk later, if you like,' Anya suggested, paying no attention to the melodramatics, knowing Lady Kathleen was merely playing to an audience. 'Nothing too tiring, just round Wishbone Lake, say, and back. We could stop by and have a look at JC's club, maybe even take a picnic? The weather is fine enough, as long as you wrap up.'

'A picnic!' Lady Kathleen grew animated. 'I'd like that. Can we have *foie gras*, oysters and champagne?'

'No. Egg and cress sandwiches and lemonade,' Anya quipped. 'The studio has cut the budget.'

'Lousy bastards!' Lady Kathleen went into Mae West mode. 'They should string 'em up.'

Anya smiled, enjoying her clowning. Despite the restless night, today was a good day. But often the pain in her back was so bad that she could scarcely raise a smile. Anya went over to Lady Kathleen's enormous wardrobe and threw the doors open theatrically. Inside, row upon row of splendid gowns jostled each other for space, silks, satins, chiffons, a veritable rainbow of colour. 'So,' she asked, with a salaam motion. 'Who do you feel like today?'

Without hesitation, Lady Kathleen pointed to a tea-dress of rosebud-sprigged white lawn, a souvenir of her Hollywood years with which she simply could not bear to part.

'Scarlett O'Hara. Definitely, Miz Scarlett. With a great big straw bonnet, don't you think? And who cares if I end up looking more like Baby Jane. Most people think I'm dead anyway.' She wrinkled her nose. 'And frankly, my dear, who gives a damn!' Energised by the prospect of an excursion, albeit just round the grounds of Castle Mac Tíre, she tossed the bedclothes to one side. 'Come along, my dear, let's get this show on the road.'

Anya winced to see how her nightgown had ridden up her thighs, exposing her sparrow-thin, frail legs.

Lady Kathleen sighed, catching the look. 'Shocking, isn't it, especially since I used to have such great legs. Dancer's pins. Now they look like two sticks of dried spaghetti.' She picked up a photograph from her bedside table and showed it to Anya. 'My daughter took after me, which was lucky since her father was built like a Sherman tank. Not that movie directors need good looks. They can have anyone or anything they desire, because they have the magic wand, the fairy dust that turns toads into princes and,' her lips twisted wryly, 'ignorant little Irish girls into movie stars.'

She tapped the glass of the photograph. 'Roisin, at eighteen. Pretty, wasn't she?'

Anya took the photograph and nodded. 'Very. I can see you in her. Same eyes. Same hair.'

Lady Kathleen looked pleased. 'I never wanted her to be an only child, didn't want her to be lonely, but ...' She shrugged. 'Man

67

proposes and God disposes. It just didn't happen. One child was my lot and one child I got.'

She took the picture back from Anya, traced a tender fingertip over her daughter's image. 'I think, perhaps, that's why she was so eager to marry and have a child herself but, sadly, it turned out to be not quite as she imagined.' Her face softened in reflection. 'Still, we had each other *and* Castle Mac Tíre. I always made sure that was protected in any divorce settlement. When life got too much for me in La La Land, or for her in Argentina, this is where we retreated to lick our wounds, Roisin and I, before making another assault on the world.' She dusted an imaginary speck of dust from the picture, replacing it at an angle, where she could see it more easily. 'There have been Ormonds at Castle Mac Tíre for six hundred years but I am the last.'

'But what about JC?' Anya asked surprised. 'As your grandson, will he not inherit?' Lady Kathleen smiled sadly. 'Yes, but he won't stay here. His heart is in Argentina.' Ever the actress, she began to sing, reminded of an old song. '*Under the Argentine sky, there with a beautiful lady, with dark and sparkling eyes.* Ah, Anya, I wish it were so. I wish there was such a lady.'

Unwilling to let her slip into melancholia, Anya was bracing. 'Maybe there is. Maybe he's just keeping her to himself for the moment.' She picked up the white dress from where she'd laid it at the foot of the bed and shook it free of creases. 'Then again, maybe the lady's eyes are blue and sparkling. And could be she's Australian and not Argentinian.'

'Orla?' Lady Kathleen asked hopefully. No, more than that, *eagerly*, Anya thought.

'Well, they certainly spend enough time together.'

'Ah, yes,' Lady Kathleen remarked cryptically, 'but there's spending time, and then there's *spending* time.'

Anya sent her a searching look. 'You're in a bit of a funny mood today,' she said. 'Tell you what, let's leave JC's love life to one side for the moment and concentrate on getting you dressed. Rhett won't wait forever, you know.'

'I'll think about that tomorrow,' Lady Kathleen smiled.

'I've got your gear,' Orla told her sister, her nose wrinkling at the smell of unwashed body and dirty bedclothes. She turned to JC, who had come in behind her. 'Ugh, we need someone to mind her. I don't want her lying in her own filth. There's got to be someone we can trust. Someone who needs the money.'

'The more people who know, the more chance there is of somebody finding out. I don't like it.' JC looked grim. 'It's risky enough having to get the shit for her. It could jeopardise everything.'

'It's a chance we have to take. Think about it, would you?' Taking a syringe filled with a cloudy liquid from her pocket, Orla walked over to where her sister was lying listlessly, her eyes staring blankly at the ceiling. She lifted one of her arms, tapping it sharply on the inside of the elbow.

'Okay, let's see if we can find a nice big vein. Ah, good, here we go.' Slowly, Orla depressed the plunger. When it was empty she withdrew the needle and pressed on the vein for a moment to stem any bleeding. 'That wasn't so bad, was it?' she said, as if talking to an infant. 'Now, how about something to eat?'

In answer, her sister rolled over and retched.

'Jesus!' Orla jumped back. 'I don't care what you say, JC, we have to get someone. What if she does that when she's on her own? She could choke to death.'

'What if she does?' JC asked callously, then thought better as he saw Orla's face. 'Oh, all right, leave it with me.'

Before they left Orla cleaned and changed her sister, put fresh sheets on the bed and made her some beans on toast, which were left uneaten.

'I wish it was all over,' she told JC as he locked the door and pocketed the key behind them. 'Sometimes, I wish we'd never started it.'

'Too late for regrets.' JC looked swiftly round to make sure there was no one in sight. 'We're both in this up to our necks.'

'I know. I was just saying.'

'Well, don't,' JC rounded on her. 'This is going to work. You're going to get what you want. And I'm going to get what I want.'

Orla wound her arms around his neck. 'You know what I want, baby. What I've always wanted.'

He unclasped her arms. 'All in good time.'

Orla rolled her eyes. 'Well, if there's nothing better on offer, I suppose I'd better be getting back to Lismore.' She looked faintly disgruntled. 'Just as well the gorgeous Fergal is there to amuse me.' It was a poor attempt to make him jealous and JC saw right through it.

'Yes, indeed,' he said. 'I'm sure he'll be more than willing to see to your baser needs.'

'Perfectly natural needs, JC,' Orla snapped. 'How I wish you didn't always have to be quite so Catholic in your thinking.'

'Damn!' JC ducked down suddenly. 'Someone's coming. Back inside, quickly!'

'Good Lord, that was close,' Orla gasped, as he just managed to unlock the door in time and they fell back inside. 'Who is it anyway?' Sidling over to the small window, she peered carefully out. 'Well, well, well. If it isn't Anya Keating and your grandmother.'

JC slapped his forehead in annoyance. 'Oh no, what are they doing here? I promised Grandmother I would show her the club when it was finished. I didn't think she'd come by herself.'

'She didn't come by herself,' Orla reminded him. 'Haven't you ever met Anya? She's Macdara's PA.'

'Yes, of course, I have. She often visits my grandmother.' JC nodded. 'But wait, did you say Keating?'

'Yes, Keating,' Orla said. 'At least, I'm pretty sure it is.'

Keating. Keating. The name rang a bell with JC. His forehead puzzled, then cleared again. Of course! The woman Liam had sent to clean the Hell Fire Club was called Keating too. Clare Keating. Curious, JC joined Orla at the window. But surely there could be no connection between that appalling individual and the beautiful young woman pushing his grandmother's wheelchair? JC scowled. Liam had better hope so. He'd been warned. There was to be no connection of any kind with Lismore.

Beside him, Orla gave a sudden snort of laughter. 'Hey, JC, don't you think Lady Kathleen looks a bit like mad old Bette Davis in

*Whatever Happened to Baby Jane?* Better hope she doesn't serve you up roast rat tonight although I guess there's enough of them running round Castle Mac Tíre.'

'Shut up!' Grabbing her roughly, JC pushed Orla up against the wall. He put his face right up against hers, so close she could feel his spittle peppering her skin. 'Do not ever make fun of my grandmother. She is a lady, an aristocrat. You are not fit to lick her boots.'

Orla wrenched herself free. 'Okay, okay. It was just a joke. I think the world of Lady Kay, you should know that.'

'Some things are not for joking,' JC snapped. 'You need to know, Orla, that in Argentina the family is sacred.'

'You do surprise me,' Orla said drily, smarting from his rough treatment of her. 'And there was I thinking only money was sacred to you.'

'Money is important to me,' JC admitted. 'But only because of what it can do to restore my family to the greatness which is rightfully theirs, both here and in Argentina.'

'I know. How could I not?' Orla gestured vaguely round. 'Isn't that precisely how we got into this mess in the first place?'

'Not a mess. A worthy cause,' JC said, a smile beginning to form on his handsome face. At the sound of vomiting behind them, it quickly disappeared.

'Oh, no,' Orla spun round and stared at the figure half on, half off the bed. 'She's bloody been sick. I knew it wasn't going to be easy, but ...'

'Better and better,' JC groaned, as below on the grass, Anya set about unpacking a picnic hamper.

'I never ever liked this place,' Lady Kathleen said, accepting a sandwich from Anya and gazing round. 'As a child I was scared to come here in case I might bump into the devil.' She smiled, dismissive of her naive younger self, letting her eyes roam over the newly restored Hell Fire Club. As in the case of Castle Mac Tíre, the club, originally a Norman church, had been added to over the years, but the most striking addition was a round tower tacked on to one side, the vision of an Ormond ancestor with more money than taste. When funds permitted, JC intended to raze it to the ground. In the meantime the structure had on it a notice deeming it unsafe, and the great studded door set halfway up the wall at the top of a flight of rickety iron steps was locked against intruders.

'Mac once dared me to come here at midnight,' Lady Kathleen remembered. 'And, although I was terrified out of my mind, I came anyway.' There was no need to tell Anya that she would have walked over hot coals naked and with bleeding feet to please Macdara, had he so wished. Her gaze climbed to a small archer's window shaped like a cross, though the tower had been built long after the age of archery. Presumably, her taste-challenged ancestor had fancied himself as a bit of a Robin Hood.

'And did you?' Anya asked, hugely entertained by the idea. 'Did you meet the devil?'

'Indeed, I did,' Kathleen laughed. 'And he looked just like Mac. See that wall over there.' She pointed to a crumbling pile of stones. 'He was crouched down behind there waiting to leap out at me. I screamed like a banshee and almost jumped out of my skin, even though I was more than half-expecting it.'

'I'm not sure I would have been so brave,' Anya confessed, goose-bumps prickling up along the bare skin of her arms. 'Even now, with the sun shining and the birds singing, it feels kind of creepy. It's that sensation of eyes watching you.'

'That'll be the ghosts,' Lady Kathleen announced matter-of-factly. 'Before it fell into disuse, generations of Ormonds were chris-tened, married and buried here. There was a crypt too, beneath the church, although whether any bodies remain there still is doubt-ful. Legend has it that my wicked old ancestor, the founder of the original Lismore Hell Fire Club, dug them all up. He planned to turn them into zombie slaves or some such, apparently.'

'Really? How horrible!' Anya gasped, as an errant cloud erased the sun for a moment, sending India rubber shadows leap-frogging across the grass and over the same wall behind which Macdara had once hidden. 'He must have been a raving lunatic.'

'I doubt it has any basis in truth.' Lady Kathleen dusted some loose crumbs off the front of her dress. 'Old places often lend themselves to fantastical stories, especially churches and grave-yards. It's probably just a tale dreamed up by the locals to frighten their children into going to bed and to warn their teens off drinking and fornicating among the ruins. You know how it is, things get embellished over the years.' She finished her sandwich and waved away the offer of another. 'Still, there's no doubt the man was a preposterous old rogue, although justice was served to a degree since he died of syphilis, I believe.' She stretched down, plucked a buttercup from the grass and twiddled it under her chin. The petals reflected gold against her skin. She smiled. 'Oh, dear, don't look so serious, Anya, child. The dead hold no power. It's the living you need to guard against.' She crushed the flower between her fingers and tossed it away. 'I must say, JC did rather well, though. The old place looks quite splendid now, doesn't it?'

Anya nodded. 'Absolutely. Perhaps he'll give you a grand tour of the inside some time.'

'Yes, I'd like that,' Lady Kathleen said. 'He raised all the money himself too – never asked me for a penny.' She rolled her eyes comically. 'Which is just as well since the piggy bank is empty, as my friendly bank manager persists in reminding me almost on a daily basis. Will you go to it, Anya, do you think? Will you trip the light fantastic, or whatever it is you kids say nowadays. Cut shapes?'

'I've no idea what they call it,' Anya confessed. 'I'm not the dancing or clubbing type. The expression "two left feet" might have been coined for me.' She topped up their beakers from a bottle of Javier's home-made lemonade. 'It's a private members' club, in any case, and far too expensive for the likes of me. And also, a little too exotic maybe.' She chose her words carefully, not wishing to alarm Lady Kathleen about the scurrilous rumours that had begun circulating in the neighbourhood concerning 'funny goings-on' at the HFC. To be fair, with its colourful history and colourful proprietor, the club was always going to lend itself to that kind of speculation. In fact, she wouldn't be at all surprised if it was all a PR stunt orchestrated by the canny JC, on the grounds that any publicity was good publicity.

'Oh, but I'm sure JC would …' Lady Kathleen began, then fell silent as Anya shook her head.

'No, Lady Kay, please don't bother. I've never been a night owl. I was born old, Sister Martha says, and she may be right since I much prefer going to bed early with a good book than going out raving.' She smiled to take the sting out of her disinterest. 'Anyway, I told you I can't dance to save myself. I'd be an embarrassment to myself and everyone else.'

Lady Kathleen looked wistful. 'I used to love dancing,' she said. 'I could have danced all night, as the song goes. JC has the body of a dancer too, don't you think? He's so strong and lithe and handsome.'

Arrogant too, Anya could have added, and cold. But knowing how much the older woman doted on her grandson, and having no wish to cause pain, she simply smiled.

'Another sandwich? More lemonade? No? Well, perhaps we'd better be moving on. I promised Javier I wouldn't tire you out.' Anya began to tidy away the picnic things, stowing them in a bag hanging from the back of the wheelchair.

'Dear Javier,' Lady Kathleen said, flicking a stray crumb from her skirt. 'Always so considerate. What a lucky day for me when JC brought him to Castle Mac Tíre, though I fear JC is not always quite as kind to him as he ought to be. I hear things sometimes, you know. Things that go bump in the night.'

It was an odd thing for Lady Kathleen to say, and clueless as to the best way of responding, Anya opted for silence. Steering the chair away from the church, she took the meandering pathway to Wishbone Lake, not at all sorry to be leaving the Hell Fire Club, with its spooky atmosphere, behind.

'Finally!' Orla said, watching as Anya began to stow away the picnic things in a basket. 'I thought they were going to set up camp. You don't think it's odd how Anya seems to make herself invaluable to the elderly and frail, my grandfather and your grandmother? A case of where there's a will, do you think?'

'No, I don't,' JC snapped. 'Maybe Anya is just a nice person.'

Orla frowned. 'Easy to be nice, when you've not been shat upon all your life.' She turned to look at the wan figure on the bed. Dead eyes met hers. 'Isn't that right, sis?'

JC followed her gaze. 'All this trouble, for what? A drug-addled waste of space. You should have just left her in Australia. She would have been dead in no time.'

'Leave it, JC. I told you, I have my reasons. Now, let's go before anyone else just happens on the scene. Mac will be wondering where I am and I'd sooner not do anything to rouse his suspicions.'

After a final check to make sure the coast was clear, they left the tower, securely locking the big door behind them. Orla glanced worriedly back.

'You will see about getting someone in to look after her?'

'Yes,' JC said. 'I said I will, but I don't like it. She was never part of the plan.' But then again Orla herself was only part of JC's plan for as long as it suited him. The scowl changed to a smile. For now, he needed to keep her on side. He softened his voice. 'Don't worry, my love, it's all going to work out beautifully.'

'Oh, look, Anya,' Lady Kathleen pointed excitedly as they rounded the little copse of copper beech trees which until now on their walk had hidden Wishbone Lake from sight. 'The Lismore lads are swimming some of the horses. Yoo hoo!' She waved furiously. 'Is this a private party, or can anyone join in?'

Equally charmed, Anya followed her gaze. Today was May Day, and the first day of the year warm enough to exercise the horses in this way. Judging from the shouts of laughter, everyone present, man and beast, seemed to be thoroughly enjoying themselves. Swimming was particularly good for any horses who had sustained injury to their joints or who had been off form and needed building up a bit. Mac raised his hand as they approached.

'Kay, my darlin', how nice it is to see you out and about and, of course, you're more than welcome to join us. We wouldn't have it any other way.' He grinned roguishly. 'And it is your land, after all.' He bent to kiss her cheek. 'I trust Anya's been taking good care of you?'

Lady Kathleen smiled fondly. 'The best. We've been having a wonderful time. I'm beginning to feel like a young girl again.'

'I always feel like a young girl.' Liam, also present, quickly ran a lascivious eye over Anya, making her cringe. He winked at Lady Kathleen. 'Though there's many a good tune to be played on an old fiddle,' he paused for a drum-roll effect, 'if you have a good strong bow.'

Lady Kathleen tinkled gaily, her flirtatious nature delighting in any flattery, no matter the source.

'Oh, Mr O'Hanlon, what a naughty man you are, and so like that gorgeous Robert Wagner. I met him once, you know.' But, like Anya, she was suddenly riveted by the sight of Fergal emerging from the water, with Glengarriff trailing behind him on a long pair of reins. Wearing only a pair of black shorts that clung to his wet skin, he was an arresting sight, although judging by his unselfconscious manner, totally oblivious to the effect his charms were having on both women.

'Lady Kathleen. Anya,' he greeted them, sweeping a displaced lock of shiny hair back from his forehead. 'Come to watch the horses, have you?'

'Not, especially, no,' Anya told him, trying not to sound like an overawed schoolgirl. 'We went for a picnic and decided to go back by way of the lake. In fact, we'd no idea you were swimming the horses today.' It was the truth, so why did she feel a flush creep up her neck? Fussing unnecessarily with the bag hanging on the back of Lady Kathleen's wheelchair, she removed an empty beaker, examined it briefly for no apparent reason, and put it back again in exactly the same place. Why, oh why, did she have to be so awkward in these situations, so tongue-tied and gauche? She imagined with envy how Orla would react, how she would tease him about his sculpted torso glistening with water diamonds, and the 'Daniel Craig in *James Bond*' fit of his swimming trunks. How she wished she could be like her, or even like Lady Kathleen, who, ever the coquette, was eyeing him up with the same interest as the main course in a three-star Michelin restaurant.

'And I must say I'm very glad that we did decide to come back this way,' Lady Kathleen said, making no effort to look away. 'The last time I saw you with so few clothes on, young man, you were about ten years of age, riding round the paddock at Lismore, playing at being Buffalo Bill.' Lady Kathleen chuckled. 'I must say you've turned out rather well. Now, if only I were forty years younger ...'

Leaving Lady Kathleen to hold court, Anya walked round to the other side of Glengarriff, who was pawing the ground. She placed a soothing hand against his neck, her fingers trembling slightly, unnerved by her proximity to the half-dressed Fergal.

'Hello, sweetheart,' she whispered. 'How are you doing? All better now?'

'I'm fine, thanks,' Fergal joked, peering round the horse's neck. 'Oh, sorry, were you talking to Glengarriff?' He grinned. 'He's tip-top. Almost back to normal, and he's loving today. You know what a water baby he is. The swimming is doing him the power of good. Thank God for Wishbone Lake, eh?'

'Thank Lady Kathleen, more like,' Macdara said, joining the conversation as he threw a grateful glance in her direction. The cost of a custom-built hydrotherapy pool ran into thousands of euros, an expense he was spared through her generosity. The lake was just the right depth, had a sloping edge and was utterly perfect for their needs.

'It's yours for so long as I have breath in my body,' Lady Kathleen had promised. Whether JC would continue to allow the Lismore horses to swim in the lake after his grandmother was gone remained to be seen. Lady Kathleen suspected not, considering how he had already raised the subject with her, insisting that Lismore's finances were healthier than theirs, and adding a somewhat bitter rider that, all things being equal, Lismore rightly belonged to Castle Mac Tíre. Arrant nonsense, thought Lady Kathleen. Following that logic, families up and down the country would be dispossessed of their land and property, on the basis that it had originally belonged to someone else. So she held firm, reminding her grandson that Macdara was a loyal and generous friend. She had only to ask and he would be more than happy to hand her a blank cheque. Indeed, he had offered more than once. As far as she was concerned, he and his horses would always be welcome at Wishbone Lake.

Now Macdara came over and placed a gentle hand on her shoulder. 'Thank you, Kay,' he said. 'You're a star in every way.'

She picked it up and pressed her lips lightly to the back. 'Mac, my dear, that's what friends are for. I'm happy to help. Always.'

Watching them and their obvious affection for each other, Anya wondered, not for the first time, why they had never got together as a couple. They were both on their own now, both lonely, and it was apparent to even the most casual observer that they thought the world of each other. Upbraiding herself for always hankering after the fairytale ending, Anya turned to look at the other horses emerging from the lake, including Amirah, the beautiful grey mare, Skibbereen, a stunning chestnut gelding and, the diva, Cashel Queen, led out by her groom, Kitty Brennan.

Cheerfully, Kitty waved at Lady Kathleen and Anya. A vivacious young redhead, she had only just turned eighteen. She was incurably horse-mad and, judging by the quick sideways glance she threw Liam's way, mad about him as well.

Surprised, Anya wondered if she was the only one to intercept the look. Certainly Liam didn't appear to notice, busy as he was with a charm offensive on Lady Kathleen. However, given his propensity to flirt with anything female, Anya thought it inconceivable that he could ignore the vision of beauty emerging like Aphrodite from the water. Certainly, Kitty's transformation from tomboy stable lass into a mythical goddess in a scarlet swimsuit skimming her slender body did not escape the notice of the other red-blooded men present. But when Kitty turned her attention back to Cashel Queen, Anya saw Liam shoot her a quick look. Surprisingly, she detected no admiration in it, nothing remotely lustful.

Thinking about it later, Anya would have described it more as a look of cold speculation, possibly even dislike. The puzzle was why? Why on earth would Liam look at Kitty in that way? Anya couldn't help but be concerned about the younger girl. Liam was not a man with whom she, herself, would like to cross swords. Despite his womanising image, the studied charm and smarm, she suspected that really he was a simmering cauldron of misogyny, a caveman who wouldn't hesitate to use his wooden club.

'Mac,' Lady Kathleen's voice, suddenly querulous, shredded her thoughts. 'You must tell Orla to visit me. She's been home for ages now and I would like very much to see how she's changed. Will you tell her?'

'Of course.' Macdara looked slightly shamefaced. 'I should have thought of it sooner.'

'Actually,' Lady Kathleen corrected, 'Orla should have thought of it sooner.' Given how she had spoiled her rotten as a child, the request was not unreasonable and Macdara acknowledged it with a slight nod.

Alerted by a sudden charge in the air, Anya left Glengarriff and Fergal, and hurried over to the elderly lady. 'Come on,' she said softly, positioning herself behind the wheelchair and releasing the brake with her foot. 'You must be getting tired. Let's get you home.'

'Ah no! What have you done to my lady? She looks *muy* tired!' Javier, who was proving to be something of a drama queen, possibly under Lady Kathleen's tutelage, glared at Anya when they arrived back at Castle Mac Tíre. He had been waiting for them in the yard, arms folded across his chest, looking for all the world like a displeased school teacher. Briskly, Javier nudged her out of the way and, taking control of the wheelchair, deftly manoeuvred it over to a ramp by the door. 'Come, my lady. I give you some nice zoop, eh? Chicken and rosemaria. Then sleep, yes? Some people,' another dirty look at Anya, 'have got no sense.'

'I am tired, Javier,' Lady Kathleen confessed, happily surrendering herself to his fussing. 'But I've had a splendid time all the same, so don't be too hard on Anya.' She blew her a kiss. 'Come back soon, darling, okay?'

'Of course.' Anya returned the gesture and shrugged an apology at Javier. 'Night, night, Miss Scarlett. Sleep well.'

# Chapter 10

Sister Martha double-checked that everything had been cleared away and that the doors of the medicine cabinets were locked, before switching off the lights and securing the door of the clinic behind her. It had been a long day and she was tired, but it was a satisfying tiredness, the kind that comes from the knowledge that you've put in a good day's work. Generally, she would have been home by now, but tonight she had stayed late to stock-take and to catch up on outstanding paperwork. Her stomach gurgled noisily, reminding Sister Martha that she'd eaten nothing but a small sandwich at lunchtime and that, as a result, she was ravenously hungry. Eagerly, she set off, anticipating supper, a hot soak and then the luxury of slipping between the crisp linen sheets of her bed. If she could nail her eyes open, she might read a chapter or two of Butler's *Lives of the Saints*, a present from Anya for her birthday and an inspiring read.

Outside, the streets were black patent, glistening from a shower of rain that had fallen sometime in the past hour, ending what on the whole had been a warm and sunny day. Ideal weather for the farmers: sun in the day, rain at night.

Pocketing the keys in her habit, Sister Martha set off upon the short walk to the convent. A rousing chorus of cheers from a pub told her that a big sporting event was under way, accounting in some part for the dearth of human life on the streets as people watched on television. It left her free to enjoy the peace and tranquillity of the evening undisturbed. The moon, a clipped fingernail, scratched at the fabric of the sky, revealing an underskirt shot through with turquoise, pink and flecks of gold, the remaining hallmarks of the exiled day. The colours put her in mind of the jewels in Doherty's window, and the diffracted light of the opals in particular. Occasionally, she liked to look at them, nestled in their satin- and silk-lined velvet boxes, admiring them as one might a precious work of art, though having not the slightest desire to possess them herself. Sister Martha was that rare thing in life, someone who was totally and utterly content with her lot, a contentment that was, perhaps, the greatest treasure of all.

Somewhere, out of sight, a door opened and banged shut again, releasing a belch of noise in the short interval. Disturbed, a dog barked once, twice, then settled down again.

A figure stepped out suddenly from an alleyway just ahead.

'Evenin', Sister Martha. Lovely night, ain't it?'

The nun's hand fluttered across her chest, as she recognised the figure as Anya's mother. 'Oh, Clare, you startled me. I was deep in thought.'

'You looked it,' the woman said agreeably enough, her eyes glowing amber in the downcast light of a street lamp. 'Thinking about me, were you?' The pleasant note turned sour. 'Thinking what an awful bloody mother I was to your precious Anya? Thinking of what a cock-up I made of everything.' Clare Keating took a menacing step forward, causing the nun to back against a wall. Her breath reeked of a stale mixture of spirits and tobacco.

'No, not at all.' Sister Martha met the aggression with mildness, long years of experience dealing with recalcitrant pupils and, more recently, drug addicts having taught her the wisdom of remaining calm. 'My mind was a million miles away.' She gave a little self-deprecating grin. 'Believe it or not, I was thinking about the moon.'

'The fucking moon!' Clare Keating brought her face right up against Sister Martha's, so close that even in the darkness the nun could clearly make out the mapping of broken veins on her cheeks and nose, and the way her features, once as delicate as Anya's, had thickened through decades of loose living.

'Or, about a poem about the moon, to be exact. "Silver", it's called.' Deliberately, Sister Martha kept her voice even, though the invasion of her personal space had caused her heart to thud in a most uncomfortable fashion.

'By Walter de la Mare. I know it.' Curiously, the other woman's face softened and she took a step backward. She almost smiled and for a split second the echo of the once pretty woman was discernible amongst the ruined face. 'I learnt it, as a kid. Listen.' Taking a deep breath, she clasped her hands low in front of her, like a compliant schoolgirl standing before the head nun. Her voice lost its grating edge, as, sing-song, she began to intone the rhyme. '"Slowly, silently, now the moon. Walks the night in her silver shoon."'

Sister Martha clapped her hands, delighted and astonished at the almost schizophrenic change in the other woman's demeanour. 'That's right, Clare. Well done. Can you recall the rest?'

'"This way, and that, she peers, and sees ... silver fruit upon silver trees"?'

'Silver fruit upon silver trees. Yes, yes, that's right.' Sister Martha's smile widened, then faded as Clare appeared to switch once more, her eyes taking on an almost feral glint. 'Clare?' Her voice wavered. 'Clare, are you all right? Only you look like ...'

'Look like what?' The last vestiges of the schoolgirl disappeared and, once more, the older Clare was in evidence, aggressive lips peeled back in a snarl. 'Look like I've taken something? Come on, you fucking Holy Mary, isn't that what you really mean? Have I fallen off the fucking wagon?'

'No. No, that's not what I meant at all.' But too late, Sister Martha realised that Clare Keating was indeed as high as a kite, and was getting higher and more out of control with every second. 'I was just concerned for you, that's all,' she said, striving to sound calm, unconcerned and in control. Show fear, her instincts warned her, and the other woman would attack like a dog.

'Concerned? Aw, how sweet!' Clare's mouth screwed up, mocking. She leaned forward and jabbed Sister Martha hard in the chest. 'Tell you what, Mother-fucking-Therese, why don't you take both your concern and your poetry and shove them both right up your holy arse? You don't fool me one bit with your praying and preaching and Good Samaritan shit. You turned my daughter against me.

I made a mistake, but so fucking what? Blame God for that. He made me human.'

She jabbed again, harder. Once. Twice, as the nun reeled back gasping. 'Everything would have been all right. Everything would have blown over, if you hadn't gone round spreading poison in the ears of the authorities. And in her ears too.' Spit flew from Clare's mouth. 'Anya is my daughter. *Mine!* Not yours, you dried up, crusty old hag. I brought her into the world.' She looked sly, almost triumphant. 'And I can fucking bring her out too!'

Terrified by these last words and what fate the woman might have in mind for Anya, the nun made a supreme effort to push past, only too conscious of the emptiness of the streets and the hopelessness of calling for help.

'I'm sorry you feel like that, Clare,' she said, still trying to hide her fear. 'My intention was only ever to protect Anya. I'll bid you good night and pray you find the strength to turn your life around.'

'Hah! Like I'm just going to let you walk away.' Clare Keating gave a mocking bark of laughter as her temper escalated. Her eyes narrowed into amber slits and she grabbed the nun with surprising strength and smashed her back against the wall. 'Right, enough with the small talk! The keys for the clinic, give them to me.'

Winded, Sister Martha struggled to catch her breath, her hand feeling for the reassuring weight of the keys in her pocket, inadvertently acting as a signpost. 'No! Go home, Clare. Please. Let's forget this ever happened. You're not yourself.'

The other woman's eyebrows rose, taunting. 'And what if I am myself, eh? And what if I don't want to go home, or to forget this?' She paused, meaningfully. 'What if I was just to take them?'

A dribble of blood ran from one of Sister Martha's nostrils. She felt the warmth of its passage, the metallic taste running over her lips, almost like a caress. 'Please,' she said faintly, feeling the world begin to spin, so that the moon suddenly looked as if it had fallen from the sky and landed at her feet. 'Please, Clare. Let's forget tonight ever happened. I won't hold it against you, I promise. We won't even mention it again.'

Clare Keating pretended to think about the offer, then screwed up her mouth. 'Nah, I've got a better idea.' Lightning fast, she pulled a knife from her pocket and held it against the nun's throat. 'How about *I* hold *this* against *you*? You know,' she said, almost conversationally, as a feeling of immense power surged through her emaciated body and, suddenly, she drew the blade across the thin neck of her quarry, 'I never did like nuns.'

As Sister Martha slumped to the ground, Clare knelt and removed the keys, before wiping the blade of the knife clean on the dying woman's skirt. She got to her feet and gazed down, almost disinterestedly as the blood pooled around Sister Martha's head in the grisly parody of a halo. 'Guess what,' she told the inert figure. 'I've just remembered some more of that stupid poem. "And moveless fish in the water gleam, by silver reeds in a silver stream".' She lashed out with her foot, kicking at the prone body. 'And, by the way, I only know it because fucking nuns, like you, beat it into me.'

Kitty Brennan sat up in bed, her eyes riveted on the bedroom door, through which she could hear raised voices. Raised, angry voices. Pulling the sheets up around her bare shoulders she wondered fearfully if Liam's wife had arrived back unexpectedly from visiting her sister in New York, then realised that since Liam had spoken to her there just a few hours earlier, such could not be the case. Curiosity piqued, she clambered naked out of bed and crept carefully to the top of the stairs and peered over the banister. In the hallway just below, Liam stood arguing with a woman whose face was hidden from view.

'You must be fucking mad.' Like someone in pain, he was holding his hands to his head, his feet jigging about on the hallway carpet as though they had a life of their own. 'I knew it was a mistake getting mixed up with you. You're off your bloody head. Jesus Christ, how dare you show up at my door like that? Anyone could have seen you.'

'No one saw me,' the woman answered. 'I swear. I was careful.' There was a raspy quality to her voice, the mark of a heavy smoker. 'Don't worry, no one can pin anything on us.'

'On *us*?' Liam's voice rose incredulously. 'On us? Listen, Keating, you mad bitch, this night's work has nothing to do with me. You did this all on your lonesome.'

'But you wanted the stuff. No questions asked, you said. So don't go getting all shirty with me.'

Her heart thudding loudly in her ears, Kitty leaned forward for a better look, even though that meant risking discovery. She could see a number of small boxes scattered on the floor below. Medicine boxes? She squinted her eyes in an attempt to see more clearly. Drugs? What the hell was going on? She already knew Liam was mixed up in something dodgy. The fact that he had stolen keta-mine from the veterinary practice at Lismore for onward distribu-tion at the Hell Fire Club was proof of that, she knew. But this looked more than just a few pills. This looked hardcore. Serious. One of the packets had burst open and a syringe lay like a pointer beside it. Recalling how he had scared her at the Hell Fire Club when he felt she had butted into his business, Kitty shrank back to a safe distance.

'I didn't expect you to top somebody for it.' Kitty suppressed a gasp as Liam grabbed the woman roughly by her shoulders and shook her violently. 'Do you even realise what you've done?' The rage in his voice was blistering and Kitty sent up a silent prayer of thanks that she was not the one in his sights. 'Has it sunk in, you mad fucking cow? You've murdered an innocent person. A nun, for God's sake! Do you really think you'll get away with it? The whole of Ireland will be up in arms till you're caught and locked up for life. I can't believe you'd try to involve me in shit like this!' Kitty watched anxiously as the woman struggled to free herself. 'It's my own fucking fault,' Liam yelled. 'I should have taken one look at you, you stinking bitch, and run for the hills. Never trust a smack-head, isn't that what they say? Christ knows, I wish I'd bloody listened.' Contemptuous, he flung the woman away, sending her crashing to her knees. Hurriedly, she began to gather up the boxes.

'Fine,' she yelled, stuffing them into a plastic carrier bag. 'I'll get out of your sight, but these are coming with me. It won't be hard to find another taker, believe me.'

'Leave them,' Liam snarled, wrenching the bag from her. 'But you'd better clear off, get yourself to England or somewhere, disappear into the wide blue yonder or fucking hell for all I care. There's to be no connection between you and me whatsoever, do you hear me? As far as I'm concerned, I never laid eyes on your ugly face. Never!'

Liam's unwanted visitor struggled to her feet. 'No fucking way. I'm listed as a patient at the drugs clinic. Now, I might not be brain of Ireland but even I know it might look more than a bit suspicious if I were to sling my hook in so timely a fashion. Much better if I stay here and bluff it out. Besides, I want to be near my daughter, ungrateful little bitch that she is.'

'You! You have a daughter?' There was profound disbelief in Liam's voice.

'Yes, me!' the woman yelled. 'I know she lives round here somewhere. That fucking busybody nun knew where, but she was as close as the grave.' She gave an evil laugh. 'But not as close as she is now, mind you. She wanted to protect her precious Anya from her own mother, the bitch.'

Anya! Kitty made the connection at the same time as Liam. Her eyebrows shot up. Macdara's PA at Lismore? It simply had to be. Anya wasn't a particularly common name in these parts. It was much too much of a coincidence. Poor girl! Kitty's heart went out to Anya, who had always been really nice to her. She couldn't blame her for keeping her mother secret. She was truly appalling.

Downstairs, Clare Keating was growing jittery. 'Enough bullshit!' She rubbed the tips of her fingers together. 'Just give me the wedge, O'Hanlon, and I'll get out of your face. Then we'll both be happy.'

'Right,' he snapped, 'but this is the last time.' He jabbed a finger at her. 'Wait there! And don't touch anything. I mean it. Don't move until I come back.'

As Liam disappeared into a room off the hallway, Kitty saw the woman grab an expensive-looking silver ornament from the half-moon telephone table and secrete in her pocket.

'Here.' He returned quickly with a small bundle of notes, which he shoved in her hand. 'Now piss off out of here and don't come back or, I swear, I won't be responsible for my actions.'

Bawling in protest at the fistful of notes, Clare struggled as Liam manhandled her out through the door and on to the driveway outside. 'It's worth twice as much, and you know it, you cheating bastard,' she screamed.

Pushing her viciously in the back, Liam sent her into a stumbling half-run. 'Yeah? Well, tell it to the guards! See how much sympathy they have for you, you murdering, low-life piece of shit.'

Slamming the door on a tirade of increasingly foul-mouthed abuse, Liam leaned against it as, unseen, Kitty made a dash back to the safety of the bedroom. Breathing heavily, a slow smile worked its way up the muscles of Liam's face. Well, well, he thought, what a night. His eyes went to the plastic carrier bag on the floor. The old hag was right, of course, the street value of the drugs was several times what he'd given her and, in its own way, the information he'd learned about Anya was likely to prove almost as profitable.

Anya Keating, the ice-maiden, who was too high and mighty to drop her knickers for him. God, he couldn't wait to get that girl on her back, which he most definitely would, just as soon as she found out he knew her dirty little secret! No one in their right mind would want such a lowly connection broadcast to the world. He had only to name his pound of flesh. Literally. The thought in itself was an aphrodisiac, and anxious to take care of his already burgeoning erection he quickly locked the boxes in his safe and then took the stairs two at a time back to the accommodating Kitty.

Muttering sleepily, Kitty turned on her back as he climbed astride and with little or no foreplay began pumping away. But something wasn't quite right, Liam realised, even as he conjured up visions of a compliant Anya to give further spice to his orgasm. Something was out of kilter. But it was only later, as he lay in the dark listening to his companion's breath escaping in little puffs from between her lips, did he realise what had been troubling him.

When he had come back to bed, Kitty's skin had been eerily cold.

Wrenched from a deep sleep just before midnight, Anya pulled on her dressing gown and went to answer a knock at the door. She wasn't unduly worried as from time to time there was an emergency at the stables that required her help. But one look at Macdara's face as she opened the door was enough to disabuse her of this notion. Looking at least ten years older than when she had seen him at dinner a couple of hours before, he was flanked on one side by a young policeman and by Bridie on the other, tears shining wetly on her cheeks. Wide-awake suddenly, Anya's heart hammered wildly in her chest and she had the strangest feeling of standing outside her own body, watching herself react.

'I knew it.' Anya's voice was tight and controlled, her emotions carefully stashed under lock and key. 'It's Clare, isn't it? So what's happened? One of her many boyfriends, was it? A drugs overdose?' Her fingers clutched nervously at the collar of her dressing gown, as though it might help anchor her in some way. She could hear herself gabbling, her words racing away like a runaway horse, but she was quite unable to stop. 'I knew it would happen one day, it was just a matter of time. You don't lead a life like hers without consequences. I won't cry, though. Not one tear.'

Horrified, Macdara realised what she thought. God! How he wished she was right and it was Clare he had come to tell her about, a woman whose passing no one would really mourn. But, Sister Martha, her beloved Sister Martha – Jesus what was that news going to do to her? He took a deep breath, steeling himself. It had to come from him. He was the nearest thing left to family. He held up a restraining hand.

'Anya. Anya, love. Stop talking just a minute. Please.' Her face crumpled as he guided her back into the room and pushed her gently down on the side of the bed. He sat beside her and, taking her hands between his, began to chafe them lightly, his voice breaking slightly. 'It's not Clare.'

Bewildered, she gazed up at him.

'It's Sister Martha,' he said softly. Macdara's own heart almost split in two as he broke the news he knew would break her heart. He would have given anything to spare her the grief he knew she would carry forever now. But there was no easy way to say it, no way of lessening the impact, and so he took a deep breath and told her straight.

And at first Anya just sat there, trembling, her eyes transfixed on the wall opposite, almost as if she could see his words sprayed there in Sister Martha's blood. When her scream finally came, it reverberated throughout the whole house and all the way down to the stables, causing the horses to move restlessly in their boxes.

'What the hell was that?' In the bedroom directly above Anya's, Fergal started for the door as, behind him, a naked Orla began picking up the clothes she'd tossed on the floor.

# Chapter 11

A great storm was raging. Five-year-old Anya lay in bed clutching her teddy bear to her chest as great flashes of lightning lit up the room, spotlighting all the scary corners. There were no curtains on the window and outside the skeleton of a gnarled old horse-chestnut tree cut obscene shapes against the glass, its monstrous tentacles playing conductor to the unearthly keening of the wind. Every now and then the wind lapsed and a mixture of raucous voices and heavy-metal music drifted up through the cracks in the bare floorboards. To celebrate Anya's fifth birthday, her mother was throwing a party for her own friends. 'Any excuse,' she liked to tell people. 'The original good-time girl, that's me.' If anyone thought it strange that neither Anya nor her friends were invited, they were wise enough to keep their opinions to themselves. Then again, Clare Keating fished her mates from a very slimy pool, where drink, drugs and loose morals reigned supreme. No one was going to bother too much about a young child, whose own mother didn't give a damn about her. No one wanted their fun spoilt. Clare may not have been good maternal material, but she was free with both her hospitality and her sexual favours, and boyfriends came and went with the frequency of city buses. Mostly, they took a leaf out of her mother's book and didn't bother with Anya.

But Clare's latest boyfriend seemed determined to be Anya's friend. Fat Ted, as his nickname suggested, was overweight and he smelt of a mixture of stale sweat, chip-oil – he owned a fish and chip shop – and beer. Watery, almost colourless eyes, submerged in deep folds of skin, followed Anya around the room whenever he came to visit and soon he took to bringing her little gifts: a bag of chips or a battered sausage, and, once, a bottle of fizzy pop. Anya took them, not because she wanted them, although she was almost always hungry, but because she knew her mother would smack her for being rude if she refused.

Time and time again she listened, close-faced, to Clare extolling Ted's virtues. He was the best thing that had ever happened to her, the first man she'd ever had who wasn't a complete loser. He had a few bob in the bank and a roof over his head that he actually owned. And if Fat Ted asked her to marry him – Clare knew he was just trying to pluck up the courage – there was no way she'd leave him kicking his heels. For Clare Keating, Fat Ted meant the good life she wanted. And nothing and no one was going to get in the way. And especially not a snotty-nosed kid. Snotty-nosed kid! The phrase rang like a constant refrain in Anya's head.

To please her mother, Anya put up with Fat Ted's tickling, his greasy kisses, though his breath made her feel sick. Obediently, she sat on his knee, freezing each time his podgy hand reached below her skirt whenever Clare left the room. And, each time, his hand moved a little higher, squeezed a little harder. Too young to give voice to the thought, Anya knew something was wrong. She just didn't know what.

The night of the storm was the first night Fat Ted actually came to her bedroom. The first, but not the last.

He never did propose to Clare Keating. Instead, Fat Ted married a widow with her own fish and chip shop – and three small daughters. At first, Clare ranted and raved, and called him every name under the sun. Then, philosophical, she moved on to the next likely prospect. If ever she took a moment to wonder why her daughter barely spoke or ate, and moved through life like a silent little wraith while doing nothing to call attention to herself, that was as far as her curiosity went.

In her own mind, Anya had become Alice. She had taken the potion and shrunk almost to invisibility. That way, when the uncles after Fat Ted came, she wasn't really there at all. She was off in Wonderland in pursuit of the White Rabbit.

The last uncle came to her room when she was ten and another party was in full swing downstairs. Someone was singing 'Bat Out of Hell' in a drunken rambunctious fashion, badly accompanied by someone else on a guitar. Guests came and went. Car doors slammed. Engines roared, then faded to a whine before distance took them out of earshot altogether. High-heels clacked on the pavement below. A man swore loudly. A woman laughed and called a cheery goodbye. Eventually, there was silence and Anya settled down to sleep. But it was not to be.

Confident that Clare was sloshed out of her skull or drugged up to the eyeballs, her latest boyfriend, a man Anya knew only as Jack, didn't even bother to close the door behind him. The first he knew of Clare's presence was when she rushed at him from behind with a kitchen knife, then chased him down the stairs and halfway up the street, screaming obscenities all the while.

Arriving back, breathless and dishevelled, Clare then attacked Anya too, casting her in the role of rival instead of victim, blaming her for luring her boyfriends away. 'You evil little bitch! You disgusting little trollop! I always knew you were up to no good. Your mimsy little ways don't fool me, madam. Sex mad, that's what you are. A sex maniac!'

Broken both in mind and body, Anya eventually collapsed. The White Rabbit had run away, disappeared off down the winding tunnel. Wonderland was no more and Alice was unmasked.

Sister Martha, her teacher, visited her in hospital every day without fail for six weeks. She sat by her bed for hours, brought her cuddly toys and fruit, held her small hand and told her stories. Lovely stories about Tir Na N'óg, the land of eternal youth, and about the Irish hero, Oisín, and Niamh of the Golden Hair. She sang to her and never ever asked her questions although, behind the scenes, she was moving heaven and earth to ensure Clare Keating never got her hands on her unfortunate little daughter again. When she was ready, when she felt safe, loved, and able to trust again, Anya filled in all the blanks and Sister Martha was able to go to the police.

Clare Keating was sentenced to one year's imprisonment – a

derisory sentence in Sister Martha's opinion – and Anya moved into a well-run and happy children's home. She continued to attend the same school where, relieved of the stresses and strains of living with her mother, she shone academically. Upon leaving, much to Sister Martha's joy, she went on to St Pat's Teacher Training college in Dublin, where she obtained her BEd. Jobs being scarce on the ground, she took a temporary job as PA to Sister Martha's cousin, Macdara, and the rest was history. As, indeed, the nun often remarked wryly, were Anya's teaching aspirations. 'Still,' she also observed, 'God spoke before us all and his ways are not ours. I daresay he has other plans for you, Anya, my dear. That said, I wish he'd told you before you spent all that time and money training.'

As the memories, some repressed for many years, rolled over her in a tsunami of grief, Anya wept for the loss of the woman she had come to think of as her real mother. She wept that Sister Martha's life had ended in such a tawdry fashion, that her body had lain like so much rubbish on the street, that such goodness could simply bleed away down a filthy gutter. Anya wept for herself too, because she didn't know how she would survive without her. Unbidden, the tail end of one of their recent conversations came back like an echo in her head, a presentiment neither had recognised at the time.

'What would I do without you?' she had asked.

'You'd survive,' had been the reply. 'You're too strong a woman not to.'

Oh, but Sister Martha was wrong about that, Anya felt. She wasn't a strong woman. Without her friend, her mentor, her mother, Anya didn't feel strong at all. She was a shadow, a wisp, a leaf helter-skeltering on the wind. Without Sister Martha, she had no anchor, no touchstone. Without her beloved saviour, she was that frightened, powerless little girl again, the one who jumped at shadows and quietly sobbed herself to sleep at night.

As her cries both of grief and rage rampaged once more through the house, Macdara, Fergal and Bridie sitting at the kitchen table below exchanged worried looks. For three days, she had scarcely left her room. She had drunk little and eaten nothing, though Bridie tried her hardest to coax her with every delicacy she could think of.

'Poor child.' Bridie paused in the act of pouring tea, put down the teapot heavily and brushed a tear away from her eye. 'It breaks my heart to hear her like that. Will she make it to the funeral, do you think?'

Fergal shook his head. 'I doubt it. Not in the state she's in. Better if someone stays home with her. I will, if you like.'

'No need for that,' Macdara said, pushing away his barely touched mug of tea. 'Anya is stronger than you give her credit for. Sister Martha knew that. She'll be there. She'll do it for Sister Martha. And we'll all be there too, supporting her and doing our bit.'

Sitting quietly in the corner with a magazine Orla frowned. She felt sorry for Anya, of course she did. But, in the heel of the hunt, she wasn't really family. Not like she was. Not like her sister was. Yet no one had been there for them when their mother died. They'd had to take care of the whole ghastly mess themselves. Tears pricked at her eyes as she recalled that fateful morning when she and her sister had entered Nessa's room bearing a surprise breakfast to celebrate their mother's birthday.

'Ding-dong, wake up, Mum,' Sinéad giggled. But Nessa hadn't woken up. And Nessa never woke up again.

Orla stared at a picture of a film star in the magazine, but she was seeing not the beautiful face before her. Instead she saw the carefully laid breakfast tray tumble to the floor in what seemed like slow motion. Transported back in time, she saw the coffee ooze in milk-brown tentacles across the floor, heard the clatter of metal strike wood, watched the red freshly plucked rose skitter mockingly across the floor. Red, the colour of danger. The colour of blood. She recalled a scream. High-pitched. Raw. Ragged. Her own. And then a second. Her sister's.

Shaking off the memory, Orla shot Macdara a searching look, turned it into a smile when he caught her eye.

'Poor Anya,' she said, betraying nothing of her thoughts. 'She's so lucky to have you, Grandy. She's so lucky to have you there for her.'

*

94

The sun shone on the day of Sister Martha's funeral, which seemed all wrong, an insult almost. Sunshine was life-affirming. It was for happy occasions, the glow that framed fond memories. It was for sunny outlooks, optimism and smiles. Anya wanted rain, rain to reflect her tears. She yearned for dark skies, thunder, rocks splitting themselves wide open, rivers bursting their banks, mountains sliding into the sea. She wanted Armageddon, destruction, the combined forces of nature conspiring to reflect the momentousness of the occasion. To her mind, Sister Martha deserved nothing less.

Macdara kept his hand on her elbow. She was conscious of its warmth, that he imagined he was holding her up. Little did he know that it was hatred and hatred alone that was keeping her upright. He imagined he was comforting her, but nothing could comfort Anya. Her heart was a frozen block, encased in ice and bitterness.

Almost dispassionate, she gazed around at the people framing the graveside. They looked grave. The word association made her want to laugh, but the laugh got caught somewhere in her throat and made her cough. The people, the mourners, she both loved and despised; she loved them for loving Sister Martha, and despised them because she had no doubt that what they had felt for her was not a microscopic fraction of what she, herself, felt.

Someone, she didn't notice who, placed some earth in her hand. There was a blood-red hue to it, iron ore in a soil that exuded dank. A piece of grass was caught in it, a strangely alive-looking root with tendrils trailing. Puzzled, she held it out before her.

'Throw it,' Macdara whispered and, when she didn't move, he took her hand and shook it over the open grave. Sieved between her fingers, the earth bounced off the polished pine of the coffin, like rain off a waxed window. The brass nameplate reflected light back up to the mourners, the inscription unreadable, though Anya knew every word by heart.

Sister Martha Fitzgerald
1938–2011
Ar dheis Dé go raibh a h'anam uasal

*May her noble soul be at the right hand of God.* And Sister Martha had had a noble soul. Indeed she had been the noblest soul Anya had ever met or felt she ever would meet again in this lifetime.

Mouth set hard, Clare Keating watched her daughter mourn another woman, another mother. No one questioned Clare's right to be at the funeral. Sister Martha was loved far and wide and, despite the heavy police presence, even the druggie contingent had turned out in force to pay their respects. The guards had questioned her, all right, the bastards. They'd searched her flat, stomping with their great big filthy feet all over her privacy, and throwing her few possessions about for no other reason than because they could. But, Clare flattered herself, she was a cool customer. She'd expected the visit. It was a given that as a patient at the rehab clinic she would automatically be close to the top of the list of possible suspects. In reality, turning her over was all just for form's sake, a box-ticking exercise to justify the bully-boys' inflated wages and pensions, and to fool the public into thinking they actually gave a shit. In truth, no one really believed Sister Martha's murder to be a woman's crime. Women weren't supposed to be that vicious. Yeah, right!

Anya didn't see her, of course. And most likely she wouldn't have recognised her if she had. Too busy channelling Our Lady of Sorrows and looking spectacular in black, Clare thought, her glorious hair swept up in a stylish chignon beneath a pillbox hat, her emerald eyes peeking tragically from behind a little net veil. It was all too clear that the bitch's star had risen, as surely as Clare's had fallen. Her beauty had blossomed, just as Clare's had faded.

And the way Clare Keating saw it, now Anya owed her big-time. She owed her for the stint served behind bars, when every day she had to duck and dive out of the way of psychos and dykes. Anya owed her for the abuse she had suffered at the hands of pig-ignorant prison guards. She owed her for moving in on Clare's boyfriends in the first place. Hell, the snotty-nosed brat owed her her very life. And Clare intended to collect. She needed now only to determine in what way and how much.

\*

Her mother's eyes were not the only ones fastened on Anya. Orla just about managed to hold back a frown as she contrasted Sister Martha's funeral with that of her own mother, where the only mourners had been the dead woman's two daughters. No one had turned out to support them in their grief. There had been no one to dry their tears and worry about whether they ate or drank, or how they were going to survive. And, most definitely, there had been no one to range themselves protectively either side like a couple of bodyguards, as Macdara and Fergal did with Anya.

Letting the almost hypnotic drone of the priest wash over her, Orla closed her eyes and let her mind drift back to that scorching day in Sydney when they'd laid Nessa to rest in a pauper's grave. She doubted she could even find it now. The days that followed had been dark, indeed. Nessa left no money and had it not been for their father eventually being alerted by social services, and whisking them off to live in Paris with him and his stuck-up French cow of a wife, they might well have ended up in care or on the streets. Not that their stay in gay Paree lasted long. Claudette, showing no sensitivity for their newly orphaned state, reminded them at every opportunity that they were there under sufferance. They were charity cases. Almost from the start, the two girls had hated her with a passion and set out to make her life a misery. And they succeeded so well that it wasn't long before the paternal-duty gene went AWOL again. Their father either couldn't – or wouldn't – make the effort to see that his daughters were grieving the loss of their mother, the woman he had cheated upon, thus changing all their lives forever. Theirs, for the worse. He refused to consider that the misbehaviour, the antics might all just be a cry of pain, a desperate scream for the attention of which they were so starved. He couldn't see that they needed him to be their father, as well as Claudette's *petit chou* husband. Most of all, they needed him to atone. He never did, so once they were of age, they equipped themselves with his credit card and bought a couple of flights back to Australia, first class, vowing to have nothing more to do with him. And thus far, they'd kept that promise. And Orla imagined that was probably a relief to him, and certainly to her stepmother.

'May her soul, and the souls of all the faithful departed, through the mercy of God rest in peace.' Bringing the requiem mass to an end, the priest snapped his missal closed on the last chapter of Sister Martha's life.

'Amen,' responded the mourners, the low, solemn hum resonating through the quiet of the graveyard. But Anya didn't join in. She had become Alice once more, and the White Rabbit was checking his watch and running off through Wonderland. And, in another second, *down went Alice after it, never once considering how in the world she was to get out again.*

And Anya didn't ever feel she wanted to.

# Chapter 12

Lady Kathleen lay in bed watching the flickering shadows leap up her bedroom walls in a variety of fantastical shapes. Castle Mac Tíre, with its thick stone walls and ancient inadequate heating, grew cold in the evening whatever the season, and so Javier had lit a small coal fire. But, tonight, it was more than normal cold that chilled her to the bone, that made her shiver and pull the covers tight around her shoulders. It was the coldness of spirits jostling for space round her bed, old memories stirred up by Sister Martha's funeral.

JC had been furious at her insistence upon going – he wasn't going himself as he was too tied up with that club of his. Instead Javier had taken her, despite her grandson snapping his head off and warning that he wouldn't be held accountable for his actions should anything happen to her. Dear JC. That was the Argentinian side of him, the high-handed autocratic attitude of master towards servant. Yet Javier was more than a servant, she knew. He was JC's everyday link with his beloved Argentina, his magic portal back into that fiery land, someone who understood the language and the customs, someone who had shared the heart-singing joy of thundering across endless acres of pampas on the sturdy back of a *criollo*, and found it to be his *raison d'être*. But she knew that JC didn't always behave well towards Javier. Sometimes he looked at him as though he hated him.

A rogue breeze blew in through a gap in the ill-fitting window. Moribund fingers of chill crept over the skin of her face, lightly tracing her worry lines as if they were Braille. The bedside lamp, already shadowy, dipped suddenly and gave a warning flicker.

Castle Mac Tíre had its own generator, ancient and bockety, totally unreliable and prone to breaking down whenever the whim took it. The shadows lengthened, crept closer to Lady Kathleen's bed like ghosts in a Hammer House horror production. She was reminded of a childhood game, 'broken statues', in which one child closed her eyes, counted to ten, and when she opened them again, the other children would have moved one step closer. When the first one reached out and touched her, she was out of the game. Poor Martha, someone had reached out and touched her, and now she was out of the game, her life forfeit forever. Kathleen's eyes filled with tears. Martha had been an honorary member of the 'musketeers', although back then her name had been Sally. Martha was the saint's name she had taken upon entering into the convent, a tradition that was dying out now, though very much a requirement when she first she took the veil. And Martha suited her, for just like her original namesake, she was a doer, a practical person who always seemed to know without being told exactly where she was needed and just what had to be done.

Although the gang were all close, Kathleen fancied that she and Martha had forged a special kind of bond, a closeness that made them the very best kind of friends. Their lives had diverged in completely opposite directions, but they kept in touch always, the actress and the nun, all down through the years and across vast continents. A wan smile flitted across Kathleen's face as she remembered how, in her anxiety to relay some drama or other, she had sometimes forgotten the time difference and phoned Martha in the wee small hours of the morning. And when, after her accident, the silver screen became tarnished and she went from being flavour of the month to being as untouchable as yesterday's dirty underwear, Sister Martha had been the buoy that saved her from going under.

Roisin! Picking up her daughter's photograph from the bedside table, Lady Kathleen perused her daughter's sweet features, feeling the usual gnawing pain of loss build in her chest, weighed down by a useless yearning to spend one last precious minute with her, to tell her, one last time how much she loved her. Sister Martha had understood her pain, her rage, her despair, even her loss of faith in Martha's own god. She'd held her in her arms, rocked and cooed and soothed. Freely, she gave of her wisdom, her time and her compassion, never ever using her religion as a licence to preach. Kathleen feared she had given very little back.

Teary-eyed, she replaced the photograph, as footsteps sounded outside her door, followed by a soft tap.

'Okay, my lady?' Javier put his head inside the door, then seeing the giveaway shine in her eyes, came over and sat gently on the bed beside her. 'You see, Javier knows when you are ...' he made a clownish sad face, his mouth turned down in an exaggerated fashion. 'My head he is thinking, my lady, tonight she is *doloroso*. Javier must go to her? Javier will bring the smiling back.' He lifted her hand and dropped a gentle kiss on the back of it. She reached up and stroked his face.

'Dear Javier. How lucky I was the day JC brought you to Castle Mac Tíre. How fortunate. You always bring the smiling back.'

'Well, I am very trying,' he nodded, and she did indeed smile, though she knew full well Javier often exaggerated his difficulties with the English language simply to make her laugh.

He went over and stoked the fire and, as sparks rasped up the chimney and the heart turned yellow, he returned to sit on the edge of the bed again.

Lady Kathleen patted the covers and moved over a little.

'No, lie down here beside me.' She waited till he had made himself comfortable, fitting his head in the crook of her shoulder, reminding her of Roisin as a child. His hair smelt faintly of rosemary and the coconut shampoo he used. 'Now, shall I tell you about the time I met Marlene Dietrich?'

'She was big bit more old than you,' Javier grinned.

'Ancient, but still gorgeous,' Kathleen confirmed, and they both laughed.

He stayed with her till she slipped into a deep dreamless sleep, never waking till well into the early hours when the noise of a man shouting woke her, followed shortly by deep heart-wrenching sobs that were quickly smothered. Poor Javier. How she longed to go to him, to bring the smiling back to his face. To set him free.

At Lismore, Macdara spent a restless night too. He felt tired and dispirited, older than he could ever remember feeling before. Fortunately, life at Lismore did not allow for wallowing. Regardless of life's dramas, the horses still had to be fed, groomed and exercised. Stables still had to be mucked out and fresh straw or wood shavings brought in for the bedding. Tackle had to be polished and mended. Fences had to be repaired, invoices had to be drawn up and bills had to be paid. There were a million and one tasks to be done each day at the yard and very little room for self-pity. To put it all into perspective, he went outside and looked around. Contrail-grey wisps, the remainders of night, were melting into the promise of another lovely day and, indeed, the air was already starting to warm up. Eastward, the sky was blushing rose-pink and orange and from all around came the life-affirming sound of birds reprising the dawn chorus.

Despite the early hour, the yard was already alive with people and horses, and a string was getting ready to go out on the gallops. Macdara frowned as he caught sight of Kitty Brennan perched high up on the back of Cavan Cate. He strode over and she jumped guiltily.

'Kitty!' Irritability honed his voice to a razor. 'What have I told you a million times about wearing your helmet? Go and get it immediately. The last thing any of us need is for you to go breaking your silly little neck! Seriously, if you don't start obeying the rules at Lismore, you're out. Got it?'

Flustered, Kitty nodded. 'Sorry, Mac. I was in a bit of a rush this morning. It won't happen again, promise.'

'See that it doesn't, because, rush or no rush, there won't be any more chances.'

Furious, Macdara stomped away. Kids! They thought they were bloody invincible. They knew nothing about the fragility of life and how it could be taken away in the blink of an eye. Like Martha's. Like Nancy's. Like Nessa's. God, the list was endless. Macdara started as Liam's Land Rover pulled in suddenly beside him, spraying gravel beneath its powerful wheels.

'Hey, Mac!' The vet stuck his head out the window. 'Nenagh Rose is in difficulty. Have you heard? I'm on my way there now. Want a lift?'

Macdara nodded and jumped in beside him for the short drive to the block of foaling boxes. He hoped it wasn't a breech birth, which could be long and complicated, and didn't always have a happy outcome for either dam or foal. He said as much to Liam, who fervently hoped the same. He'd had a heavy night and had the hangover from hell to prove it.

As they pulled up in front of Nenagh Rose's stable, Fergal emerged looking shattered, his face creased with worry.

'It's not good, Mac. She's really struggling.' He scowled at Liam, as he dismounted from the vehicle. 'Of course, if our trusty vet here had bothered to show his arse before now, things might not have got so out of hand.' The scowl deepened into naked aggression. 'So, where the hell were you, Liam? Eh? Why didn't you pick up your phone and answer? I was ringing half the night. Correct me if I'm wrong, but isn't that what you're bloody well paid for?'

Because he was rat-assed, that's why, Liam acknowledged to himself. Not that he was going to tell Fergal that, the sanctimonious tosser.

'Battery died,' Liam said, giving the explanation he had prepared earlier, conveniently ignoring the fact that he also had a landline he had deliberately left unplugged. He shouldered his way past Fergal. 'Now, if you don't mind, I'd like to see what's going on.'

Inside Nenagh Rose lay on her side, bloated and in pain. Her eyes rolled frantically and sweat covered her neck and flanks, making her chestnut coat appear almost black. Her contractions, though rapid and intense, were ineffective, and of the foal only the hind legs were visible. It was, as they feared, a breech birth and the only thing that would save them both was careful human intervention.

'There now, girl, there, alannah,' Macdara crooned, gentling the mare, as all three men endeavoured to coax her to her feet to make manipulation easier. 'It'll be grand, so it will. It'll be all right.'

'It had better be!' Fergal shot another glare at Liam. 'Because, so help me, if either of them dies ...'

'Enough, Fergal!' Macdara said. 'Draw back your horns. Let's just concentrate on the job in hand.' He positioned himself for a further attempt. 'Steady now. Let's try again, one, two, three.'

And at last the mare was standing, enabling Liam to insert his arm into the birth canal in order to pull and twist and gently ease the passage of the foal. Anxious, the other two men watched the progress, scarcely daring to breathe, as inch by inch the foal emerged and flopped finally, still swaddled in its birth membrane, on to the straw below. Tense, all three leaned in for a closer look, relaxing as, with a sudden twitch, the foal's tiny ribcage started to move rhythmically up and down.

'Thank God,' Fergal said, exhaling relief. 'He looks healthy enough.'

'He does indeed,' Macdara crowed with delight. 'And he's a real beauty, what's more. Who's a clever girl, eh?' He patted Nenagh Rose's neck, as she turned and gently began to snuffle her newborn son. Despite having witnessed hundreds of births, the sight of a newborn foal never failed to move him and, today, it felt especially poignant, underlining as it did the whole cycle of life and death.

'Thought of a name yet?' Fergal asked slightly husky, every bit as moved as Macdara, though desperate to hide it lest it undermine his masculinity. 'Martha?'

Macdara shook his head. 'No, Martha wouldn't have cared for us to break with tradition. What do you think of Derry Oak?'

'I like it,' Fergal said. He smiled down at the little foal. 'Hello, Derry Oak. Let's hope that despite your rough beginning you grow up to be every bit as strong as your namesake.' Good humour restored, he grinned at Macdara. 'Although, I suggest we call him Little Acorn to begin with.'

For his part, Liam couldn't give a toss if they called the animal every swear word under the sun. He was feeling as sick as a parrot, desperate for his bed and a fistful of painkillers. In no mood for maudlin sentimentality, he just about managed to suppress a sigh of relief when Macdara, with a final pat on Nenagh Rose's flank, headed for the exit.

'We'll leave him in your capable hands now, Liam,' he said. 'As for you, Fergal, what do you say we head back to the house for a bite of breakfast? I don't know about you, but my stomach has been growling this past hour or more.'

'I'm ravenous too,' Fergal confessed, his mouth beginning to water at the thought of a full Irish breakfast. Bacon, eggs, tomatoes, mushrooms, black pudding – the lot. 'And, with a bit of luck, Bridie will have baked some of her brown soda bread.'

'Dripping with butter.' Macdara's mouth salivated, his mood much improved from that of earlier. New life. That's what did it. That's what gave everyone the hope, the impetus to just keep on going, despite the slings and arrows pitched their way.

Liam just about managed to wait till they were out of sight and earshot before chucking his guts up in a corner of the stable. That fucking Kitty! It was all her fault he'd got off his face. But Kitty Brennan was just a silly little girl who'd played with fire. And soon, the flames were going to flare up and burn her, smack, bang on her cute little arse.

One of the stable cats, a striking ginger, pottered in and sniffed round the pool of vomit. Viciously, Liam lashed out at it with his boot. Seemed like everyone wanted a piece of him.

# Chapter 13

Life slowly began to return to normal for Anya, although memories of Sister Martha sometimes assailed her at the most unexpected times, sending her spiralling back into a deep depression that could last for days. The first forty-eight hours of an investigation were said to be the most important, after which time the chances of catching the killer grew markedly less. As far as Anya knew, the guards had few, if any, leads to go on. She was beginning to doubt anyone would ever be brought to justice, an idea that caused her so much anguish she sometimes felt she would go mad simply thinking about it.

Concerned for Anya's health, both physical and mental, Lady Kathleen spoke to Macdara.

'She needs to get away for a bit, Mac,' she told him. 'She needs to get completely away to recharge her batteries and take stock. You know what Anya is like. She's a brooder. She internalises things till they build up inside like a pressure cooker. I'm worried that one day it will all get too much and the weasel will go pop.'

Macdara frowned. 'I know, I'm worried about her too. I'd hoped that Orla might help bring her out of it a bit, take her shopping and do girly things with her. But, and don't take this as a criticism of Anya, I suspect Orla finds her hard work sometimes.'

'Really?' Despite the stricture, Lady Kathleen bristled immediately. 'How so?'

Macdara fiddled idly with the strap of his watch. 'Oh, I'm not entirely sure. You know the workings of women's minds have always been beyond the comprehension of mere mortals such as myself. Still, reading between the lines, I wonder if maybe Anya might be a bit jealous.' He held his hand up. 'Oh, not that Orla said so in as many words – she's far too sweet-natured for that. But, well, I suppose Orla is so exceptional in every way, others girls are bound to feel at a disadvantage around her.'

'Nonsense!' Lady Kathleen pooh-poohed the idea waspishly. 'What on earth has Anya to be jealous of? She's every bit as beautiful as Orla. Her colouring is divine.' And entirely natural, she might have added cattily. It hadn't escaped her notice at Sister Martha's funeral that Orla had taken to supplementing the blond in her hair, though she had only viewed her at a distance on the far side of the grave. However, Lady Kathleen had been around the 'beautiful people' of Hollywood so long that she could give a masterclass in all the little ruses people used to enhance their looks, no matter how subtle. She could spot a dye job at fifty paces, and pinpoint with deadly accuracy every nip, tuck and syringe of filler that had passed their way.

'Oh, I'm not denying that!' Macdara said hastily. For God's sake, he'd made an eejit of himself proposing to Anya only a few months before, and he was honest enough to admit that had she looked like Quasimodo, the offer might never have been made, *retinosa pigmentosa* or no *retinosa pigmentosa*. He looked faintly wistful. 'Naive though it sounds, I suppose I was hoping they'd become bosom buddies. It's that old thing about wanting the people you love to love each other. Pathetic, isn't it?' He ran a despairing hand through his hair. 'Tell me, do we ever leave off believing in fairy tales, Kay?'

Kathleen shook her head. 'No. Eternal optimism is all part of the human condition. It's what makes us get out from under the duvet in the mornings.' She reached out and stilled his hand, as he continued to twist his watch strap, round and round. 'Still, it's been a difficult few months and, you know, the dynamics at Lismore were bound to change with Orla's return. It takes time for people to get used to each other, and for normality to reassert itself.' She raised an eyebrow. 'Speaking of which, has Orla decided what she wants to do with her life yet? Any mention of getting a job?'

Macdara shook his head. 'No, and, to tell you the truth, I'm not inclined to push her on the subject. Life hasn't been easy for her over the years. From what I can gather, the poor child only just managed to scrape by, doing a bit of waitressing here and shop work there. Even worked in some sweatshop at one point, working her fingers to the bone sewing cheap clothes for the masses.' He put his hand across his heart, *mea culpa*. 'My fault, Kay. I condemned them to that. Nessa, God rest her, didn't have much when she packed up and left and seemingly things didn't improve any. She died penniless, and Orla and her sister were pretty much left to shift for themselves.' His look veered between guilt and defiance. 'Yes, yes, I know it might look as if I'm spoiling her, but should I live to be a hundred, I could never make up for a fraction of the pain she's experienced in her short life. Never!'

'You're a good man, Mac,' Kathleen said softly. 'And it's high time you stopped turning yourself into the devil incarnate. We've all made mistakes and we've all done things we're not proud of.' She wagged a finger. 'But we're none of us born with a crystal ball in our hands. All we can do is make a judgement based on the knowledge to hand at that time, that's all.' She smiled, a sparkle in her eye. 'Yes, Mac, my old friend, I hate to break it to you, you're human like everyone else. And both Orla and Anya are blessed to have you.' She wagged her finger again. 'Which brings us back to the immediate problem of Anya, and how to extricate the poor girl from the slough of despair.'

'A holiday?' Macdara suggested. 'Somewhere warm, where she could just lie on a beach and soak up the sun. I'll happily pay for it.' Lady Kathleen threw up her hands in horror. 'Good Lord, no!' That would be a recipe for disaster. With so much time on her hands she'd be bound to brood even more. What she actually needs is something to keep her so busy she has no time to think.' She frowned, clicking her thumb and middle finger together to aid the thought process. 'Come on, Mac, think. There must be a horse fair coming up in Kentucky or somewhere? Don't you go on different horsey junkets every year?'

'Not this year. My days of junketing are over, I'm afraid. All that change in cabin air pressure – not good for the condition, you know.' Although he tried to look blasé, Lady Kathleen caught a fleeting look of worry cross his face.

Her heart aching for her old friend, she leaned across from her chair and patted his knee. 'Oh, Mac, I'm so sorry. How insensitive of me. Sometimes I could cut my tongue out. Honestly, I could!'

Macdara shrugged. 'It's okay, I often forget myself and then something happens to remind me.'

'Or *someone* happens, and puts their big stupid foot in it.' Lady Kathleen looked furious with herself.

'It's all right, Kay,' Macdara insisted. 'Don't beat yourself up over it. To be honest, I really am more concerned about Anya at the moment. It wouldn't surprise me if she was heading for a nervous breakdown.' He snapped his fingers. 'Eureka!' His face cleared suddenly. 'I have it. Dubai!'

'Dubai?' Lady Kathleen echoed.

'Yes. The Dubai horse fair. I was intending to send Fergal over on a scouting mission for a new stallion I read about in the sales catalogue. A real beauty, with a bloodline second to none. Now, just suppose I was to ask Anya to accompany him?'

Lady Kathleen clapped her hands. 'Excellent idea! Perfect.' She sounded a note of caution. 'But you know, you have to make it sound like work, Mac, or she'll never agree. Anya doesn't do pity. For some unfathomable reason, she thinks she has to plough a lonely furrow through life, carrying everything on her own shoulders, narrow little things that they are.'

'I'll make it sound like a matter of life or death,' Macdara promised. He rose and dropped a kiss on her brow. 'You're a rock of sense, Kay, do you know that? If I were forty years younger, I'd marry you.'

But you didn't, Mac, she thought ruefully as she waved him off, a much cheerier man than when he had first arrived. You married Nancy instead. On a happier note, perhaps things would work out better for Anya, who, despite her best efforts to hide it, was clearly in love with Fergal Fitzgerald. And now, on their own, away from Lismore, the romance might have the chance to develop. Perfect couple. Perfect setting. And, hopefully, perfect ending.

There was only one big fly in the ointment,' Kathleen thought, wheeling herself over to look out the window. Fergal himself! After all, he'd already had a whole seven years in which to make his move. She didn't understand what on earth was holding him back.

'Dubai? Me?' Startled, Anya looked up from where she was replacing the toner cartridge in the photocopier. It was a messy, dirty job and she jumped back slightly as some of the black powder spilled out on to the floor. She knew from bitter experience that if it got on her clothing, it would never come out again. 'But why, Mac?'

'Because I need someone to accompany Fergal to the horse fair.' Rifling through a stack of paperwork, Macdara schooled his features to innocence. 'Someone competent to organise the nitty-gritty, do the paperwork, take notes and what have you. Fergal's strength, as I think we are all well aware, is in horseflesh, not admin.' Macdara cleared his throat. 'So, what do you think, Anya? I'd go myself, but you know how it is.' Deliberately, he left her to fill in the blanks, noting sardonically that he was beginning to shine at emotional blackmail. This time, however, it was for her own good, and he felt not one iota of guilt about slathering it on with a trowel.

Fergal and Dubai? Anya's wariness turned to suspicion. Did Macdara know how she felt about Fergal? The idea made her blood run cold. Dear God, was this some clumsy attempt to give Cupid a hand? Head averted, she took her time adjusting the toner cartridge, aware that her cheeks were twin pyres of embarrassment. On the other hand, she couldn't discount the fact that it might just be her guilty conscience jumping at shadows because, on the face of it, Macdara's request seemed reasonable enough. It was true what he said about Fergal. His avoidance of all things administration-wise was legendary. In fact, he made a virtue out of it. And yet Anya couldn't quite bring herself to believe there was no ulterior motive.

'Why me?' she persisted, whacking a lever into place with unnecessary force. 'Why not Orla?' Even as she posed the question her stomach churned at the idea of Macdara's blue-eyed girl and

Fergal disappearing off to exotic Dubai together.

'Orla's not my PA,' Macdara said simply. 'You are. Plus you know the ins and outs of the business, almost as well as I do. Besides, Orla is too easily distracted.' He gave a forgiving grin. 'Imagine the effect Dubai, that Mecca of shopping malls, would have on her. Shoes and designer gear everywhere.' He mimed backing off. 'No. No, it would be cruel to send the poor girl there, like putting a drunk in a brewery and telling him to abstain from touching a drop.'

Anya's ears pricked up. Oh, so he'd noticed that, had he? Anya was beginning to wonder if she was the only one who found it peculiar that finding a job seemed not to feature on any of Orla's to-do lists. Not whilst she could indulge her taste for shopping, at Macdara's expense. A certain pair of expensive shoes came to mind, Orla casually swinging the strappy, red-soled shoes off the ends of her feet and declaring them to be a snip at only five hundred euros. The following day, she purchased a second pair in a different colour. Perhaps it was mean spirited of her, but Anya couldn't help but wonder why someone who, by her own admission, had spent her entire life missing Macdara and Lismore, chose to spend so much of her time disappearing up to Dublin on shopping trips, or gallivanting with JC somewhere or other. As for poor old VIP, the elderly horse spent far more time in the company of people other than her mistress. Macdara's frequently vaunted assertions that Orla was 'born on horseback' had begun to wear a little thin, for Anya saw little evidence of her love of horses. When everyone turned out to view Derry Oak recently, the latest addition to the stables, Orla had been conspicuous only by her absence. In fairness Anya had to acknowledge that Orla was hag-ridden by her own demons. But times change. Tastes change. Little girls grow out of teddy bears and dolls. Why not horses as well? Hand on heart, Anya couldn't honestly be sure that her criticisms of the other girl weren't simply rooted in her own petty jealousy and fear of the ripples Orla could spread in what had, up till now, been a relatively smooth pond.

'So? Will you go for me?' Macdara looked anxious because, busy with her thoughts, Anya had remained silent. 'Seriously, Anya, you really would be doing me a favour.'

'Okay.' Anya took a deep breath as she made her decision. She smiled slightly tremulous. 'But only on condition that you run it past Fergal first. It's got to be okay with him.'

'And why wouldn't it!' Macdara said, trying to hide his relief at her acceptance. 'But, of course, if it makes you feel any better.'

'It would,' Anya said firmly. 'Please, Mac. I don't want to feel I'm only there under sufferance.'

Macdara set a sheaf of papers to one side and looked at her curiously. 'Well, I don't know why you would think that. You'll be deputising for me, Anya. Fergal's opinion really doesn't come into it, though why you think he'd be anything other than delighted is a mystery to me. Don't the pair of you get on like a train on a track?'

Anya nodded. 'Yes, but ...'

'Yes, but nothing!' Macdara said firmly. He pounced suddenly on a bit of paper as though it was of monumental importance and waved it triumphantly in the air. 'Ah, here it is. The invoice for all that new tackle we bought last month. I'd better go and deal with it right away.' Disappearing into the inner office, he closed the door behind him. Leaving an open-mouthed Anya to wonder why on earth he needed to do anything at all, considering she had settled it weeks before and Macdara himself had signed the cheque. With a shake of her head, she replaced the side of the photocopier, did a quick test to determine all was working as it should be, and went off to Google Dubai.

In the office, Macdara picked up the phone and dialled Castle Mac Tíre. 'The eagle has landed!' he said, before Lady Kathleen even had a chance to finish her greeting. 'The target is going to Dubai.'

Fergal and Dubai! At her desk, Anya experienced a rush of intense happiness, only to come crashing down moments later as she realised that the one person she normally would have shared her excitement with was no longer around. But, almost as quickly,

Sister Martha was in her head, wagging her finger and laying down the law.

'Now, you listen here to me, Anya Margaret Mary Keating. This is the opportunity of a lifetime, so no snivelling, do you hear me? Go out and make your mark on the world, child. Life is a cornucopia. Full of good things, for those who have the wit and wisdom to see it.'

God, how Anya missed her!

She got through the rest of the day on autopilot, performing her everyday tasks without even noticing, emotions see-sawing between elation and anxiety. Apart from a couple of trips to London and a long weekend in Paris, she had never been abroad otherwise, and Dubai sounded so exotic. She hoped Fergal wouldn't think her a complete hick or, worse still, a damn nuisance. What if he'd been planning to do the nightspots, hook up with a woman or something? Bridie always maintained it was better not to ask too many questions when the men came home from their trips abroad, though she'd hazard a guess that more than one kind of filly had caught their interest, married or single. The thought brought Anya out in a cold sweat. What if he thought he had to babysit her, mind his Ps and Qs around her when, really, he just wanted to let his hair down and party hard? Soon one negative thought borrowed another and by the end of the day Anya had managed to talk herself out of the trip. She couldn't go through with it. Macdara would just have to find someone else.

'Ah, Anya,' Fergal greeted her, when she came in for dinner. 'Great, isn't it? Two whole weeks in sunny Dubai.'

'Two?' Anya looked questioningly at Macdara, who was innocently helping himself to a large portion of Bridie's steak and kidney pie. 'I thought the horse fair only ran for a week?' Not that she was going for even one hour, so it didn't make a lot of difference to her either way.

'Change of plan.' Macdara speared a piece of steak on the end of his fork and waved it like a baton. 'Amirah's owner has invited the pair of you over for the first week, to stay at his palace, if you don't mind.' Macdara looked stern, though he couldn't quite mask the twinkle in his eye. 'He would be mortally offended if you threw his kind offer back in his face. And then he might take his business away from Lismore, which wouldn't be good at all. Very hot on honour, is old Sheikh Faisal Bin Rashid!' Macdara popped the meat into his mouth and chewed, sending Bridie a 'pure heaven' look as she bustled about topping up plates.

'Imagine it,' Fergal enthused, 'you and me, Anya, a couple of greenhorns from County Tipp, lording it up in a palace in Dubai. You must have been born under a lucky star, because the best I've ever had before was a two-star fleapit in the Ali Baba and the Forty Thieves district.' He accepted a second helping of mash from Bridie and dug in with his fork.

'Rubbish!' Macdara pretended umbrage. 'It was three-star, and there were only thirty thieves. You even had running water – from a well in the back garden.'

Fergal rolled his eyes. 'Yes, well this time we're doing Dubai in style and, hopefully, the water will run from a tap in my luxurious en suite or, failing that, be poured from silver ewers by sultry maidens wearing little more than a welcoming smile.'

'Dubai? Someone going to Dubai?' Orla asked, coming into the room and catching the tail end of the conversation. Several shopping bags swung from her hands, which she dropped unceremoniously on to the floor.

'We are. Anya and me.' Hastily, Fergal swallowed his food, as she pulled up a chair beside him. 'We're off to the horse fair there on a scouting mission for Mac. He has his eye on some stallion.'

'Haven't we all?' Bridie deadpanned, coming out of the scullery and setting Orla's dinner before her. 'Most of us, though, are doomed to disappointment.' She patted Orla's shoulder. 'There, love, get that down you. You must be worn out carrying all those heavy shopping bags.'

'Oh, I am,' Orla laughed and gestured to the bags on the floor. 'You wouldn't believe how much that little lot weighs.'

'Or costs,' Anya thought, as Orla smiled widely round the table and caught her eye.

'So, you're off to Dubai, Anya? Lucky you, that's one place I've always wanted to go.' Actually, she didn't. In her days of shimmying round poles for a living, she'd a bellyful of smelly Arabs pawing her, but that was classified information, known only to the privileged few. 'Although, from what I've heard, Western women don't always have an easy time of it over there. They think we're all prostitutes. No, really,' she nodded her head, as Anya looked horrified. 'They think we're all on the game.' And she should know. They'd treated her as a hooker because, well, she was. But, in Orla's defence, she'd desperately needed the money and selling her virginity over and over again had proved a lucrative source of income. Far more lucrative than waitressing, shop work or other menial jobs. It made good business sense to trade what assets you had, in her case her looks. And although it wasn't a career choice she would shout about, she wasn't ashamed either. At the time it had been a very necessary means to an end. A life and death situation. Literally. If called for, back then, she would even have sold her soul without a second thought. Or maybe she had done, without really noticing.

'That's nonsense, Orla.' Worried that Anya might be put off going, Macdara rubbished her claims. 'Dubai is like any other Muslim country. Dress modestly and behave with a bit of decorum and there's no problem whatsoever. It's hardly unreasonable to expect people to behave in a respectable and courteous fashion. The pity is that they've forgotten how to here. This country's gone to rack and ruin.'

'Well, it doesn't matter to me, anyway.' Anya hoped her voice didn't sound as nervous as she felt. 'Because I don't think I can go after all.'

'Why not?' Macdara and Fergal blurted in tandem, forks frozen almost comically mid-air.

'Because, I've far too much to be doing here. It wouldn't be right, Mac. You don't pay me to go gadding about.' Anya set her mouth, more to stop her lips trembling than from inner strength. She was aware that she was letting Macdara down and the knowledge was painful. 'I'm more than happy for Orla to take my place, if that's what she wants.' She smiled tremulously at Orla, wondering if the other girl had any idea of what it had cost her to make the offer, or how her heart was thudding against her ribcage.

'No, Anya!' Orla's eyebrows shot up. 'That wasn't what I meant at all. I've no intention of taking your place.' Panicked, she injected as much sincerity into her voice as possible. Her jetting off to Dubai played no part in JC's plans for the two of them. Christ, she could just imagine his face if she dropped that little bombshell: now you see me, now you see me in Dubai! 'Please don't let Grandy down. As for what I said about Western women, he's right, these things are often exaggerated, blown way out of proportion.' She shot Macdara a heartbreaking smile. 'Oh, look, Dubai will always be there, and I've only just got back to Grandy and Lismore. I couldn't bear to leave again so soon.'

'No reason why you should.' Macdara returned her smile in full measure.

Fergal rolled his eyes and pretended to be sick. 'Stop. Stop, Orla,' he pleaded. 'Any more of that and Mac will melt and disappear beneath the chair in a pile of soppy goo.'

'Why? Jealous, are you?' Orla laughed, but there was a slight edge to her voice that made Macdara look at them both speculatively. Anya, on the other hand, was too fraught to notice anything other than the problem, as she saw it, with Dubai. Which, in truth, was not so much a problem with Dubai, as with Fergal. Wildly torn in two directions, she was half-terrified they would convince her to go, and half-terrified they wouldn't.

'What about my work at Lismore?' she insisted. 'Who's going to do that?'

'It can wait,' Macdara said reassuringly. 'And, I daresay, if anything urgent presents itself, Orla will step in and lend a hand. Isn't that right, Orla?'

'With pleasure,' Orla nodded. 'I used to help you out all the time when I was little. Do you remember?'

'I do indeed,' Macdara said fondly. 'And now that that objection has been overturned, Anya, is there anything else standing in your way?'

Anya shook her head, a small smile creeping over her face. 'No.

Nothing at all. I guess then that I'm going to Dubai.' For better or for worse.

'Hooray,' Fergal said, 'I'm glad we got that settled.' He broke into an appalling impression of an Arab prince. Hey, habibi, 'ave yourself stripped, vashed and brought to my tent.'

Anya blushed as everyone chuckled, but once more Orla's laughter seemed to grate slightly on Macdara's ear. He pondered on it briefly, wondering if it wasn't just simply his imagination, or his sense of hearing over compensating for his failing eyesight. It was common knowledge that where one sense failed, the remainder became more acute to make up for it. Whatever the case, he told himself as Bridie placed a steaming bowl of apple pie and custard before him, he intended to keep a close eye on all the young charges under his roof.

That evening, when everyone had split up and dispersed about their business, Anya went outside to her favourite spot under the oak tree in the back yard. The air was heavy and warm, with barely breath enough to stir the leaves. Bridie had planted a big tub of scented stocks close by and their perfume, released by the night, hung heady on the air. Hidden in the clouds above came the sonorous drone of an airplane, en route to who knew where – Dubai perhaps? Until today, the name had barely crossed Anya's radar, except for the odd mention on the news and a vague recollection that David and Victoria Beckham owned a spectacular house there on some man-made, palm-shaped island. Of course, she'd Googled the city earlier, her excitement mounting as virtually every click of the mouse presented yet another feast for the eyes. Dubai. The name itself was a warm whisper, a promise of enchantment issued from between Scheherazade lips and carried on the desert air.

Anya smiled at this flight of fancy and closing her eyes went to that quiet place inside her where she could be tranquil and think through the day's events without any outside interference. It was a trick Sister Martha had taught her and the rest of the class, which she encouraged them to do whenever she thought they were tired or losing focus. 'Now, girls, rest your heads on your hands, listen to this, and simply be. That's all you need to do, simply be. Go inside yourselves and find the quiet core there.' And she would put on Ketèlbey's 'In A Monastery Garden', and after a few seconds any initial shuffling or coughing would stop and Sister Martha would have achieved the near impossible, thirty unruly schoolgirls, draped across their desks, communing with their own souls and learning simply To Be.

Orla, coming out into the yard for a late cigarette, stood and watched Anya for a moment, eyes closed, smiling softly to herself. The other girl looked so contained, so happy in her own skin that Orla experienced an unexpected frisson, a stab almost of jealousy. She could barely remember the last time that she herself had felt happy in her own skin, if in fact she ever had. But, then again, her life hadn't exactly been sugar and spice and all things nice. Not since her grandmother died in the fire, and the whole house of cards had come tumbling down.

She drew on her cigarette, willing herself to stay in the moment and not time-travel backwards, but it was useless. The past was a different country, but it hadn't loosened its grip. Wherever Orla went, the tentacles were always there, always ready to yank her back, probing for weaknesses beneath the hard shell she had purposely grown, exposing the vulnerabilities of the hurt child in the grown woman.

How she used to envy the Anyas of this world back then, the uncomplicated products of a loving nuclear family: Mum, Dad and a complementary sibling. A nice house. Clean clothes. Regular meals on the table. Christmas with all the trimmings. Peace and goodwill to all men! Orla's share of that particular goody bag had come to an abrupt end. Gone was her grandmother. Gone was her mother, ravaged by unhappiness and illness. Gone was her grandfather, Macdara, to a place of grief where no one could reach him. Gone was her father into the arms of another woman. All were gone now, leaving only quicksand in their place. And everyone knew you couldn't put down roots in quicksand, although her mother had tried her best.

In an effort to mend her broken heart and, as Orla learned later, in protest against her father's entrenched opinions on divorce, Nessa whisked her daughters away from Lismore, smuggling them out in the dead of the night because 'it was easier that way'. Though very young, Orla could still recall every detail of that night: the sting of rain on her face, the moon crushed between gigantic boulders of black cloud, the glistening scariness of the monstrous shadows preceding them, the isolating yet exciting sense that they were the only ones left alive on the planet. At first they'd moved to Dublin to stay with some of her mother's friends, but when that sympathy-bank ran out of funds as it inevitably had, they'd moved on, first to Spain, then to Italy and, finally, to Australia.

'We're like gipsies,' Orla recalled her mother kidding them, trying to make light of the situation. 'Wherever we lay our hats, that's our home.'

And at first it had been fun, a novelty, but then the gloss wore off and Orla and Sinéad had wanted nothing more than a proper home, somewhere they could settle down, go to school and make friends they didn't have to leave after a few months. They just wanted to be ordinary, not gipsies. Not nomads.

Shaking off the memories, Orla flicked her cigarette away and went over to sit beside Anya.

'So,' she said, startling Anya out of her reverie, 'are you looking forward to going to Dubai?'

'Yes and no. It's out of my comfort zone,' Anya admitted, feeling slightly awkward about opening up. As a rule, she and Orla didn't do cosy talk, the hoped-for friendship having amounted to little more than a few shopping trips and small talk across the kitchen table. Orla's bouncy outgoing personality, Anya had begun to realise, was more front than reality. There was a certain reserve about her too, an invisible electrical fence which prevented anyone from going too near. And Anya respected that, empathised even. There were whole parts of herself and her world which were keep-off-the-grass areas. 'I can't help worrying that I'll somehow make a fool of myself.'

'Why?' Orla slanted her a look. 'Is it something to do with Fergal?'

'Fergal! No, why should it be?' Her armour pierced, Anya's hands rushed to touch her suddenly heated cheeks.

Orla was slightly mocking. 'Because you do rather seem to hang on his every word. He's not some sort of guru, you know. He doesn't hold the key to the universe.'

'Fergal's a *friend*, that's all,' Anya said, smarting at the accusation.

'Yeah, right!' Coolly, Orla lit up another cigarette, squinting her eyes against the burning sulphur of the matchstick. 'Oh, don't get me wrong, I don't blame you. Honestly, I don't.' She jerked her head around the yard. 'Let's face it, compared to most of the hay-seeds round here, cousin Fergal is a veritable god, the Brad Pitt of County Tipp. But, do yourself a favour, Anya, and look elsewhere.' She blew smoke from her nostrils. 'He's really not for you.'

'Because?' Anya bit her lip, her heart suddenly thundering in her ears. It was as she feared. Orla wanted him to herself, and what Orla wanted, Orla got. Or so it would appear. Anya steeled herself for the no-holds-barred official warning off but, in the event, Orla took her completely by surprise.

'Because he told me,' she said flatly.

'Told you? How? When?' Oh God. The humiliation! The betrayal! The thought of the pair of them gossiping behind her back made her head reel. Anya bit her lip to prevent herself from crying aloud. Goosebumps erupted up along the skin of her arms and pulled the hair on her scalp into little peaks.

'Not in so many words,' Orla admitted. 'And look, Anya, I take no pleasure in telling you this. I just don't want you to make a fool of yourself.'

A fool of herself! Better and better. Anya's stomach heaved to the point where she truly felt like she might lose her dinner. Nevertheless, she gritted her teeth and urged Orla to continue. 'Go on. The genie is halfway out of the bottle. Too late to let sensibility stand in your way now.'

Orla shifted uncomfortably, looked down at the ground, then up at the sky as if seeking divine guidance. 'I'm sorry I started, really I am,' she said. 'Shoving my foot in my mouth is something of an occupational hazard with me.

'Well, you did start,' Anya's chin came up bravely, 'so now you might as well tell me all. What exactly did Fergal say?'

Orla tapped her cigarette against the side of the bench, releasing a clump of ash. It fell to the ground, glowed a final act of defiance and died. She threw up her hands. 'Okay, if you insist. It was the day you had glammed yourself up a bit, remember? You had on a slightly too tight dress – nice, but definitely a bit snug, and all the men were bug-eyed ...'

Anya remembered all right. She remembered thinking she looked great, when, if Orla was to be believed, she looked like an overstuffed sausage. Her eyes stung with humiliation.

'... and I asked Fergal if he fancied you, just teasing him. Childish, I know.' Orla closed her eyes, and exhaled a twist of grey smoke.

'And he said?' Anya prompted, her inner masochist encouraging the fall of the axe.

'He said,' Orla turned troubled eyes on her, 'he said that he didn't think of you in that way. That you were like Bridie, part of the furniture, the hired help.'

Part of the furniture! The hired help. The blade cut cleanly, slicing through any residual pride she had left. Anya felt choked, mortified. Her heart lay like a dead weight in her chest. Her thoughts churned, whizzed as though in a blender, filling her with confusion, with despair and an aching disappointment. There was no way now that she could go to Dubai with Fergal. Not now she knew he viewed her merely as an employee. And to think she had been foolish enough to believe that they were friends, good friends, and even to hope that one day perhaps things could change between them.

'Oh, listen, don't worry!' Orla gave Anya a supportive nudge, as she struggled to contain her emotions. 'I told him you were already spoken for anyway, and by a man who could give him a run for his money. That took the wind right out of his sails, I can tell you.'

'You told him what?' Anya's voice skidded with disbelief. 'What on earth are you talking about? I'm not seeing anyone.' Elbowing aside a cloud, the moon panned, for a split second, across Orla's face, a trick of the light that twisted her features and made her look almost frightening.

'No? Well, how do you explain Liam O'Hanlon, then?' Orla chuckled softly. 'Oh, don't worry, your secret is safe with me.'

Anya frowned, genuinely mystified by the accusation. 'Orla,' she said, 'I have no idea what you're talking about. I wouldn't touch Liam O'Hanlon with a barge pole. Besides which, he's married.'

'And I think the lady is protesting too much. Anyway, I saw you, Anya, after dinner on the first day I came back to Lismore, sneaking round the side of the house. It was quite amusing really. Then I saw you get into Liam's Land Rover and drive away with him.' Orla reached across and patted Anya familiarly on the knee. 'Hey, don't sweat it. He's a good-looking guy. Rugged, with a dangerous edge, just my type actually, except I'd never muddy another woman's field.' Leaving Anya open-mouthed with disbelief, she pitched her cigarette butt into the tub of night-scented stocks, got up and stretched. 'Anyway, I'm off to bed. Sweet dreams.'

Sweet dreams? Sweet dreams! Dear God, what a nightmare. Appalled, Anya stared after her departing back. Whoever Orla had seen, it certainly hadn't been her. Besides which, Liam gave her the creeps. The back door of the farmhouse opened, throwing a rectangle of light across the ground. A moment later Orla stepped inside, the door closed and the light was swallowed up. Anya shivered, more from the effect of the other girl's words, than from the cool breeze that had begun to eddy round her shoulders.

Scenarios, each one worse than the last, chased themselves around her brain. What would Fergal think of her? What would everyone think of her should Orla divulge what she thought she saw? What if it came to the ears of Liam himself? Or his wife! Anya felt like she might die. Not even the attentions of Yeats, her favourite tomcat, could console her, as he ambled across the yard and jumped heavily on to her lap, his claws kneading through the material of her jeans. He looked up quizzically as a tear splatted on to his head. 'Oh, Yeatsy, what am I going to do?' Anya moaned, rubbing it away with her finger, only to immediately replace it with another. Dismayed that his place of comfort was so invaded, the cat jumped back down and stalked away with his head held high. Anya turned her face up to the sky. 'Sister Martha? Anyone?'

On his way back from the stables after a final check to make sure the horses were settled for the night, Fergal caught sight of Anya sitting alone on the bench. His first thought was to go and join her, but then she looked up briefly and he saw that she was crying. He walked on, presuming she was weeping for Sister Martha and not wishing to intrude upon her grief. It felt wrong, though, all wrong. It felt as though he should be able to go over, take her in his arms and … No, he reminded himself. That road was forbidden.

Macdara had put him in no doubt about this right from the start, making it clear that Anya was off limits. She was fragile, damaged in some way, though he had never done more than hint at the reasons behind the latter. As far as Fergal was concerned, she was china, breakable, handle-with-care. Not as other girls. But he knew that already, and had known it almost from the moment he first set eyes on her, being squired around Lismore by an avuncular Macdara, smiling shyly as he introduced her to all the staff.

'Now that's what I call a bit of all right,' Liam had leered, as Macdara whisked her onward, and Fergal had felt himself wanting to set about the man and not leave off until he was dead on the floor at his feet. The sheer violence of his emotions had taken Fergal aback. But that's what being near Anya did to him from the very first moment he set eyes on her. And still did to him. Every day. But his hands were tied.

Feeling someone's eyes on her, Anya looked up just as Fergal turned away. Her tears came thick and fast then, spurred on by the pain of loving someone who valued her only as an extra pair of hands around the place and nothing more.

# Chapter 14

'Mrs Keating,' JC instructed. 'Come and see me later when you're finished cleaning up. I'll be in my office, and I'd be obliged if you would kindly knock before you enter.'

Clare Keating doffed an imaginary cap to him. 'Yes sir, three bags full, sir!' She screwed up her face as, ignoring her sarcasm, he walked away, leaving her in the middle of what looked like the destruction left behind by a particularly violent hurricane. The rich kids had excelled themselves this time. JC was clearly making a mint if he could afford to sustain this kind of damage to the club week after week. And what she could see right now, Clare knew, was only the tip of the iceberg. In the private ante-rooms, there would be worse, much worse, including the discarded paraphernalia used by those who wanted to get a bigger high than that afforded by mere alcohol. Not for the first time she thought of selling JC out to the newspapers. They'd pay a mint to have the in on this little lot, and she'd be set for life. But no sooner was the thought born than it died again, not because of the principle but because she instinctively knew that, when it came to JC, she would live to rue the day if she didn't play fair by him.

Resigned to always being bottom of the food chain, she pulled on her rubber gloves, armed herself with a bucket, mop and bleach and got to work, pondering on why JC wanted to see her. Contact between them was, for the most part, kept to a minimum. He made no secret of his contempt for her, flinching whenever they passed, as if the very sight of her inflicted physical injury upon his person. Silly up-himself sod! Still, Clare wasn't too proud to take his money, and if there was more on offer, she'd happily kiss his toffee-nosed arse.

JC had left his office door half-open, in anticipation of their meeting. Nevertheless, she knocked and waited for the command to enter. JC pointed to a seat opposite the desk, behind which he was sitting on an oversized carved chair resembling a throne. Big head. Big chair!

'Coffee?' JC raised an eyebrow.

Clare nodded. Jesus, he was really pushing the boat out, though by the contorted look on his face it was hurting him to do so. JC poured a mug for her, the delicate china cup on its matching saucer sitting before him being, apparently, not for the likes of her. She recognised the make, Spode, their classic Blue Italian design, not to be confused with the even more famous Willow Pattern. It amused her to think how surprised he would be if he knew just how much Clare Keating understood about the finer things in life. Like everyone else, he assumed she was just a skank, flotsam, but actually she hailed from good stock, people of breeding and wealth.

'Thanks.' Deliberately, she slopped a bit over the edge on to the tooled Moroccan leather desktop and looked at him enquiringly, vastly amused by the warring expressions going on behind his sophisticated veneer. When he remained silent, she grinned. 'Earth to Mars. I assume I'm not here because you want to look at my beautiful face.'

JC glared at her. In truth he still had grave reservations about involving this woman in any more of his business. It was tantamount to giving her a big stick to hold over his head. Nevertheless, things couldn't continue as they were. Orla risked discovery every time she rode or drove over from Lismore, and discovery would mean that all their plans would have been in vain. He sighed irritably, wrestling with the pros and cons. The situation was far from ideal but, for now, at least, the only solution was to put their trust in the verminous creature sitting opposite, and pray that money would buy her silence. He took a deep breath, hating the fact that every word he now uttered would place him deeper in Clare's debt.

'Well, I'll be damned.' Clare whistled through her teeth as his narrative drew to a close. 'I can see why you need a fairy godmother's help. And I will help. For the right price.' She gave a screech of disbelieving laughter, as she thought over what he'd revealed. 'Fuck me! You're a right one, you. All that poncing about like Little Lord Fauntleroy, looking as though butter wouldn't melt, looking down on the rest of us like we're shit. And all the time, hidden beneath your designer duds, beats a heart as villainous as any I've ever come across. And I've come across many in my time.' She dabbed at her streaming eyes. 'You know, any more little revelations like that and I might actually start to like you.'

JC's brows beetled together. Truly, the woman was worse even than he'd realised. He steepled his hands on the desk and rested his chin on the top of his fingers, lancing through her with his dark eyes. Though he seemed composed enough sitting there in his dandified Dries Van Noten suit, the real impression Clare had was of a serpent, poised and ready to strike. She could almost hear him rattle.

'You will not speak of this to anyone.' The words were both instruction and threat. '*Comprende*? Just keep your mouth closed, do what I ask, and I will make it very much worth your while.'

'You're talking my language now.' Clare rubbed the tips of her fingers together. 'So how much worth-my-while are you actually offering?'

Swiftly JC named a sum of money that made her eyes almost pop out of their sockets. 'And, of course, you would still continue to clean the club. It's important to have a valid reason for your presence there. Are we agreed?' His stomach revolted at the alliance, but just as in the case of Liam, he knew it was sometimes necessary to dance with the devil.

'Done!' For her part, Clare would have not only danced with the devil, but bedded him too if it furthered her interests. Her eyes darted to the drinks cabinet behind him. 'Now, how about we spit on it with something a little stronger? Just to seal the deal.'

JC eyed her with distaste. 'I think not.' His gaze moved to the spilt coffee. 'And, before you leave, I would be grateful if you would clean this up.' JC stood up quickly, his chair grating on the costly Minton-tiled floor. 'Cross me, Mrs Keating, and you will find out just how hard I can be.' He bared his teeth, more snarl than smile. 'Do I make myself clear?'

'As fucking crystal,' she nodded, as she walked out of his office and back into the club, which suddenly smelt fresher than a whole field full of daisies.

'And you're sure you can trust her?' Orla asked, plucking at the material of her skirt with nervous fingers.

JC shook his head. 'I don't trust anyone. You should know that. But she is a greedy woman and so her silence can be bought.'

'Well, if it can't, all of this will have been for nothing.'

'Your fault,' JC snapped, his face thunderous, a muscle twitching madly in his cheek. 'It was only ever supposed to have been the two of us, you and me.' He pointed at the third occupant of the room. 'And yet you chose to jeopardise it all for what? For that! *Madre de dios.*' He made a gesture of disgust. 'You must be crazy.'

'Fuck you, JC,' Orla retorted. 'I did what I had to do, so please stop harping on.' She took a deep breath and willed herself to calmness. 'I suppose we have simply to hope that this woman you've found is on the level.' She too turned to the third occupant of the room. 'For all our sakes.' Walking across to a cupboard, she opened it up and extracted an ampoule of medication and a syringe, still wrapped in its cellophane cover. Swiftly unwrapping it, Orla attached a needle to the end, snapped off the top of the ampoule and drew the liquid up into the body of the syringe. Carefully, she checked for air bubbles, flicking it to make sure. She replaced the needle with a butterfly infusion set and laid it on a metal tray, together with a packet of antiseptic wipes and spot plasters. 'Right,' she said. 'It's that's time again and please don't make a fuss. Remember, it's for your own good.'

Kitty was crying and Liam was angry. Women! Why did they always have to be such drama queens? It was a fling, for God's sake, not the love affair of the century. He fancied her. She fancied him and one thing led to another. Now, why couldn't she simply leave it at that? But, oh no, that would have been too easy. Instead, she lay on the bed gazing at him with her big teary eyes, looking as if her world had exploded and he was the terrorist who had detonated the bomb. Admittedly, his timing could have been better. He shouldn't have screwed her first. That was a mistake.

'Listen,' he tuned his voice to woman-friendly. 'It's been fun, Kitty, but it was never for keeps. You went into this with your eyes wide open. You knew I was married. We were never going to be Winslet and bleedin' DiCaprio.'

Sniffling, Kitty sat up in the bed, clutching the covers tight around her naked breasts in a pathetic attempt at salvaging some dignity.

'But, I thought—' she began, only to be cut off abruptly by Liam as, turning his back to her, he zipped up his trousers and reached for his shirt.

'You thought wrong. Really, Kitty, I never promised you anything other than a good time. I never led you to believe I would leave Jenny.' Why would he? Jenny was an excellent wife, the kind who knew how to turn a blind eye and keep her mouth shut, the kind who understood that one woman simply wasn't enough for some men. He waved an impatient hand. 'Now get dressed, would you? Keep the memories, sweet as they are, but accept it's time to move on.' He combed his fingers through his tousled hair to flatten it. 'Anyway, you won't be in mourning long. You're a hot little number. Don't think I haven't noticed the way Fergal and the lads at Lismore look at you.'

'Fergal's in love with Anya,' Kitty said. 'Any fool can see that.'

Maybe, Liam thought, but that particular bird wouldn't fly. Thanks to her low-life mother, Anya was as good as his.

Kitty swiped at her tears, smearing her mascara across her cheeks. 'Anyway, what if I don't want to move on? What if I *can't* move on?'

Liam's patience, always limited, was rapidly nearing its end. He rolled his eyes. 'For God's sake, what kind of nonsense is that? You're how old, eighteen? I'm very flattered, Kitty, but I doubt very much if your life is ruined because of me. I'm more than twice your age. Go and get a young fella for yourself.'

'And who'll want me, Liam?' A bitter note in Kitty's voice brought his head spinning round. 'Who'll want me at eighteen years of age, pregnant with another man's child?'

Horror dawned in Liam's eyes. The shoe he had lifted thudded to the floor. 'But you were on the bloody pill. You told me you were on the pill.'

Kitty shrugged, pretend-defiant. 'I lied,' she said. The pretence fell away and her face crumpled. 'I know it was stupid, but …'

'You didn't think you could get pregnant.' Famous last words. Liam let out a howl of rage. 'You fucking little idiot. How could you have been so bloody stupid? Haven't you been round Lismore long enough to know what happens when the stallion covers the mare?'

She shrugged, looking so absurdly young that for a moment he almost, but not quite, experienced a flash of conscience.

'You'll have to marry me,' she said, trying for strict, but looking bereft. 'My parents will go demented otherwise.'

He rounded on her in amazement. 'Tell me, what part of "I'm already married" don't you understand, Kitty? What part of I have already been up the aisle and plighted my troth to another woman?'

Kitty looked hopeful. 'You could leave her. You cheat on her anyway, so you can't possibly love her.'

Liam slapped his forehead in despair. 'Never! Never in a month of Sundays. You'll just have to get rid of the brat. I'll pay, of course.' Kids, he reflected bitterly, had never been on his 'to do' list and he was damned if he was going to play Daddy-effin-Day-Care now.

'I will *not* get rid of it,' Kitty yelled, metamorphosing much to his amazement from Kitty the cat into Kitty the tiger, claws fully extended. Her green eyes blazed fire. '*You* are going to marry me, Liam, because *you* did this to me and it's the right thing to do. Your wife will understand.'

Liam's amazement grew in direct proportion to her anger. Never in his entire life had any woman, including his own mother, spoken to him like that. He almost laughed in disbelief. The sensation was that of being bossed about by a pink marshmallow, Jonah telling the whale to piss off. Nevertheless, his voice was cold, laced with something which, if Kitty had been less het up, she might have flagged up as danger. 'Otherwise?'

'I know things, Liam.' Kitty took a deep breath, aware of teetering on a very steep ledge, but stepping forward all the same. 'I know a lot of things that could get you into trouble.'

Liam went statue-still. The little bitch was threatening him, blackmailing him. Blackmailing *him*! Suddenly the blood was rushing, pounding furiously in his ears. Shaking off the paralysis, he bounded over to the bed. Grabbing her viciously by the wrists, he brought his face down to hers, so close she could see the beginnings of his five o'clock shadow pushing through his skin.

'*What* do you know, Kitty?' He drew out the words, increasing the pressure till her bones almost snapped and she screamed in pain. 'Tell me. Tell me it all.'

'I know about the ket,' she faltered, struggling uselessly to free herself.

'The ket.' Liam laughed in relief. Was that all? 'We discussed that already, in the club, that night? Remember?' As an aide memoire, he transferred one of his hands to her throat, almost lovingly stroking the skin with his thumb, before applying slight pressure. 'And I warned you then what I would do if you opened that mouthy little gob of yours.' He spread his fingers, grasped her neck. 'And pretty Kitty, I wasn't messing around.'

Kitty's heart was in her mouth, her eyes wide with fear. But greater than her fear was her obsession with her lover. Bad though he was, dangerous though he was, she wanted him at any cost, even if that meant using his dirty secrets to bind him to her. And so she said, 'I know something else too, something far worse than the ketamine.' Kitty paused, and it seemed as if even the air around them also paused in expectation. 'I know about the nun.'

'The nun?' Liam's voice was deceptively soft, so soft it barely made a dent in the air. 'And tell me, sweetheart, what nun would that be?'

'The one who was murdered.' Kitty felt almost triumphant at the disclosure. 'Oh, don't deny it, Liam. I was there when that woman came to your house. I heard her talking to you. I saw the drugs. I saw you give her money. I saw it all. Everything!'

'Did you indeed?' Liam's head reeled, though he had suspected as much when he came back to bed on the night in question and her skin had been cold to the touch.

'Yes.' Kitty nodded, almost drunk now on the heady mixture of power and adrenalin coursing through her veins. 'So you see, Liam, you'll have to marry me now, or I'll go to the guards and they'll lock you up. You, and that woman.'

If Liam had ever felt a modicum of anything other than lust for Kitty, it fled completely and forever in that moment. Every instinct told him to throttle her where she now lay, to shut her up once and for all, to stop the damning stream of invective issuing from between her fatuous lips. But using all the self-control he possessed, Liam curbed the instinct and willed himself to calmness. Kitty's saving grace was that she was so very stupid. Unbelievably thick. An eejit! For a moment Liam felt almost insulted that he had actively chosen to sleep with someone whose very existence was a snub to the gene pool. But gallingly, eejit or not, right at this moment his balls were in the vice-like grip of her eighteen-year-old hands and the sensation was far from pleasant. Liam held his palms up in surrender and attempted a smile, though his face felt as though it had been coated with several coats of quick-drying plaster of Paris.

'Congratulations,' he said. 'You've got me between a rock and a hard place. My fate is completely in your hands. If marriage is the price for your silence, then so be it.'

'Oh, Liam!' Kitty gave a squeal of excitement. 'Do you mean it?' Too foolish to sniff out the wolf in sheep's clothing, she was ecstatic that the risk she had taken in admitting the extent of what she knew had paid off. Wedding bells chimed in her ears. A series of stills from the film reel running in her head flashed before her. Pink and blue booties. An angelic-looking child. Liam, the older husband, besotted with his young and beautiful wife, the happy couple posing on the steps of a fairytale cottage. Everyone saying how well they looked together.

'Say it again,' Kitty commanded flirtatiously, suddenly overwhelmingly confident in her new power over him. 'Say we'll get married.' She needed to hear the words again, so she could hug them to herself later, remind herself that it wasn't a dream, that she really had got what she wanted.

'Yes, we'll get married.' Liam tried not to flinch as she threw herself into his arms. Her perfume, appearing suddenly overpoweringly sickly, caught at the back of his throat and made him almost retch. 'But, Kitty, you do realise we'll have to keep it a secret for the moment. I'll have to tell my wife before we tell anyone else. That's only fair, isn't it? She deserves to hear it from me. So not a word to anyone. No one at all. Promise me?'

Magnanimous in victory, Kitty beamed widely. 'Cross my heart and hope to die. Now, why don't you come back to bed and we can celebrate our engagement?' She giggled, unaware that the sound grated like an out-of-tune violin on his already frayed nerves. She stuck her hand out before her. 'You'll have to buy me an engagement ring, to make it official. A solitaire diamond. Or, maybe an emerald, to match my eyes.'

Liam smiled, as he bent to kiss her, the smile of the cobra before it strikes.

Lady Kathleen smiled down at Javier's bent head, as he applied a coat of nail varnish to her toenails. He looked up.

'You like?'

'I like,' Lady Kathleen agreed.

'Hollywood Red.' He grinned. 'I see it in a shop and I am thinking of you.' He sat back to admire his work. 'Good. Very good. But now, your fingers, eh? It is *muy importante* that you look beautiful. Maybe soon you will make another movie?'

Lady Kathleen suppressed a smile. 'Oh, indeed. I hear Richard Gere is looking for a new leading lady for his latest film. Apparently Julia Roberts let him down.' Bless Javier, there was as much chance of her flying to the moon on a broomstick.

'*Pretty Woman*. Good movie,' Javier said with satisfaction. 'Tell me about Hollywood.'

It was his normal refrain and usually Lady Kathleen was more than happy to indulge him. However, today she was determined to find out a bit more about him.

'No. You tell me about Javier, where he comes from, who he is, what he wants out of life.'

Javier drew carefully around her cuticle, careful not to smudge the nail varnish.

'Javier, he is nobody. You like Richard Gere? His eyes are too close together, no?'

Lady Kathleen ignored the blatant attempt at side-stepping. 'Javier is not nobody. Javier is most definitely somebody. Now, come, tell me all about your family. Let's start with the easy stuff. Where were you born?'

Javier sighed. 'It is very boring. Not like Hollywood.' Lady Kathleen made a warning face and he capitulated. 'Okay. Okay. I was born in San Antonio De Areco, a small town near Buenos Aires. *Mi padre,* he is a gaucho. *Mi madre*, she works in the fields. We are very poor, not much food. One day, everybody get sick and die, except Javier. Me, I am not dying. That is all.'

That is all? Everybody get sick and die! 'How awful.' Lady Kathleen glanced at him, not quite sure whether to believe such a harrowing tale, but Javier was looking perfectly composed, the only sign of emotion being his breathing which had grown slightly uneven. But then again, this wasn't the kind of thing people lied about. 'Javier, my dear, I am so sorry,' she said quietly. 'I shouldn't have pressed you. Can you forgive a nosy old woman?'

'It is a long time ago,' Javier said dismissively, beginning work on one of her thumbnails. 'Now, tell me about Hollywood. You like Tom Cruise?'

'Is it true all Javier's family died?' Lady Kathleen demanded, as she and JC ate dinner together that evening.

JC nodded. 'There was a lot of poverty in Argentina at that time; in fact, there still is in places.'

'But what happened?' Lady Kathleen stabbed desultorily at a piece of chicken on her plate. Her appetite, never strong, had almost vanished since her discussion with Javier. Her heart was in pieces for the poor boy. He was lovely. So gentle.

JC was dismissive. 'Oh, you know, big Catholic family, a child every year and no money to feed them.' He popped a piece of chicken in his mouth, his own appetite undimmed by any concern over Javier's past. 'Then, one day his father, Eduardo, fell from his horse, landed awkwardly and broke his neck. After that there was no money at all, only what his mother and the older children could earn working in the fields. There was an outbreak of dengue fever, not uncommon in that area, and one after the other they succumbed, except Javier.' He sounded so factual, so completely unemotional in the telling that he might as well have been singing that old song about twelve green bottles hanging on the wall.

'Why not Javier?'

'Because he was twelve then and had already moved away to start work at Estancia Del Fin Del Mundo.'

Lady Kathleen noticed how her grandson's face softened when he mentioned his family's beloved ranch. The ranch at the end of the world. His Achilles heel. How he loved his Argentinian home – almost as much as his poor mother, Roisin, had hated it. Lady Kathleen dragged her thoughts away from her unfortunate daughter and back to Javier.

'And so you became friends,' she said. 'How kind. I expect he needed a friend more than ever then.'

JC's face took on a shuttered look. 'Javier is a servant, Grandmother,' he reminded her. 'An employee. That is all.'

'I understand, JC,' she said softly. And she did, far better than he realised.

# Chapter 15

Macdara signed the sheaf of letters and passed them back to Anya.
'Is that it?'

'For the moment. I'm just popping into town to post them. Anything I can get you while I'm there? No? You, Orla?'

'No thanks.' Orla smiled over at her grandfather. 'I've got everything I always wanted right here. I know, I know,' she grinned at Anya. 'Pass the sick bucket! But it's true.'

Anya gave a tight smile. 'Right then, I'll be off.' Since the Liam episode in the back yard, she had felt distinctly uneasy around Orla and so spent as little time as possible in her company. Perhaps, Anya thought a little guiltily, as she closed the office door behind her, she was making too much of it. Being too sensitive, too thin-skinned. It was perfectly possible that Orla had seen someone else get into Liam's vehicle and genuinely mistook that person for her.

As if thinking about the man conjured him up, Liam stood before her suddenly, smiling his slightly loose-lipped smile. His glance went to the letters in her hand.

'Off to the village, are we?'

'I am, yes.' Anya emphasised the singular. A flash of something crossed Liam's face, but his smile never wavered.

'I'm going that way shortly, myself. Can I give you a lift?'

Anya shook her head. 'No, thank you. I have my own car.'

His smile disappeared. 'Right so. Well, I'll get out of your way.' He narrowed his eyes, as she walked swiftly over to her little car, her head held high, as if she was something special and not just the by-product of a scumbag mother. The stuck-up bitch really had it coming.

Liam turned away to find himself under the intense scrutiny of Fergal, who was standing on the opposite side of the yard. How long he'd been there was any one's guess.

'Everything all right, Liam?' the other man called, giving him a searching look.

'And why wouldn't it be?' he replied testily, stalking over to his Land Rover. It would be even better as soon as he brought Miss Hoity Toity Anya Keating to heel.

Fergal gazed speculatively after him. He'd never liked Liam, but these days the vet was seriously beginning to get on his nerves. What had he said to Anya, he wondered? More importantly, what had Anya said to him? Judging from the look on the vet's face and his cranky mien, nothing good. Maybe he'd tried it on with her, as he did with almost every female with a pulse, and been rejected. Fergal certainly hoped so. The thought of Anya succumbing to a man of Liam's calibre filled him with dismay. She was much too good for Liam. And much too good for himself too, judging by the way Macdara had warned him off.

As the Land Rover barked into life and Liam drove away at far too high a speed, Fergal resolved to keep a closer eye on him.

'Sorry, Grandy, did I embarrass you?' Orla asked, when Anya had left. 'I don't mean to, you know. It's just that I'm so happy to be back at Lismore, I know I go over the top sometimes, which is why I'm in here skulking round your office today.'

Macdara stuck his chest out. 'Embarrassed? Not at all. Sure, isn't it flattering to an old fella like meself.' He winked. 'You just keep on telling me how great I am. And one day, I might just believe you.' His eyes went to the novelty clock on the wall, a recent present from Orla, who had spied it in a shop in Dublin. Instead of a cuckoo, a racehorse popped out and whickered. Only four o'clock, but already he felt dog-tired and more than ready to put his feet up.

'Weary?' Orla asked, watching him suppress a yawn.

'A bit,' he admitted. 'More and more lately. I'm afraid it's all getting a bit beyond me, Orla. I'm far too long in the tooth to manage Lismore for much longer. This is a young man's game. I'm looking forward to the day when I can just hand over the reins in every sense of the word and take a back seat.' He felt slightly guilty at misleading her, blaming everything on his age, but until he had a firm prognosis from the doctor regarding his failing eyesight, it didn't seem fair to burden anyone else with his problems, especially Orla, who had already been through so much.

'Who will take over?' Orla queried lightly, knowing full well it was bound to be Fergal which, after all, made perfect sense. Nevertheless, her stomach turned flip-flops at the thought that he would get everything, leaving her, once again, to draw the short straw.

'Fergal,' Macdara confirmed, trying unsuccessfully to suppress a yawn. 'Who better? He knows the business like the back of his hand, and I wouldn't want Lismore going to a stranger. It would be safe in his hands.'

Orla looked pensive, paused long enough for Macdara to realise something was wrong, then asked with a slight break in her voice, 'Why doesn't Fergal like me, Grandy?' Taken completely off-guard, Macdara's slowly closing eyes snapped wide open again. 'Is it because he resents the fact that I came back?'

'Is that what you think, love?' Macdara looked shocked and upset. He had no idea she felt like that, had even thought that for a moment, apart from the odd bit of sniping, she and Fergal seemed to get on fine. Yet, here she was, struggling to hold back tears. Macdara shook his head. 'No, you've got it all wrong, Orla. Fergal's an open book. There's not a begrudging bone in his body. I can assure you he's every bit as delighted as the rest of us.'

Orla blinked rapidly and cleared her throat. 'I'm sure you're right, Grandy, and that I'm just being a silly billy.' She smiled tremulously, her anxious expression telling the true story, which was that she was far from convinced. 'I just thought he might be worried about me muscling in on his territory, which is understandable, especially as he does tend to be rather sensitive about the fact that he's adopted.'

'Does he, indeed?' Macdara looked astounded. 'That's never been an issue. I've never thought of him as anything other than my grandson.'

'Maybe not for you, Grandy, but it is an issue for him,' Orla insisted. She sprang lightly up from the settee. 'Anyway, I'm sorry I brought it up and I'm sure you're right and it's all just my imagination.' She clapped her hands together. 'Tell you what, instead of exercising my imagination, I'm off to exercise VIP instead. In fact, I think I'll ride over to Castle Mac Tíre. Any message for Lady Kathleen?'

'Just give her my regards,' Macdara said, his brow furrowed with thought.

'I will. See you later, Grandy.' Orla dropped a kiss on his forehead, and headed for the door.

Macdara sat on long after she left, his frown deepening as he replayed their conversation, dissecting every word and each nuance. He hoped he hadn't been too cavalier in dismissing her concerns. Though Macdara felt it unlikely, it wasn't beyond the realms that Fergal was experiencing some trepidation about Orla's return. And simply because he, Macdara, never gave the matter of Fergal's adoption a thought, didn't mean, as Orla had pointed out, that Fergal himself wasn't conscious of the lack of blood ties. Irritated with himself, Macdara felt that he had let both Fergal and Orla down. Indeed, the more he thought about it, the more it made sense that Fergal might worry about the new brush sweeping clean, and that that anxiety might well manifest itself in less than pleasant behaviour towards Orla. That he, himself, had never witnessed anything other than the odd bit of bickering didn't mean it didn't happen. He made a note to ask Anya if she had noticed anything amiss.

Disturbed, Macdara rose and poured himself a finger of whiskey, then returned both to his seat and his ruminations. There was no question but that Lismore would go to Fergal. He had been Macdara's right-hand man since he was barely out of nappies; he had been there through thick and thin. He had earned the right. Unlike Orla, however, Fergal hadn't been forced to flit halfway across the world. Looked at it that way, Macdara told himself, if anyone had the right to be resentful, it was she. He smiled to himself, as there wasn't one mean or resentful bone in her entire body. He scratched his head as another problem presented itself.

Orla had little more than the clothes she stood up in and, reasonably, could look to him to settle something upon her too. But there was only so much money in the pot and, of necessity, the bulk would go to Fergal for the upkeep of Lismore. Nevertheless, Macdara vowed to find a small sum to put her in the way of setting up a business or of training for a career. Still only in her twenties, she had ample time to make her own way in life. He would like to have been able to do more for her, but she would understand the situation. Wouldn't she?

Lady Kathleen was sitting in the garden reading a biography on Marilyn Monroe. She was having what Anya teasingly referred to as a librarian day in that she had forsaken her usual glamour for a dark-green tweed skirt and white cotton blouse. Her hair was swept up in a tidy chignon and half-moon spectacles rested on the bridge of her nose. The only nod to her love of froufrou was the pussycat bow with which her blouse was decorated.

'Hi, Lady Kay,' Orla called, coming round from the courtyard, where she had left VIP tethered to one of the old hitching posts.

Laying down her book, Lady Kathleen shaded her eyes against the evening sun. 'Orla!' Her face creased with pleasure. 'What an unexpected though very lovely surprise.' She gestured to a wrought-iron patio chair. 'Come, pull up a chair and let me look at you properly. Heaven knows I've been dying to see you since your return and we hardly had a chance to do more than nod to each other at poor Sister Martha's funeral.' She wagged a finger, mock angry. 'JC's fault. The boy would insist that Javier took me straight home afterwards. He does so worry about my health.'

'I know. I feel so guilty. I should have come long before now.' Orla made a helpless little gesture with her hands. 'But it's all been a bit fraught, as you can imagine.' She leaned over and kissed the older woman on the cheek, then dragged up the chair next to her wheelchair. 'Strictly speaking, though, and since we're apportioning blame, it's all down to Grandy.' Pretending annoyance, she rolled her eyes. 'Honestly, Lady Kay, he hardly lets me out of his sight.'

Lady Kathleen laughed, though in her own mind she was comparing Orla's version of events to that of Anya's. No mention of all the shopping trips to Dublin, the weekends away.

'I'm not surprised,' she said. 'The poor man still can't believe you're back. I think for a while he thought he was hallucinating or entering his dotage.' Her sharp eyes scanned Orla's face. 'What a pretty thing you are, my dear. And so Australian-looking.'

Orla gave a deliberately cheesy grin. 'I hope that's a good thing.'

'Oh, very good. You've got that sun-kissed-blond Kylie look off to a fine art. I bet the male population of Tipperary doesn't know what's hit it. I expect they're queuing up for the chance to give you the guided tour and show you what you've been missing all these years.'

'I doubt it.' Orla gave a little deprecating shrug. 'In any case, I'm not interested in men at the moment. I'm just getting used to being back home again, and enjoying every second. So much has changed and yet so much remains just as I remember.'

'It must have been very hard for you and your sister being so far from home, especially after your mother died,' Lady Kathleen said softly, her eyes full of compassion for the young woman.

'It was,' Orla said honestly. 'Made worse by the fact that our father really didn't give a damn. Mother dying was a real inconvenience for him. It took him out of his happiness bubble for a while, reminded him that he had a life before his precious Claudette and gay Paree, *and* that he had two daughters.' She smiled, but there was pain in her eyes, real and raw. Sensing that she needed to just speak, Lady Kathleen stayed quiet. 'Oh, for a while, he stepped up to the plate. We went to live with him in France, but we weren't really wanted there. His half-his-age bimbo wife made it abundantly clear that becoming stepmother to two bothersome teenage girls was definitely not the role she had signed up for.'

'I'm guessing it didn't end well,' Lady Kathleen said when Orla fell silent.

'Nope. In the end, we left them to their little love nest, and returned to Australia. I daresay it was the happiest day of Claudette's life.' Lady Kathleen reached out and took Orla's hand, played absent-mindedly with the bracelet on her wrist. 'Did you never consider coming back to Lismore?'

Orla nodded. 'Often. We dreamed about it. But, Lady Kay, you know what the situation was like. My mother left under a cloud and then there was all that business with the fire, and Grandy blaming Sinéad for Grandmother's death.' She lifted her chin slightly, looked slightly defiant. 'He wouldn't have welcomed her back. You know that, Lady Kay. And one thing our mother taught us was that sisters should stick up for each other, and stick together.'

'So what happened?' Lady Kathleen asked gently. 'You're here, but where's Sinéad? Are you in touch still?'

A shutter came down over Orla's face. She cleared her throat, and extricated her hand from Lady Kathleen's kind but firm grip. 'If it's okay with you, I'd sooner not talk about it.'

Already feeling guilty over forcing Javier to bare his soul, Lady Kathleen didn't hesitate to drop the subject. If Orla wished to open up about her sister, she would do so when she was good and ready.

'My dear, I understand completely. Just remember I'm always here if you do wish to talk.'

'Thank you,' Orla said softly. 'I appreciate it.'

'Oh, look,' Lady Kathleen said, breaking into a sudden smile. 'Here comes JC, just in time to rescue us from the doldrums.' She waved at her grandson, who was walking across the lawn towards them, looking impossibly handsome in riding breeches and a white shirt with several of the buttons undone. A lock of his blue-black hair lay like an inverted question mark over one eye, almost as if it had been artfully stuck there, rather than as the entirely natural result of a recent bracing ride over the fields on Tango Lass. Heathcliff, eat your heart out! 'Hello, darling,' Lady Kathleen called, as he approached within hearing distance. 'Look who's come to visit. Isn't that a nice surprise?'

JC flashed them his charming smile and nodded in greeting. 'No surprise. I saw her horse tethered in the yard, and where VIP is, Orla is never far behind.'

Orla smiled back. No, she did more than smile, Lady Kathleen thought, she positively glowed back. Interesting. Anya had hinted recently that she felt there might be a mutual attraction between Orla and JC but until this moment Lady Kathleen hadn't given it any credence. The two had known each other since childhood and their shared history gave them a bond, an ease in each other's company which to an outsider might appear as something greater. But seeing Orla's reaction now, however, Lady Kathleen was forced to acknowledge that Anya may have been right. Orla and JC were no longer children, but two exceptionally good-looking young adults. No good could come of it, she thought worriedly, as JC pulled up a chair. One heart was already spoken for.

JC stretched his long legs out before him, crossing one Spanish-leather-booted foot over the other at the ankle. 'So, Orla, to what do we owe the honour?'

Orla smiled archly. 'I've been most neglectful of your lovely grandmother. It was high time I paid a visit. And it's obvious she's got a portrait in the attic, because she's hardly changed a bit since I saw her all those years ago.'

'Dear child, how sweet of you to say so, although it's patently untrue,' Lady Kathleen preened a little at the compliment. 'But you know, JC, I was just saying what a beautiful young woman Orla has grown up to be. Don't you agree?' She scrutinised him sharply.

'Orla!' JC let out a disbelieving shriek. '*Ay, dios mio*! You need your eyes tested, Grandmother. Beautiful? Yes, if a cow is beautiful, or a goat is beautiful, or a pig.' He broke off, laughing, as Orla jumped up from her chair and launched herself at him, sending his chair flying backwards, so that the two of them ended up in a tangled heap of arms and legs on the ground.

Amused, Lady Kathleen watched the horseplay, but behind her smile, her eyes were anxious and alarm bells were going off left, right and centre in her head. There was something wrong with the little tableau. Something off-kilter. She just couldn't put her finger on quite what it was.

Breathless, JC and Orla picked themselves up as Javier came out of the house with a cup of tea for Lady Kathleen.

'Ah Javier, the very man,' JC called, his arm wound loosely round Orla's waist. 'Have you met, Orla, Macdara's granddaughter, lately exiled from Australia?' And to Orla, 'Meet Javier, Grandmother's companion, nurse and all round handyman at Castle Mac Tíre.' JC waved a casual hand. 'Fetch us some drinks, too, if you would, Javier. There's a particularly nice bottle of chilled Chablis I've been saving for a special occasion.' He dropped a light kiss on Orla's hair, his eyes locked on to Javier's, with something cool and challenging in their depths. 'Is this a special occasion, Orla?'

'Definitely.' She clapped her hands together quickly. 'Chop, chop! *Rapido*, Javier. Don't spare the horses!' She giggled as he went back into the house. 'Mm, nice bum. Nice everything. Where did you pick him up?'

'Buenos Aires. He used to work for us on the ranch,' JC said tonelessly, as he watched Javier depart.

'And now he works for me,' Lady Kathleen said, a distinctly frosty note in her voice. 'And I expect him to be treated with the utmost respect.'

Orla looked immediately contrite. 'Oh, I'm sorry. I didn't mean to offend him, honestly. I'll apologise, shall I, when he comes back?'

'No need,' JC said, rounding on his grandmother. 'Really, Grandmother, if I've told you once, I've told you a thousand times, Javier is a servant. It is a mistake to let him become too familiar.'

'That, Javier, dear,' Lady Kathleen retorted, the chilliness still evident in her voice, 'rather depends on your definition of familiar, doesn't it?'

The atmosphere had suddenly become charged. Confused, Orla glanced from one to the other. What the hell was going on? And then a notion struck her, so outrageous she almost laughed aloud. Lady Kathleen and Javier? Christ on a lollipop stick! Had JC's grandmother turned into a cougar? Was Javier her toy boy? Orla gazed at him with even more interest when he returned with the wine on a silver salver and two crystal glasses.

Anya drove into the village and quickly found a parking space in the usually crowded square, which was enough almost to restore her good humour, dented by her encounter with Liam. More than ever she felt uneasy around him, felt under his scrutiny increasingly often as she went about her business, added to which he seemed to materialise all too frequently in the same places as she. Although he had always flirted with her, as was his wont with anything in a skirt, he seemed definitely to have upped the ante lately, his remarks escalating past the point of merely flirtatious to the downright suggestive. Anya found it difficult to fathom why. It wasn't as though she encouraged him in any way. In fact she went out of her way to avoid him as much as she could and, when that proved impossible, she was polite to him and no more. At no time had she ever given him any reason to believe she might be interested in his attentions. And so why Liam persisted in creeping her out was something of a mystery, especially as he must know that Fergal and Macdara would not approve of any lewd behaviour under their roof. Anya gave herself a little shake. The solution to this problem would have to wait though because right now there were letters to post and purchases to be made. Climbing out of the car, she locked it with the zapper and made her way across the street to the post office.

'Hi, Anya. Long time no see.'

Anya suppressed a groan as she emerged some minutes later and bumped into Suzy Walsh, a former classmate with a reputation as both a gossip and a troublemaker. From personal experience Anya knew both epithets were well deserved.

'Oh, hi, Suzy,' she returned the greeting in what she hoped was a suitably rushed manner. 'Can't stop, I'm afraid. I've got to pick up a bit of shopping for Bridie at Lismore. For the dinner,' she added a bit desperately, as the other girl planted herself directly in front of her like a small tank.

'Sure, I won't keep you a minute,' Suzy promised, although it came across more as a threat. 'Isn't it only civil to stop and pass the time of day with someone you haven't seen for a long time?'

Which of course was a dig at Anya for being a rude bitch. She groaned internally again as Suzy, with a quick look to either side, as if they were engaged in the exchange of state secrets, leaned slyly towards her.

'So how are things at Lismore? How is the granddaughter – Orla, isn't it? – settling in?'

'She's fine,' Anya answered shortly, loath to gossip about Lismore or any of its inhabitants.

'A bit of a funny one, she is, if you ask me,' Suzy said, not in the least put off by Anya's froideur. 'She might look like an angel with that tan and blond hair and everything but, Jesus, the woman's got a temper on her like Beelzebub himself.'

Anya raised an eyebrow, her attention caught despite herself. 'Whatever do you mean? I'd no idea you even knew her.'

'I don't, and after what I witnessed in Klassy Kutz last week, I've no wish to know her, what's more.' Taking the moral high-ground, Suzy jerked her head up the High Street in the direction of a hair salon that was popular with the younger crowd. 'Getting all blonded up she was, and the poor junior accidentally got suds in her eye when she was washing her hair, so she had to take her contact lens out.' Suzy rolled her eyes expressively. 'Well, anyone would think she was being murdered. The fuss she made had to be seen to be believed. And the language out of her! The air was blue. Cut a long story short, they ended up not charging her a penny.' She chuckled, a sound with no real humour in it.

'It must have been a knee-jerk reaction. It probably was very painful.' Anya felt compelled to defend Orla, though she wasn't quite sure why. For Macdara's sake, she guessed. But if what Suzy said was correct, it sounded like Orla had completely over reacted to what was, after all, a minor accident.

Suzy looked at her mock pityingly. 'Have a word with your-self, Anya,' she said. 'We're talking a few suds in the eye, not a feckin' knife through the heart. She's a spoilt madam, if you ask me, stamping her feet and demanding that the poor kid be sacked.' She huffed a little. 'Ah well, I suppose it's one law for the rich and another law for the rest of us gombeens. Isn't it always?' Satisfied that she'd given that lot over at Lismore a good rubbishing, she nodded briefly. 'Anyway, I'll be off now since you're in such a tear-ing hurry. See you around.'

'Yes, okay,' Anya said faintly, as Suzy marched off suddenly, humming some old song beneath her breath and brandishing her shopping bag like a weapon. She felt slightly winded after the encounter, almost as if she had been picked up by a mini tornado and set back down again, a little bruised and shaken. Suzy had not mellowed with age, and her gossip radar was as deadly as ever. She'd certainly given Anya food for thought, and she couldn't help but wonder what Macdara would say should he learn that Orla had been making herself unpopular amongst the locals. But then, as usual, Anya's sense of fairness kicked in to point out that you couldn't believe the gospel out of Suzy Walsh's mouth: no doubt she had exaggerated the whole episode hugely, and probably had done so out of jealousy. Yes, that was more than likely it. A beautiful girl like Orla would always bring out the green-eyed monster in some people. Even herself. Putting Suzy firmly out of her mind, Anya headed for the butcher's, Bridie's instructions ringing in her head.

*Now, don't let Mr Egan pass you off with any old rubbish, Anya. I want only the leanest steak, marbled, but not fatty. Orla hates fatty meat.* And suds in her eye too, apparently, she mused as she pushed opened the door of the butcher's shop and an old-fashioned bell tinkled her arrival. Mr Egan stood behind the counter chopping meat. He looked up, smiled and wiped his hands on his bloodied apron. 'Hello, Anya, love. What can I do you for?'

She laughed obediently at the tired old joke and gave him her order.

When Anya returned to Lismore, the house was in a state of bedlam. Bridie, normally unflappable, seemed to have undergone a personality transplant, and was frenziedly chucking clothes into a suitcase, whilst issuing instructions non-stop to a dazed and confused Macdara.

'Anya! Anya! Thank goodness you're home.' She threw a look of gratitude up to Heaven. 'At last, someone with a decent head on their shoulders.' She rolled a towel into a sausage shape and jammed in the case. 'Listen, pet, my daughter's been taken poorly and has been rushed into hospital. I'm needed straight away to look after the children.'

'Oh, dear, poor Karen.' Anya hurried over to make herself useful. 'What's the matter with her? She hasn't … ?'

'Miscarried? No, but she's got that pre-eclampsia thing, high blood pressure, which is very dangerous for both mother and child. They want to keep her in for observation.' Bridie looked harassed. 'I don't know how long for. Anyway, the long and the short of it is that Bill, her husband, can't manage on his own, what with work and rushing in and out of the hospital, so I'll have to leave you all to your own devices.' Her glance went to Macdara. 'I'm really sorry to leave you in the lurch like this, Mac. Will you manage all right?'

'Fine,' Macdara assured her. 'So, don't you go worrying your head on that score, Bridie. Your place is with your family. We'll manage grand, and if we have to send out for the odd take-away in the evening, it won't kill us.'

'No need for that, Anya's a great little cook,' Bridie said. Unable to close her suitcase, she resorted to sitting on it in an attempt to get the two sides to meet. She beckoned to Anya. 'Try doing the zip up now, will you?' She gave a relieved sigh as with Anya's help the zip slid obligingly up the track. 'Good. That's that done.' She stood up, slightly breathless. 'Now, does anyone know where Orla is?'

'She's gone out with JC, I think,' Macdara said. 'I'll go and look for her, shall I?'

Bridie shook her head. 'No, no time. The taxi will be here at any minute.' She sent a glance out the window. 'I'll just nip up to her room and leave a note. I feel like I'm deserting her when the poor little thing has only just come home.' Her glance veered worriedly to Anya. 'And what about you, pet, will you be all right?' Quickly, Bridie picked up a biro and began to scribble a note on the writing pad she used for making shopping lists.

'Of course. I'm a big girl now,' Anya laughed. 'I can even tie my own shoelaces. Just tell Karen to get well soon and give the children a kiss for me.'

'I will,' Bridie promised, then finished off the note to Orla with a couple of kisses at the foot of the paper. 'Right,' she said. 'I'll just pop this upstairs and have a last-minute check round to make sure I haven't forgotten anything.'

'I'll take your suitcase outside,' Macdara offered. 'That way, you won't lose any time when the taxi arrives.'

'And I'll get on with making the dinner,' Anya said, as Bridie headed for the stairs. 'See, no need to panic, everything is under control.'

Upstairs, Bridie made a cursory check of her own bedroom before going into Orla's with the note. It was in a right old mess with clothes strewn on the bed and on the floor, drawers half open, clutter everywhere. She smiled affectionately. Some things didn't change. Orla and her sister had been as different in that respect as in every other, one neat as a pin, the other chaotic as a whirlwind. She propped the note on the dressing table, which was a jumble of cosmetics, perfumes and odds and sods, sliding it upright between a bottle of expensive-looking perfume and a box of what looked like some kind of medicine. Her eyes ran curiously over the label, but there was no time for investigation, as she could hear the taxi pulling into the yard below, and a moment later Macdara yelled up the stairs.

'Bye, Orla, love,' she blew a kiss into the empty room, and went down to the waiting car.

'God bless, Bridie.' Macdara gave her a peck on the cheek and helped her in. He closed the door behind her and banged on the roof in a signal to the driver that she was ready. 'We'll miss you.'

'I'll miss you too,' she called, her eyes suddenly swimming with tears. 'Stay safe, all of you, do you hear me?'

'Well, we'll try anyway, won't we Anya?' Macdara waved after the car as it disappeared down the long sweeping drive of Lismore and out on to the main road. 'Poor Bridie, I hope her daughter will be all right.'

'So do I,' Anya said quietly, and she knew he was thinking of his own daughter, Nessa, and wishing he had been there for her when she needed him, in the way that Bridie was there for her daughter.

# Chapter 16

Lady Kathleen was thinking of her own daughter too, and how she wished she could have been there for her at the end. But then no one expected the end to come as it had, out of a clear blue sky, when the plane she and her husband were travelling in collided mid-air with another. Human error, they said at the inquest. Someone had screwed up and that screw-up had cost her her daughter, and JC his parents.

Methodically, Lady Kathleen worked her way through photograph album after photograph album, each one containing a pictorial history of Roisin, flimsy paper milestones marking her daughter's transition from babyhood right through to motherhood and beyond. But really, she didn't need the photographs, not with a cine reel of Roisin's life playing on a continuous loop in her head. Scene one, the opening shot: Roisin at her baptism, round-faced, angelic, swathed in the same antique lace gown that she herself, and generations of the Ormonds had worn before her, and JC after. Titles flashing across her mind: 'The First Holy Communion'; a white dress and veil, Bible held carefully between gloved hands, Roisin's beautiful fair hair teased into ringlets and crowned with a wreath of orange blossom. Cut to: eighteen, and a beautiful debutante now. The ringlets replaced by a sophisticated French pleat, her first ball gown, a fairytale confection of white tulle and satin. Lady Kathleen remembered, as if it were only yesterday, the special trip they had taken to London in quest of the perfect frock. Trekking up and down Oxford Street, in and out of shops, finding nothing suitable. Nothing that made her daughter sing, which Roisin insisted was the litmus test. Into a black cab then, and off to Knightsbridge to sample the joys of first Harrods and then Harvey Nichols; pink champagne and prawn ceviche in the fifth-floor restaurant. Happy and triumphant when they finally found the Holy Grail of dresses in Lindka Cierach's boutique in South Kensington. Roisin, aglow with excitement, because Linda was the designer of Fergie's wedding dress. And her own, only one year later.

Lady Kathleen's face darkened. She had never liked Eduardo, her daughter's husband. At thirty-six, he was seventeen years older and a man of the world. Oh, she could well understand the attraction. He looked very much as JC did now, a cliché almost, in his tall, dark perfection, charming almost to a fault, and super-wealthy. He owned properties all over the world, but his favourite, the one he called home, was his *estancia* near Buenos Aires. Spreading across several thousand acres of land, it was one of the largest and best known in Argentina. A well-known figure throughout the equestrian world, he bred both race-horses and polo ponies, along with the sturdy work horses, known as *criollo*, which were used to round up the several thousand head of cattle he kept grazing out on the pampas.

He had first encountered Roisin at a dinner party thrown in his honour by Macdara, whilst visiting Lismore on business. Roisin, still very much an ingénue in matters of the heart, had come away from the table wide-eyed and smitten. Lady Kathleen, wiser by far, had disapproved right from the beginning. For nineteen years, she had hot-housed her daughter, staying ever vigilant against the Lolita-loving sharks that swam in the waters of Hollywood. Never for a moment did she suspect that when danger came, it would be in the place she always thought of as their safe haven. Unreasonably, she blamed Macdara, ranting and raving till he gently pointed out the truth: Roisin was in search of a father-figure. She it was who had failed her daughter, she who had run through four husbands and a succession of lovers, leaving the girl feeling rudderless and insecure. When Eduardo Fernandez de Rosas, Latin lover and father-figure all rolled into one, happened along, her beautiful daughter was ripe for the plucking. He simply reached up and down she tumbled into the palm of his hand. And from that moment she was under his thumb.

The cine reel in Lady Kathleen's head rolled relentlessly on. A close-up on Eduardo's handsome face, arm possessively encircling Roisin's slender waist, something hooded, almost triumphant flashing in his night-shaded eyes.

Admittedly, he'd treated Roisin well, in the material sense at least. To make her feel at home, he'd even pulled down the old ranch house on the *estancia* and replaced it with a house in the English Georgian style. But, knowing her daughter as well as she knew herself, Kathleen had often sensed something sad about her, an emptiness, the kind that comes from dreams unfulfilled. Loneliness too. Eduardo, she guessed, found it easier to open his wallet than to open his heart. But such was the culture of machismo in Argentina. A man who was soft with his woman was seen as less than a man, a figure of fun, disrespected in a land where respect and honour were worth dying for. Or killing for. Or banishing one's only son for.

Final scene. Cut to: Roisin, faded-pretty now, a sign above her head, swinging eerily to and fro, heralding the legendary Santa Rosa storm that whirled across Argentina every year, sweeping all in its path before it. Estancia Del Fin Del Mundo, the sign announced grandly in painted letters, now so worn in places the original grain of the wood shows through. The ranch at the end of the world. Prophetic words. Lady Kathleen often wondered if it had, indeed, proved to be the end of the world. Roisin's world. And fade to black.

With a sigh, she put down the last album and lay back against her pillows. Today was the anniversary of her daughter's death. Three years. Sometimes it felt like only a day, sometimes an eternity. But always, always there was an emptiness, a gaping void, a suppurating wound that would never heal.

Outside her window voices drifted up. Harsh. Masculine. A volley of Spanish, staccato bullets grazing the air. JC and Javier. Her thoughts turned to her grandson, conjuring him up as she had seen him earlier today out in the garden with Orla, smiling, charming, a master of mind games. He had, she feared, inherited most of his father's characteristics and little or none of his gentle mother's.

Weary, almost unto death, Lady Kathleen closed her eyes.

Stars flickered like votive candles in the sky as JC left Castle Mac Tíre behind and stepped on to the lane that led to Wishbone Lake. Opaque ribbons of cloud coiled around the moon like the string on a child's spinning-top, setting it to rotate gently on its axis. A bat sped like tracer fire across his path, its black-patent coat filigreed by night and, in the distance, a single cry marked the passing of the soul of some poor creature.

'In the midst of life, we are in death.' The words travelled through time and space, a three-year-old echo resounding in JC's soul. Three years since he had buried his parents, together with the hoped-for reconciliation with his father. Blinded by sudden tears, he turned abruptly into the little copse of woods skirting the lake, kicking out savagely at the creepers flailing with skeletal fingers across his path. Reaching the lake, he stood and looked out across the expressionless expanse of water, unmarred by even a single ripple. The air was thick and warm.

'Why?' A whisper. He turned his teary face up to the sky, arms outstretched, embracing nothingness. 'Why?' A shout, a howl of rage that ricocheted off the water into the lap of the sky, falling back to earth unanswered. JC slumped to his knees, his body jerking like an out of control marionette. He buried his face in his hands and let the grief come, wave upon juddering wave until, at last, his tears ran dry. From the shadow of the woods, Javier watched silently, patiently, showing himself only when JC rose unsteadily to his feet.

Their eyes met and held for a moment. Then, Javier turned and walked back into the woods. A moment later, JC followed.

# Chapter 17

Liam O'Hanlon was sick of being snubbed. He was a good-looking man, for God's sake, not Quasimodo. Whatever he'd lacked in his life, it certainly wasn't the attentions of the fairer sex. He had only to click his fingers and they came running. Until now, that is. Far from falling into his arms, let alone his bed, Anya Keating looked at him like he was just shit on the bottom of her shoe. Well, not for much longer, because Liam was going to up the ante. Removing Kitty from the picture would create a vacancy, one that Anya was more than qualified to fill. He looked forward to the first time, and smiled.

'Share the joke,' Fergal said, coming into the stable where Liam was checking on Derry Oak's progress.

'You wouldn't appreciate it,' Liam said, smiling wider than ever. 'Believe me, you wouldn't appreciate it at all.'

No doubt he was right, Fergal thought, not bothering to reply. There was nothing he found amusing about the man. Absolutely zilch!

Macdara advertised for a temporary housekeeper at Lismore although in the meantime Anya pretty much took over the running of the house. In theory, Orla was supposed to chip in. In practice, she did little but bat her baby-blues and laughingly bemoan the fact that she could even burn water and that she would never make a domestic goddess. Anya didn't mind in the least. Running the house made a change from her usual work and she enjoyed the creativity involved in cooking and the opportunity to expand on Bridie's tasty but limited repertoire of recipes. Sister Martha would have been amazed to witness her adroitness in the kitchen, considering how her first attempt at cooking, a birthday cake for the nun's birthday, was a disaster of epic proportions. Not only did it sink like a stone in the middle but, when she turned it out, it was as hard as concrete. Sister Martha declined to go near it on the basis that her teeth hadn't got that much life left in them. They had giggled over it many times in the years since, and Sister Martha had crossed out the original recipe name in the book, substituting it with Anya's Rocky Millstone Cake.

Though still grief-stricken about the loss of Sister Martha, Anya occasionally found that her grief was tempered with the sweetness of memories that made her smile: a funny recollection such as the cake incident, a snatch of music, or one of Sister Martha's many wise proverbs falling from another's lips. The rage of the early days had become diluted, mixed as it was now with a sense of gratitude that in her life she had had Sister Martha at all, let alone for as long as she did. Many children, with backgrounds far worse than hers, were never so blessed. And, because of this, because she felt she owed Sister Martha, Anya resolved to make the most of her life and not, as the saying went, sweat the small things. Like Fergal thinking of her as just the hired help. Although actually that didn't seem to be quite such a small thing. It hurt. It really hurt. And what was even more injurious was the thought that, thanks to Orla and her fairytales, he might actually believe her to be involved with Liam. Not too long ago, Anya had thought they were friends and that he knew her too well ever to imagine that was true. Now, sadly, she wasn't so sure.

But bustling about the kitchen she consoled herself with the thought that at least she wasn't deluding herself any more, and nor was she wasting her time on girlish flights of fantasy and dreams of Fergal that would never come true. Ironically, she had Orla to thank for that. The fact that a great big empty pit seemed to have opened up in Anya's stomach, a yawning loneliness, was just something she would have to get over. But it wasn't easy, especially since Fergal had started looking at her in an odd sort of way.

She placed a saucepan in the sink, picked up a scourer and began to scrub more brutally than was necessary, growing hot at the thought that he might be imagining her and Liam together. Her chin came up and the scourer moved at twice the speed, almost removing a layer of aluminium. Oh well, let him believe what he damn well wanted. The help didn't have to explain herself to anybody.

Macdara pushed his chair back from the table and patted his stomach. 'Well, Anya, that was very nice. Very nice, indeed. What did you say it was called?'

Anya looked pleased at the praise. 'Jambalaya. It's a Creole dish. The name means jumbled up.'

'Like my brain,' Macdara smiled. 'What do you think, Fergal, will we keep her on?'

'Without a doubt.' Fergal mopped the last of the sauce up with a piece of bread and pushed his plate away. 'Good help is hard to find these days.'

Anya froze. There it was. The 'H' word, and straight from the horse's own mouth this time. It was an effort to restrain herself from lifting up his plate and smashing it down over his head. Instead she contented herself with snatching it noisily from under his nose and bearing it off to the scullery for washing.

Fergal sent Macdara a puzzled look.

'Women! Ours is not to reason why,' Macdara said, in answer to the unasked question. He pushed his chair back and rose to his feet. He picked his jacket up from the back of his chair and shrugged it on. 'I'm off to check on Glengarriff. Liam gave him a clean bill of health earlier, but I'm still in two minds as to whether to race him next month. Coming?'

Fergal jumped up hastily as a cacophony of crashing dishes sounded from the scullery. He raised his eyebrows. 'Come home, Bridie, all is forgiven, eh?'

Macdara laughed. 'Show me a woman without a temper and I'll show you the eighth wonder of the world.'

'Yeah, but Anya? Anya's not like other women. She's kind and sweet.' Fergal caught himself as Macdara sent him a quizzical look.

He grinned, slightly shamefaced. 'Ah, who am I kidding? You're dead right, Mac. They're all the same.'

'Which is why you like to keep your options open?' Macdara thumped him jovially on the back. 'You're still young, Fergal. Plenty of fish in the sea, eh?'

But the one Macdara didn't want caught was Anya. Fergal was only too aware of this, and he was beginning to find it extremely irritating. Whilst he understood that Macdara considered himself *in loco parentis*, Anya wasn't a child any more; she was a grown woman who, presumably, could make up her own mind about who she did or didn't want to go out with. There was something more to it, Fergal suspected, some reason why Macdara took his role of protector to extremes, but he was damned if he knew what. For a moment, Fergal toyed with the idea of quizzing him outright, but Macdara looked in no humour to share confidences, so he settled for believing all would be made clear in time.

'I've never been too keen on fish,' he said jokingly. 'But I know what you mean. Why settle for a minnow, when you can have a shoal. Right?'

'Exactly right,' Macdara nodded. 'Play the field while you can, Fergal. Time enough to tie yourself down.'

'And yet you did,' Fergal remarked impishly, unable to resist calling him on his double standards. 'You married Nancy when you were much younger than me.'

Macdara huffed a little. 'I was lucky,' he said. 'I met the right woman early. That doesn't happen very often.'

'But how do you know she's the right woman,' Fergal persisted, 'if you haven't, to use your own words, played the field?'

'You just do,' Macdara said with certainty. 'You will too.'

'And what if I already have?' Fergal asked, bringing Macdara up short as they walked across the yard towards the stables. 'What if I have already met the right woman?'

'You've never mentioned anyone special.' Macdara thought about it and started to walk again. 'Anyway, you're married to Lismore. Tell me, when was the last time you actually went out on a date?'

'Not for a while,' Fergal admitted. He pushed the stable door open and stood aside for Macdara to pass. 'But, then again, maybe I don't need to go any further than Lismore.' Now what on earth had possessed him to say that, he wondered, as Macdara swung round, a look of shock on his face.

'Is that supposed to be a joke, Fergal?' Macdara snapped, his voice suddenly strained. 'Because if it is, I'm not laughing. You'll have respect for the women under my roof, do you hear me? I'll have no one playing fast and loose with their feelings. They've been hurt badly enough as it is.' Signalling that the conversation was at an end, Macdara walked over to Glengarriff and bent down to examine his leg.

Curiouser and curiouser, Fergal thought. He was familiar with the story of Orla's background and he knew exactly why Macdara might be concerned about her feelings. But when it came to Anya, the mystery deepened. Nevertheless Fergal let the subject drop. There was no point in baiting Macdara any further. One thing Liam was right about was that Macdara was like a bear with a sore head these days. Fergal was beginning to think he couldn't do right for doing wrong, which was a puzzle because Macdara was generally the most even-tempered of men. Worried as well as slightly put out that Macdara could think him capable of playing fast and loose with either Orla or Anya's feelings, Fergal joined him at Glengarriff's side.

Liam had been waiting impatiently for just such an opportunity to come along. His pulse quickened as he saw Fergal and Macdara leave the house and walk towards the stables. Orla had left with JC earlier and so, putting one and one together, Liam knew that Anya was home alone. He waited for a minute to make sure the men were well clear of the house, before letting himself into the kitchen. It was empty, but he could hear Anya clattering about in the scullery. He went over to the door and leaned casually against the jamb. She was standing with her back to him at the sink, furiously scrubbing the pots and pans. Clearly her hackles were up about something. Liam smiled. He had nothing against a woman with spirit, so long as that spirit was amenable to breaking. In fact, there was nothing like a good tussle to put him in the mood.

As if sensing his eyes on her, she swung round suddenly, her eyes widening in surprise. Christ, she was looking bonny, Liam thought, all rosy-cheeked from the heat in the kitchen, with little strands of hair plastered to her forehead, precisely as he imagined she might look after a turbulent bout of bareobics. One of Kitty's words.

'Liam?' He was gratified to hear a slight tremble in her voice. 'Were you looking for Macdara? If so, he's over in the stables with Fergal. I heard them say something about checking out Glengarriff.'

'Good,' Liam said. 'They'll be a while so, which means that you and I, my darlin', have time for a nice little chat before they come back.'

Recognising the predatory look on his face, Anya blanched, despite the heat of the kitchen. In a flash she was back in her bedroom, a terrified child with nowhere to run. Sick to her stomach and more than a little frightened, she considered screaming, but one look at Liam was enough to disabuse her of the notion. There was an air of barely suppressed violence about the man. She had sensed it that day at Wishbone Lake, when she had seen him look at Kitty in a way that had made her worry for the young woman. And now she was worried for herself.

'What about?' Trying hard not to show her fear, she picked up a tea towel in a poor attempt to hide the shaking of her hands.

'Oh, this and that,' Liam said casually. 'Your mother, perhaps.' Good Lord, Liam thought as she reeled back, clutching at the sink to prevent herself from falling, whatever reaction he'd expected, it hadn't been one of such magnitude. Anya had gone ghost-white. In fact, had she seen an actual ghost, she couldn't have gone any paler. Whatever that bitch Clare Keating had done to her daughter, she'd freaked her out good and proper. Better and better, from his point of view. 'Hey. Hey.' Liam held his hands up soothingly. 'There's no need to take on like that.' He caught her arm, steadied her. 'Here, come and sit at the table. Let me get you a glass of water.'

Anya shook her head, hating the feel of his hands on her as he led her out to the kitchen and helped her into a chair. 'No. No. I'm all right,' she said. But she knew that she wasn't. She was far from all right. As usual, the mere thought, the mere mention of her mother had sent her into a tailspin, and this time there was no Sister Martha to buy her off.

Liam pulled up a chair beside her, took hold of one of her hands and held on to it, despite her trying to pull away.

'Jesus,' he said, mock concerned. 'What's wrong with you, Anya? I thought you'd be pleased to hear your mother is in the neighbourhood and looking for you.'

'She's here? Here in Lismore?' If Liam had thought it impossible for Anya to turn any whiter, he was proved wrong, for now her face resembled nothing so much as a bleached bone, her eyes staring at him, transfixed.

'Oh yes, she's here all right.' He licked his lips and even in her state of terror, Anya was reminded of a snake about to attack its prey. 'But she doesn't know where you are. Yet.'

'Don't tell her!' Anya begged. 'Please, Liam, say you won't tell her.'

'I won't,' Liam said. 'But remember, Anya, one good deed deserves another.' Deliberately, he reached out and drew a hand slowly across her breast. 'Know what I mean?'

She knew what he meant, all right. Only too well. And suddenly despite her fear of him, despite her fear of his mother, Anya was furiously angry. Jumping to her feet she sent her chair hurtling clattering backward on to the floor. The colour rushed back into her face and her voice trembled again, but this time from pure rage.

'Get out, you bastard,' she yelled, pointing to the door. 'Get out, you filthy bastard!'

Leaping to his own feet, Liam grabbed her hand and twisted her wrist, pulling her so close into him she could see her terrified reflection in his eyes. 'I'm the one holding all the aces here and don't you forget it. One word from me and the whole world and its aunty will know your dirty secret. So think on, Miss High And Mighty, before you go shouting the odds.' He froze at the crunch of footsteps outside, heralding Macdara and Liam's return from the stables. Violently, Liam threw Anya away from him. 'Not a word, do you hear me? Not one word to anyone, or you'll find your mother standing on the doorstep before you can say Liam O'Hanlon is a dirty bastard.'

He walked towards the door, just as it opened and Macdara, followed by Fergal, came in. 'Ah, there you are, Mac,' Liam said jovially, as though he had only just arrived himself. 'I was just about to go up to the stables to find you.'

'Why?' Macdara looked at him in surprise. 'Is something wrong?'

'No, not at all,' Liam said. 'It's just that I forgot to tell you I have to take a trip to Dublin in the morning for some medical supplies. I won't be back till the evening.'

'Fine. Fine,' Macdara said. 'You should have just phoned.'

'Probably on the blink again, Liam, eh?' Fergal said sarcastically. 'Like the night Nenagh Rose went into labour.'

Ignoring this remark, Liam shouldered his way past.

'I wish you'd stop stirring it with him, Fergal,' Macdara remarked. 'We've all got to work together.'

'More's the pity,' Fergal said. 'He might be a good vet but, as a human being, he falls far short of the mark.'

'Stags! That's what the pair of you are like. Always locking horns, trying to get one over on the other. Wait till you get to my age, you'll be content to settle for a nice cup of tea.'

But Fergal was no longer listening to Macdara. His focus had shifted to Anya, who was half-leaning against the table, looking shaken and ill. 'Anya?' he asked. 'Anya, are you all right?' The concern in his voice alerted Macdara, who hurried over and pressed her gently into a chair.

'Good heavens, Anya child, you look awful. Has something happened?' He shared a look with Fergal.

Anya took a deep breath, Liam's threat ringing in her head. 'I'm all right, really. It's just a touch of migraine, that's all.'

'Well, can I get you anything?' Macdara asked, his brow creased with anxiety. 'I've got some Migraleve somewhere.'

'I already took some,' Anya lied. 'I'll just go up to bed, if you don't mind, and have a bit of a lie down.'

'Of course. Come on, love, lean on me.' Grateful for Macdara's support, because she did indeed feel as though her legs might buckle, Anya leant heavily on his arm.

'I hope you feel better soon,' Fergal said, as they passed on their way to the stairs.

'Thanks,' Anya said, in little more than a whisper, unhappily aware of a slight edge to his tone. She could guess what was in his mind. He thought she and Liam had had a lover's tiff. Dear God, he couldn't be a million miles further from the truth.

Fergal went to the fridge and took out a can of lager. He popped the ring and went to stand by the window, where he stood gazing out into the darkness beyond. He could see the red tail lights of a vehicle receding into the distance. Liam on his way back to his poor put-upon wife, Fergal guessed. The lager tasted bitter on his tongue but he drank it all the same, his mind busily trying to fathom what exactly had gone on between Anya and Liam. Macdara may have swallowed the whole migraine business but he didn't, not for one minute. More than ill, Anya had looked frightened, scared to death, and it didn't take a genius to figure out that Liam was at the back of it. Fergal drained the remainder of his lager in one gulp, then flung the can with far more force than was warranted into the bin. So help him, if he found out that Liam had touched so much as one hair on her head, he wouldn't be responsible for his actions. He looked up as Macdara came back into the room.

'Is she okay?' he asked.

Macdara nodded. 'She says she is, but I've never known Anya to suffer from migraines before. Still, I suppose there's a first time for everything.'

As well as a last time, Fergal thought, and this had been the last time Liam O'Hanlon would get the chance to get next or near to Anya, even if it meant watching him twenty-four hours a day.

Macdara left his consultant's office in Dublin and stood outside for a moment, letting the doctor's words sink in.

'I'd think about retiring sooner, rather than later, Mr Fitzgerald. There is some noticeable deterioration since your last visit, and although it's impossible to say for certain whether you will lose all your sight, it would be unrealistic to rule it out completely.'

It hadn't come as a shock, not really. It was just that hearing the words said aloud gave Macdara that feeling of cold water trickling down the back of the neck. It meant that he couldn't prevaricate any longer. The time had come to shit or get off the pot.

He headed off down St James's Street, home to many of Dublin's historical landmarks, including the old St James's Gate Brewery, where the famous 'black stuff' had been brewed since 1901. Tempted, he hesitated, then thought better of it and continued on down along Thomas Street into Temple Bar, Dublin's cultural quarter, where over priced restaurants and pubs competed for a share of the tourist market and a motley assortment of street entertainers vied with each other for the few euros left in their pockets. Macdara stopped for a moment to watch a tribute act, four young lads dressed as the Clancy Brothers in cream Aran sweaters. Not a patch on the real thing, of course, with reedy little off-key voices, but they were proving popular with the locals and tourists alike. Macdara threw a few coins into the flat cap at their feet and walked on with no real agenda, just following where his feet took him. At Trinity College he turned right up along Grafton Street, crossed over the road at the top and headed into St Stephen's Green, where he sat for a while by the duck pond.

Around him life fizzed and buzzed with normality. Office workers popped out of their stuffy offices for a cigarette and a gossip. Others were glued to their mobiles phones or texting, fingers flying over the keys as if their very lives depended on it. Exhausted mums pushed tired toddlers in buggies and dragged others by the hand. Holidaymakers took photographs, shiny happy smiling people, pleased as punch to be away from the humdrum routine of their everyday existence. One young couple snogged in the maternal shade of a weeping willow, enveloped in a magic cloak of love that rendered them invisible to everyone else. Or so they appeared to think. An educated tramp, who had fallen or jumped off the establishment ladder many years before, shambled over and began reciting poetry to the ducks. '"Romantic Ireland's dead and gone,"' he declaimed in a voice sonorous with grief. '"It's with O'Leary in the grave," so it is.' Unimpressed or uncaring, the ducks swam away.

'September 1913' by William Butler Yeats. Macdara smiled, recognising it from his school days. Romantic Ireland. Looking at the young couple, engrossed in each other almost to the point where they needed to get a room urgently, he wasn't so sure romantic Ireland was in the grave at all. Not if you took it in its literal sense anyway.

Macdara closed his eyes and let the heat of the sun penetrate his bones, allowing himself to drift back to a time when he too was young and in love, and old age and *retinosa pigmentosa* were merely words with little power to hurt him. Nancy and him, in the bluebell woods. Nancy Devine. Divine Nancy. After a while, his breathing slowed and he dozed off, hands folded peacefully across his lap, completely oblivious to the world carrying on around him.

'Excuse me.'

Sometime later, Macdara woke with a start. He blinked rapidly, taking a moment or two to get his bearings. The bench, empty when he sat down, was now also occupied by a young woman, blonde, attractive, foreign judging by her accent. Polish, probably.

'Yes?' Macdara looked at her curiously.

'I am sorry I woke you. You looked so peaceful. Like a little baby.'

'Not at all, I'm glad you did.' Macdara felt slightly foolish and hoped he had neither snored nor drooled in his sleep, though he feared he had done both. He glanced at his watch. 'I have to catch a train soon. If you hadn't come along, I might well have missed it.'

'Oh!' Her face fell. 'You are going away already? But we have only just met.' Suddenly she reached out and drew a long suggestive finger down along his hand. 'Are you sure you don't want to stay with me a while?' She leaned close to his ear, her breath warm against his cheek. 'I have a room, you see, not so far from here.'

Macdara's eyes widened as he took in the implication.

'Please.' The faux disappointed look in her eyes changed to one of desperation. 'I am very good. I will do whatever you want. And cheap.'

'Enough!' He pushed her hand away. 'I'm sorry, love, but you've got the wrong man.' Up close, he could see that her attractiveness was all on the surface. Her teeth were yellowed, her skin spotted and pasty under a thick layer of badly applied make-up. Beneath her too low, too short mini-dress, she was little more than a bag of bones. A tell-tale line of purplish dots marched up the inside of her skinny arm. His heart turned over as he realised that she couldn't have been older than her twenties. Not far from Orla's age. Or Anya's. There but for the grace of God, he thought, possessed of a sudden and violent urge to get home, back to his girls, back to Lismore. He took out his wallet, pulled out a bundle of notes and, without even checking the value, pushed them into her hand. 'Go home, darling. Buy yourself a ticket back to wherever you came from. Go back to your family. There must be someone who loves you. Will you do that for me?'

She took the money, but looked at him as if he were crazy. 'You are a good man,' she said, stuffing it into a cheap plastic handbag and clicking the clasp closed. 'But not everyone is good, mister. And not everyone has someone who loves them.'

Macdara wanted to cry as she walked away, her head bent forward as if slightly too heavy for the delicate stem of her neck. There was something so vulnerable about her, so helplessly childlike and fragile. Inexplicably, his thoughts turned to Sinéad. A child when he had seen her last. Fragile. It hurt him to think of her now. A cold breeze blew in from the River Liffey a short distance away, making him shiver in his short-sleeved shirt. Somehow, when he hadn't been looking, the sun had been mugged of its fire.

Feeling every one of his seventy-four years, Macdara left St Stephen's Green and its abundance of life behind and headed for Heuston Station.

On the train, he leaned back into his seat, head turned to where the brown and green fields of the countryside and the grey buildings and mean houses of the towns flashed by. His eyes were open, but his thoughts were turned inward, mulling once more over the whole Fergal/Orla problem, and what to do for the best. Bridie had started him thinking one day when she'd made an off-the-cuff remark about what a lovely couple the pair of them would make.

He hadn't paid much attention at the time, but thinking about it now he had to admit that Orla and Fergal falling in love would have been the perfect solution. He would happily have handed Lismore over to the pair of them and retired to a nice little cottage by the sea. Cupid, however, obviously hadn't received this particular memo because far from falling in love, Orla seemed to be under the impression that Fergal didn't even like her. Macdara knew that despite his best efforts to persuade her to the contrary, she absolutely believed this to be the case, only now Orla seemed to be downright frightened as well. He'd noticed her stealing nervous glances at Fergal several times lately and, concerned, he'd raised the subject with a clearly flummoxed Fergal who, at first, looked shell-shocked, and then, bizarrely, laughed his head off at the very idea. Macdara had ended up feeling like a complete fool.

The train pulled in at a station. A number of the occupants got off and a number of others got on. If any of them had been put in a line-up later, Macdara would not have been able to pick out one face, so wrapped up was he in the eternal cat chasing its tail cycle. In his heart, though, there was no doubt but that Lismore should go to Fergal. Orla's return had muddied the waters, that was all.

Morally and in every other way, Fergal was the rightful heir to Lismore. He knew every inch of it as well as he knew his own face in the mirror. He was, as he used to joke to Macdara, a centaur, half-man, half-horse. 'Whole idiot!' Macdara had once replied, and they'd ended up laughing like a couple of hyenas. Lismore would be safe in his grandson's hands, Macdara knew. He would hold it in trust for the future generations of Fitzgeralds so that the greedy property developers who, in Macdara's opinion, were devastating the land roundabout, would never get their hands on Lismore, as they had with several neighbouring farms and stud farms. The fields of beautiful horses grazing on sweet Irish grass had been replaced with endless rows of soulless, ticky-tacky houses, many now unsold as the fingers of the financial recession tightened their grip. The landowners had been paid well, of course. But Lismore represented more than just money to Macdara and Fergal. Macdara had invested a whole lifetime in the estate, his very heart and soul, and Fergal was in a fair way to doing just the same.

Macdara was completely worn out by the time he got back from Dublin. Even so his heart lifted, as it never failed to do, when the cab drew up in front of the imposing wrought-iron entrance gates to the estate. They had been made to his own design and featured a gold centrepiece of Pegasus, wings extended, with 'Lismore, Home of Winners' inset in matching gold italic script beneath. These gates were Macdara's pride and joy, a fitting entrance to the home he thought of as heaven on earth.

'You sure you don't want me to drive you right up to the house? You've a fair old walk ahead of you, Mac, and if you don't mind me saying so, I've seen you look better,' said the taxi driver.

Macdara waved away the offer. 'No thanks, John-Joe, it'll do me good to stretch my legs after being cooped up on the train for so long.'

'Fair enough.' The taxi driver, a man whose services they often called upon, sketched a half salute, reversed the car and drove back the way he had come.

Macdara fumbled in his pocket and located the zapper that opened the gates, watching with childish satisfaction as they swung slowly open. A memory came to him and his face softened. Orla and Sinéad, skipping up this very avenue, arms linked, singing a song from their favourite *Wizard of Oz* video. Faces bright with innocent glee as they danced down the yellow brick road, turning round and beckoning him, pigtails and pink gingham dresses, their summer school uniform. One of them, he couldn't remember which, with a gap where her front tooth had fallen out. 'Hurry up, Grandy, don't let the Wicked Witch of the West catch you.'

The avenue was long and winding, almost a mile long, with a different view round every bend. Apart from the neatly fenced fields, paddocks and stables, several acres had been dedicated to creating a wonderful, partially landscaped garden, with pretty little terraces, a water sculpture and the wishing-well the girls had begged and begged for. The rest of the land had deliberately been left to revert to nature and, year after year, it self-seeded producing a vast array of wildflowers and plants. Macdara kept a small flock of sheep, some Jersey cattle, and a couple of bad-tempered, evil-eyed goats, Beelzebub and Lucifer, for no other reason than that he liked animals.

Every summer, Lismore held a series of open days when the public were free to come and view the house, estate and stables. Macdara enjoyed those days very much and spent a great deal of time strutting round, according to Lady Kathleen, just like a turkey-cock.

He knew he would be heartsick when the time came to leave it all behind. But leave it Macdara felt he must, as he strongly believed the next generation should be free to look after Lismore without him breathing over their shoulder. And, come tomorrow, when he was rested, he would break the news to the family that he would soon be leaving.

'Jesus, Mac!' Shocked, and full of pity, Fergal dropped his head in his hands, unable to look Macdara in the eye. 'I don't know what to say, except that the doctor must be wrong. Some of them are eejits, you know. Did you get a second opinion?'

'And a third,' Macdara said drily. 'No, there's no mistake, Fergal lad, I'm going blind.'

Fergal risked a look. 'How long?'

'Before the final curtain falls?' Macdara shrugged, his gaze going out the window, where life was carrying on with its usual frenetic pace. He could see young Kitty Brennan cuddling one of the stable cats, laughing as it tried to escape, Anya unloading shopping bags from her car, Liam talking to a groom, tapping his muddy welling-ton boot with a bit of stick, clearly laying down the law about something or other. The everyday sights and sounds of life at Lismore. 'I don't know.' He answered Fergal's question honestly. 'It's that old piece of string. Sooner. Later. I might not go entirely blind at all. It's a guessing game.' He brought his gaze back to Fergal. 'But here's the crux of the matter. I can't carry on at Lismore. So I need you to take over from me.'

Fergal's head snapped up fully. 'What? No, you can't mean that,

Mac. Lismore means everything to you. You can't just give up on it like that.'

Macdara nodded. 'It does. I'd be a liar if I said otherwise. But do you not see, Fergal, I might as well be dead if I can't be a part of it? If I can't be the same as before?' Despite himself, a small groan escaped his lips. 'Put yourself in my shoes and imagine yourself having to be led around the place you used to know like the back of your hand, to be part of it still, yet not part of all. To become a burden to other people. An object of pity. No, lad, I'd sooner put it in safe hands, your hands that is, and feast off the memory.'

'But where would you go? Have you got somewhere in mind?' Fergal looked distraught. His eyes ranged from Macdara, round the room, and back again. His hands felt suddenly too big. Every now and then they made independent motions, half-rising, then falling back like dead weights into his lap. He clenched them into fighting fists, unhappily aware that Macdara's condition was one opponent he could never hope to get the better of.

'No, not yet. And I don't much care where I go, to be honest,' Macdara said. 'A little place by the sea, maybe.' He gave a little mocking laugh. 'The sea air is supposed to be a great cure for all sorts, though maybe not for blindness.'

'On your own?' Fergal stared at him in disbelief. 'How would you manage?'

'Not on my own, no, I'll get a companion. There's always someone desperate enough for the money to come and look after an old curmudgeon like me. Orla, maybe.'

Fergal shook his head. 'Not Orla, Mac. Orla's not the ...' he paused for a moment, choosing his words with care, 'well, she's not exactly the domestic type, is she? You'd see more mealtimes than meals on the table. Besides, she's like a butterfly, always flitting off somewhere or other.'

'She's young,' Macdara pointed out, bristling slightly, as always, at the faintest hint of any criticism of his favourite. 'It's allowed.'

'And I'm not denying that,' Fergal said, although, in his opinion, twenty-seven was plenty old enough to get your house in order. And Orla had had several months since her return to make a start.

But, as far as he could see, to date she had made no effort at all to find a job or to fend for herself in any way. But that was not a point he was going to pursue at this moment with Macdara, who had already wrong-footed him lately by implying that Orla felt uneasy round him, which was news to Fergal, considering how in his experience she was more than happy to get up close and personal. Still, these were thoughts best kept to himself, particularly as Macdara had more than enough on his plate right now. 'That's exactly my point, Mac,' he pointed out gently. 'Orla is young and she wants to go out and have fun, which is why I think you might be better off with somebody else. Someone older, and more reliable.'

'Possibly,' Macdara said, but the obdurate line of his mouth suggested he was far from convinced. 'But, you know, Orla's made of sterner stuff than you give her credit for. And so kind. That girl would give you a piece of her heart.'

And more, Fergal thought wryly, remembering how, on the night Sister Martha had been stabbed to death, he had found her waiting in his bed, wearing a come-hither look and not much else. But whilst most men might have thought all their birthdays had come at once, Fergal had, quite simply, been shocked rigid. And not in a good way! He wouldn't deny that he enjoyed flirting with Orla, exchanging banter tinged with innuendo – what red-blooded male wouldn't? – he genuinely didn't believe she'd taken it seriously. Now, it struck him that maybe his rejection of her that night accounted for the supposed fear she had of him. What better way to avenge herself than to turn Macdara against him? The retribution of a woman scorned was a story as old as the hills.

In any case, a dalliance of a sexual nature between them had never been on the cards, even if Fergal had been so inclined. It was far too complicated. For starters, he had to see her every day, share the same house. She was Macdara's granddaughter, and his cousin. Not to mention that she was flavour of the month. Fergal baulked at the thoughts of the flak he'd have to take were they ever really to fall out. His life wouldn't be worth living as everyone, from the horses in the stables to Lady Kathleen at Castle Mac Tíre, would be hot on his case. With an effort Fergal wrenched his thoughts back to the present and the man before him, who was not only his grandfather but also his mentor and, let it be said, his hero too. Macdara didn't need to hear Fergal's possibly baseless suspicions; and the indisputable fact was that she brought Macdara great joy. And for that alone Fergal felt as if he should get down on his knees and thank her.

A great wave of emotion took hold of him, grief mixed with anger, in turn mixed with despair. 'Are you sure nothing more can be done, Mac? Is there anything I can do? Anything at all? You know you've only got to ask.'

Dejected, Macdara shook his head. 'The answer is no and yes. No, there's nothing more that can be done, and, yes, there's something you can do for me. And I've already told you what that is.'

Despite his best efforts to hold it together, Fergal's voice cracked. 'Okay. But, one thing, Mac, you're not an old curmudgeon. You're the best man that ever lived, and I feel privileged to have known you.'

Macdara gave a crack of laughter, trying to lighten the mood. 'Well, don't go writing my eulogy just yet, will you? I'm not quite dead.'

Fergal laughed too, hollowly, but it was still a laugh. 'I pity the devil when you are.'

They smiled at each other. An understanding had been reached. Love sparked between them but of course, being men, it was necessary for them to disguise this with either humour or insults.

'What are you going to tell Orla?' Fergal raised the thorny issue which, did he but know it, had also been weighing heavily on Macdara's mind in recent weeks. He cleared his throat, steeling himself to say the words that cut him like a knife. 'She is your *real* flesh and blood.'

Macdara forestalled him. 'Stop right there, Fergal!' He raised his hand. 'Have I ever treated you as anything less than my own flesh and blood? No! So, let's make this absolutely clear and then I want the matter dead and buried. There has never been any distinction in what I feel for Orla and what I feel for you. Family is about far more than shared genetics. You are my grandson, just as Orla is my granddaughter. And that's that!' His eyes teared up. 'Now get out of here, would you, before I disgrace myself by telling you how much I love you.'

Shakily, Fergal walked to the door. He gave a weak grin. 'And if I wasn't afraid of being called a sissy, I might tell you I love you right back.'

# Chapter 18

Fergal found Anya in the kitchen preparing a shoulder of lamb for slow roasting. He stood for a moment watching as, biting her lip in concentration, she massaged olive oil into the joint before studding it with sprigs of fresh rosemary and whole cloves of garlic. Her face was flushed from the heat of the kitchen and little springs of hair had broken free from her ponytail and were waving softly round her face. She lifted the roasting tin towards the oven, caught sight of him and almost dropped it. Shakily, she put it back on the table, her hand flying to her throat.

'God almighty, Fergal! You put the heart crossways in me! You shouldn't go sneaking up on people like that. It's not funny, you know.'

Fergal mimed backing off. 'Whoa! Sorry. I really didn't mean to scare you, though nobody's ever jumped out of their skin at the sight of me before. Doesn't do much for the old ego.' Jesus, he thought in amazement, he really had frightened her. Her hands were actually trembling, her chest rising and falling as if her heart was, indeed, engaged in some sort of aerial aerobatics.

Anya struggled to regain control. 'No, I'm sorry. It's just that I was a million miles away, that's all.' She smiled shakily. 'Anyway, come for elevenses, have you?'

'Elevenses would be nice. But, in fact, that's not why I'm here. I came to talk to you about something serious, and I suspect you already know what it is.'

'Oh?' Anya's heart rate had just begun to slow, but now it speeded up again. Dear God, please let him not talk about Liam. Her nerves were already in tatters. She'd hardly slept a wink since the vet had made his indecent proposal and, though he hadn't approached her again, she'd been constantly aware of him lurking like a malign presence around Lismore, his eyes boring right through her skin into the vulnerable flesh below. If Fergal was to so much as mention his name, she'd have a complete meltdown.

'Macdara,' Fergal prompted, having absolutely no idea of the tortuous path down which her thoughts were careering.

Macdara! Anya's brow cleared with relief. She picked up the roasting tray and slid it into the oven, adjusting the temperature slightly, before turning back to Fergal.

'He's told you, then?'

'Yes, and also that you knew.' Fergal sat down at the table, picked up a salt cellar and idly twisted it in his hands. A few grains fell out on to the deal surface. He puffed them away. 'It must have been hard keeping it to yourself.'

'It was, but it was what he wanted.' Anya sat down opposite, folding a teacloth over and over in her hands, until it was just a small square. She let it unravel and began the whole process again. 'I think he just needed to come to terms with it, you know, and sort everything out in his own head before breaking the news to everyone else.'

'Except you. He didn't keep it from you.' Fergal's voice was faintly accusatory.

Anya nodded. 'True, but only because I keep his diary and make his appointments and such like. And Mac, as you know, is not exactly computer literate. There were things he needed researching such as treatments, hospitals, information about the condition, etc. Believe me, Fergal, it wasn't because he thinks I'm anything special or because he wanted to exclude the family in any way.'

Fergal put down the salt cellar and covered his face with his hands. 'I know. I'm sorry for sounding like a jealous idiot. It's just that I feel so bad that I wasn't there for him. So bad, that he's had to struggle with this and act like everything is normal. He should have been able to trust me.'

Anya got up and came around the table. Tentatively, she put her hand on Fergal's shoulder, rubbing it comfortingly. 'Trust has nothing to do with it. He just needed to make sure that what the doctors said was right. What would have been the point of worrying everybody unnecessarily? Mac is not a selfish man. He needed to explore every avenue before breaking the news.'

'And is there really nothing that can be done? What about treatment abroad? Maybe the States, or even Russia? The Russians have all those eye hospital ships, haven't they? They've got a great track record when it comes to pioneering eye surgery.' Fergal looked almost feverishly hopeful.

'*Retinosa pigmentosa* is a genetic eye condition,' Anya told him gently. 'There is no cure, or certainly not at the moment. The best we can hope for is that Mac retains at least some of his sight. But it is degenerative and it will, undoubtedly, get worse. You have to be realistic and prepare for that.'

With a groan Fergal turned, put his hands around her waist and buried his face against her. Surprised, Anya's first instinct was to pull away, but then almost of their own volition, her hands reached out to stroke his hair. She was surprised to feel how soft it was as the black curls sprang back against her fingers, soft yet strong, just like their owner. Her face was serene and compassionate as she gazed down at his bent head. Loving.

Like a fucking Madonna, Liam thought angrily, as he stood in the doorway watching them. After a moment, he cleared his throat, causing them to jump apart so fast it was almost laughable.

'Sorry,' he said. 'I didn't mean to interrupt.' Casually, he walked across and slumped into one of the chairs. 'Still, I'm sure you can put the passion on hold just long enough for me to grab a cuppa. A time and a place and all that.'

The colour fled Anya's face and she hurried into the scullery ostensibly to put the kettle on. Fergal though was quick to anger. Jumping to his feet, he rounded on the other man.

'Just for once, O'Hanlon, why don't try to keep your mind above sewer level?' In stark contrast to Anya's, his own face was flushed, but from anger, not shame. 'And, in future, try knocking before entering this house? You don't live here. You're not family. You're an employee, and you're far too familiar.' His look, hard as glass, cut right through the other man. 'Do I make myself plain?'

'Yeah, maybe, if I was listening,' Liam sneered. 'Only my orders come from the organ grinder, not the adopted monkey.'

'Not for much longer. Maybe not at all.' Fergal's hands bunched into tight fists by his side, the tendons on the back standing out like knotted ropes. Liam had been winding him up for ages. He shirked his work and was far too touchy-feely with the female members of staff. Ugly rumours had come to his ears about the vet and little Kitty Brennan. He hoped, for O'Hanlon's sake, that it was smoke without fire. Kitty was only eighteen, and a very young eighteen at that. He would not stand by and see her taken advantage of by a man more than twice her age.

'And what exactly is that supposed to mean, big fella?' Liam scoffed. 'Going to go running to Macdara, are you? Going to tell tales out of school?' He scrunched his face up mockingly. 'Daddy, Daddy. Liam pulled my hair. Liam robbed my dolly. Liam spat in my Ribena.'

'No, Liam.' Macdara's voice splashed between them like a pail of cold water. He had been standing outside the door during the better part of the altercation, the raised voices from inside bringing him up short. 'What it means is that Lismore is changing hands.'

'Changing hands?' Liam shook his head, as though there was interference in his ears preventing him from hearing properly. His brain simply refused to process the news he might lose his cushy job at Lismore before the big pay-off with JC came to fruition. It had always been so ideal. He pretty much came and went as he pleased, it paid well, and then there were the perks of the job, the tumbles in the hay with a willing stable lass or two, and unlimited access to medical supplies for the horses that didn't always reach their intended destination. Liam's eyes widened disbelievingly. 'You're never telling me you sold Lismore, Mac? You swore blind no property developer would ever get his hands on so much as a blade of grass.'

Macdara laughed thinly. 'Blind is exactly the right word, Liam, because that's what I'm going and soon, by the sound of things, I won't be able to see my own hand in front of my face, much less run the stables.'

'Jesus!' Liam looked stunned. 'You're codding me!' But even he, with his warped sense of humour, doubted anyone would joke about a thing like that. He pursed his lips in a soundless whistle. 'So you are selling up then?'

'Not selling, no, I'm passing it on to my *grandson* and heir, aka the new organ grinder.' Macdara fixed him with a look. 'So, from now on, if Fergal says jump, you ask how high.' The threat hung heavy in the air.

Abruptly, Liam leapt to his feet, his hand automatically reaching out to steady his chair, which very nearly toppled over. His eyes narrowed. 'I see. So that's the way the wind blows, is it?'

'That's the way the wind blows,' Fergal confirmed. 'Think of me as the new brush, Liam, the one that sweeps clean. You've taken advantage of Macdara's kindness for far too long.' He glanced at Anya as she came tentatively back into the kitchen. 'And another thing, stay out of Anya's face, do you hear me? Save your charm and smarm for those that ask for it. It's not wanted in this house.'

'Is that right, Anya?' Liam turned to her, his deceptively pleasant expression decidedly at odds with the coldness of his eyes. 'Have I over stepped the mark with you? You see, Fergal,' he said as, numb, Anya shook her head, 'you've got things arse-backward. Anya and I are friends. So I tease her a bit. That's what friends do. It's not like I've been shoving my hand up her skirt. Lighten up, man.'

Seething, Fergal pointed to the door. 'Go now, Liam, before I lose both my temper and my boot up your backside.'

Ruddy with a mixture of rage and humiliation, Liam held his hands up. 'Oh, don't worry, I'm going. But, remember this, sonny Jim, you might be cock of the walk right now, only don't crow too loudly or someone might come along and wring your scrawny neck.'

'Bastard!' Fergal swore, as the door banged behind the other man. 'Honestly, Mac, I don't know why you didn't give him the boot long ago. I've always felt there was something shifty about that fella. I wouldn't trust him with a third-world charity box for crippled orphans.'

'Misplaced loyalty.' Macdara looked tired, wrung out. 'His father worked at Lismore, and his father before him. You know how it is, a mixture of tradition and feeling beholden. But, you're right: Liam is a bad apple. Anyway, like I said, it's your call. Lismore comes with no provisos. You run it your way and I won't interfere.' Macdara clapped his hands. 'Now, we've wasted enough time on O'Hanlon. Anya love, be an angel and fetch me a cuppa.' In an effort to lighten the mood, his nose wrinkled. 'And what's that gorgeous smell? God, we're really going to miss your cooking.' He smiled. 'By the way, I've just had a call from the employment agency. Bridie's replacement starts tomorrow. That's what I was coming over to tell you.'

As Anya hurried to put the kettle on, her mood had changed completely and her heart was singing. Surely if Fergal thought she was romantically involved with Liam, he wouldn't have warned him off like that. Which had to mean that either Orla hadn't told her the truth, or that Fergal wasn't stupid enough to believe she would ever get mixed up with Liam. However, if Orla had lied to her about that, it begged the question as to whether she had also lied about Fergal seeing her only as the hired help. Yes, he'd made that joke the other night about good help being hard to find, but wasn't that the kind of jokey remark people made all the time? Previously, Anya knew that she wouldn't have given any weight whatsoever to the remark, and just laughed along.

Now, taking the tea caddy off the shelf, Anya tipped a couple of spoonfuls of Barry's tea into the teapot and poured on freshly boiled water, ducking back as the steam whooshed upward. So, if Orla had lied, then *why* had she lied? The obvious answer had to be that, despite Orla's protestations to the contrary, she wanted Fergal for herself. Anya stirred the tea, popped the lid back on the teapot and placed it on a tray, together with a strainer, three mugs and a plate of fresh-baked chocolate macaroons. For the first time since *that* conversation with Orla, she allowed herself to daydream about the up-coming trip to Dubai, and the delicious possibilities once again opening up before her. Whilst she didn't pretend to be Einstein, it didn't take a genius to figure out that if Orla felt the need to resort to such deceptive measures, that could only be because she saw Anya as a threat.

In the kitchen, Fergal and Macdara fell on the macaroons like starving savages, each outdoing the other in his cries of ecstasy.

'Manna from heaven.'

'Food of the gods!'

Anya poured out the tea in a long amber stream, smiling indulgently at their boyish antics, but her smile quickly faded as Liam appeared framed in the window behind them. Slowly, deliberately, he waggled his tongue at her in an obscene gesture. She jumped, almost scalding herself with the hot liquid, then she burst into tears, both of rage and frustration, banged the teapot down on the table and ran from the room. Macdara and Liam stared at each other as her footsteps went clattering up the stairs

'There's something very wrong there,' Fergal remarked as they heard the door to her room slam. 'She's been like a cat on a hot tin roof recently, and she nearly had a fit when I came into the kitchen earlier. Twitchy isn't the word for it.'

'Probably all this business with Sister Martha,' Macdara said, gazing forlornly at a macaroon. 'It takes a long time to get over a shock like that. And the fact that they haven't caught the murderer makes it that much worse.'

'No, it doesn't help,' Fergal agreed. 'But I can't help feeling there's something more. Haven't you noticed the way she sometimes looks? I don't know, she looks haunted, hunted even. She's so private, though, it's difficult to figure out what's going on inside her head. She keeps her emotions firmly under lock and key.'

Macdara nodded shrewdly. 'Well, maybe you can do a bit of delving when you're in Dubai. Talk to her like a brother. She might find it easier to open up when she's away from Lismore.'

'I'll try.' Fergal put down his half-eaten macaroon, Macdara's words resounding in his ears. Talk to her like a brother! He checked his watch. 'Listen, I'd better run, Mac. We have a new boarder arriving shortly. I want to double-check all the preparations are in place.'

Macdara simply nodded, his mouth full. He eyed the younger man speculatively as he made for the door, a slightly dejected droop to his shoulders. Macdara's glance travelled to the half-eaten cake. Like himself, Fergal was not a man to go off his grub easily. In fact the only time Macdara could remember ever being off his food was when … when he found himself in love with Nancy. On auto-pilot, Macdara froze with a macaroon half way to his mouth.

Orla and JC sat side by side, more than half way up the slope of Slievenamon, leaving VIP and Tango Lass tethered to an old gate post a short distance away. The air was crystal clear, perfumed with the mingled scents of yellow gorse and wild flowers. Below them, the skirt of the mountain billowed out in a crinoline of patchwork greens and browns on this beautiful summer afternoon. Dog-daisy sheep cropped methodically at the verdant grass.

'So?' JC plucked fastidiously at his shirt where a burr had become caught on the sleeve. 'How did Macdara approach the subject and how did you handle it? With an Oscar-level performance, I hope.' He made an exaggerated expression of wide-eyed shock and fell back on the grass, clutching at his heart.

'Not funny.' Orla gazed down to where a Lego-sized Lismore nestled snugly in the valley below, complete with dinky people, vehicles and animals, reminding her of a farm set she'd once had as a child. Beyond, densely shrouded in the forest, lay the Hell Fire Club, its old tower just visible above the tree tops jabbing evangelically at the sky. Orla shifted uncomfortably. 'It wasn't my finest hour, if you must know. Actually, I felt a bit grubby, almost as if I'd read his diary behind his back, and was privy to his deepest secrets.'

'Bit late in the day now to develop a conscience, isn't it?' JC observed caustically, springing back Weeble-like into a sitting position. 'You embarked on this little escapade of ours with your eyes wide open, precisely because of his little secret. Baling out now is not an option.'

'I have no intention of baling out,' Orla snapped. 'But that doesn't mean I'm totally inhuman. I do have some compassion, you know.'

JC shrugged. 'Oh, right, I'd forgotten Macdara was such a saint.'

Orla made a pissed-off face. 'Don't be such a smart-ass. I didn't say that, but he has some redeeming features. *Everybody* has some redeeming features. Even you, JC!'

'Really? I'm pleased to hear it,' JC said drily. 'Now, let's cut to the chase. When did Macdara break the news to you?'

Orla picked up a blade of grass and poked absent-mindedly at an insect crawling up the leg of her jeans. 'After dinner, yesterday when I came back from one of my,' she made inverted commas with her fingers, '"trips to Dublin". We went for a walk.' And it had been pleasant enough, she recalled, wandering round the estate with Macdara, reminiscing in the pinky-yellow light of evening about times gone by, even though their memories didn't always accord. They sat for a while on a fence with a particularly nice panoramic view over the estate, and Orla laughed as a wild rabbit popped its head out of a burrow only inches away from her swinging feet, panicked and disappeared beneath the ground again.

'You always liked bunnies,' Macdara reminded her affectionately. 'I bought you and your sister one each, do you remember? You called yours Loppy Lou?'

'Loppy Lou and Rabbit, I remember,' Orla smiled.

Macdara frowned. 'Oh, yes, Rabbit. As I recall, Sinéad didn't bother naming hers, probably realised it was pointless, considering how she released it into the wild almost immediately.' His frown deepened. 'And as for poor Loppy Lou.'

'Please, Grandy,' Orla flushed. 'Can't we forget about that? It was all such a long time ago.'

'Of course,' Macdara said. 'That was insensitive of me. But, you know, I've been thinking a lot about Sinéad lately.' He turned his face up to the evening sun, enjoying the warmth on his skin. 'Which, I suppose is only natural, considering how much you remind me of her.'

'Really?' Orla's voice came out sharper than she intended. She tried to soften it. 'In what way?'

'I suppose because you were always together.' Macdara turned to look at her, noting the tightness of her expression and the way her chin had lifted, almost defiantly. 'Wherever you were, she was never very far behind. Or vice versa. In spite of you being very different, personality-wise.'

'Good girl–bad girl?' Orla looked away from him.

'Something like that, all right,' Macdara said quietly. 'Have you been in touch with her recently?'

Orla shook her head. 'No. I told you before. We went our separate ways.'

'Any specific reason?'

'This and that. Things happen. You should know that, Grandy.' She made a little moue. 'Better than most, I should think.'

Macdara hung his head. 'You're right, of course. I didn't mean to pry. I suppose I've been doing a lot of thinking lately. Going back and forth over things, rehashing the past.'

'But you still blame her for starting the fire that killed Grandmother?' Orla said bluntly. 'You haven't changed your mind over that?'

'No,' Macdara admitted. 'Time and time again, we warned her against playing with matches, and she didn't listen.' A rook swooped low across their line of vision, flapping so hard they could almost feel the back draught from its wings. They stayed silent a moment, following its flight, its shadow whooshing along the field, liquidising as it slid over the wooden posts of the fence opposite, then shape-shifting back into a flat black echo of the original bird.

'I'm going blind, Orla,' Macdara announced suddenly, striving to keep his voice in neutral. 'There's no easy way to say it and I think that's why I've been so much engaged in mulling over the past recently. Major bombshells in life tend to have that effect. Make you stop and take stock. That's what I've been doing. Taking stock.'

Orla turned towards him, steadying herself on the fence with both hands to keep from toppling over. 'Blind? You're going blind?' Her face collapsed into folds of concern. 'Whatever are you talking about, Grandy?'

*

'Yes, I think it qualified as an Oscar-worthy performance,' Orla told JC. 'He would have been shocked to know that I already knew about it from you. I don't suppose he expected Lady Kathleen to tell anyone.'

'She was upset,' JC said. 'She needed to talk to someone.' He grinned. 'And of course my ears pricked up. The plan was born shortly after.'

Orla peered at him intently. 'Ah yes, the plan. As it happens we don't have anywhere near as much time as we thought, because Macdara is intent on handing over Lismore, lock, stock and barrel to cousin Fergal, with almost immediate effect.' Savagely, she knocked the insect she'd been poking on to the ground and squashed it beneath her clenched fist. 'Oh, don't look so shocked, I've got the consolation prize. A couple of quid and the satisfaction of knowing the future of Lismore is secure for the next generation of non-bloodline, bastard Fitzgeralds.'

'*Ay, dios mio*! This cannot be.' Angrily, JC jumped to his feet and began to stride about kicking at the grass, his face suffused with anger. 'Fergal is a cuckoo in the nest, a usurper, just like my uncle Rodriguez. But he, at least is blood. He is a Fernandez de Rosas.' Viciously, JC booted a loose stone, sending it hurtling down the slope. 'Fergal has no right to Lismore. No right at all.' He loomed over Orla. 'That he should get his hands on what is rightfully mine. That I should be disinherited yet again? No. It shall not be!'

'It won't be,' Orla said quietly. 'Believe me, I have already set the wheels in motion. Cousin Fergal would be wise not to count his chickens. Not just yet, anyway.' She looked up at JC. 'Just one thing. Lismore may have belonged to the Ormonds a couple of hundred years ago. But it belongs to the Fitzgeralds now. It is not your inheritance, my darling. It's mine.'

'Yes, yes. But our agreement?' JC looked slightly flustered.

'Still stands,' Orla said. She looked at him quizzically. 'You do trust me, don't you? As I trust you.' She patted the grass next to her. 'Now, sit back down beside me and I'll tell you exactly what I've got in mind.' She grinned at him. 'Don't look so worried. The future's bright. The future's Lismore.'

# Chapter 19

Lady Kathleen laughed, delighted, as Macdara stuttered out his suspicions that Fergal might have feelings for Anya.

'Do you think that's likely?' Macdara asked, his expression comically bewildered, as he pushed her wheelchair towards the orangery where she liked to sit on summer evenings.

She bent her head back to look up at him. 'Dear Mac, you are so completely clueless. Not only do I think it likely, but I think it an absolute certainty. The only puzzle is why he's held off doing anything about it before now. He's not shy, surely?'

'My fault, I suspect,' Macdara admitted guiltily. 'I pretty much warned him off from day one. I just didn't want her getting hurt again, and young men can be so thoughtless. You know how it is, all the blood rushes out of their brains and into another part of their anatomies entirely.'

'Oh, Mac. You can't put her in a glass case, you know.' Lady Kathleen clutched at the tartan rug about her knees as it threatened to slip off, and tucked it more securely down the sides of the chair. 'Regardless of what happened in the past, she has a life to live, which may involve getting hurt now and then. But Anya is a woman now and not a child. If she is to move forward, my dear, then you will have to step back.'

Macdara fell silent, thinking about what she said, and knowing in his heart that it made perfect sense. 'I don't like taking the risk,' he said finally.

'But it's not your risk to take,' Lady Kathleen pointed out. 'You can't live her life for her, and everyone deserves to make their own mistakes. If a mother bird never allows her baby to leave the nest, how will it ever learn to fly?' She reached back and patted his hand. 'Dear Mac, no one could have done more for Anya, than you. Loosen the reins a little. Have faith. She won't stray far.'

They had reached the orangery, and Macdara pushed the chair through the French doors and positioned it by a table facing out on to the meadow beyond. He pulled up a chair for himself and gazed out.

'So I should encourage Fergal, is that what you think?'

'Perhaps not discourage him,' Lady Kathleen said gently. 'Besides, Fergal never struck me as anything other than a perfect gentleman.'

Macdara looked appalled that anyone might think otherwise, then slightly queasy as he thought back to the rather insulting and not to mention high-handed stricture he had delivered to Fergal about playing fast and loose with the women under his roof. Kathleen was perfectly right. Fergal was a gentleman through and through, so much so he had allowed himself to be slighted that evening without ever hitting back. Under consideration, Macdara could think of no better match for Anya, assuming she shared Fergal's feelings. 'What about Anya?'

'Without shadow of a doubt,' Lady Kathleen smiled and tapped her nose. 'She does a very bad job of hiding it, but you only have to mention his name and she blushes like a rose. I am rather hoping something might come of it all in Dubai.' She grinned naughtily, looking all of a sudden years younger than her actual age. 'You know how it is: hot sun, hot sand, hot bodies.' She clapped her hands. 'Oh, I do so love a romance and, you must admit, they make a perfect couple.' Her mood altered slightly, saddening a little. 'Sister Martha would have approved. Anya is still quite lost without her.' She took a deep breath, knowing that what she said next was bound to meet with resistance from Macdara. 'You know, I've often wondered if it was worth finding out more about Anya's family. Her mother's family, that is. And nobody seems to know anything at all about who her father is, her mother most of all, I daresay.'

As expected Macdara looked horrified. 'No, Kay, you can't be serious. Not after what that Keating woman put her through.'

She sent him a withering look. 'Oh, I wasn't thinking of her. Good riddance to bad rubbish. However, I understand her people were from decent stock. Sister Martha knew a bit about them. Evidently, Clare broke her mother's heart when she went off the rails. She brought so much disgrace on the family and trouble to their door that eventually they had no option but to completely disown her.' She scanned his face intently, hopefully. 'Anya's so lovely that I can't help but think that if they were to meet her it could be a good thing.'

'No, Kay.' Macdara held firm. 'Let's not complicate the poor girl's life any more than it is already. She's suffered enough rejection. We can't risk subjecting her to more.'

'But who's to say they would reject her?' Lady Kathleen set her mouth. 'For all we know, they might be delighted.'

'And hang out the bunting, and bring on the brass band.' Macdara threw his hands up. 'Kay, you're a hopeless romantic, but this is real life and not one of your Hollywood movies. Now, please put it out of your mind. If it works out between Fergal and Anya, surely that will be enough.'

'A start, certainly.'

'Enough!' Macdara countered, knowing his friend of old, and how once she had the bit between her teeth she was reluctant to let go. 'Don't meddle, Kay. Promise?'

'So boring,' Lady Kathleen complained, but decided to drop the subject.

The evening sun slanted in through the long windows, bathing them in primrose and tangerine light. Macdara looked round approvingly at his surroundings which, until recently, had been in a pretty ruinous state. Following through on his promise to restore Castle Mac Tíre to its former glory, it was clear to see that JC had ploughed some of the profits from the nightclub into some restoration work, so his grandmother would have somewhere nice to sit during the summer. Victorian Gothic in style, the building was constructed around an intricate metal framework ornately embellished with finials and decorative castings. The façade was glossed in royal icing white, giving it the look of a fancy frothy wedding cake. Fourteen magnificent fanlight-topped windows gazed out over the East Meadow, at present a riotous tapestry of poppies, scabious, corn marigolds, lupins and dainty pink meadowsweet. Sloping away at the end of the meadow stood the small wood that screened Wishbone Lake from view, and rising just above the tops of the trees was the spire of the Hell Fire Club.

Each with their own thoughts, Macdara and Lady Kathleen fell into a companionable silence, rousing only when Javier bustled in with tea and mini blueberry muffins still warm from the oven.

'How perfectly splendid!' Lady Kathleen looked pleased and Macdara's eyes lit up as he served them both. 'Thank you, Javier, dear. I really don't know how I managed before you came along.'

Macdara added a gruff thanks as with a slight bow from the waist, Javier left them.

'Baked by his own fair hands?' Macdara bit into one of the little cakes, nodding appreciatively.

'But of course.' Lady Kathleen's tongue darted out and rescued a stray crumb from the side of her mouth. 'The boy has many talents.' She gave a gurgle of laughter as Macdara slanted her an old-fashioned look. 'Good grief, Mac, what a mind you have. I don't mean in the bedroom, although that may well be the case. How flattering that you should think that I, in my decrepit state, could still pull someone of Javier's tender years.'

Reassured, Macdara found it easy to be magnanimous, though strictly speaking Kay's private life was none of his business. Still, she was a friend, one of his oldest and dearest, and he would never forgive himself if she were to fall victim to some young Argentinian gigolo on the make. 'Oh, I don't know. You're still a good-looking woman, Kay. You could have anyone you want, young or old.'

Lady Kathleen laughed. 'Silver-tongued devil.'

A movement between the trees caught their eye and a moment later, JC and Orla ambled into view, leading their horses on slack reins. Looking as though she had just stepped through the frame of a Rossetti painting or, perhaps more fittingly, a 1970s Athena poster, Orla was wearing a white cheesecloth dress, through which the evening sun shamelessly silhouetted her slender body. Her hair was loose, sexily tangled about her shoulders, and a large straw picture-hat decorated with raffia flowers was looped by a ribbon around one wrist. Just before they veered off in the direction of the courtyard and the stables, Orla waved her hat aloft at Lady Kathleen and Macdara, and JC raised his hand in acknowledgement.

'How perfect they look together,' Lady Kathleen sighed, a somewhat wistful note in her voice, as she waved back. 'A casting director's dream, Orla, the blonde angelic ingénue, and JC, dark, piratical, the strong-jawed hero who eventually bends her to his will.' She clasped her hands together. 'So romantic, like Romeo and Juliet, Tristan and Isolda, Heathcliff and Cathy.'

'Star-crossed, each and every one,' Macdara interrupted the litany with a chuckle. 'Luckily for their health and well-being they're only friends.'

'Dear oh dear, Mac, your naivety is showing again.' Lady Kathleen picked up her delicate china cup a little too forcefully, causing a mini tidal-wave of tea to splash up against the rim. Her eyes roved disbelievingly over his face. 'Are you so entirely ignorant when it comes to love? Can you not see your granddaughter is madly in love with JC? Just look at her,' she urged. 'Can you not see the aura of passion about her?' Her eyes grew dark and seemed to be looking inward towards a picture only she could see. 'But it's a destructive passion, the kind that burns too brightly, the kind, which if not carefully tended, is liable to go out of control and destroy everything and everyone in its path.'

Macdara threw back his head and laughed. 'Kay. Kay. You're priceless. Are you never off the stage? Orla and JC have been friends since childhood. They're like sister and brother. Thick as thieves, I grant you. But love? Not at all.'

Lady Kathleen sent him a quelling eye. 'Your vision has obviously deteriorated more than we realised, considering you can't even see what is directly beneath your nose. First, Anya and Fergal, and now Orla and JC. Must everything be spelled out in big neon letters before you get the message?'

Macdara spluttered a bit more, then subsided as her face remained grave. 'You're serious, aren't you?' His eyes flew back to

Orla and JC, just disappearing from view. He shook his head in complete denial. 'No, you've got it all wrong. Typical woman! You look for romance in everything and if you can't find it, you inject it anyway.'

Lady Kathleen sulked a little, his 'typical woman' comment rankling somewhat. *Typical* women weren't movie stars, and certainly she wasn't so asinine as to satisfy some pathetic Mills & Boon urge for romance with a customised slice of make-believe. Her eyes gleamed as her mind delved deep in the past and surfaced triumphantly with a memory which, until now, she had almost completely forgotten. As had Macdara, apparently.

'I'm simply telling you what I see,' she said through narrowed lips. 'And it is you who are mistaken. Far from being childhood friends, Orla and JC spent their time squabbling. Both, if you recall, were spoilt silly and both wanted to hog centre-stage all the time, which hardly made for happy playmates. Sinéad was the little acolyte. She it was who worshipped JC. She it was who dogged his steps, trailing him everywhere like a little dark-eyed shadow. Truly, that child would have done anything for him.' She finished her tea and set her empty cup back on its saucer with a definitive clink. Macdara offered a refill, but she shook her head. 'Nancy was quite concerned at one stage as she seemed to think JC was something of a mini Svengali, if you remember.' Lady Kathleen's mouth twisted wryly. 'I, being JC's grandmother, might quite rightly have felt offended had the whole idea not been so utterly preposterous. And so I told her,' she smiled, 'in no uncertain terms, I might add.'

Macdara nodded sadly. 'Poor Nancy. She was always ready to take up the cudgels on Sinéad's behalf.' A picture rose up to torment him: Sinéad on Nancy's lap, cuddled into her breast, Nancy's hand stroking the child's hair, a shaft of sunlight refracting the light from her diamond engagement ring around the room and Bluebeard, the old tom cat, transfixed by, but too lazy to try and catch the darting rainbow of colour. 'There, there, my little one. Come now, dry those big tears for Nanna, and let's go see if we can find you a nice big bun.' Despite the softening of his feelings lately, the old bitterness reared its head. "'She's just a child, Mac." That's what Nancy used to say. "You're too hard on her. She doesn't mean any harm." Famous last words, eh?'

'Did it ever occur to you that Nancy might have been right?' Lady Kathleen asked softly, watching closely as a range of emotions chased themselves across Macdara's face. Denial? Doubt? Anger? Guilt? She endeavoured to interpret them. 'Did it never occur to you that Sinéad's misbehaviour was, perhaps, most of all just a cry for attention?' She splayed her hand on the table top, examining her nails but without seeing them at all. 'Please don't take this as a criticism, Mac. But to an outsider it might well have looked as though you were playing favourites. Neither of the children were saints, but perfectly ordinary little girls, each as capable of naughtiness as the other. Yet, Orla seemed to get off scot-free most of the time, while Sinéad was always in trouble.'

'Don't take it as a criticism!' Macdara pushed his chair back from the table and rose to his feet where he stood glaring down at his oldest friend. 'What else should I take it as? It's hardly a compliment. Besides, it's not true. Both girls were treated exactly the same. I did not play favourites. On the contrary, I was even-handed to the point of stupidity. Maybe if I had raised my hand to Sinéad more often, her grandmother would still be alive today.' Breathing hard, he retrieved his jacket from the back of the chair and shrugged it on. 'I think maybe I'd better go now, before we both say something there's no coming back from. Thank you for a lovely evening, Kay, though it's ended badly, and I'm not entirely sure why.'

'Of course you know why.' Lady Kathleen glared back with slatey eyes. They had been friends far too long to lie to each other. 'It's that old adage, remember? The one about the truth. Sometimes, it's bitter.' She softened, feeling as though she might have been slightly harsh, though truthful. 'Poor Mac. You know, I think guilt is eating you up deep inside.'

Vehement in denial, Macdara tossed his head. 'No way, Kay, don't try to lay the burden of guilt on me. I wasn't the one who set fire to the barn. I wasn't the one who killed my wife.'

'No,' Lady Kathleen said, grown suddenly weary. 'The burden of guilt was laid on Sinéad's back, a heavy burden, indeed, for such a small child. And, what happens when that back can no longer bear it?' Like ectoplasm, the question floated between them, a restless spirit in need of exorcism.

'Goodnight, Kathleen,' Macdara said with finality, and moments later she watched him stalk across the meadow, head arrogantly upright, shoulders rigid, his whole mien one of affronted dignity.

'God bless you, Mac,' she whispered, sad for her dear friend and the blindness that was afflicting him in more ways than one.

She sat on in the orangery till the thief that was darkness came and filched the sky of its summery pastels. An ink-bellied cloud shifted slightly, revealing a crescent-shaped segment of moon and directly beneath, as if attached by an invisible chain, hung one bright star. Black on black across the meadow night creatures came out to play and hunt, squealing, chirruping and snuffling amid the vegetation. An insect, drunk on nectar or, perhaps, the sheer wonder of flight, blundered clumsily against the window and, stunned, flew erratically away again.

Outside, a breeze sprang up from nowhere, setting the grasses and tall night-shaded poppies to wavering, reminding her of a couplet from a pretty old poem: *Summer set lip to earth's bosom bare, and left the flushed print in a poppy there.*

In the wood, she could just about make out the shapes of the trees dancing in pagan ritual. For a split second, as they hula-hooped their branches, Kathleen thought she saw a pinpoint of light. But then the trees closed ranks again and the light, if such it was, was swallowed up by the dark. After a while she drowsed, waking only when Javier erupted through the door.

'*Ay, dios mio!*' he exclaimed indignantly. 'The Señor Macdara, why does he not tell me he is leaving? I shall talk to him.' He jabbed at his chest 'Me, Javier, I will tell him of my deep unhappiness.' He looked so mournful, it was all Lady Kathleen could do not to laugh. Not since she had played opposite Tyrone Flynn in *The Longest Knight* had she seen such a display of outraged, over-the-top chivalry. 'Ah, my lady, but you are cold and tired. And hungry too.'

'Just weary, Javier,' she told him, a little catch in her voice. 'These old bones are longing for their bed.'

'Do not worry.' Javier positioned himself behind her wheelchair and released the brake. 'Javier is here now. Bed, he is coming most immediately.'

# Chapter 20

*The girl lay on the bed, her head turned towards the postage-stamp piece of sky she could see out the little window, summer blue, streaked with cotton buds of fluffy cloud. Perfectly framed, for a moment, a jet streaked past high in the sky. She could hear the distant whine of its engine as it toured the heavens en route to distant climes.*

*Rolling on to her other side, she gazed at the woman slouched at a table on the far side of the room. Clare. Clare something or other, the woman who had been entrusted with her care. Who knew? Who cared? As usual, the skaghead was as high as a kite, eyes glazed, her body jerking occasionally as if she had been wired up to the mains and was the recipient of irregular but continual shocks to her system. Oh, how her clever-clogs sister had cocked-up there. It was never a good idea to put a junkie in charge of another junkie. For the last week the drugs had gone directly into Clare's own veins, and though she, herself, had spent days virtually climbing the wall as she was forced to go cold turkey, today for the first time in years she felt strangely at peace, strangely together, as if the fog that had clouded her brain for so long was on the verge of lifting. She held an arm out in front of her. It was painfully thin and twig-like, but it was steady. Her skin felt cool to the touch, with no sign of the fever that usually gripped and held her down in a world of hellish delusion. Experimentally, she pulled herself up into a sitting position. It took every ounce of strength, and her head reeled, forcing her to lie back down again. But she wasn't discouraged. It was a start. Her body was weak, but her mind and willpower were stronger than they had been for a very long time and, later, she vowed to try again. And again and again. Until one day, she would be strong enough to get up and walk out of this place. And no one and nothing would stop her.*

*Across the room, Clare looked up groggily. 'What the fuck you lookin'
at?'*

*'Nothing.' The girl closed her eyes and lay weakly back on the bed. 'I'm
looking at nothing.'*

Orla wished in vain that JC's fingers would fly across her own
body, as quickly and assuredly as they flew across his computer
keyboard. But tonight, as usual, he kept her at arm's length, roughly
unclasping her hands from round his neck when once more she
had tried to seduce him.

'How many times, Orla?' Little candles of rage burnt in his eyes,
as with one of his elaborate Argentinian gestures he made his position clear. 'How many times need I tell you that we must wait till
we are married? I do not want a *putana* for a wife. Understand?'

Orla laughed sarkily at that. 'Then you've chosen the wrong
woman for your wife. Honestly, JC, you know my history. You
know what I had to do. My virginity belongs to a whole other century, not to mention a whole host of other men.' Disconsolate, her
mouth turned down. 'If it's Mother Therese you're looking for, then
I'm afraid you're all out of luck.'

'That,' JC said, 'was in the past. And the past is where we will
leave it. I am a Catholic, *querida*, and I believe in forgiveness. But
I also believe in waiting until after the ceremony, so God will smile
upon our marriage. It does not mean that I do not love you, or
desire you. I do.' He sighed inwardly; really, he couldn't be doing
with this constant massaging of her ego. The bigger picture, he
reminded himself, as he hoisted a repentant smile on to his face.
The bigger picture, that's what was important. His ranch at the end
of the world.

He stood up and backed Orla on to the bed. 'I'm sorry, truly
sorry,' JC said, sitting down beside her, picking up her hand and
kissing each fingertip in turn. 'I know it's difficult. You are so passionate. So hot-blooded, and so very distracting.' There was a flash
of the boyish Hugh Grant smile that never failed to melt her. 'I just
don't think I can afford the distraction right now.' Good! He could
already see her turning to mush, lapping up the flattery and every

honey-coated lie that tripped from his mouth. For a woman of the world, she was incredibly stupid and naive. 'When we are married, it will be a fresh start for us both. It will be as though we are newly born, belonging only to each other. Trust me on this, my darling. I won't make you wait much longer.' His beautiful eyes took on a dreamy look. 'Think of how it will be in Argentina. You and me, dancing the tango under a wonderful scraffito sky.'

Orla had no idea what a scraffito sky was or how to do the tango. But it sounded good, and she wanted some of it. Face alight, she smiled her adoration. 'Oh, I do love you, JC. And, truly, I'd wait forever if I had to, although I'd rather not.' She gave a rueful smile. 'It's just that I get so frustrated sometimes. And it's hard to remember you love me when you barely kiss me, let alone touch me.'

'Because I cannot be sure I would be able to control myself,' JC smiled, looking equally rueful. He stroked a finger tenderly down her cheek. 'Still, I am not an unreasonable man. I don't wish to entirely deprive you of your fun. So for now, should you come across a nice toy on your travels, I give you full permission to pick it up and play with it.' He turned her hand, kissed the palm. 'But, when you are my wife, all that must change.'

Orla looked glum. 'Trust me, there's an acute shortage of nice toys around, especially of the Action Man variety. Cousin Fergal was the only real contender on that score and, as you know, he's been chucked out of the ring.' She brightened suddenly. 'Perhaps Javier though. I wouldn't throw him out of bed for eating biscuits.'

'Out of the question.' JC's response was quick-fire. 'How can you think to humiliate me with my own servant?' His mouth contorted angrily. 'Anyone else. You can have anyone else at all, but Javier is out of bounds. Understand?' He gripped her face tightly between hands that smelt faintly of his signature Eau d'Orange Verte. 'I said, do you understand?'

'Yes!' Angrily, Orla jerked her head free and rubbed at her cheek, which had reddened under the pressure of his grip. 'Honestly, JC, I don't see what your problem is. All that servant and master crap is so outdated. Wasn't slavery abolished?'

'Javier is out of bounds.' It was a clear warning as the words hissed through JC's teeth like bullets. 'Do not disobey me on this, Orla.' Dismissive suddenly, he rose to his feet. 'Go now!' His face was wiped clean of all expression. 'This conversation is over and I have work to do.'

*As do I, patently.* Orla thought the words, but did not speak them. Childish, she stuck her tongue out at his back. Telling her what she could and could not do was tantamount to waving a red flag at a bull. Yes, she was engaged to him, but that didn't make her his possession, any more than working for him made Javier his possession. Although she had really only thrown Javier's name into the pot for mischief's sake, the fact that JC had deemed him so off-limits had suddenly made him a very desirable proposition. Showing nothing of her thoughts, she slid off the bed, went over and dropped a kiss on JC's bent head. 'Okay, babe, I'll let you get on with cooking the books. Catch you tomorrow, okay?'

JC didn't bother even to look up but just waved a casual hand, which only served to strengthen her resolve. Orla didn't like being taken for granted. By anyone. 'Ready or not, Javier,' she said under her breath as she closed the door behind her and started down the stairs, 'here, I come.'

It was late and Castle Mac Tíre was badly lit, but Orla didn't need lighting to find her way round the maze of passages and corridors. As a child she had often played in the castle and she still knew the way like the back of her hand. The servants' quarters were in the basement, alongside the cavernous stone kitchen, where modern equipment and utensils marched cheek-by-jowl with their antique counterparts. There were no fewer than seven ovens, each used for a different method of cooking: two for stewing, two for baking, a hot plate, a boiling stove, and a roasting fire where whole suckling pigs and haunches of venison had once rotated on a spit. In the 1940s these ovens had been replaced by a massive cream Aga, once state-of-the-art but also now a geriatric in its own right and sadly battered-looking.

A pine table, fully twenty feet long, dominated the centre of the room, suspended above which was a wrought-iron rail hung with enamel cookware, as well as bunches of herbs, strings of onions and vivid red and yellow Argentinian chillies. Jars of preserves and pickles lined the shelves and a banded oak barrel containing balsamic vinegar sat like a squat Friar Tuck in one corner.

As Orla pushed the heavy kitchen door open and peeked in, the light from the corridor sparked warmly off the fluted sides of a display of copper jelly and pie moulds decorating the wall opposite. She took a step inside, her nose wrinkling appreciatively at the lingering smell of fresh baked bread overlaid with the pungent, slightly medicinal smell of rosemary.

Javier had clearly been busy, but hopefully he was not so tired from his exertions that he wouldn't be in the mood to cook up a little mischief with her. If her suspicion that he was playing hide the chorizo with Lady Kathleen was correct, she reckoned he'd be only too pleased to get his hands on something smelling less like death and more like YSL's Young Sexy Lovely – her, in other words. Orla hoped fervently he hadn't already turned in for the night with his pension-drawing lover.

Exiting the kitchen, she stood for a moment with ears pricked for any signs of life, and she was rewarded by a muted trill of music emanating from further up along the corridor. In a burst of nervous excitement she followed it, the strains becoming louder and louder as she neared the source. Rodrigo's *Concierto de Aranjuez*. Orla recognised the piece as a favourite of JC's, though why anyone should be so besotted by a lot of old Spanish guitars weeping and wailing left her baffled. He had tried to explain it to her once, animatedly detailing the complexities of the three movements, waxing lyrical about the inspiration the composer had taken from the gardens at Palacio Real de Aranjuez, thrilling over how he had managed to encapsulate within the notes 'the fragrance of the magnolias, the singing of the birds, and the gushing of the fountains'.

Outside the door, Orla waited for a lull in the music, took a deep breath and tapped lightly, arranging her features into a seductive expression and shuffling her neckline lower to reveal the top of her lace-trimmed bra. When, after a moment or two, no reply was forthcoming she tapped again, turned the knob and pushed the door slightly ajar.

Fresh from the shower, Javier was standing with his back to her towelling himself dry. From what she could see of it, his body was truly beautiful, slender, yet honed and muscular, his skin a wash of pale gold, accentuated by a darker bronze in the little creases and folds. Had Orla's knowledge of art been anything other than scant, she might have compared him to Michelangelo's *David*, or Myron's athletic *Discobolus*. As it was, Conan the Barbarian was the rather more mundane, but equally gratifying image that sprang instantly to her mind. Spying on her own private dancer, Orla's tongue ran appreciatively over her lips. Firm thighs. Taut buttocks. Loving it. Loving it! Like Herod waiting for Salome's seventh and final veil to fall away, she watched with almost breathless anticipation the teasing motion of the towel shimmying across his upper back and shoulders. But when the big reveal finally happened and Javier whipped the towel away, screwed it into a ball and flung it from him, it was all she could do not to gasp in shock. Clapping her hand over her mouth, she turned and fled back up the corridor. Within seconds, she was outside, her breath leaving her body in heavy gasps.

Macdara shot upright in bed, his heart pounding and body drenched in sweat. For a moment, as his eyes strove to focus, he could still see the wall of flame, the vicious red, yellow and white-hot flames that had devoured the barn on that sunny June evening all those years before. And with it, his beloved Nancy. It was the talk with Kay that had stirred up his mind, of course, that had brought the memories leaping thick and fast so that they invaded his dreams and turned them into a feverish nightmare from which there was no escape. Swinging his legs over the side of the bed, Macdara sat for a moment, head in hands, willing his heart to quietness, his breath to evenness and his mind to emptiness, but all to no avail. Transported back into the past, he couldn't help but stare in horror at the pall of thick black smoke over the hay barn, the voracious flames shooting random sparks in every direction, causing the terrified horses in their stables nearby to kick desperately at the doors.

'Mac! Mac! Nancy is in there. She's gone after Sinéad!' Fateful words shouted by whom he knew not. Then nothing but heart-stopping confusion, and Macdara beating his way forward, only to be wrested back by strong arms; then fighting to break free, mouth screaming again and again, 'Nancy! Nancy! Hold on, love, I'm coming.' And above the crackle and roar of the flames, the sudden shocking, banshee screech as the whole roof caved in. Five men it took to hold Macdara back then, possessed as he was of an almost demonic strength. 'Stop, Mac! It's too late, there's nothing you can do. Nancy's gone. She's gone Mac,' they said.

Defeated at last, he fell to his knees and, as his head tipped hopelessly forward on to his chest and the tears rained down his scorched and blistered face, the remains of his heart shrivelled to a hard black fossil encased in layer upon layer of bitterness. And over the years he clung to that bitterness like a lifeline, because soon it seemed to be the only thing that kept him strong, that spurred him on and kept him from going entirely mad.

How could Kay turn the tables like that and accuse him of being in the wrong, of being *guilty*? That she had done so astonished him. Of course Kay had not been there when they dragged the blackened remains of Nancy from the burnt-out shell. Kay had not been there when eventually he'd staggered to his feet and found Sinéad standing next to him, a box of matches in her hand. The very Sinéad whom Nancy had gone into the blazing barn to rescue. Sinéad, alive and well, the girl who had yet again ignored the warning about playing with matches. Sinéad, the bad seed. Sinéad, the firestarter.

'Sorry, Granddad.' That's what Sinéad had said. 'Sorry, Granddad.' As if sorry could unwind time. As if sorry could restore his beautiful, adored Nancy back to life. They had had to restrain him once more then because, child or not, he'd have strangled the life out of her, if he had managed to get his hands round her neck.

No. Kay had not been there. She had been away in Hollywood or Monaco or somewhere exotic, playing at being someone else, warming herself on the adulation of strangers, while the body of her best friend cooled on a mortuary slab. It was easy for her to be so forgiving.

Macdara put on his slippers and dressing-gown and went down-stairs, walking on tiptoe so as not to waken anyone else. But some-one else was already awake and crying her heart out at the kitchen table. In his concern for her, Macdara immediately forgot his own troubles.

'Orla? Orla, love, whatever is the matter?'

Orla, half prostrate across the table, didn't look up, just sobbed louder as he approached and gently laid his hands on her shoulders.

'Nothing! Everything! Oh, I don't know, Grandy.'

Macdara levered himself down beside her. 'Lovers' tiff?' he asked gently, recalling the picture of her and JC together earlier, and Kay's assertion that the pair were more than just good friends. Although she didn't answer, Macdara took the sudden stiffening of her shoulders for assent. 'JC?' he queried gently.

Orla sat up, knuckling her eyes like a child. 'Yes. No. Yes and no,' she sniffed, the tears coming thick and fast.

'Do I need to get my shotgun out?' Macdara asked, only half-joking.

There was a pause, then a very watery giggle. 'No. No. It's nothing really. You must think I'm such a baby.'

Reaching for her hand, damp from her tears, Macdara cradled it between his own. 'Yes. Yes, I do, silly old fool that I am, even though I know full well you are a grown-up young woman who can handle her own affairs. But, you see, to me you will always be that precious little baby, all pink and blonde and angelic. The baby that your mother carried home from hospital and who stole my heart away with her first gappy smile.' His voice broke a little, the result of too much emotion in one night. 'I suppose what I'm trying to say and am making a complete hash of, is that I'm here for you if you need me now, even if I haven't been always. I am now and I always will be. And if ever you want to speak to me about whatever happened tonight with JC, or anything else, I will always listen and do my best never to judge.' He kissed her cheek lightly. 'Okay?'

Orla batted back a sudden yawn, and rose to her feet. 'Sorry, Grandy,' she said. 'I think the day has caught up with me.' She bent down and kissed the old man's cheek. 'Thanks for the pep talk. I do appreciate it.' She headed for the stairs. 'Don't stay up too long, eh? You need to take care of yourself, especially now.' She left him to fill in the gaps himself.

This Macdara did. As if he could forget his encroaching blindness.

Upstairs, Orla picked up the old one-eyed teddy Bridie had put on her bed and began rhythmically to bash its head against the bedstead, till the sawdust filling began to pour out through a small rip in his fur. Finally, she kicked the toy clear across the room and, feeling the need to calm her nerves, went to her underwear drawer where she extracted a spliff from a stash she kept in an old tampon box. For emergencies. She lit it, threw open the window, and leaned out over the edge, inhaling deeply. The night air was thick like Marmite, the sky a gloopy black. Longingly, she thought of JC's promised scraffito sky, imagining herself whirling in his arms, following wherever he led.

She stayed for a while, quietly smoking, eyes searching the darkness as if perhaps she could divine her future. But she couldn't see anything really, and especially not a future. Not after tonight. The joint made her suddenly nauseous, or was it the recollection of what she had seen? She cursed herself for a stubborn fool, for the contrary streak that had made her search out Javier against JC's wishes. She stubbed out the joint, returned the remains to the tampon box and went and lay fully clothed on the bed. Her glance went to a poster on her wall, a jokey one she had picked up in Australia years before, featuring a cork-trimmed-hat-wearing kangaroo. 'Don't worry about the world coming to an end today,' advised the speech bubble coming out of its mouth, 'it is already tomorrow in Australia!'

Sleep finally captured her. She dreamed. There was a party, lots of noise and laughter, blaring music. A rhythmic thump, thump, thump, like a heart beating. And drugs. A small mountain of snowy cocaine on the table. Weed. Heroin. Her sister, flirting with a boy she'd introduced her to, head thrown back and laughing like she hadn't for a long time, eyes sparkling. Fear striking at her heart as she caught sight of her sister later, arm compliantly outstretched, the glint of a syringe, the skin puckered as the needle made contact. Tears, so many tears. Blame, so much blame. She tossed, turned, woke up panting, eventually falling back asleep straight into the coils of another nightmare.

Macdara gazed at the empty space where Orla had been, then at the clock on the wall. It was three o'clock, the time when life was reckoned to be at its lowest ebb, when the veil between this world and the next was at its thinnest. It certainly seemed that way tonight as Macdara felt as if Nancy was in the room, her presence surrounding him, reaching for him, comforting. And, God help him, he needed that comfort badly. Through the kitchen window he idly watched the sky change from mourning-gown black, to semi-mourning grey, punctuated with hopeful touches of mauve. From somewhere came the sound of a cockerel heralding the start of another day. He shivered, realising he was cold. Thoughts of Nancy faded, and he found himself back with the living once more.

# Chapter 21

'You must think me such a baby.' Anya pulled a deep-red satin gown out of Lady Kathleen's wardrobe and held it up for inspection.

'Vintage Valentino,' Lady Kathleen said with satisfaction. 'I wore it to the première of *Swans Like Us*. Meryl was green with envy, but I told her that going with an unknown is all very well and good, darling, but one simply can't beat a tried and tested.' She giggled. 'Blackwell had her on his ten worst-dressed women list that year. Dear Richard! Not everyone was sorry when he died, you know.'

Anya laughed dutifully, but having heard the tale a hundred and one times before, she reverted immediately to the subject that was uppermost in her mind. 'It's just that, apart from a couple of shopping trips to London and a long miserable wet weekend in Paris, I've never been abroad before. And Dubai is so far away, and so foreign.'

'Foreign? Hah!' Lady Kathleen snorted. 'In Dubai, my dear, it becomes something of a game trying to spot the native. The place is quite simply overrun these days with tourists and foreign contract workers clogging up the posh hotels and vast shopping malls. I should know, I've been there. Think London or Paris, only with more sunshine, a lot more gold and, quite often, a lot less clothing.'

Disbelieving, Anya pulled a face. 'But isn't it a Muslim country. Aren't there strict laws governing that kind of thing?'

'Oh, to be sure and, outside, it is advisable to be seen to observe those laws. Hence absolutely no necking in public, no drunken shenanigans, or the like. But behind closed doors, it can be a different story.'

Anya replaced the red dress in the wardrobe and pulled out a purple velvet gown, with a full skirt and a deep sweetheart neckline.

'Never liked it,' Lady Kathleen waved a dismissive hand. 'I only wore it as a favour to Christian. But *Vogue* likened me to Morticia Adams and Meryl phoned me up especially to tell me.' She grinned wickedly. 'Old movie stars never forget. They simply wait their cue.'

'Oh Lord, am I doing the right thing?' Anya asked. 'I'm so confused. I keep changing my mind every five minutes.'

'Would it make a difference if Fergal wasn't part of the equation?' Lady Kathleen asked slyly.

'No. Why should it?'

'You're absolutely sure?'

Anya's hesitation was an eloquent answer.

Lady Kathleen smiled kindly. 'Listen, my dear, I haven't reached my age without learning a thing or two en route, and one of the things I've learned is that chances for happiness don't come along all that often. When they do, you have to pounce with both hands, because she who hesitates is an absolute mug. And are you a mug, Anya?'

Anya smiled and shook her head.

'Good,' Lady Kathleen said. 'So you're going, and that's all that's to it, okay?'

Anya nodded and substituted an apple-green silk column dress for the purple.

Lady Kathleen clapped her hands with delight. 'Première of *The Lady of Shallnot*. I was nominated for an Oscar for that, you know. What a night! Camera bulbs flashing left, right and centre, the paparazzi positively crawling all over each in a bid to take my picture, thunderous applause like a great tsunami and, best of all, waiting at the end of the red carpet with eyes only for me, George, beautiful George.'

'Not Clooney?' Anya asked breathlessly.

'No, silly. Hamilton. A wee bit older, but every bit as gorgeous.' Lady Kathleen burst out laughing as Anya looked disappointed. She waved a hand, as the younger woman went to the wardrobe again. 'Leave it. Enough reminiscing for the day.' She wheeled her chair over to a low table where, thoughtful as ever, Javier had placed a bottle of her favourite red wine and a couple of crystal glasses. 'Now, how about a nice glass of wine. I reckon after that let-down, you need it.' She poured for them both, then raised her glass. 'To Dubai. Cheers, my dear.'

'To Dubai,' Anya returned the toast, her eyes drawn magnetically towards her handbag in which nestled the Emirates ticket she had received by post earlier that morning. No going back now. The die was cast.

Lady Kathleen smiled into her glass as an idea occurred to her. Her little black book contained hundreds of useful contacts, including Sheikh Faisal Bin Rashid's. He was, as she recalled, quite star-struck, and she had been his guest on more than one occasion. Perhaps she would speak to him about her two young friends. Cupid occasionally needed a push in the right direction.

'I hope you have a wonderful time in Dubai,' Macdara huffed, helping to load Anya's rather large suitcase into the back of the cab booked to take her and Fergal to Dublin airport. 'Make sure you come back, that's all.'

Anya smiled tearfully round at the small crowd that had gathered to see them off. Now that the moment had arrived, she felt more nervous than ever. It had been so long since she had left Lismore, her safe haven, for any length of time, as well as the wonderful people she had come to think of as her family.

'Bring me back a sheikh,' Kitty laughed, tossing her glossy hair which was caught up in a high ponytail, mirroring her love of horses. She wondered what everyone would say if they knew she had already caught her sheikh, although sneaking a peek now at Liam, whose face was grim in the midst of the otherwise cheery-looking group, he looked more satyr than sheikh. Still, he was hers and soon everyone would know it.

'I'll settle for a millionaire, nationality unimportant,' Orla added drily.

'And I'll settle for a nice winning stallion,' Macdara added with heavy emphasis, reminding them of the real point of the trip.

'I'll do my best, Mac,' Fergal promised. 'If Persian Prince

measures up to his sales pitch, he's as good as yours.' He held the door of the taxi open for Anya, then slid in after her.

'Only at the right price,' Macdara warned, closing the door behind Fergal. He rapped smartly on the roof and the cab moved off.

Anya struggled round in her seat to wave, her vision blurred with tears. 'Goodbye,' she called. 'Look after yourselves. Please. Look after yourselves, all of you.'

'Anya,' Fergal laughed, giving only a casual backward wave himself. 'I think they can survive for two weeks without us, don't you?'

She turned back to him, feeling slightly foolish. 'Of course, it's just that, well, you know.'

'You love them. I know.' Fergal grinned suddenly. 'Even Liam?'

Anya shuddered. 'Definitely not. Never in a month of Sundays. It beats me what Kitty sees in him.'

Fergal looked concerned. 'Isn't that all just a rumour?'

Anya shrugged. 'I'm not sure. But I wouldn't put it past him to take advantage of her. She's very young and very silly sometimes.'

'I'll keep a close eye on him when I get back,' Fergal said, his face forbidding. 'While Kitty is working at Lismore we have a duty of care towards her, morally if not legally. I'd hate to see her ruined by the likes of O'Hanlon.'

Anya shot him a look of gratitude. Not all men were the same. Thanks to Macdara and Fergal, she had learned that much. 'Kitty's a sweet girl. She deserves so much better than a married man more than twice her age.'

The car slowed as it reached the electronic gates, which swung slowly open. And then they were out on to the main road, and off on the first leg of an eighteen-hour journey that would eventually deposit them in sunny Dubai.

'You okay?' Fergal asked, as the driver put his foot down and the car picked up speed.

'Fine. I'm just finding it hard to believe that this is actually happening. I mean, I'm not the kind of girl things like this happen to.' She made a little moue. 'Does that sound pathetic?'

'Why shouldn't good things happen to you? You know, Anya,

you really need to get over this "I am not worthy" attitude you carry round. Aren't you as good as anyone else, and a damn sight better than most?'

Anya flushed. 'Good heavens, do I really come across like that? I certainly don't mean to.' Oh Lord, inside she was dying at the thought that she might unconsciously be portraying herself as one of life's no-marks, forever a victim of her past. Not that Fergal knew about her past, of course. That was a dark secret known only to the trusted few: Sister Martha, Macdara, Lady Kathleen. But to everyone else, Anya hoped fervently, her background was as boringly ordinary as that of the vast majority of people, and that's exactly the way she wanted things to stay. You're right, of course,' she said now, making a deliberate attempt to respond to Fergal's banter, 'I'm great, fantastic, amazing, one in a million. I just don't like to boast about it.'

'You are that,' Fergal said quietly. 'The shame is that you really don't know it.'

Unused to flattery and at something of a loss as to how to respond, Anya turned her head away and gazed out the window at the Irish countryside as the car whizzed along. Lush, fertile and forty shades of green, according to popular legend. Up front the driver turned on the radio, fiddling with the dials until he reached a popular music station. His eye caught Anya's in the rear-view mirror.

'Off on your honeymoon, are you?' He winked playfully at Anya.

Fergal grabbed Anya's hand, silencing her as she started to correct the driver's assumption. 'Yes, we're off to Dubai. But I'm thinking of trading her in for a camel or two. Any idea how many I could get for her?'

'Camels? Good grief, I wouldn't know about that, sir. But I've got a pig and a goat I'd be interested in trading myself.'

Anya laughed, all tension dispelled. 'Oh, be quiet, the pair of you, and turn up the radio, please. I love this song.' As the driver obliged on both counts, she sat back and closed her eyes, letting the strains of 'Fields of Gold' wash over her.

They were leaving fields of green behind for fields of gold, and on a sudden burst of happiness Anya felt like anything at all could happen. A grin came to her face as she recalled an Arabic proverb she had chanced upon while researching their trip: *Throw a lucky man in the sea, and he will come up with a fish in his mouth*. Fergal didn't look much like a fish though.

'What's so funny?' Fergal asked, turning to her and catching sight of the grin.

Anya opened her eyes. 'Nothing, everything. Fish.'

In the rear-view mirror, the driver grinned and turned an imaginary screw in his temple. 'Sorry, mate, the price has just come down. You can have the pig and that's my final offer.'

'A masked ball at the Hell Fire Club?' Kitty's face, already flushed from frantic love-making, lit up as though a lantern had been switched on inside. 'That's a fabulous idea. JC is so clever. I thought that kind of thing only ever happened in books and films.'

Propped up on one elbow, Liam gazed dispassionately at her pretty, excited face. He felt no guilt about continuing to lead her on. A man had his needs, after all, and hoity-toity Anya was off the menu, at least for now. His philosophy, as he often boasted to his mates down at the pub, was simple – a bush in the hand was worth a flock of birds fluttering out of reach.

'And later,' he told her, 'I've got a little surprise lined up for you.'

'Really?' Kitty's excitement mounted. 'Oh, Liam!' She wound her arms around his neck, hoping to pull him back down on top of her, but he wriggled away. Their recent bout of love-making had been perfunctory and not at all satisfactory from her point of view. Not that she was complaining as she knew how much pressure Liam was under since finding out that Fergal was to take over Lismore. That, coupled with the stress of working up to telling his wife that their marriage was over, was understandably affecting his performance. And while other women might accuse him of being selfish and of thinking only of his own pleasure, Kitty congratulated herself on her maturity and understanding. She clapped her hands suddenly, thinking she had guessed the surprise. 'Oh, yippee, you've told your wife about us? That's the surprise, isn't it?'

'Not yet.' Liam tensed, though his face remained impassive. Pushing. Always bloody pushing. If it was an Olympic sport, Kitty would take the gold. 'I have to pick the right time. After all, we're going to be turning her whole world on its head. Jenny is the married-for-life type.'

'Yes, I know all that,' Kitty said, finding it increasingly difficult to hide her impatience. 'But, honey, I'm getting so tired of waiting.' She reached out, caught his hand and brought it down to the bare skin of her still flat tummy. 'And Junior here is going to start showing sooner rather than later.'

Liam made a big show of checking his watch. 'Look, I'll do it soon. I promise. Maybe even after the ball. In the meantime …'

Kitty sighed and made a zipping motion in front of her mouth. 'It's our secret, I know. Don't worry, I'll be as silent as the grave.'

# Chapter 22

*Dubai*

The plane chased its own reflection across the aquamarine waters of the Arabian Gulf as it made its final descent into Dubai International Airport. Looking down at the jewelled expanse of water below, and the mile upon mile of talcum-white beach, Anya gasped in delight. Apart from in the movies, she had never seen water so crystal-clear, so beautifully tinted, as if an Old Master had specially blended it to a wash, one part azure, one part indigo, teal fading to turquoise where the colours overlapped. And rising just beyond on the skyline was Dubai, a vast etching of skyscrapers, each one jostling for superiority over its neighbour. Beside her Fergal was as openly excited as a little boy on his first trip to Disneyworld.

'Wow, look at that!' He leant across and singled out a magnificent concrete and glass sail-like structure looming in the near distance. 'That's the Burj Al Arab Hotel where all the big noises stay. Seven stars! It's designed to resemble the sail on an Arabian *dhow,* and it's even got its own helipad. See, there's a chopper taking off now. How the other half lives, eh?'

Squashed back in her seat, Anya followed his pointing finger to where a dainty-looking helicopter was rising gracefully into the air. With the bubble of glass at the front and silvered rotary blades glinting in the evening sun, it reminded her of the mayflies hovering above the little river that slewed through Lismore. Fergal and Macdara sometimes went fishing there for speckled brown trout, and occasionally she would accompany them, content simply to sit and watch, surrounded by the gentle sounds of nature, the mossy perfume of the earth and the sense of safety she always felt in their presence.

It's very impressive,' she said, surprising herself with a sudden jolt of homesickness. 'But I'm not sure about all those skyscrapers. There's something a bit soulless about them, don't you think? All that concrete, steel and glass.'

'An urban jungle,' Fergal admitted. 'But, what an urban jungle! What you see before you, Anya, is a smorgasbord of some of the world's very finest architecture, the futuristic concepts of the most skilled architects and visionaries. A tribute, if you will, to mankind's skill and ingenuity.'

Anya gazed at Fergal with new eyes, impressed by his passion and not a little surprised by this hitherto hidden aspect of his persona. She joshed him gently, 'Hey you, what have you done with the real Fergal?'

Laughing good-naturedly, he rumbled her at once. 'Confess it, you thought I was just about wellies, horse manure and handicap races? But a man's allowed to have more than one interest, isn't he?' His eyes looking softly into hers suggested that another one of his interests might lie very close to hand, and when his gaze dropped suddenly to her lips, Anya thought for a moment that he might kiss her. All she had to do was tilt her head slightly towards him. But she couldn't because she still couldn't tell if she had read the signs correctly, and the humiliation would be unbearable if she were wrong. Flirting was for the Orlas of the world, women who were confident in every way, who were sexy, sassy, sure of their place in society and in men's hearts. Women who, as children, had slept soundly in their beds at night, never fearing the sinister turning of the doorknob.

Wrenching her head away, Anya fastened her gaze on the fast-approaching skyline as if it was suddenly the most important thing in the world. 'I suppose it is rather lovely,' she said, a slight tremble in her voice. 'Quite fascinating really.'

If Fergal was disappointed, he chose not to show it. Instead he chuckled, 'Now, say it like you mean it.'

'I do mean it. It's just that it's so different from Ireland, and Lismore.'

'I should hope so. I, for one, intend to enjoy every single second of our time here. We'll be back in rainy old Ireland soon enough.'

'Oh, me too,' Anya reassured him hastily, plagued once more by the suspicion that Fergal might have preferred to travel alone. She set her lips, determined. On no account must she allow her own insecurities to turn her into a clinging vine.

As the plane dipped lower, she braced herself for the inevitable bump as it touched down on the runway but in the event it landed with barely a wobble. With a sigh of relief, she hoped that the rest of her visit to Dubai would go as smoothly.

On the tarmac they were enveloped in a warm blanket of petrol-scented air, and within seconds Anya could feel a trail of perspiration working its way down her forehead.

'This is nothing,' Fergal warned her, wiping beads of moisture from his own brow. 'During the day, the temperatures can reach the mid forties, and even the sea temperature gets up to around thirty-seven degrees. Believe it or not, this is actually low season, as most tourists simply can't stand that kind of heat. Did you remember to pack lots of sunscreen?'

Anya nodded, feeling very glad of her cool cotton dress, even though it was moulding itself to her body in a most revealing way. They retrieved their luggage and navigated passport control in a surprisingly short time, before emerging on to the main concourse where the Sheikh's chauffeur, an affable Filipino, awaited them. Efficiently, he took charge of the baggage and ushered them out to a sleek black limousine with personalised number plates and a gold figurine of a horse in place of the usual Mercedes emblem.

'Now this is what I call living,' Fergal drooled, revealing himself as something of a petrol-head. Between that and his hitherto un-guessed at love of architecture, he was full of surprises, thought Anya. His hand stretched out to stroke the soft-as-doe skin cream leather upholstery. 'I think I've died and gone to heaven, and we haven't even got to the palace yet.' Enveloped in luxury, he lounged back as the air-conditioned car pulled smoothly away with only the gentlest hiss to show it was moving at all.

'Boys and their toys!' Anya smiled, though a moment later even she was amazed by the array of upmarket vehicles travelling down the wide tree-lined roads. Here Ferraris, Lotuses and Aston Martins were seemingly ten a penny, while the other cars on the road seemed either to be swish limousines or Rolls Royces. Like the Mercedes in which they were travelling, many of the vehicles they passed had personalised number plates and were trimmed with gold and, in the case of a Lamborghini that sped by them, what looked to be diamonds spelling out the owner's name.

'Flash Harry!' Fergal said admiringly, though Anya was less impressed and indeed somewhat dismayed by such a vulgar and ostentatious display of wealth. Her own bit of research on the internet had thrown up the fact that Dubai's treatment of its immigrant workers sometimes left a lot to be desired. Her brow wrinkled.

'Oh, Fergal, surely this can't be right? Isn't it all a bit let-them-eat-cake-ish?'

'Maybe,' Fergal agreed. 'But I'm afraid 'twas ever thus. The haves and the have-nots are the eternal two sides of the divide. And, personally, right at this minute I have nothing against enjoying a little luxury.' He reached across and patted her knee gently. 'Hey, come on. You can't change the world all by yourself.'

Anya forced a smile and reminded herself that this would be a good time to try to be more like Orla, to be light-hearted and to ease her foot off the angst pedal a bit. No one liked a party-pooper, and Fergal deserved this break. In times to come, when he looked back upon this visit, she wanted him to have happy memories and to feel that having her along had increased his enjoyment, rather than had put a damper on things. She forced herself to relax, and soon she found herself smiling and laughing along as Fergal pointed out the many splendours of the beautiful city through which they were driving. She ended up having such a good time that she was almost disappointed when they reached their destination.

'Now, there's an entrance that would leave Mac green with envy,' Fergal grinned, as the limousine nosed its way through the heavily guarded, key-hole shaped archway leading to the estate.

They set off down a serpentine driveway set in exquisitely landscaped gardens, many themed, as in the case of a pretty little Japanese garden framed by intricate topiary and hedging. Anya could see no sign of any gardeners although she was sure a whole army must be employed to keep the grounds so fertile and abundant in so arid and unforgiving a climate. Turning her head to look back, she inadvertently found the answer as, like the Munchkins hiding from the Wicked Witch of the West, one figure after another emerged from various hidey-holes once the car had passed.

'Anya!' Fergal said warningly, noticing her frown. 'I know you don't approve, and neither do I, as it happens. But please keep your thoughts to yourself. It's considered unpardonable here to insult the host or to criticise his way of doing things.'

'I have no intention of insulting our host,' Anya said, stung that Fergal might think her so ill-mannered. 'But no one, including you, has the right to police my thoughts, and right at this very moment they're not very charitable.'

'I wouldn't dream of it,' Fergal said drily. He looked away and once again Anya could have kicked herself for her being such a misery-guts. She was glad when the car navigated a final bend and the palace was revealed in all its glistening-white splendour. Anya, who had been expecting a building more in the Islamic style with domes and turrets, was surprised to find that the palace was built along classical lines, with Doric columns and topped by an elaborately carved entablature reminiscent of a Greek temple. A flight of marble steps, inscribed with passages from the Koran, led gracefully down to an expanse of velvet-green lawn, so impossibly verdant one might have suspected it to be a *trompe l'oeil*. Vast urns, spilling over with exotic flowers, were artfully placed for maximum impact, while high-stepping amongst them was a flock of peacocks, tails fanned out in iridescent glory.

Almost before the car had come to a halt, the driver scurried round to open the doors for them, bowing slightly as he did so. Two servants, dressed in traditional white *djellabas* and with nut-brown faces, appeared out of nowhere and took charge of the luggage, disappearing again in almost an instant. A little at a loss, Fergal and Anya gazed after them, then jumped as a door opened at the top of the steps and an elderly man dressed in the uniform of an English butler appeared in the opening. Somewhat flustered, he hurried down the steps and bowed from the waist.

'I am Manning,' he introduced himself in a cut-glass English accent. 'Forgive me. I am running a little behind. So many guests, you see. I did not mean to keep you waiting.'

'You didn't,' Fergal assured him. 'We've only just arrived.' He glanced at the man curiously. 'I must say I didn't expect to find an English butler amongst the Sheikh's staff.'

'The Sheikh was educated at Eton,' the butler told them. 'He likes the idea of having an English butler, feels it helps him keep his English up to standard.' He waved a hand. 'Of course, there are staff here from many other countries too. Understandably, the upkeep of the palace requires a large number of employees.' He made an impatient motion. 'But enough of my chatter. You must be tired after your journey, Mr and Mrs Fitzgerald. Let me show you to your suite.' Turning, he led the way up the steps, dignified as an elder statesman.

'Mr and Mrs Fitzgerald?' Anya mouthed in horror at Fergal, who put a warning finger to his lips and shook his head.

She nodded her understanding. Fergal was right. There was no need to embarrass the poor man by pointing out his error – he looked the sort to take it to heart. Besides, it was an easy enough mistake to make considering all the guests he had to deal with. All would become clear soon enough, Anya imagined.

The interior of the palace was as magnificent as the outside, a continuum of the classical theme with marble columns, ornately plastered ceilings and gilt cornicing. Pale, ankle-thick, utterly luxurious rugs were scattered about the marble floors, while the furnishings were a made-in-heaven fusion of the best of antiquity and contemporary, sourced from all over the world by an obviously expert eye. Similarly the works of art were eclectic, a mixture of the old and the new, Rembrandt marching side by side with Turkey's foremost artist, Ismail Acar; Bacon rubbing shoulders with Van Gogh. A wonderful sculpture with all the appearance of a Rodin stood juxtaposed with a rather bizarre Henry Moore, each somehow doing the impossible in managing to complement the other.

Manning led them through a maze of rooms and corridors, each one more sumptuous and sinfully luxurious than the last.

'Magnificent,' Fergal enthused, as they followed behind and up a flight of marble stairs wide enough for a jumbo jet to taxi down.

A further straightening of the butler's already ramrod straight back showed that he was pleased by the compliment. He turned slightly and gave Fergal an approving look. 'Indeed it is quite splendid and one of the foremost residences in Dubai. The Sheikh has spent many years refining the architecture, as well as amassing treasures from the four corners of the earth. What you've seen so far is but a small sample.'

'Really?' Anya said, her attitude one of barely concealed censure. It seemed wrong that one human being should have so much, while so many others had nothing. Fergal nudged her gently in the ribs, and whatever criticism she was about to make died on her lips. Annoyed though, she glared at him and Fergal grinned back, turned his eyes piously upward and sketched a halo over his head. Anya stuck her chin out. She might be a Holy Mary, but that didn't necessarily make her wrong.

Oblivious to undercurrents, Manning continued to extol the Sheikh's virtues all the way to the top of the stairs and along the corridor until they reached a pair of ornate double doors. Proudly, he threw them open. 'Your suite. I trust you will find everything in order but, if not, you have only to tell Monique, who will be your maid for the duration of your stay.' He smiled at Anya and his face, which up until that point had been rather grandly immoveable, relaxed into more avuncular lines, charmed perhaps by her good looks. 'Monique will also help you dress for dinner. I am told she is something of an expert with hair.' With a bow from the waist he was gone, leaving a somewhat indignant Anya in his wake.

'Good heavens!' she snapped, as his footsteps echoed their retreat on the stairs outside. 'Is that his oh-so-genteel way of telling me I look like I fell out of a skip?'

But her words fell on deaf ears because Fergal was exploring their suite. A moment later she followed, all residual indignation quickly replaced by a sense of wonder.

'My God, it's like something out of the *Arabian Nights*!' she breathed aloud, as she took stock of her surroundings. It was difficult to know where to look first. Everything was so perfect, from the fabric-covered ceiling, draped and folded to give the impression of an opulent Bedouin tent, to the Moroccan-style banquette that was upholstered in jewel-coloured silks and running the length of the semi circular shaped room. Carved sandalwood tables laden with bowls of tropical fruit, flowers and incense were scattered about, and the mingled smells of roses and wild jasmine was intoxicating. By one of the arched windows, a pair of sweetly canoodling lovebirds swung from a silver swing in a huge golden cage. Anya was just about to go over to them, when Fergal called her to take a look at the bathroom, which was jaw-droppingly gorgeous. A huge sunken bath, mosaicked with pictures of Neptune and other mythological deities, was in the middle of the room, whilst either end was taken up with an enormous space-age shower and a full-sized Scandinavian sauna. A mountain of fluffy white towels lay folded neatly on a silk-covered chaise longue. Luxurious Bulgari and Annick Goutal toiletries lined the shelves.

'Wow! Now I think I've died and gone to heaven,' Anya laughed, picking up a bottle of Eau d'Hadrien and examining it as though it were a rare jewel. 'Fergal, have you any idea how expensive this stuff is? You need to take out a small mortgage for even a tiny bottle of this Eau de Parfum. Fergal?' She looked around, but he was exploring once more.

'Houston,' she heard him call from another room a moment later, 'we gotta problem.'

'What?' Anya asked, unable to resist spritzing herself with perfume before going in search of him. She came to a sudden halt at the door to the bedroom. 'Oh!'

'Yes, oh!' Fergal said, gesturing quite unnecessarily. 'Only one bedroom and only one bed. Looks like somebody cocked-up somewhere.' He didn't appear particularly unhappy.

'The butler!' Anya looked annoyed. 'This is your fault, Fergal. We should have come clean outside and told him we weren't married. What will we do now?'

Fergal picked up a card propped against a bottle of champagne on the bedside table and waved it at her. 'Dear Fergal and Anya,' he read. 'Many congratulations on your recent marriage. I trust you will enjoy your honeymoon in Dubai.' He raised his eyebrow at a thunderstruck Anya. 'It's signed by the Sheikh.'

Anya looked at him disbelievingly. She felt dizzy suddenly. She groped for the side of the bed and sat heavily down on the side. Where on earth did the Sheikh get that idea? For a fleeting moment, she wondered if Macdara had something to do with it. But no, he would never set them up like that. 'We'll have to tell him,' she said firmly. 'This place is so big, I'm sure they'll have another room spare.'

'We can't.' Fergal was just as firm. 'It would embarrass him hugely. We need to be gracious about this, and not let on.'

'But there's only one bed.' Anya flushed, and then gave a careless, if unconvincing, shrug in an effort to sound less prissy. 'Well, never mind, I can sleep on the banquette. It's plenty big enough.'

'Don't be silly.' Impatient, Fergal tossed his head. 'That bed's the size of a rugby pitch. You could sleep seven prop-forwards in that, a couple of wingers, and still have enough room left over for half the spectators.' He sighed as still she looked unconvinced. 'Look, we can put a Berlin Wall of cushions down the middle for modesty, if you're worried. There are certainly enough of them around.'

'I'm not worried.' Anya's fearful eyes gave the lie to her words.

'Good.' Fergal threw himself headlong on to the mattress and splayed out like a contented starfish.

'So that's it,' Anya said waspishly. 'We're doomed to play Mr and Mrs, just to keep the Sheikh happy.'

'Mm, that's about the strength of it.' Fergal closed his eyes and shuffled deeper into the mattress, for all the world, Anya thought crossly, like a contented cat.

'Supposing they expect us to act all lovey-dovey,' she said in a tiny voice.

Fergal opened one eye. 'This is Dubai, Anya. Decorum at all times, remember? Even a peck on the lips is frowned upon.' He grinned. 'I don't know about you, but I have no intention of spending *my* honeymoon in a filthy prison, so your virtue is safe.' He struggled up on one elbow, his hair mussed, giving him a messy little-boy look that was very appealing. 'Besides, it could be a whole worse. I mean, it's not like we hate each other, is it? Close proximity for a week won't kill us. On one condition.' There was a silence, heavy with meaning.

'Which is?' Anya asked alarmed.

'That you remember that over here it's the man who's the boss. So, you just do what you're told like a good little girl and—'

Fergal never got to finish as, picking up a heavily embroidered cushion, a mock-enraged Anya attempted to smother him.

As they play-fought on the bed, Anya had no idea that the heady scent of her perfume and her close proximity was sending Fergal crazy, or that his willpower was being sorely tested.

Outside, day collapsed suddenly into the arms of night, the cicadas struck up their harmonious chirruping, and a beautiful low-hanging Middle Eastern moon tipped silver stars all over the land below.

# Chapter 23

*Clare was talkative. She sometimes got that way before the full effect of the drugs hit her, and she crashed and burned. Usually it was maudlin stuff, endless complaints about how badly the world had treated her, escalating in pitch and fury whenever she embarked, as invariably happened, on the topic of her daughter. The girl had learned to listen, and play along, dealing sympathy cards as they were called for, stroking her jailer's injured ego. But all the while an escape plan was hatching in her mind and taking shape, hour by hour, day by day.*

*'She did this to me,' Clare spat now, yanking on a makeshift tourniquet as she probed for a usable vein on her own skeletal forearm. 'That little bitch, Anya.' Glassy-eyed, she gazed around the bare brick walls of the room. 'I was somebody once. Oh yes, I had everything. You wouldn't know that to look at me now, would you?' Her eyes returned to challenge the girl on the bed. 'But it's true. And I was a good mother, the best. But she destroyed me with her lies and accusations. Her, and that mealy-mouthed nun.' She found a likely vein, picked up the syringe and depressed the plunger. Her eyes closed in anticipation of the exquisite hit to come, then snapped wide open again. 'She better watch out though. I'm not out of the game yet. Not by a long chalk.'*

*The girl nodded understanding and so Clare talked on, her voice slowing as the drugs worked their way into her system and gradually sent her into a deep stupor. Her jailer was becoming careless, but not quite careless enough. Yet. Longingly, the girl gazed at the set of keys on the table by Clare's elbow. Temptation beckoned, but only for a moment. A buttermilk page pressed against the window outside told her it was still light. Soon, though, she promised herself, when the time was right. Night-time, ideally, when she could blend with the shadows, slipping quietly back to freedom and a life long since left behind. Fail to prepare, her mother always said, and prepare to fail. With hope as her beacon, the girl could manage a while longer. She would concentrate on staying positive, using the remainder of her incarceration to build her strength and hone her plan.*

*Clare stirred, murmured something unintelligible, and quieted again. Her prisoner glanced sharply at her, then back up at the window, longing for the time when she would be free to look up at it from the other side. She stayed focused on the small patch of sky until the buttermilk soured to ashy grey. Then her eyelids drooped and she slept deeply, more deeply, more calmly than in an age.*

'So can you forgive an old fool, Kathleen?' Macdara reached out tentatively and took Lady Kathleen's hand in his own. Her skin was thin almost to the point of transparency, the fine tracery of veins clearly visible beneath, another unwelcome reminder that they were both another rung higher on God's big ladder to the heavens. He was shocked at the change in her since the last visit, which had ended with him storming off like a sulky child. Her face had taken on a yellowish cast, the cheeks sunken and drawn across cheekbones so sharp they looked as if they might cut right through the flesh. Only her eyes were unchanged, and were as mischievous and twinkling as ever.

'No fool like an old fool, eh?' Lady Kathleen smiled, looking suddenly years younger, although her breathing was a little laboured. 'Of course I forgive you, provided you forgive me too. I spoke out of turn and I'm sorry, Mac.'

'No, it did me good. I need someone to pull me up short every now and then.' Macdara grinned ruefully. 'Nancy never had any time for what she called my toddler tantrums and she would send me away with a flea in my ear too.'

Kathleen's lips twitched. 'She always did have you wrapped around her little finger. But you were lucky, Mac. You had a marriage made in heaven, which is what everyone aspires to and only the lucky few manage.'

'I know. That's why I took her passing so hard.' Mac's face

twisted, as though in physical pain. 'Oh, God, Kathleen, I felt as if half of me had been ripped away. Still do. The nights are the worst. Sometimes I wake up and imagine she's still beside me, that I can hear her breathing, softly. I turn and reach across and there's nothing, nothing at all. And memories just aren't enough.' His eyes fell in sudden shame. 'You know, sometimes I have to pick up a photograph to remind myself of what she looked like. Isn't that terrible?'

Lady Kathleen said nothing, just squeezed his fingers gently in sympathy, recognising his need to talk, to unburden himself. For too long he had kept his pain inside, stoking his anger to keep his heart from breaking altogether, focusing instead on fall-guy Sinéad. Only by sacrificing her to his anger had he managed some semblance of normality. But the dam had cracked at last. Calmly Lady Kathleen waited for the walls to tumble, hoping she would be strong enough to keep her friend's head above the churning waters of his emotions, to help him navigate a safe passage and emerge safely on the other side.

'Kathleen!' His cry when it came was like the cry of the damned. 'What have I done? Sweet Jesus, what kind of selfish monster am I? Nancy was not only my wife, she was Nessa's mother too. I wasn't the only one grieving. Why couldn't I see that? It wasn't all about me. I should have been there for Nessa and the children. Instead, I added to Nessa's pain, piled on the guilt and then, even worse, cast Sinéad in the role of devil incarnate.'

Sweat sprang to Macdara's brow as he fought to come to terms with his conscience. 'Oh, but you were right, Kathleen. I got it all out of perspective. Sinéad wasn't a devil, just a child, a stupid disobedient child with a box of matches. You can't put an old head on a child's shoulders – how many times did Nancy tell me that, whenever I moaned about one of Sinéad's misdemeanours? Stupid little misdemeanours, like putting salt in the sugar or pulling the cat's tail? Bad behaviour, certainly, but not evil. "Kids will be kids!" That's what she used to say. "You'll see; she'll grow up to be a young woman we can be proud of." But she never got the chance! *I* never gave her the chance.'

Macdara jumped up out of his chair and strode up and down

the room. 'I drove Nessa and the children away. Away from what should have been their safe haven. Contemptible, selfish, stupid man that I am! I sometimes wonder if this blindness isn't some kind of karma visited on me for being wilfully blind in other ways.'

With an effort, Lady Kathleen pulled herself up in the bed and reached out to him. He came and knelt beside her, placing his head on her blanketed lap, his shoulders heaving with the sobs so long suppressed.

'There, there,' she comforted him like a child, her palm stroking circles across his shoulders. 'There, there. It will be all right.'

Eventually, he was still.

'What's that?' Lady Kathleen asked, as he muttered something into the blankets.

His head came up, his tortured eyes seeking hers. 'I said, it will never be all right, Kay, because in my heart of hearts I know Sinéad is dead. And I'm the one that killed her, as surely as if I had put a gun to her head.'

'We don't know that.' Lady Kathleen deliberately made her voice crisp. 'For all we know she might be living a perfectly nice life somewhere with a banker husband and a couple of lovely children.'

'Then why is she not in touch with Orla? They were inseparable as children. Where one led, the other was never far behind. And Orla won't be drawn on the subject.'

Kathleen shrugged. 'Times change. Things happen. Misunderstandings, who knows? But, Mac, do remember there is nothing to suggest that Sinéad is dead.'

A gleam of hope flashed in Macdara's eyes. He pulled himself to his feet, leaned across and lightly kissed Lady Kathleen on the lips. 'You know, Kay, you're an amazing woman. I don't know what I'd do without you. I'll talk to Orla, ask her where she last saw her sister. That would be a start.' He straightened his shoulders. 'Time to make amends, eh? God grant I'm given the chance.'

Kathleen smiled and gestured towards the door. 'Go on, then, scoot. No time like the present.' She gazed thoughtfully after him as the door closed, wondering what he would have said, had she voiced the suspicion that had been growing upon her day by day, the suspicion that maybe Sinéad was nearer than he thought. Tired almost to the point of exhaustion, Lady Kathleen sank back upon her pillows just as the door opened again and a scowling Javier let himself in carefully, so as not to upset the tray in his hands.

'Macdara, he is a very big menacing. Always he is making you tired, no?'

'No,' Lady Kathleen smiled. 'And I think you mean menace, Javier.' Her nose wrinkled appreciatively. 'Let me guess, chicken zoop with rosemaria?'

'No!' Javier looked offended. 'Tomato and basil zoop. But, if you no like …'

Lady Kathleen held up her had. 'I like.' She gazed tenderly at him as he fussed with the tray, placing it just so across her lap and tucking the napkin bib-like into the neck of her nightgown. Dear Javier. She had come to think the world of him. With him watching approvingly, she picked up her spoon and began to eat.

*Dubai*

'Pax!' Fergal yelled, as Anya, showing no sign of tiring, continued to beat him about the head with the cushion. He was saved by a knocking on the door.

'To be continued,' Anya said menacingly, as she went to answer it.

A girl, her own age or slightly older, and very pretty, stood outside dressed in a French maid's outfit.

'Hi,' she said in an Australian accent. 'I'm Monique, your maid for the duration of your visit. I expect Manning mentioned me.'

'Oh yes, he did.' Anya stepped back to allow her to enter.

Monique giggled. 'Your face,' she said. 'I'm obviously not what you were expecting.'

Anya looked slightly embarrassed. 'I suppose not,' she admitted. 'To be honest, I was never sure French maids actually existed outside of films and books.'

'Well, I'm not French, as you can tell by my accent,' Monique said. She ran her hand down along her starched white apron. 'This is all the idea of the Sheikh's youngest wife.' She gave a naughty wink. 'To be honest, I think the Sheikh quite likes it too. What red-blooded man wouldn't?'

Would Fergal, Anya wondered, her old insecurity rearing its head. Immediately she quashed the thought and set off after Monique, who was heading for the bedroom.

'Let's unpack your suitcases first,' she was saying, 'and then—' She came to a dead halt as Fergal sat slowly up on the bed and smiled. 'Hi,' Monique said, extending her hand to him. 'You must be the husband. I'm Monique, your personal maid.'

Anya stole a quick glance at her. Was it her imagination, or had the other girl put the slightest emphasis on the word 'personal'?

'Monique, this is Fergal,' Anya said, possibly a bit more sharply than intended. 'And I'm Anya.'

'Pleased to meet you both,' Monique said, her eyes straying speculatively to the somewhat rumpled bedclothes. 'I hope I'm not interrupting,' a slight pause, 'anything. I can come back later, if you like.'

Anya knew that her face was flaming. 'No! Now is fine. Absolutely fine. Isn't it, Fergal?'

'Of course, my dear,' Fergal said, managing to inject such disappointment into his voice that she wanted to hit him.

She glared at him, as Monique barely managed to suppress a smirk. How dare he give the impression that anything untoward had been afoot.

'Right then. Let's get you unpacked,' Monique said, belatedly it seemed, now remembering her role and going into efficiency mode. 'Then you might want to have take a walk or a nap before dinner, or something.'

Anya didn't ask what the 'something' might be. She was feeling a bit bewildered by Monique. The girl behaved nothing like Anya would have expected a maid to behave, not that she would expect anyone to kow-tow to her or anything.

'What time's dinner?' Anya asked.

'Eight-thirty,' Monique said. 'Would you like a hand getting dressed, Mrs Fitzgerald?'

Although the question was directed at her, Anya couldn't help but notice, Monique's eyes were firmly fixed on Fergal.

'No,' she said, not caring if she sounded ungracious. 'I can manage perfectly well by myself.'

'Who are the other guests, do you know?' Fergal asked. He propped himself up, to the manor born, against the pillows on the back of the bed.

Monique extracted a dress from Anya's suitcase, shook out the folds, looked at it admiringly and stowed it away in a cedarwood wardrobe that was giving off a delightful scent.

'It's a bit of an eclectic mix tonight,' she told him. 'An American woman big into gee-gees, a minor movie star, a boy-band popstar turned soloist, and a pair of Russian businessmen with Roman fingers, if you get my drift. And, of course, you two, the Irish newly-weds.'

Fergal pinioned Anya with a look, knowing she was dying to set the record straight. 'Sounds interesting,' he said.

Monique nodded. 'The Sheikh's banquets are famous. Sometimes they go on all night. And, believe me, no expense is spared.'

'Better and better,' Fergal said. 'And what about you, Monique? Tell me, how does an Australian Sheila end up working as a French maid in a palace in Dubai?'

Monique seemed to hesitate as she folded an item of clothing into a drawer. 'I could tell you,' she said a moment later. 'But then I'd have to kill you.'

Fergal laughed and held up his hands. 'Sorry. Sorry. I didn't mean to be nosy. No offence intended.'

'None taken,' Monique smiled. She held up the dress Anya intended to wear to dinner that evening. 'This is beautiful,' she said, with a rapid change of subject. 'You'll look stunning.' She tipped her head to one side, considering. 'You should wear your hair up.'

When she had gone, Fergal looked thoughtful. 'Not quite what you'd expect, is she? Typical Aussie though. Outspoken, full of fun.'

Anya nodded, but instinct told her there was much more to Monique than met the eye. There was a story there and her guess was that it wasn't entirely happy.

'I'm going to have a soak in that amazing bath,' she said. 'Might as well enjoy the luxury while we can, and there's ages to go before dinner.'

'Hmm, you do that,' Fergal said, sliding down on the bed and closing his eyes. 'I'll just stay here and grab forty winks.' For reasons she couldn't explain, this annoyed Anya intensely.

She injected a note of steel into her voice. 'By the way, I didn't appreciate your implication earlier.'

'What implication?' Fergal kept his eyes firmly closed.

'The one you made to Monique.' Anya felt her blood begin to bubble. 'You know, that we were, well, at it! Well?' She challenged him, but the only answer was a gentle snore.

Picking up a cushion she threw it at his head, before stalking out. Yet, inside, she didn't feel annoyed at all. Quite the opposite.

'You look amazing!' Catching sight of Anya, Fergal turned from the mirror where he had been engaged in the tricky business of tying his bow tie. 'Monique was right. That's a gorgeous dress. You surely didn't get it from Betty's Boutique,' he said, referring to the only local dress shop near Lismore, an establishment favoured by old-fashioned farmers' wives with a penchant for man-made materials and elasticated waists.

Anya shook her head happily. 'It's one of Lady Kathleen's.' She burst into a fair mimicry. 'Vintage Oscar de la Renta. I wore it in *Cabbages and Queens*. Dear Jane was up for the part, you know. But I wiped her eye for her. Such a wonderful emerald green. How fabulous it will look with your glorious red hair. No! No! You must wear it. I insist!'

Fergal laughed, enjoying this more flippant side of Anya, one she displayed all too rarely. 'Which Jane was that? Fonda? Seymour? Russell? Eyre?'

'I don't know. There are so many I get confused.' Shyly, she gave a little twirl. 'Does it really look okay? It's not like I'm used to dining with royalty. I don't want to make an idiot out of myself.'

'You look amazing,' Fergal told her truthfully, wishing Anya was not so self-effacing and that she knew her own self-worth. The other girls of his acquaintance would have been prancing and preening and full of themselves. 'The Sheikh's four wives had better look to their laurels.'

Anya batted the compliment away. 'Don't be silly. I'm sure they're all doe-eyed, raven-haired beauties. They're unlikely to be threatened by the likes of me.'

'Even in Lady Kathleen's vintage Oscar de la Wilde?' Fergal joked.

'De la Renta!' Anya laughed. Leaning closer to the mirror, she fastened her diamond earrings, also on loan from Lady Kathleen, with matching necklet and bracelet. When she had satisfied herself that the butterfly backs were in no danger of falling off, she turned back to Fergal, who was still tugging futilely at his bow tie.

'Here,' she offered. 'Let me do that for you. Talk about a dog's dinner.'

He stood quietly as deftly she pulled the wayward ends into a tidy bow, stepped back and smiled triumphantly up at him. God, she was truly ravishing, he thought, assailed by a sudden urge to forget his scruples and her modesty, rip the dress from her there and then and make passionate love to her. Shaken by the sheer strength and suddenness of his desire, he turned quickly away, pretending to search for his watch, perfectly aware that it was already on his wrist. What the hell was the matter with him? Macdara's instructions were quite clear: he was to think of her as a sister. Except, she wasn't his sister, and his thoughts were far from brotherly. With an effort Fergal brought himself under control and with a little cry of surprise pretended to discover the watch already on his wrist. 'What an idiot I am,' he grinned self-deprecatingly. 'Imagine, I was wearing it all along.' He offered Anya his arm, 'Shall we?'

As they reached the door to the suite, it opened as if by magic to reveal a child-sized Arab servant waiting outside who, judging by the maze of wrinkles on his walnut-brown face, might have been aged anywhere between eighty and a hundred. He gave them a toothless smile and gestured for them to follow him, which they did down staircase after staircase, and along what seemed like acres of marble corridor till they reached a majestic set of doors which, upon their approach, again opened seemingly by magic.

'Open sesame!' Fergal whispered, following their diminutive guide into a cathedral-sized ballroom, decorated throughout in white and gold.

'Scary,' Anya whispered back, as they found themselves at the top of a shallow flight of steps and the focus of all the other guests, who were already seated at a formal dining-table marching the centre of the room.

'Welcome! Welcome!' Bowing from the waist, the Sheikh rose to greet them. As was customary in Arab cultures, his greeting was effusive. 'Welcome to my poor house. Please forgive me if it is not all you would have wished.'

Feeling gauche and very much out of her depth, Anya was very glad of Fergal's firm hand on her elbow as he ushered her down the steps to meet their host.

'How lovely to see you again, Sheikh Faisal,' Fergal said smoothly. 'Thank you so much for inviting us to stay in your amazing palace. We are truly honoured.' Having had previous dealings with the Sheikh and others of his ilk, Fergal knew exactly which buttons to press to keep everyone happy. It was a game, but a game he was happy to play in order to smooth the wheels of business.

Playing his part, the Sheikh looked scornfully around. 'A hovel! A stable! I am ashamed. What must you think of me?' He clapped his hand across his breast, sorrowfully.

'No. No,' Fergal protested. 'It is quite stupendous. We are overwhelmed.'

The Sheikh nodded in a way that told Anya that Fergal had got the tone exactly right, and they were at last allowed to take their seat at the table with the other guests.

Anya was seated with Fergal to her right and one of the Russian businessmen to her left. Directly opposite was the actor, who introduced himself as Clive, with an 'of course you know me from the telly' wink. If asked, Anya would have had to admit that she had never seen the man before in her life. The other Russian was seated further along the table, opposite the popstar, a pretty-boy with a hairstyle that defied gravity, whilst the American woman who was in Monique's words, 'big into gee-gees', was seated on Fergal's left, and already whickering into his ear about bloodlines and racing form.

His sharp eyes missing nothing, the Sheikh presided at the head of the table, diametrically opposite his favourite and much younger wife, Somaya, who was as glamorous as any film star. Somaya sent a sweet and friendly smile in Anya's direction, making her feel immediately a little less awkward.

After a brief nod of greeting, the Russian reserved his attention for the extravagant feast laid before them. Anya's eyes roamed over the vast platters of spiced meats, the bowls of stuffed aubergines and artichokes, the artfully arranged golden pyramids of couscous and mountains of warm pitta bread. Little plates of olives, stuffed peppers and vine leaves studded the table like jewels, and Lalique bowls of gold-sprayed lilies paraded regally down the centre.

Being Muslim, the Sheikh and his wife did not drink alcohol, although the foreign guests were presented with a stunning array of exquisite wines, among them Château Margaux and Domaine de la Romanée-Conti of excellent vintage, each one retailing for several thousand pounds. Fergal, who knew a little about wine, decided it was a very good thing that Anya didn't, just in case she would feel it incumbent upon herself to remind the Sheikh about starving children in Africa. His lips twitched at the thought. His own philosophy was that denying himself the rare pleasure of a glass or two of Château Margaux wasn't going to do the little children in Africa one bit of good. Fergal nodded thanks as a servant meticulously topped up his glass before it was quite empty, and then inclined his head towards the American woman. Bunny Bradbury, *not* Bunny Boiler, she had introduced herself as, with something approaching a leer. 'I'm sorry, I didn't quite catch what you were saying.'

The woman smiled, revealing a row of large, unnaturally white teeth. 'I was just inviting you folks to come visit my ranch in Kentucky any old time at all. See what *real* training is all about. *Real* horse flesh.'

'Oh, we do all right in Ireland, thank you.' Fergal mopped up some delectable sauce with a piece of warm pitta bread. 'We've had several big winners over the last year or two, both in Ireland and the UK, and acquit ourselves pretty well across the rest of the world, though unfortunately the Dubai World Cup still eludes us.' He gazed into his glass, reflecting on the prize of $6 million, the largest purse in the world for a horse race. 'As a matter of fact, we have one of the Sheikh's horses in training at Lismore.'

'Yes, Amirah.' The Sheikh, who seemed to be effortlessly fielding several conversations at once, nodded delightedly in their direction. 'She is in good form?'

'Tip-top,' Fergal assured him. 'Macdara's delighted with her progress. You've got a real chance there. I wouldn't be surprised if she shows all the other horses a clean pair of heels.'

'Most gratifying.' Content, the Sheikh sat back, his glance bouncing now appreciatively from Anya to his wife and back again. Such white skin the Irish girl had. Such green eyes. Such red hair, as if it had caught the dying sun in its strands and held it prisoner there.

'I take it you've come here for the sales?' Bunny raised an over-plucked eyebrow in Fergal's direction.

'Indeed. And you?'

She nodded. 'Got my eye on a real beauty.' Deliberately, she stroked the stem of her wine glass, ran her tongue over lips too full to be entirely natural. 'And I'm gonna get him!'

Anya, unused to seeing an openly predatory woman in action, translated the 'him' to 'you', as in 'I want you, Fergal, and I'm gonna get you, no matter what the cost'. Taken aback, Anya took a long swallow of delicious wine, though her enjoyment of it was some-what marred by the other woman's vivaciousness, which left her feeling dull as a little brown sparrow. It was easy to believe that Bunny, with her golden tan, tumbling blond locks and long, thor-oughbred limbs, could get any man she set her sights on. She was dazzling, brimful of the self-confidence Anya lacked.

Bunny, Fergal thought meanwhile, was about as real as Barbie, and most definitely not his type. Too fake-baked, too plastic, too over-the-top. But the Kentucky woman certainly knew her horse-flesh, and he was enjoying their well-informed chat. It didn't take long to surmise that Bunny was, most probably, his main competi-tion for the purchase of Persian Prince. And although she looked as if she had major bucks behind her, Fergal couldn't help but think that forewarned is forearmed. As he nodded at this thought, a serv-ant materialised immediately beside him, bottle in hand. Fergal beamed and held his glass out for another expensive top-up.

Feeling unsure and unable to compete with the predatory Bunny, Anya made small talk with the other guests, whilst hoping fer-vently the dinner would not turn out to be one of the marathons of which Monique had spoken. She was picking desultorily at a fresh fig marinated in an orange and mango sauce and sprinkled with edible gold dust, when her ears pricked up in sudden horror.

The Sheikh was on his feet, lofting a glass in her direction.

'Ladies and gentlemen, I would ask you please to raise your glasses in a toast to my young, newly married friends, Fergal and Anya. May Allah shower you both with his blessings.'

Anya wanted nothing more at that point than to slide under the table as the other guests smilingly held up their glasses and echoed the Sheikh. Helplessly, her eye caught Fergal's, but he was nodding his thanks at both the Sheikh and the guests, playing his role of newly-wed to perfection. She almost cried with relief when the voices died away and the guests returned to their various conversations. After that, the meal seemed to drag on inexorably.

Anya almost sighed with relief when Fergal eventually caught her by the hand and drew her gently to her feet. He glanced at their host and grinned bashfully.

'Time my wife and I retired, I think, as it's been a long day. Thank you, Sheikh Faisal, for a truly memorable dinner.' Fergal gave a small bow round the table. 'Ladies and gentlemen, enjoy the rest of your evening.'

Fergal fought to suppress a chuckle when, on the way back to their suite, Anya gave vent to her dismay, the words tripping over themselves in her haste to get them out.

'That was horrible, Fergal. Awful. We should have come clean. It's wrong to mislead people like that. Imagine what they'd think of us if they knew the truth.' She stopped for a moment to take off her shoes which were pinching like mad. Clutching them by the straps, she quickened her pace, eager to put as much distance between herself and the banquet room as possible.

'Oh, don't take it so seriously,' Fergal said. 'Think of the good story it will make when we're back home in rainy Ireland.'

'Good story nothing!' Anya stamped her foot and immediately regretted it as the blister on her heel protested against such rough treatment. Fergal shrugged. 'Look, if it makes you feel better, I'll go and have a discreet word in the Sheikh's ear. Or, maybe we can make our excuses and leave early.'

'No. No.' Anya waved the idea away. 'That would be like throwing his hospitality back in his face.'

Fergal tucked Anya's arm in his. 'Right. So let's just make the most of our time here.' He yawned, obviously. 'Now, come along. Time to face the Berlin Wall.'

And now that they were finally in bed, they were each acutely conscious of the other, as well as the flimsy wall of cushions separating them. They listened, ears cocked, to each other's every breath, slightest movement, flicker of an eyelash.

For her part, Anya longed for the confidence of the Orlas, Bunnys and Moniques of the world, who would, she thought, simply reach out and grasp what they wanted. They were, after all, the beauty queens Janis Ian had written about in her rite of passage song 'At Seventeen.' Golden girls, one and all, born with a sense of entitlement. And just for one night Anya longed to be like them. She yearned to kick down the cushions, lean across and ask Fergal what the hell he was waiting for. But Anya knew that she could *never* be like them. She was small-town, not cosmopolitan; gauche, not sophisticated; and a downright idiot for dreaming, even for one second, that she could be anything other than the country Irish girl that she was.

Miserable she rolled onto first one side, then the other, wondering what Lady Kathleen might have to say about the matter. Here Anya was in the textbook perfect romantic setting, the man of her dreams no more than a satin cushion away. Yet he might as well have been on the opposite side of the world. Anya squeezed her eyes tightly shut and willed sleep to come in the way it had so easily to Fergal.

Fergal was wide awake too, plagued by the thoughts of Anya, so close and yet so far. Every now and then he caught a waft of her perfume, the stuff she had raved over in the bathroom, something light, tangy, grapefruity. He wasn't one for describing smells, but he did know it was sending his libido into orbit. The mattress dipped slightly as she shifted position, her breathing deep and regular, sleeping the sleep of the innocent. Fergal's eyes sought out the moon, peering like a Peeping Tom through the window. If only he had been brave enough to take full advantage of their beautiful surroundings, and had made it a romantic night to remember.

But he couldn't lose sight of the fact that Anya was like one of the shyer ponies at Lismore, in need of lots of patience, gentle coaxing and sugar lumps before she would ever give her trust. She wasn't the throw-it-all-to-the-wind and seize the moment type. She was an old-fashioned girl, really, the marrying kind, as Bridie would have put it when she used to lecture him in his days as a hormonal adolescent, 'Some girls do, Fergal, as that old song goes, and some girls don't. Just be careful not to get them mixed up, that's all.' It had been good advice and though he was no saint and had had a few dalliances – another of Bridie's words – over the years, he had always been careful not to string anyone along or to take unfair advantage. And he was damned if he was going to be so crass as to break that rule now, especially with someone as vulnerable as Anya.

Still, as his body insisted on reminding him, he was a man, with a man's urges. In a bid to oust his sleeping companion from his mind, he thought of pretty Monique in her French maid's uniform – but a moment later he was transfixed once more by the memory of Anya adjusting his bow tie, her serious green eyes on a level with his chin, leaning slightly forward so that her hair brushed soft as a whisper against his lips. Soft as a kiss. Exasperated, he threw off the covers, dressed quickly and, careful not to wake Anya, tiptoed out the door.

Anya heard the door close, then gave way to bitter tears. She felt such a failure.

Feeling oddly adrift, Fergal walked through the jasmine-scented pagoda garden, trying without success to make sense of his thoughts. Wind-chimes harmonised sweetly with the low warbling of a nightjar performing solo in a mango tree. He paused on an ornamental bridge straddling a small stream and gazed thoughtfully in at the drowned reflection of the moon on the water. He placed his hand on his forehead searching for signs of a fever, something that would rationally explain why he suddenly felt the urge to re-evaluate his life and where it was going.

Turning away, he trudged on past a pair of Japanese dragons, whose stone faces seemed to snarl at him in contempt. Feeling slightly foolish, he flipped them an 'up yours', walked on a little further, then sank down on a low wooden bench, oblivious to the now-you-see-me, now-you-don't glow of a cigarette tip nearby.

Half-hidden behind a Japanese frangipani bush, Monique drew a final time on her cigarette, before grinding it out beneath the heel of her shoe. Dear, oh dear, all did not appear well in the land of the beautiful couple, Anya and Fergal. She debated with herself, but only for a moment. It had been a long time since she had found herself attracted to a man, but Fergal Fitzgerald was definitely a bit special. It didn't faze her that he was newly married. Any scruples she might have had once were now long lost in the mists of time, which is what came of selling your body in low-budget porn flicks or to well-heeled business men around the world. Her life up to now had been no bed of roses. Who could blame her if she took her pleasure where she found it?

The decision made, Monique stepped out into the moonlight, her hair loose about her shoulders, her button-through gown diaphanous. Without speaking a word, she undid the buttons slowly, one by one, shrugged off the gown and stood naked before Fergal, the material spread out at her feet like a pool of mercury. Inviting, she held out her arms.

Savagely, Anya swiped her tears away, angry at her inability to do other than play the victim. But, she realised, to play this passive role in her own life was to give Fat Ted and the succession of men who came after him the power to keep on abusing her. It was allowing them to dictate her life and her happiness, to keep her caged in the mind of her five-year-old self. To remain forever the disenfranchised keeper of secrets never to be told.

No more! Tonight, vowed Anya, the spectre of Fat Ted hanging over her was going to be buried once and for all. Tonight she would reclaim her life – all of it – mind, body, and her sexuality. She was going to take control; and Fergal, wonderful, gorgeous, amazing Fergal, was going to help her.

With a new-found determination, Anya swung her legs over the side of the bed and reached for her dressing-gown and slippers, so fired up that she was anxious not to waste one more second. So what if she bumped into anyone and they thought she was crazy, a mad, red-eyed woman in rumpled nightclothes, with hair like a bird's nest. Her slippers slapped against the marble flooring as she walked. In the distance, a staccato burst of female laughter followed by a rough male guffaw signalled that dinner was still under way in the banqueting hall. Pausing for a moment, Anya cocked an ear towards the racket, wondering if Fergal might have returned there. But Fergal was a man of the soil and far more likely to be found communing with Mother Nature.

After one or two false turns, Anya found the great doors that led to the gardens outside. A servant, too used to the vagaries of the Sheikh's guests to show any surprise, smoothly undid the bolts to allow her through.

'Excuse me.' Half-in, half-out, Anya faltered a little. 'I wonder if you've seen my husband?' The word lodged painfully in her throat as, even now, she felt it necessary to keep up the pretence. 'Tall. Dark hair. Perhaps you saw us arrive earlier?'

Impassive still, the servant waved a vague hand. 'You will find him where moon meets water. In the Japanese garden.'

Where moon meets water – only someone from the East could get away with that, Anya thought, smiling bland thanks. Pleased that her instincts were correct, she set out for the Japanese garden, only to discover moments later that her instincts had been no more than half-right.

For Fergal had not only found solace in Mother Nature, but also in the slender arms of the beautiful Monique. Unnoticed, except by the nightjar practising its scales in the mango tree, Anya retreated quietly back from whence she had come.

When Fergal eventually returned to their suite, night had paved the way for a taffeta sky of chartreuse yellow and the nightjar had long since fallen silent. Anya, broken-hearted, pretended to be deeply asleep.

# Chapter 24

*The Hell Fire Club*

Kitty's heart was beating fast as she slipped through the doors of the Hell Fire Club where the masked ball was already well under way. Adjusting her black satin eye mask, she sought Liam amongst the mêlée of partygoers thronging the dance floor but, of course, it was impossible to tell who was who beneath the many weird and wonderful disguises. She whisked a glass of champagne from a tray borne aloft by a Harlequin-clad waiter, and waited for Liam to find her instead. Sipping her drink, she let her eyes stray admiringly around the room, which had been turned into a replica of a Doge's palace, undoubtedly at great expense. But, then again, JC's clientele were minted, spoilt 'beautiful people' who expected and got only the best, paying through their surgically enhanced noses for the privilege. Her eyes skittered shyly away from the great tapestries draping the walls, in which all sorts of erotic scenes involving fauns, satyrs and voluptuous naked maidens were being played out. Kitty wasn't a prude; becoming Liam's lover had quickly put paid to any inhibitions she might have had. Still, one didn't like to be caught actively looking. Flambeaux set high into sconces on the walls threw mellow pools of light on to the dancers below, picking out the gold and silver threads in their costumes and setting them a-shimmer like a million fireflies. Gondolas, many with a small cabin known as a *felse*, had been placed at strategic points around the room, and amorous couples were already taking advantage of the privacy the *felse* afforded. Living statues, naked but for a skilful application of marbling on their skin, stood unmoving on plinths set into plaster alcoves, whilst around the edge of the room, a couple of stilt-walkers in full Venetian carnival costume carefully negotiated safe passage. Looking closer, Kitty saw that they were trying hard to avoid a pair of court jester dwarves, who had clearly earmarked them as their next joke.

Kitty finished her drink far more quickly than was wise, and her head spun slightly as she looked about for somewhere to set her glass. She jumped as a sinister figure materialised beside her, then breathed a sigh of relief as she recognised Liam's voice.

'Here, let me,' he said, whipping away her empty glass and replacing it with a full one.

Her fingers trembling slightly with heady excitement, Kitty accepted the glass from his hand. Eschewing the gaudy feathered and spangled creations much in evidence elsewhere, Liam had come dressed as a plague doctor. His mask, covering only half his face, was bone white and featureless, except for two glassed-in eyeholes and an immensely long beak-like nose that threw his mouth and chin into shade. An old-fashioned tri corn hat, Phantom of the Opera cloak and knee breeches finished the ensemble, lending him the menacing air of a Venetian Marquis de Sade.

Amused and pleased by her reaction he threw back his head and laughed.

'Handsome, eh?'

'As if!' Kitty gave a spirited toss of her head, but her fingers still shook a little.

'Ah!' Liam tapped the side of the beaky nose. 'This little fellow is called after the Medico Della Pest, a French doctor who invented it in the belief that it would protect him from the disgusting diseases carried by his filthy plague-ridden patients. A kind of prototype gas mask, I suppose.'

'And did it protect him?' Kitty asked. 'Or did it just frighten his poor patients to death?'

Behind the mask, Liam raised his eyebrows. Really, Pretty Kitty could be quite amusing at times, comical even. It was a shame the flipside was a petulant and demanding child with the power to screw up his nice, shortly to get even nicer, life.

'I don't know,' he told her, 'but his creation at least lives on, and has proved very popular amongst the carnival goers of Venice.' He leaned close to her ear, or as close as the mask would allow. 'Know what, Pretty Kitty, I'd like to fuck you while wearing this get-up.' The idea gave him a real frisson, made him hard beneath his tight satin breeches. It was just as well the cloak covered the evidence.

Predictably, Kitty simpered, a painted-on beauty spot dimpling prettily beneath her own demi-mask. 'Well if you really can't wait, we could always go for a gondola ride.' She gestured to where an inebriated, half-dressed couple were falling out of one of the vessels. No prizes for guessing what they had been up to.

Liam shook his head. 'No, the naughtycal mile club is not for me. Later will have to do.' A commotion on the far side of the room diverted their attention. A stilt walker had divested himself of his stilts and, urged on by the increasingly unruly crowd, was using one as a weapon against his erstwhile dwarf protagonists. The unscheduled entertainment was short-lived, however, as only moments later a posse of burly bouncers ejected them all from the club.

'Never trust a man with a big stick,' Kitty quipped, with a sly glance at Liam.

Liam barked a laugh, glad of the mask concealing his humourless face from view. His eyes slewed away, following a sparkling Snow Queen vision in white, whose face was completely hidden behind a doll-like Columbine mask. Orla, without shadow of a doubt and, beside her, JC, regally clad in cloth of gold, but sans mask. But, then again, a mask wasn't necessary. JC's own expression was habitually inscrutable, his thoughts and feelings well hidden behind his almost impossibly handsome exterior. There was something between the pair, Liam suspected, some skulduggery, and he doubted it was something as simple as plain animal lust. It took one to know one and JC Ormond was a cold bastard. Narrow-eyed behind the glass sockets of his mask, Liam followed their progress across the room and watched with interest as they climbed aboard one of the gondolas. What he would give to be a fly on the wall of that *felse*.

'Dance with me, Liam,' Kitty begged, tugging at his hand as the live band of minstrels struck up Flogging Molly's 'If I Ever Leave This World Alive'. Without a shred of either conscience or remorse at what he had planned for later, Liam led his young lover out on to the dance floor.

Settling herself in the gondola, Orla arranged her skirts around her on a velvet-covered banquette and patted the seat invitingly. 'God, what a relief it is to take five. This place is worse than Bedlam.'

'Which is as it should be, since it's bringing the pesetas rolling in,' JC said, taking a seat beside her. He reached across and pulled a heavily embroidered curtain across the entrance to the *felse*, and turned to Orla, his expression slightly accusatory. 'Which is more than you're doing. I can't help but wonder if, despite our recent conversation, you've gone cold on our little plan. Have you, Orla dear?'

'No, I have not!' Orla slipped off her mask and glared at him. 'I haven't gone cold on anything. Macdara threw me a curve ball with the whole Fergal thing, that's all. Never in a million years did I think he would hand over his precious estate to someone who wasn't a blood relative, or with such unseemly haste as he's told me the paperwork is already under way.' She spun the mask on its elastic tie, screwing her lips up in disgust. 'Christ! It doesn't half piss me off to think of how he used to bore us all rigid with derring-do tales of the illustrious Fitzgeralds. Yet, when push comes to shove, he blithely decides to forget all that and throw *my* inheritance away on some smooth-talking blow-in, whose own family disowned him.'

JC made a gesture of impatience. 'Yes. Yes. We've already discussed how unfair it is. But what are you doing about it, that's the question? Those wheels you were telling me about, have they been set in motion yet?' He took hold of her hand, squeezed her fingers almost to the point of bruising them. 'Need I remind you that time is of the essence. I need that money. Like yesterday.'

Orla snatched her hand back, nursed her crushed fingers. 'Have some patience, will you? I'm working on it. You know, behind the scenes. Drip. Drip. Drip, pouring poison into Macdara's ears. Take it from me, cousin Fergal will soon be as good as dead.'

'Dead is good,' JC said. He leaned forward and dropped a light kiss on her angry mouth. 'But buried is even better. And the sooner, the better.'

Annoyed still, her fingers stinging, Orla narrowed her eyes. 'What's that expression, you know the one about the female of the species being more deadly than the male. Well, it's a damn shame more men don't remember that.'

JC's expression darkened. 'Are you threatening me, Orla?' he asked silkily, though he was perfectly certain that he himself had nothing to fear, and especially from someone as stupidly naive as his fiancée. It still amazed him how easy it had been to spin his web and snare her in its silky but deadly net, to bend her to his will even after so many years spent on different continents without so much as a phone call or email between them in all that time. JC let his mind drift back to the very start of the plan, feeling once more the all-consuming anger, the disbelieving sense of powerlessness, the shame and humiliation heaped upon him when his father had dispossessed him in favour of his worthless uncle. As if he would simply walk away, turn like a cowardly dog kicked once too often, and slink away tail between legs into the night. The sky would fall down first.

'I was talking about Fergal.' Seeing the barely suppressed rage kindle in JC's eyes, Orla was almost panicked in her denial. 'I've worked out a way of dropping him in the shit. It still needs a bit of fine tuning but, believe me, if all goes according to plan, Macdara will kick his adopted grandson's butt from here to eternity.'

JC mulled over what Orla was saying. 'Well, go to it, my dear. Fine-tune, and perfect.'

'Twiddle. Twiddle,' Orla grinned. She mimed turning a dial. 'What's that? I'm picking up the Lismore frequency. Coming in now, loud and clear.' She bent forward. 'Now, my darling, how about a kiss to seal the deal?'

Lismore, salvation of his ranch, the ranch at the end of the world. JC tried not to show his repulsion as her greedy, seeking tongue curled itself round his and she placed his hand upon her breast, her nipple immediately hardening to his touch. How much longer, he wondered, could he put up with this?

'Liam, I'd know that nose anywhere,' the normally humourless JC joked as Liam came up and asked for a word. Excusing himself to Orla, he led the way to his office, glad-handing the punters en route. 'I am very glad to see you're not with that Lismore stable girl tonight.'

'I told you, JC, that's dead in the water.' Apt choice of words. 'Kitty was never more than an opportunity that presented itself one night when the missus was away.'

'I'm pleased to hear it,' JC said, closing the door behind them and taking up his usual position behind his big penis-extension desk, as Liam had come to think of it. JC steepled his hands and leant slightly forward. 'What is on your mind?'

'The stuff,' Liam said. 'It's getting harder to find a regular, reliable supplier. It means me having to put my ass on the line more and more. I'm putting myself in danger.'

'And for this you want a bigger cut? Is that what you're trying to say?' JC leapt up suddenly, half-lunged across the desk towards Liam, his eyes sparking with sudden rage. 'You want my balls! I warn you, Liam. Don't get too greedy. There are others only too happy to take your place.'

'None like me.' Liam's voice rose. 'Hey, come on, JC. I've always been straight with you, haven't I?'

'As a corkscrew is straight.' JC sat back down, his glance roving distastefully over the man opposite. 'Think carefully, my friend. Do not rock the boat unless you are a very good swimmer.'

'It was just a thought, that's all. No offence intended. Mates still?' Liam leaned across to spud JC, then dropped his fist, as the other man made no attempt to complete the gesture. Scowling, JC pointed towards the door.

'Go home, Liam. Fuck off out of here. Now! And the next time I see you, we'll pretend this conversation never happened, eh?'

Liam made no reply, just stood up and retrieved his mask from where he had laid it on the desk. But as he turned away from JC and towards the door, he was smiling. Mission accomplished. He had got what he wanted from the Argentinian prick, and it was something more important than JC could ever guess – an alibi. Should the police roll up asking questions about Kitty, he could testify to this conversation and the fact that JC had sent him home long before the stupid cow came to grief. It was just a precaution, just common sense, a way of covering his arse in case Kitty had blabbed about going to the masked ball and, somehow, his name got bandied about in the mix.

Kitty was tipsy, quite drunk in fact, as over an hour later she made her way down to Wishbone Lake and the surprise Liam promised was awaiting her there.

'You leave here at midnight,' Liam had instructed much earlier in the evening. 'I've got business to discuss with JC, and then I'll meet you there. Besides, we can't take the risk of anyone seeing us together, even if we are in disguise. Remember, Kitty, discretion at all times.'

Swaying from side to side, she giggled as the branches bordering the path down to the lake lunged at the voluminous skirt of her gown as though trying to rip it from her body. Her high heels drilled holes in the muddy ground, threatening to send her arse over tit more than once as they got stuck. Arse over tit! She giggled aloud at the expression, one of Liam's. Lord, he was so funny and she was so lucky. She couldn't wait for the surprise, whatever it was.

Behind her the music from the Hell Fire Club grew fainter, while the curtains of night thickened to ebony, concealing her in their folds. A fox barked somewhere, answered crossly a split second later by his own echo. Something crashed nearby in the undergrowth and moments later Kitty caught the flash of two green eyes peering at her from a bush. Unfazed, she lurched on. A country girl born and bred, it took more than things going bump in the night to scare Kitty, especially when her senses were already dulled by a surfeit of cocktails and champagne.

By the time Liam found her, Kitty was sitting on a large flat rock by the edge of the lake, dabbling her bare toes in the water. She had taken off her dress and under garments and was completely nude. Her hair, free from all constraining hairgrips, rippled loosely around her shoulders. Wanton and sexy, she looked like an erotic version of the little mermaid of Copenhagen. Liam stood and watched her for a moment, feeling himself grow hard as her hand came up and played absently with her breast. But sex couldn't be any part of the plan. There must be no evidence when Kitty was found, no tell-tale particle of DNA that might point the finger in his direction. Forensic science was so advanced these days that even immersion in water was no guarantee that the white-coated nerds wouldn't turn up something. Narrowed-eyed, Liam watched her a moment longer, his mouth curving in a cruel smile.

'Aaagh! Liam! You startled me.' She spun round suddenly as his footfall sounded behind her, then leapt to her feet and threw her arms around his neck.

'Kitty, you'll catch pneumonia,' he warned, firmly disentangling himself from her grasp. 'Put your clothes back on, there's a good girl.'

Hands on hips, she adopted a brazen top-shelf stance. 'But aren't you going to warm me up first?'

'All in good time, sweetheart,' Liam promised. 'All in good time. Now, how about I give you your surprise?'

Kitty clapped her hands, a reverberation of the little girl she had been not too many years before. 'My surprise. Ooh, yes please! What is it? A ring? Is it a ring, Liam?'

In the moonlight, Liam looked handsome. Handsome and mysterious. 'Maybe,' he teased. 'But first, look what I made earlier.' Moving away a short distance, he pulled a wicker work picnic hamper out from behind a bush.

Kitty squealed with excitement. 'A picnic! A midnight feast. Liam that's so romantic!' Hurriedly, she put on her clothing as he unpacked the basket, carefully arranging the contents on to a white linen cloth. Blinis with caviar, chocolate-covered strawberries, a magnum of champagne he waved in the air.

'Look, Kitty, Cristal! Only the best for my fiancée. Special edition too.' This meant laced with ketamine. When, or if, her body was found it would look like she'd suffered an accident whilst under the influence of drugs and alcohol. Liam congratulated himself on the simplicity of his plan. After tonight Kitty would get to take her place on the roll call of tragic statistics.

There was a horrible moment as Kitty seemed belatedly attacked by conscience, and it looked like his plans might fall at the final hurdle. Waving the bottle away, she said, 'Oh dear, I'd better not. I've been drinking all night and I shouldn't really. It's not good for the baby.'

Fuck the baby. There was going to *be* no baby! Liam strove to keep the irritation out of his voice. 'Don't spoil the night, Kitty-kat,' he cajoled. 'You can go on the wagon tomorrow. Another one or two won't hurt at this stage.' He hoisted a big smile on his face. 'And later we can get down to the real business of the evening. Bet you've never done it wearing nothing but a diamond ring. Let's drink a toast to us first.'

At the mention of the ring, Kitty's conscience fled. 'Oh, Liam, I do love you.' He filled her glass right to the top and watched her drink. 'You, me and Junior are going to be the happiest family that ever lived,' she said.

'Oh, to be sure,' Liam said drily, 'the Waltons in miniature.' Picking up a chocolate-covered strawberry – a nice touch that; women went mad for them – he popped it into his mouth and leaned back on one elbow.

Kitty pointed to the sky. 'Look, a shooting star. The angels are putting on a fireworks display, just for us.' She wriggled her way into his arms. 'You know, I could die happy, now.' With a dramatic sigh, she raised the poisoned chalice to her lips once more.

'Good,' Liam said soothingly, hypnotically stroking the bare skin of her arm. 'That's very good, Kitty.' Mentally, he began the countdown from a hundred. At twenty-two, her slight frame went limp in his arms.

Checking that the coast was clear, he lifted her up as though she weighed nothing, waded out to where the water was waist high and dropped her. It was a shame, but it had to be done. Pretty Kitty had become a walking liability.

# Chapter 25

Kitty had been missing for several days and concern was mounting for her safety. When she failed to arrive home or even to call, her anxious parents turned up at Lismore to find Macdara equally perplexed. Kitty adored her job and on the very rare occasions she had been ill or unable to attend work for some other reason, she had always made sure to telephone first thing in the morning. It was completely out of character, everyone agreed, for her simply to disappear without a word to anyone. Distraught, her parents called in the *gardaí*. Once satisfied she had taken nothing from home, such as clothes or passport, and that no activity had taken place on her bank accounts during the period of her absence, the *gardaí* instigated a full-scale search of Lismore, Castle Mac Tíre and the surrounding areas. Posters were put up in the local towns and villages. The press and media were alerted. White-faced and fatigued to death, her parents made a personal plea on television. But of Kitty, there remained no sign.

Assisted by a group of local volunteers, among them Kitty's co-workers at Lismore, the guards performed an intensive sweep of the area, beating with sticks in the hedgerows, peering half-fearfully, half-hopefully beneath bushes and into ditches, searching every inch of the pine forest, as well as the slopes of Slievenamon. Soon there remained only one place left to search, Wishbone Lake.

'It doesn't look good,' Macdara observed to Liam, as they stood side by side, watching the divers suit-up. 'Kitty isn't the type simply to take off with a boyfriend or something. She's got a good head on her shoulders. I've got a horrible feeling this will all end badly.'

'Ah, I wouldn't write her off just yet,' Liam was dismissive. 'She wouldn't be the first young girl to vanish, and then turn up several months later large as life and with a babby under her arm.'

'Not Kitty,' Macdara said with certainty. 'I'm telling you. I don't like it, Liam. I don't like it one little bit.'

'Should we come home?' Fergal asked, when Macdara phoned with the news. 'I don't like staying on here in the lap of luxury, knowing poor Kitty is missing, not while I could be out helping to look for her.'

'Me too.' Frantically, Anya conveyed her own feelings, signing at him to pass them on to Macdara.

'No point,' Macdara told him honestly. 'Everything that can be done, is being done. You and Anya might as well stay where you are. There's more than enough people looking for her as it is.' He cleared his throat. 'They've begun to dive Wishbone Lake. Nothing so far, thank God, though it will take a few days to be certain.'

'Thank God is right,' Fergal said. 'And I assume they've questioned everyone about her movements.'

'Everyone,' Macdara confirmed.

'Including O'Hanlon,' Fergal pressed. He cleared his own throat. 'You do know, Mac, that there were rumours about the two of them. Liam and Kitty. I wouldn't trust that sod as far as I could throw him. I know for a fact he gave his wife a black eye one time.'

'Including Liam,' Macdara told him. 'And, to be fair, Fergal, I know you don't like the man, but that doesn't mean he's capable of murder. There's a helluva jump between dishing out a black eye and killing a young girl. Not,' he added hastily, 'that I condone either.'

'I know,' Fergal said. 'It was just a thought. You will keep us posted, won't you?' He rang off as Macdara assured him he'd be on the phone at the first hint of any news.

'Poor Kitty.' Anya stared glumly at the floor, tears gathering in her eyes. 'I wonder what's happened to her. God, I hope she's all right.'

'So do I.' Fergal walked across to the window of their suite and peered grimly out. 'I've got a bad feeling, though, Anya. People don't just disappear into thin air. Not people like Kitty with a solid family background and people who care about her. There's nothing dysfunctional in her background that I know of. Her parents worship the ground she walks on, and she always speaks highly of them. She loves her job. She's popular. Why would she just run off? It doesn't make sense.'

Anya shrugged. Suddenly her own troubles seemed very small by comparison. 'I think we should go home, Fergal,' she said, her lower lip trembling. 'There must be something we can do.'

Fergal shook his head. 'No, Mac is right. There's no point in everybody running round like headless chickens. If we can be of any use, he'll let us know. In the meantime, we should at least make sure that this has not been an entirely wasted trip.'

Anya nodded, but her eyes were wet as she started to pack her bags in readiness for their move to a hotel the following day. Poor Kitty. A vision of her in her scarlet swimsuit on the day they'd been swimming the horses at Wishbone Lake came to mind. Anya wondered whether to mention the odd look she'd seen on Liam's face as he looked at her, but thought better of it. It was, after all, just that, a look. It could have meant something or nothing at all.

Bags packed, she went for a final walk round the palace to try and compose herself. She paused in the art gallery in front of what had become her favourite painting, Goya's portrait of the actress Antonia Zárate. The woman had such expressive eyes. Such sad eyes. Anya recalled seeing the painting once before in the National Art Gallery in Dublin, and now it had somehow found its way into the Sheikh's private collection, where only a privileged few would get to enjoy it.

'That's my favourite painting too.' Quietly, Monique had come to stand beside her. 'She looks like she's in mourning, with her black lace mantilla and gown. Mourning her lost love, do you think?'

Anya wondered if the other girl was sniping at her with regard to Fergal, but Monique's face showed nothing but real interest in the painting.

'Possibly,' Anya conceded. 'Or perhaps she's just reflecting on life in general, or listening to a perfect piece of music played on a piano just out of sight. Beethoven, maybe. "Moonlight Sonata".'

'Maybe,' Monique said and grinned. 'You really are a dewy-eyed romantic, aren't you?' Her expression changed from warmth to something more complex. 'That's not always a good thing, you know. Romanticism is all very well and good, so long as it's backed by a good old dose of reality.'

Anya turned and looked at Monique face to face. She was off-duty and dressed in a simple shift. Her face was without its usual coating of thick make-up, making her look considerably younger, and plainer too.

'Too much romanticism means you leave yourself wide open to being hurt,' Monique said, sounding as if she knew what she was talking about. She walked over to a cream leather, button-backed settee opposite the painting and sat down. She patted the seat next to her invitingly. 'You know, Anya, you're very nice, but you're very innocent too. The sooner you realise that all men are dogs, the better.'

'I don't think I ever want to be that cynical. Besides I saw you with Fergal,' Anya said. But she went to sit by Monique, albeit a little reluctantly. Ever since the incident she had seen in the Japanese Garden, Anya had found it increasingly difficult to be around Monique and so had given her as little as possible to do.

And yet the reality was that Fergal and Monique actually hadn't done anything wrong. Fergal was free to do as he wished, as was Monique.

Still, a little voice insisted Monique hadn't known that. So much then for female solidarity. Monique had been totally pre-pared to sell Anya down the river and that Anya found very hard to forgive.

Oblivious to the increasing tension in Anya's body, Monique continued, 'Oh, I was like you once, wide-eyed and innocent, will-ing to look for the best in everybody.'

'But?' Anya prompted, as Monique drew to a halt, seeming dis-inclined to go on.

'But life,' Monique said simply after a moment. 'Life and reality woke me up to myself. Especially the reality of how men really think.' She stretched her hands high above her head, linked her fingers together. 'I'm so tired of it all.'

She stood up suddenly, shook herself as if physically casting off her gloom and pulled Anya to her feet. 'Hey, come to my room. You're off tomorrow, aren't you? Come and have a farewell drink with me.'

Sudden naked loneliness flashed across the other girl's face, and so Anya hesitated from walking away from her. She had spent such hours torturing herself with images of Fergal and Monique lying coiled together in naked intimacy, that it was difficult to see her other than in the light of someone who had betrayed her.

Monique misread the hesitancy. 'I see,' she said. 'You're worried about consorting with the help, is that it?'

The help! Lord, that stirred some memories. Monique couldn't have hit on a word more guaranteed to change Anya's mind, since she had no difficulty at all in remembering how small and insignificant she had felt in the bad old days when Orla had led her to believe that to Fergal, *she* was merely the help.

'Not at all,' Anya said hastily. 'It's just that I've been gone some time. Fergal will be wondering where I've got to.'

'No bad thing,' Monique replied brusquely. 'You're your own woman. It won't hurt him to know that.'

Anya gazed at her curiously. Was that anger in her voice and, if so, who was it directed at: men in general or, specifically, Fergal? A glimmer of hope fanned suddenly like a small candle in Anya's heart. Perhaps Monique's stolen night of passion had not gone entirely to plan.

Monique's room was squirrelled away at the top of the palace. Although pleasant, it was a far cry from the honeymoon suite Anya and Fergal had been allocated, being furnished simply with a single bed, a narrow settee, a small fridge, and not much else. The one window overlooked a view of the kitchen garden. It was partially open, allowing a pleasant breeze into the otherwise stifling room. In an effort to make it more homely, Monique had added some scatter cushions and a pretty Kelim-type throw. A vase of flowers stood on the windowsill and she had made several collages of photographs to take the bare look off the walls.

Anya looked around. 'This is nice,' she said, bending to smell the flowers. 'And these are lovely. Anemones, aren't they?'

Monique went to the fridge, took out a bottle of water and poured them each a glass. She waved Anya onto the settee and handed her one of the glasses.

'Not exactly the Ritz, though, is it? Or the honeymoon suite.' As Anya looked away, embarrassed, Monique smiled. 'Actually, this place is luxury compared to some of the dives I've lived and worked in. In comparison to some of my previous incarnations, being the hired help is no bad thing. At least it's respectable work.' She got up and pulled a photograph off the wall and handed it to Anya. 'Me, in a former life, dancing naked with a python around my neck. *That* was one of my better jobs.' She sighed and pinned it back up again. 'To be truthful, there's not much I haven't done in the past to earn a crust, but finally I have the chance to make something of myself.'

As Anya looked surprised, she shook her head. 'Oh, I don't mean here at the palace. But this job has allowed me to save a bit of money. I'm going home soon, Anya. I'm going back to Australia and I'm going to open my own business. What do you think of that?'

'I think it's wonderful,' Anya said truthfully. She had guessed correctly that Monique had a story to tell, and now she guessed further that still Monique had not divulged the whole, although what she had revealed was bad enough. 'I'm sorry you've had such a hard time of it,' Anya added, unable really to contemplate the kind of life the other girl had led.

'Don't be,' Monique shrugged. 'It's not your fault. And really I should be apologising to you. I shouldn't have targeted Fergal.' Her lips tensed. 'My mother used to say I was born bad. That every family had a bad seed and I was the bad seed in ours.'

'I don't believe that,' Anya brushed the notion aside. 'All babies are born innocent.'

'Maybe,' Monique said mildly, going over to another collage on the wall and scrutinising it closely. 'But a lot of people share the belief. Her, for instance.' She unpinned a photograph from the mix and handed it to Anya, stabbing with her forefinger at a picture of a lithe blonde woman, pole-dancing for a group of men. 'She was the bad seed in hers although I forget why. But that girl was seriously messed up. Made me look like a model of sanity. She had a sister too, as I recall. A serious junkie. All dead now, I expect.'

Anya gave the picture a cursory glance and then, visibly startled, examined it more closely. 'Good lord, I think I know her,' she said, a frown gathering between her eyes. 'Isn't that Orla Fitzgerald? No, not Fitzgerald.' Anya screwed up her forehead in an effort to remember, but drew a blank. She wasn't sure, in fact, if she had ever known Nessa's married name.

Monique pinned the photograph back in place. She shook her head. 'Not Orla, definitely not. Some other odd name though. And we rarely traded surnames. In the transitory world I lived in back then, no one bothered with surnames. Nobody cared that much. I'm lucky I managed to escape before it completely destroyed me.' Monique stretched out a hand, laid it softly on Anya's arm. 'Listen, I really am sorry about Fergal. Sometimes, I look at girls like you, ordinary girls with ordinary lives, and I wish I could have a piece of that. A man who would love me for more than the few minutes it takes for him to have his end away. Babies. A house in the country.'

Anya stood up, touched by Monique's simple wistfulness and the honesty in her eyes.

'Listen, Monique,' she said impulsively. 'If I leave you my telephone number, will you keep in touch with me? I really would like to know how you're getting on.'

'Really?' Monique looked doubtful, and then a genuine smile creased her face. 'You know, you're a funny one. I've no idea why you'd be bothered, but okay, sure. Only now and then, mind. I'm not much good at playing the friendship game, I'm afraid.'

'Good enough,' Anya smiled back, thinking with gratitude of the love of Sister Martha, and how she had rescued Anya from a life that could well have turned out like the Australian girl's. 'There, but for fortune, Anya,' the nun had often pointed out, 'go you or I.' Anya left Monique then and went back to the suite, where she found Fergal pacing up and down like a caged tiger.

'Oh no! Please no!' Anya cried, drawing her own inferences and staggering over to the banquette. 'It's Kitty, isn't it?' She let herself fall heavily on to the seat. 'They've found her. Is she dead?'

'God no!' Fergal hurried over and clasped her hands between his. 'That's just it. They haven't found her. They've been all over Wishbone Lake now, dragged and dived it, and nothing. It's almost as though she's vanished into the ether. No one has seen hide nor hair of her.'

'Well, that's got to be a good thing, hasn't it?' Hope lit up Anya's eyes.

'Yes, of course,' Fergal agreed. 'Until we hear any different, there's always hope.'

The person who wondered most where Kitty had got to was Liam. Where the blue blazes in hell was she? Liam had panicked as the last diving team arrived back empty-handed on the bank of Wishbone Lake. There was no way she could have swum to safety. She was out cold when he dropped her. The pity was he hadn't been able to hang around a while to make sure she didn't surface, for to do so would have meant risking discovery, particularly with people wandering in and out of the Hell Fire Club all night. Other than that, though, he'd made sure of everything, he was certain.

But where on earth was she? What could have happened to her? Had some fucker seen them? Was he gearing up right at this moment for a spot of blackmail? Where had he hidden the body? Like a carousel of crazy horses, the questions to which there appeared to be no answer galloped round and round in Liam's mind. Though it was a cold enough day, one of those rogue late-summer days when the sun was boycotting the sky, Liam felt himself break out in a sweat.

'And you're sure, there's nothing?' Macdara asked the diver in chief. 'Only there are some hidden shelves on which a body might easily get caught up and not be found. I remember them well, from when I used to go swimming as a boy. A couple of small under-water caves too.'

Liam felt hope surge through him at Macdara's words. Of course, that was the simplest and sanest explanation. Kitty was probably caught on a shelf somewhere, weighed down by that big ball-gown of hers. Jesus! The sweat intensified. What an eejit he was not to have destroyed her clothes. When she did turn up, it would take them all of two seconds to figure out that she must have been at the masked ball after all. And though his little altercation with JC had furnished him with something of an alibi, he wasn't entirely convinced that it was anywhere near enough to prevent the finger of suspicion pointing in his direction.

'No. She's not down there, sir,' the diver assured Macdara. 'There's not an inch we haven't been over at least twice, reeds, shelves, caves and all. Wherever that young woman is, she's not in Wishbone Lake. I can assure you of that.'

'Thank God,' Macdara bowed his head in relief. 'But where could she possibly be, then?'

Beside him, Liam silently echoed the question. If Kitty really wasn't in the lake where the hell was she? Somehow he had the feeling he wouldn't much like the answer.

# Chapter 26

*Dubai*

The second week of Anya and Fergal's week in Dubai flew by in a flurry of race meetings and horse auctions. They left the palace and moved to a small but also luxurious hotel, on a palm-lined boulevard, although not before the Sheikh enquired after Lady Kathleen, who was, apparently, an old friend. Anya found it strange that she had never mentioned the fact. Lady Kathleen was normally so forthcoming about name-dropping, as often she cheerfully admitted herself. The rest of the guests had also dispersed about their various businesses, except for Bunny who seemed to be hot on their heels at every auction.

Anya did not see Monique again before they left the palace, although she found time to slip her mobile number under the door of her room and she genuinely hoped the other girl would stay in touch occasionally. Despite Monique's hard shell, Anya sensed in her something of a kindred spirit, a sister-under-the-skin whose life might have taken a different turn had fate and fortune been a little kinder to her. And if Monique had been fortunate enough to have her very own Sister Martha guiding her.

Despite regular bulletins from Lismore, there was no further word regarding Kitty's mysterious disappearance and soon, because there was no evidence either of foul play, the guards seemed more and more inclined to believe that she had simply taken off with a boyfriend and that she would turn up in her own good time.

'I hope they're right,' Anya remarked to Fergal for the thousandth time, as they sat eating dinner on a restaurant veranda overlooking a sapphire-blue infinity pool, round the periphery of which beautiful people strolled like models on a catwalk.

'Me too,' Fergal said, his eyes scanning their surroundings as if Kitty might suddenly appear in front of them. 'And could be they are right, in which case that girl is going to have an awful lot to answer for, especially to her poor parents.'

'But, if they're wrong …' Anya toyed absently with her salad, pushing it round and round her plate. 'Fergal?'

A note of hesitancy in her voice brought his focus sharply to her face. 'What?'

'I can't get Liam O'Hanlon out of my mind, you know, and the rumours about him and Kitty.'

'I don't like him either,' Fergal said. 'But to be fair, he has been questioned. Mac says there's nothing to connect him to Kitty's disappearance at all.'

Still, Anya couldn't forget the dark look he'd bestowed on Kitty the day they were swimming the horses. It disturbed her then and it disturbed her now. Slightly hesitant, because she was aware that Fergal might well accuse her of making a mountain out of a molehill, she told him what she had seen. 'I'll never forget it,' she finished. 'It was, well, so cold. Calculating, almost. I remember wondering if Kitty had done something to piss him off and actually feeling quite frightened for her.'

Fergal speared a piece of fish on the end of his fork, paused with it halfway to his mouth and then put it down untouched. 'Yes, but at the end of the day, it *was* just a look. In real terms it doesn't mean a damn thing. And yet, gut instinct tells me that O'Hanlon is involved. Or maybe it's just that I want him to be the culprit, if culprit there is. But a look, no matter how chilling, simply isn't proof.' He narrowed his eyes. 'That said, when I get back to Lismore, I intend to do some digging. This is about more than just a clash of personalities, him not liking me or me not liking him. O'Hanlon is a thug and I believe he's capable of all sorts.'

'He is.' Giving up all pretence at eating, Anya pushed her plate aside. She took a deep breath, aware that Fergal was looking at her intently. Feeling slightly dizzy at her own daring, or foolishness, she then told him about the awful night when Liam had come into the kitchen and propositioned her. Or, rather, blackmailed her. 'So you see,' she said as she came to the end of the sorry tale, 'I believe you're right. I believe Liam is capable of, well, just about anything.'

'Jesus Christ!' Fergal banged his fork down on the table, eliciting disapproving glances from several other diners nearby. 'The bastard!' His expression was thunderous. 'Why the hell didn't you tell me, Anya? Or Mac? Seriously, do you think so little of yourself that you thought we wouldn't kick his arse from here to kingdom come?'

'I was ashamed,' Anya confessed, her voice very small. 'You don't know my mother, Fergal. She really is the lowest of the low. Pond life. I couldn't even begin to tell you the things she did, both to me, and to others. Her own family disowned her. *I* disowned her.'

'And do you think people would tar you with the same brush?' Fergal reached across the table and took her hand. 'For God's sake, Anya, have a little faith. We know you. We know what you're like. You should have told us what that low-life O'Hanlon was up to.' His face darkened further as a thought struck him. A thought too horrible to contemplate. One that made him want to lash out and start breaking things left, right and centre. 'You didn't, did you? Please, Anya. Please, please, please, tell me that you didn't sleep with him.'

She dipped her chin. 'No. But I'll be honest. I did consider it for all of about five seconds. But he did frighten me, Fergal. Badly.' Her voice trailed off. 'I can feel his eyes on me all the time, boring into me. It's like a nightmare I can't wake up from.'

'He's dead!' Fergal vowed, his stomach turning somersaults at the thoughts of Liam's filthy hands straying anywhere near Anya. She was so pure, so fragile. And most likely a virgin still. Fergal had never seen her, not once, with a boyfriend. 'When I get back to Lismore, he'd better start running, because, if I catch up with him, he'll rue the day he was born.'

'Please no, Fergal,' Anya pleaded. 'He's not the type to be thwarted. He'll carry out his threat to tell my mother where I am. And then my life won't be worth living. I'll have to start running.'

He stared at her for a moment, frustrated almost to the point of bursting. 'Anya, have you not been listening to a word I said?

Do you think Macdara and I are going to let anyone, anyone at all, including your bloody mother, walk casually in and destroy your life? She'll have to go through us first to get to you.'

'She's devious,' Anya warned. 'Totally callous. And she hates me. She tried to kill me once.'

Fergal regarded her steadily. 'There's a lot more to this story, isn't there, Anya?'

'Yes,' Anya said, a shutter coming down over her face. 'But that's all I can tell you right now. I don't like to talk about it. And please don't ask me any more.'

Fergal watched her sip from an ice-cold glass of San Pellegrino, her fingers trembling on the stem of her glass. He wouldn't force her. Besides Macdara was bound to be able to fill in some, if not all, of the blanks. Fergal placed a finger under her chin, tipped it up so that her eyes were on a level with his.

'Okay, that's your right. Just believe me when I say I'm here for you. And I know Mac is as well.'

'Thank you,' she whispered softly, then with a huge effort smiled tremulously. 'Now, let's change the subject, shall we? How high will you go in the bidding on Persian Prince at the auction tomorrow?'

Fergal raised an eyebrow, willing to play along if it made her feel better, but inside he was still seething, still boiling over with fury at Liam. 'Do you mean, is it worth it knowing moneybags Bunny is in the running?' He tapped his nose and grinned. 'Of course, especially since I have a dastardly plan.'

'Oh? And what exactly might that be?' Anya looked intrigued.

'Can't say,' Fergal grinned. 'Might dilute its potency.'

Below, a girl in a black monokini sauntered by, halting for a moment directly in Fergal's line of vision. She flicked him a saucy smile and waggled her fingers in a tiny wave.

'Heavens, you're a quick worker,' Anya said, careful to keep her voice neutral, though inside she felt her stomach begin to tie itself in knots. Since the night she'd seen him in Monique's arms, she'd made herself the subject of a sharp reality check. Fergal wasn't for her. She simply wasn't his type. It wasn't his problem. It was hers! And she vowed to get over it. But, Anya acknowledged to herself, she had loved Fergal for a very long time and he was proving a damn hard habit to break.

'What?' Fergal followed her glance. 'Oh, that's Malika from reception.' He waved back at her. Reluctant to rain on his parade, Anya yawned and stood up. 'Well, I think, I'll have an early night. You have a good evening. Enjoy yourself.' With a twiddle of her own fingers, she left him to the delights of Malika, damned if she was going to be sidelined as yet another woman made a play for him. Maybe one day it wouldn't hurt quite so much, she thought. But that wasn't today. Today it throbbed like an amputated limb.

Fergal sat brooding, replaying their conversation in his mind, growing angrier and angrier as he thought about Liam and his disgusting, low behaviour. From what Fergal had witnessed, Liam had more than enough stupid women offering themselves on a plate to him. Why go after Anya? He gave a mental click of his fingers. Of course, that was exactly why. Anya wasn't available, which made her even more of a prize for scum like Liam, men who revelled in despoiling beauty and innocence.

'Hi, Fergal, mind if I sit down here?'

Fergal gave himself a little shake as Malika, a silk multi coloured sarong draped around her waist, appeared at the table.

He stood up rather abruptly. 'No, not at all. I was just going.' He pointed to an empty chair. 'Please, it's all yours.' Smiling absently, he strolled away, leaving her staring a little open-mouthed after him.

The following morning, the auction was heaving with both buyers and observers. Fergal had been round to the stalls earlier to check out Persian Prince and to watch him being put through his paces in the training ring. He checked him thoroughly for anything that might ring alarm bells, but came away perfectly happy that the horse was just as described, a true thoroughbred with bucketloads of potential. There was no doubt about it, it would be a real coup were Fergal to bring him home to Lismore

'I don't see Bunny anywhere,' Anya observed, searching the crowd for the American woman.

Fergal cleared his throat, looking slightly guilty. 'Er, Bunny might be otherwise engaged.'

'Doing what?' Anya asked surprised. 'She seemed pretty determined to bid for him.'

'Let's just say, she got a better offer.' Fergal couldn't stop the grin from spreading across his face. 'As of now, I'd say Bunny is happily engaged in a different kind of riding, with a good-looking, very accommodating stable lad.'

'Good lord, how on earth do you know that?' Anya eyed him suspiciously.

'Because,' Fergal, confessed, 'I bribed him. Handsomely. After all, all is fair in love and horse dealing.'

'Fergal!' Shocked, Anya smacked his arm, but then a little bubble of merriment rose in her chest and suddenly she was laughing her head off. 'Oh, dear,' she said, when she finally managed to bring herself under control. 'Poor Bunny.'

'Poor? Far from it, I'd say,' Fergal laughed too, completely unrepentant. 'If anything, I'd say she's a very happy bunny indeed.'

The sudden ringing of a bell indicated that the sale was about to start and suddenly there was a crush of people towards the rails, all anxious to get closer to the action. Persian Prince was the sixth horse into the ring.

'He really is beautiful,' Anya remarked, watching the horse being led around by a groom.

'Yes,' Fergal said. 'But you know what they say, beauty is as beauty does. He needs to do more than simply look beautiful. Though from studying his bloodline, I'd say he's in with a better than average chance of being a real winner. Hold up! The bidding is about to begin.'

Tense, Anya watched what seemed like a frenzy of bidding break out, number cards shooting up in the air, bids being taken over the telephone and internet and gradually, one by one, the bidders falling away till only two remained, Fergal and an internet opponent. She closed her eyes, unable to watch, her lips moving in silent prayer till, beside her, Fergal let out a yell of triumph.

'Yes! Yes! Yes!' His fist punched holes in the air.

'Oh, Fergal,' her eyes lit up. 'You did it. You got him.'

'Yes I did, didn't I?' Grabbing her, Fergal kissed Anya full on the lips. Then he looked deep into her eyes, before he pulled her closer and kissed her deeper.

'Oi! You could get arrested for that over here.' They sprang quickly apart as Bunny's braying voice, coming out of nowhere, acted like a shower of cold water.

'Congratulations.' Bunny extended her hand to Fergal. 'I believe you are the new owner of Persian Prince.'

Looking slightly shamefaced, Fergal nodded, but Bunny just laughed. 'Nice one!' She winked. 'In fact, *very* nice one. Next time, though, could you make him blond. And I'd appreciate it if he could speak a couple more phrases in English.' Bunny shrugged her shoulders expressively. Not waiting to hear any more, Anya strode away.

Fergal had kissed her, yes. But already she was convincing herself that it was only because he had got carried away by the excitement of the auction. She mustn't read any more into it than pure spur of the moment exuberance, or expect him to declare undying love for her. She wasn't that much of a fool. But oh! How very sweet it had been, and how her lips still tingled!

Perplexed, Fergal stared after her retreating back..

'There's always me,' Bunny pointed out, not at all perturbed at the idea of being a consolation prize.

# Chapter 27

'I wish you had come home to better news,' Macdara told Anya and Fergal the morning after they returned home. 'The guards have all but given up on finding Kitty.' He spread some marmalade on a piece of toast, then changed his mind about wanting it and pushed his plate to one side. 'Although the rest of us haven't given up hope.'

'I'm not convinced O'Hanlon didn't have something to do with it,' Fergal said, and quickly filled Macdara in about the look Anya had intercepted between Liam and Kitty.

'Truly, Mac,' Anya added, 'it made my blood run cold.'

'Could have been about anything,' Macdara was dismissive. 'Besides, he was questioned like everyone else. The last time Kitty was seen was early on the evening of the masked ball. She told her friend, one of the other stable lasses, that she had a bit of a headache and intended to have an early night. Moaned a bit about how she would have loved to have had an invite to the ball, herself, and about how it was just for the privileged few, it wasn't fair and so on.'

'But Kitty didn't go home,' Fergal guessed. 'So where did her parents think she was?'

'Here,' Macdara said. 'She told them she was working late, possibly staying over. But when she didn't ring, or come home the next day, and there was no reply from her mobile phone, they came over to Lismore to check that everything was all right. That's when all hell broke loose.'

'So it sounds as though Kitty might have had something up her sleeve,' Fergal remarked. 'She lied to her friend and to her parents.

Small wonder the guards might suspect she had orchestrated her own disappearance.'

'I just don't believe it,' Anya shook her head. 'Kitty never struck me as being anything other than a sensible girl. Fairly flighty around men, granted, but that was just her age. It just doesn't make sense that she would up sticks and leave everyone and everything she loves behind.'

'Stranger things have happened,' Macdara said. 'According to the guards, nearly eight thousand people are reported missing in Ireland every year. Most are eventually traced or return of their own volition. Others never return. Of those, it's reckoned only a tiny percentage fall victim to foul play.'

'So it's a waiting game really,' Fergal said. 'My heart bleeds for her parents. They must be going through hell.'

'Yes they must,' Anya agreed sadly.

Macdara pushed his chair away from the table. 'In the meantime, callous though it might seem, life goes on. When you're ready, Fergal, we'll potter on down and have a look at how the horses are doing. Glengarriff, you'll be delighted to hear, is one hundred per cent back on form. When the import papers are through for Persian Prince and we can bring him home, there won't be a stable in the land able to boast the equal of either of them.' Macdara collected his coat from a peg on the back of the door. 'Say what you like, O'Hanlon might be shady, but he's a damn good vet.'

'True,' Fergal said, following him out. 'His only redeeming quality. Still, there's nothing on earth will ever make me like him.' He turned back and a look passed between him and Anya. She flushed slightly and gave a little shake of her head. At her request Fergal had held off regaling Macdara with regard to the vet's sordid attempts at blackmailing her. Macdara had enough on his plate, she reckoned, and she was probably right. And to keep her happy, Fergal had even agreed to postpone beating the bastard to a bloody pulp, though this left a vile taste in his mouth. Postpone being the operative word though. O'Hanlon's day was coming faster than the Derby winner, and Fergal couldn't wait to take him apart at the seams.

As they neared Glengarriff's stable, a wild-eyed, breathless, somewhat dishevelled Orla came running up to them. She pointed urgently behind her.

'Grandy! Fergal! There's a couple of dogs worrying the sheep in the East Meadow. I saw them when I was out for a walk. There's blood all over the place.'

'Jesus!' Fergal shouted, spinning on his heel and making a run for the house. 'I'll get the shotgun. Quick, Mac, start up the Land Rover! It'll be much quicker than going on foot.'

'And you, young lady, go into the house and get Anya to make you a cup of tea. You've had a nasty shock.'

'Oh, Grandy, it really was horrible,' Orla looked sick. 'All that barking and snarling. But will you be okay?'

'I'll be fine. Go on now, Anya will take care of you.' Macdara fished in his pocket for the keys and hurried off towards the vehicle as Fergal, a shotgun broken over his arm, raced full-pelt back out of the house. Tyres spinning, they screeched away.

'You poor thing,' Anya said, setting a cup of steaming, well-sugared, coffee before Orla. 'You've had a nasty shock. Thankfully, that kind of thing doesn't happen that often but, occasionally, a dog will stray and end up in a field of sheep. Bad enough when it's just one. But if there's two or more, you can guarantee it will end up in a blood bath.'

'It was awful,' Orla admitted. 'They were in a complete frenzy. I screamed and threw stones, but they took no notice of me at all. I thought it best then to come back and find Mac and Fergal.'

'And quite right too,' Anya soothed. 'The pack instinct is an awful thing to witness. Even the gentlest family pet can turn savage in those circumstances. And once they get the taste for it, there's nothing for it but to shoot them.' She bent a kindly look on the other girl. 'Now, come on, drink up. It will help steady your nerves.'

Orla shook her head. 'I'm all right. I just hope Mac and Fergal can save those poor animals.'

'They'll have lost a few, that's inevitable, but hopefully most will be fine, thanks to you.' Anya poured herself a mug of coffee and took a seat opposite. 'Anyway, what on earth possessed you to go out walking so early? You're generally more of a night owl than an early bird, aren't you?'

Orla stared thoughtfully into the murky depths of her coffee. 'I just had one of those restless nights where I couldn't sleep.' There were many very good reasons why she couldn't sleep, JC for one, Javier for another, but that was something she could hardly bring herself to think about, let alone share. In fact, she felt like she'd spent so much time lately with her head buried in the sand that she should change her name to ostrich.

'I was actually standing by the window watching the dawn come up, when I realised that I'd never really seen it before, well, not unless I was falling home drunk from a nightclub or party.' She looked slightly awkward, as if caught in the act of some misdemeanour. 'Don't laugh, but suddenly I had an intense urge to be out there, in the open, walking through the fields, brownnosing Mother Nature and all that poppycock.' She rolled her eyes. 'Must be something in the water at Lismore. A surfeit of hayseeds, maybe. Anyway,' she said brightly, uncomfortable with the direction her thoughts were taking, 'let's change the subject. How did you like Dubai? And,' Orla gave a coy wink, 'more importantly, did anything happen with Fergal?'

'Dubai was fine,' Anya said, happy to change the subject if it helped calm her down. 'Although, it's a bit of a fur coat, no knickers society. You know, gold and glitz on the outside, grime and poverty beneath.' She stirred the liquid in her mug. 'As for Fergal, you surely didn't expect anything to happen there, did you?' Anya regarded her coolly. '*Not* with the hired help.'

Orla's eyes slithered away, as good an admission as any of her guilt. Although the timing could have been better, Anya decided to call her on it while the opportunity presented itself.

'Of course, Fergal never said that at all, did he, Orla? So why? Why would you tell me that?'

For a moment, Orla looked as though she might deny it, then her mouth twisted. She leaned across the table and said roughly, 'You want to know why? I'll tell you why. It's because I'm sick to the stomach of girls like you always getting what they want. Mealy mouthed do-gooders, fucking Pollyannas still sucking on the silver spoon you were born with.' She hammered her hand against her heart. 'I'm fed up with always getting the raw deal, being lied to and conned, having to fight tooth and nail for every blessed thing I get.' Ablaze with challenge, she glared at Anya. 'So, yeah, I threw a spanner in your works but, you know what, it damn well serves you right. If you were woman enough, you would have had Fergal long ago. You had every opportunity and so, to my mind, you don't deserve him.'

'And you do, I suppose?' Anya returned her glare in full measure.

'Fuck Fergal!' Orla snapped her fingers. 'Believe me, if I wanted him, I could have him. Easy as that!'

Anya made to retort, but broke off as suddenly tears began to cascade down Orla's face. Covering her eyes with her hands, she rocked backwards and forwards. Anya rose and came round the table. Bewildered, she put a tentative hand on the other girl's shoulder. Orla shrugged her away.

'Leave me. I'm all right.'

'Clearly you're not,' Anya said, but withdrew her hand all the same. 'Look, what's the matter? Is there anything I can do?'

Perplexed, Orla shook her head. 'Jesus, Anya, do you never get tired of playing the Good fucking Samaritan? Don't you ever feel like letting loose or hitting back?' She pushed her chair back with a screech and gazed at the other girl through tear-drenched lashes.

'Sometimes,' Anya admitted. 'Except I can't seem to allow myself that luxury.'

'Because?' Orla challenged. 'Mummy dearest taught you to have nice manners, did she? Daddy dearest taught you that nice girls were to be seen and not heard?'

Anya's face darkened. Her mouth trembled and found its echo in her voice. 'No. Because Mummy dearest beat any hint of rebellion out of me. And Daddy dearest could be any of a hundred men. I don't suppose I'll ever know.' She drew herself up, as Orla started, incredulous. 'That silver spoon you were on about? Not mine. I

267

ate with my fingers. When there was anything to eat, that is.' She turned and walked out of the kitchen, leaving the other girl to gape disbelievingly after her.

Orla gave herself a little shake. Christ! You never really knew people. Who would have thought that Anya was hiding such a dark background. Secrets and lies! They were everywhere, and she was in the thick of them herself. Reflective, Orla finished her coffee and was just about to leave when Anya came back to pick up her purse from the kitchen. Her expression was calm, but, in the light of her recent revelations, Orla had the sense that it was a forced calm, perfected over a lifetime of holding-back.

'Anya, I'm sorry,' she said, surprising herself with how heartfelt the apology was. 'I had no idea.' She gave a helpless little shrug.

Anya picked up her purse. 'No reason why you should. It's not something I like to broadcast.'

'No, but I wouldn't ... I mean, if I'd known I wouldn't have wound you up about Fergal.'

'Why? Because we're sisters under the skin, is that it? You share my pain.' Anya looked sceptical. 'We're bone fide paid-up members of the same misery club?'

'Maybe.' Orla ignored the sarcasm. 'But you always came across as being so goody-two-shoes, it set my teeth on edge. I suppose I was a bit jealous too. Grandy has such time for you. And Fergal. And Lady Kathleen.' She looked contrite. 'Not to mention Liam O'Hanlon.'

Anya's eyes hardened. 'Oh yes, Liam! My fictitious lover.'

'Yeah, I'm sorry about that too. Of course, later I realised it was Kitty I saw sneaking round that night and getting into his car.'

'Kitty!' Anya gripped her purse very tightly, her fingers whitening at the knuckles. 'Are you sure? Did you mention it to the guards?'

'Pretty sure, and yes, I did mention it, but since I couldn't be a hundred per cent positive, I'm not sure how seriously they took it. Anyway, it's no great secret that Liam has a way with the ladies or, should I say, has it *away* with the ladies. That doesn't mean he's guilty of anything other than cheating on his wife.' Orla shrugged.

'Anyway, I suppose there is a minute chance it was someone else. It happens.'

Reminded of Monique, Anya nodded. 'I can't argue with that. In fact, a funny thing happened when I was in Dubai. There was an Australian woman, Monique, working at the palace. She showed me a photograph of a girl she once knew and she bore more than a passing resemblance to you. Honestly.' She looked mildly rueful. 'Except she was a pole-dancer and her name wasn't Orla. But, seriously, she might have been your doppelgänger.'

'A pole-dancer? How amusing.' Orla's lips quirked slightly. 'Sadly I'm not quite that flexible. I can hardly stand upright on two feet, let alone dangle by my ankle from a pole.' She topped up her coffee. 'Plus I don't think I've ever met anyone called Monique.'

'Oh, I think that might have been just her "working name".' Anya made quotes of her fingers. 'Anyway, we're planning to stay in touch, though I'm not entirely sure why. It's not like we have that much in common.' Plus Monique had spent the night with Fergal, which really ought to have put her beyond the pale. That particular morsel, however, was one Anya chose not to share with Orla. It still hurt to think of it, even though, as Anya reminded herself constantly, she had no claim on Fergal and so who he chose to sleep with was none of her business. None at all.

'Really?' Orla banged her mug down with a jolt splashing some of the coffee on to the tablecloth. She fanned her fingers in front of her mouth. 'Oops. Clumsy me. Should have put more milk in it. What?' she asked, as Anya shot her a searching look. 'It's just a drop of spilled coffee. It'll wash out.'

'I'm sure it will,' Anya said. 'It often amazes me what comes out in the wash.'

Orla narrowed her eyes. 'And that cryptic shit means what exactly?'

'I've no idea what you're talking about,' Anya said. 'Anyway, I'll fetch a cloth, shall I?' She left and went into the scullery. When she returned a moment later, Orla had vanished, leaving her mess behind.

'Something I said?' Anya joked to a marmalade cat, poking his head through the doorway in the hope of receiving charity scraps from the breakfast table. Her brow knitted. 'Actually, maybe it *was* something, I said.' And, step by step she began to replay in her head their conversation.

When Macdara and Fergal returned they were half-triumphant; only half, because one of the two dogs had managed to get away.

'I'll go back out later,' Fergal vowed. 'He won't have gone far. He'll be hiding somewhere no doubt, biding his time before coming back for another bite of the cherry.' He looked up as Orla, alerted by the sound of the returning Land Rover, came back into the kitchen. 'Well done, Orla, for spotting those dogs this morning. If you hadn't, God knows how many sheep would have been mauled. I'm going out later again, since one of them managed to do a runner.'

'Probably skulking in the woods,' Macdara suggested. 'Plenty of places to lie low there.'

Fergal nodded. 'It's worth a look. I'll flush him out if he's in there, even if it takes all day and all night.'

'How many did they kill?' Anya asked, drying her hands on a teacloth.

Macdara looked grim. 'Two dead, four injured. And we might have to put two of those down.'

'How awful,' Anya said, on the verge of tears.

'Terrible.' Orla too looked like she might cry. 'I hope you don't mind, Grandy, if I go to my room for a while. I feel kind of sick.'

Macdara waved her away. 'Of course. Go and lie down for a bit, love. Then, if you feel better later, maybe go out and have a bit of a walk for yourself. Put the roses back in your cheeks.'

'But not near the East Meadow,' Fergal warned. 'Although, after this morning, I can't imagine you'd want to go anywhere within a million miles of the place.'

Orla gave them both a weak smile. 'A walk. Yes, we'll see. If I feel up to it.'

She left and Macdara sighed deeply, his face etched with worry.

'Soft. That's what she is, that girl. Too soft for her own good. It's impossible to live in the country and not accept there's two sides to nature. She was away too long to remember it's not all primrose paths and gambolling lambs.' He shook his head, regretful that such were the facts of life, and then stomped off to his office.

Fergal nodded at the shotgun he was still carrying. 'I'd better put this away for the moment.' He smiled grimly. 'Just in case O'Hanlon hoves into view and it *accidentally* goes off.'

'And I had better go and do a bit of work for Macdara,' Anya said. 'He doesn't pay me just to stand around looking pretty.'

'I would,' Fergal said softly. 'And I'd pay you double the going rate, what's more.'

Anya's eyes dropped to the floor. Hell! Why did she have to make that remark! It sounded like she was fishing for compliments. And why did he have to flirt with her, anyway, when they both knew it was nothing more than a game to Fergal? Just like the kiss in Dubai. She'd been over that stupid kiss in her mind a thousand times, relived every exquisite second of it, analysed it till she thought her brain would burst. But ultimately, to read any more into it other than the unthinking exuberant gesture it was, would be to label herself a fool. And Anya already felt foolish enough around Fergal, awkward and self-conscious. Thankfully, his phone rang out its merry tune, relieving her of the need to say anything witty or otherwise. For a moment he looked almost annoyed at the intrusion, but then he clicked the answer button and she took the opportunity to walk smartly away.

In her room, Orla was smiling down her mobile phone. 'So, what do you think?' she asked JC. 'Is it a good plan or is it a terrific plan? The dark-haired boy versus the blue-eyed girl. Gather round, ladies and gents, and place your bets.' As an appreciative chuckle sounded from the other end, her finger hovered above the off button. 'Now, say you love me,' she commanded. It was the way she ended every phone call only, this time, she listened more intently than ever to the response before breaking the connection.

She placed her mobile on the bedside cabinet and sprawled back on her duvet. The August sun, reflecting on something metal outside, bounced light on to the white paint of her ceiling creating a perfect circle. A circle, the symbol of infinity and, in some cultures, the symbol of female power. And in her case, ever-growing female power. Absent-mindedly, Orla traced the shape of the reflection in the air. She conjured up an image of JC and thought of how she loved him, how she'd loved him since she was knee-high to a grasshopper, as the saying went. Soulmates, she had heard someone say once; soulmates recognise one another almost from the cradle. She believed that too. Orla thought about the little tests she'd been setting him, of late. And how he'd been failing. She thought about him and then she thought about Javier, the two linked inexorably in her mind since the awful night she'd spied on Javier at Castle Mac Tíre. As always, the memory deeply shocked her. Her eyes rose once more to the reflection on the ceiling. The rules of the game had changed, although JC didn't know that yet. No more than he knew that he had broken her heart and that, by dint of doing so, the power had transferred out of his hands directly into hers. The woman scorned now sat plotting revenge. Outside, the sun moved across the sky and the circle on the ceiling above flickered and dimmed.

JC was making plans for yet another extravaganza at the Lismore Hell Fire Club, an Egyptian theme this time, champagne-spouting pyramids, servants dressed as Egyptian slaves, an abundance of Tutankhamuns, King Ras, Cleopatras and Nefertitis among the guests, no doubt. Plus the odd gladiator or two to satisfy the gay clientele. JC could almost hear the melodic ker-ching of money piling up in his bank account. Nevertheless it rankled that he had to expend his energies on such trivia when they could have been far better employed restoring his Argentinian ranch to its former glory. Assuming, that is, he could wrest it from Rodriguez's feckless grip.

Soon, he promised himself, going over to the window of his office and gazing out. Soon all would be well, providing Orla, the stupid bitch, didn't cock things up for him. She, of course, had always been the weakest link in his plans, though a necessary evil. He could rely on her for only so long as she thought he returned her feelings. One hint that it was all a sham, that she was in effect just another chess piece on the board, and JC knew he could kiss goodbye to his future. And so he was determined to keep her sweet for as long as it took. And not one second longer.

He turned away from the window, then back again instantly as a crack sounded in the distance. Followed closely by another. And another. Gunshots! The dark-haired boy versus the blue-eyed girl. Game on!

Macdara and Anya were in the office working their way through some paperwork when the first gunshot sounded. Startled, both their heads jerked up at the same time.

'Fergal!' Macdara said. 'Must be. He said he was going out to look for that hound again. Sounds like he located him.'

Anya hurried over the window, scrying in the distance. 'I think it's coming from the wood or just beyond.' She flinched at the sound of another two shots in rapid succession, then screamed aloud as a bloodied and crumpled-looking Orla stumbled into view below. 'Mac! Mac! Dear God, it's Orla. She's bleeding. She must have been shot.' Spinning round, she made a mad dash for the stairs, Macdara thundering down behind her a split-second after.

'Grandy! Grandy!' Orla screamed, staggering across the stable yard towards them, her arms stretched out imploring. 'Fergal shot at me! He tried to kill me.' Her knees buckled suddenly and Macdara caught her just before she collapsed to the ground. A moment later both he and Anya gazed astonished as Fergal, shotgun still cocked, emerged through the trees and hurtled towards them.

'Jesus! What's wrong? What happened? Orla, are you all right?' He pounded breathlessly to a halt, staring in apparent astonishment from one to the other. He waved a vague hand. 'I heard somebody scream.' Macdara shot him a very strange look.

'Anya,' Macdara instructed, 'call an ambulance, quick.'

Orla's eyes flickered, then half-opened. 'No, don't,' she groaned in a voice weak as a kitten. 'I'm all right. Really. He missed me.'

'Who missed you?' Fergal asked, looking round in bewilderment. 'What are you talking about, Orla?' His glance went disbelievingly to his gun, shifted rapidly to Macdara. 'Oh no, you don't think … Did she think …? What did she say? God almighty, Mac, you don't think I tried to shoot her, do you?' Fergal turned to Anya, beseeching. 'Anya? Anya, you don't believe I did that, surely?'

Macdara's face gave nothing away. 'First things first,' he said. 'Let's get Orla inside where we can assess the extent of the damage. We'll figure out what happened later.' With Anya's help, he carried Orla into the house, leaving a dumbfounded Fergal to face the stares of a small crowd of employees drawn by the noise.

'Listen,' he told them, his face white beneath his normally healthy tan. 'I didn't do anything. I swear, I never even saw her, much less shot at her.'

Indoors, Macdara and Anya gently laid Orla on the settee in the living room, and Anya got busy cleaning her wounds which, fortunately, turned out to be little more than scratches where rogue branches had caught her on her flight through the trees. None were deep enough to require stitches or any kind of medical intervention, other than a dab of antiseptic and a few Band-Aids. Of far more concern was Orla's mental condition. She shook and cried in Macdara's arms, insisting over and over again that Fergal had tried to shoot her.

'I told you, Grandy,' she hiccoughed, her chest rising and falling in distress. 'I told you he didn't like me. He never wanted me to come back. He was angry.'

'There, there,' Macdara crooned, rocking her in his arms like a small child. 'Fergal doesn't hate you. You've got it all wrong. Most likely he heard you in the trees and thought you were the stray dog. He wouldn't deliberately shoot at you. Not Fergal.'

Orla sobbed louder than ever. 'Oh, yes he would, Grandy. I know he's your dark-haired boy, but he wants me out of the way.'

'But, why?' Macdara asked. 'Why would you believe such a thing?'

'I told you before, because of Lismore,' Orla said in a tragic tone.

'Oh, I'm not sure—' Macdara began.

Anya cut him off. 'Look, everyone's overwrought and in shock at the moment,' she said. 'Better if you go to bed and rest, Orla. You've had a nasty shock, one way or another. We can discuss it later, when you're more yourself, okay?'

Orla sniffed. 'I do feel tired.' Her lip trembled. 'And a bit shaky. Will you give me a hand, Anya?'

'Of course. And in the meantime, Mac, you might want to go and have a word with Fergal. I'm sure he's beside himself.'

As she settled Orla into bed, Anya felt sick inside. She simply could not believe Fergal was capable of such a thing. And yet Orla wasn't the first one to imply that Fergal's inheritance was a matter of monumental importance to him. She recalled how Liam had once taunted Fergal regarding her own relationship with Macdara, winding him up about the effect a marriage might have on his inheritance prospects. Although in a rage with Liam, Fergal had restrained himself, she also remembered. Whatever happened out there in the woods, Anya was staunch in her belief that Fergal Fitzgerald had not shot at Orla, and absolutely not deliberately. As she tucked the covers up around Orla's neck and checked to see that her water glass was full, she could hear raised voices from the yard outside. Macdara and Fergal were going at it hammer and tongs, by the sound of things.

'I'll be up to check on you in a little while, all right?' she said, going over to close the curtains. 'In the meantime, try to get some sleep, eh?'

Orla gazed plaintively up at her. 'Thanks,' she said. 'I will. And Anya, I know you don't want to believe it, but Fergal did try to shoot me. Why on earth should I make something like that up?'

Indeed, Anya wondered, as she went back downstairs. Why would she make it up? It didn't make sense. None of it did.

Macdara had come indoors and was striding up and down the kitchen as he waited for Anya.

'How is she?' he asked, looking both weary and defeated.

'She'll live.' Equally weary, Anya sat down at the table. 'Do you believe Orla's story, Mac? Do you really believe Fergal to be capable of something like that?'

'No. I don't know.' Distraught, Macdara rubbed his eyes. 'Yet we saw the state of her. We saw Fergal follow her out of the woods. We saw the gun in his hands.'

'Yes, on the face of it, it looks pretty damning,' Anya admitted. 'But, come on, Mac. Is it likely he'd come chasing after her in full view of everyone, waving his shotgun around willy-nilly? How daft would that be? Fergal is anything but stupid. Seriously, would you not credit him with a bit more sense? If he wanted to get rid of Orla, I'm sure he could have come up with a more creative, less public method of doing so.'

Macdara frowned. 'That thought had occurred to me too. Could be he heard her in the woods, thought she was the stray dog and fired off a couple of shots. Orla panics, thinks he's shooting at her and goes screaming and crashing through the woods. He hears the hullabaloo and takes off after her to find out what's wrong.'

'That sounds a lot more likely,' Anya agreed. 'Except for one thing. Fergal is far too conversant with gun lore ever to fire off a pot-shot without making sure of the target.'

Macdara dropped into the chair opposite. 'Aye, and there's the rub. So, Anya? What really happened in the woods today?'

'Search me, but I would bet my own life on it that, Lismore or not, Fergal did not try to kill Orla.'

'It's as good as his, anyway.' Macdara smiled sadly at her. 'Oh yes, I was working my way round to telling you that. I'm planning on taking a back seat and handing it all over to Fergal. My solicitor is already drawing up the paperwork. As soon as the last i is dotted and t crossed, I intend to take my leave of Lismore.'

Anya's eyes filled with tears. 'Oh Mac! I hadn't realised things had deteriorated so much with you. But are you sure this is the right decision and you're not just rushing things? Is it not better to hold off for a while? Wait, and see how things pan out.'

'No. I think it's better to face the inevitable whilst I can still see, to some degree anyway. And I'm getting used to the idea. Slowly. It's not like I've got much choice.' Macdara twisted his wedding ring round his finger. He had never taken it off, not even for a moment, either before or after Nancy's death. 'And I don't want you to worry about your job, Anya. That's safe. Fergal is more than happy to keep you on, I know. I, on the other hand, will be very sorry to lose you.'

'Mac, I'm not bothered about me.' Anya felt choked by Macdara's kindness. 'I just wish things could stay the same.' She trailed off, embarrassed by the childishness of the statement, and the futility of railing at fate as though it was hers to control. Her brow knitted as a thought struck her. 'Does Orla know, Mac? Did you tell her you were handing Lismore over to Fergal?'

Macdara nodded. 'She's fine about it. Glad, actually. She had some notion that Fergal might feel uneasy about accepting on account of being adopted.' He steepled his hands on the table. 'Funnily enough, that thought never entered my mind. I always assumed he knew he was just as much part of the family as anyone else. It just shows you never really know what's going on in anyone's head.'

'Doesn't it just?' Anya said heavily. 'I must say it's very decent of Orla to be so selfless. Not everyone would be so sanguine about an adopted child coming into the family and copping for the lion's share of the inheritance.'

Macdara examined his fingertips. He pursed his lips and looked worried. 'In retrospect, I'm beginning to wonder if perhaps I should have given it more thought. Maybe I should have split it between the two of them. It's just that Fergal has always been so hands-on at Lismore, my right-hand man. Handing it over to him is the logical thing to do. He'll look after it exactly as I would myself. It will be safe with him.' Macdara smacked his hands flat down against the table top. 'Oh God, why is nothing ever simple! It's true what they say, all good deeds will be duly punished.'

'Where is Fergal now?' Anya asked, worried about how he must be feeling.

Macdara sighed. 'Damned if I know. After our bawling match, he stormed off somewhere. He'll be back.' Macdara looked ill, his face an unhealthy shade of grey. 'He will be back, won't he,

Anya?' he asked anxiously. 'Lismore is his home.'

'Yes, of course he will,' Anya soothed, but inside she felt anything but confident. Fergal was proud. He wasn't the kind of man to take easily to being accused of attempted murder. No more than he would take easily to the people he loved most in the world doubting his innocence. Especially his hero, Macdara. If ever Fergal had felt different because of his adoption, an outsider, a cuckoo in the nest, call it what you would, Anya imagined he was feeling it now. And in spades.

Orla stood eavesdropping on the landing at the top of the stairs. After a while, she tiptoed quietly back to her room and picked up her mobile phone. She scrolled to JC's name in the address book and fired off a text. *Dark-haired boy* 0, *Blue-eyed girl* 1.

Fergal returned later that evening, but only for so long as it took him to throw a few belongings into a rucksack. Then he went to take his leave of both Macdara and a tearful Anya, both of whom were waiting in the kitchen.

'I'm sorry, Mac,' he said, when Macdara pleaded, almost in tears, for him to stay and discuss matters. 'I'm sorry I have to leave you, especially at this time, but you must see that my position at Lismore has become untenable. I don't give a toss what others think of me, but if you think for a minute I could do this, Mac, then I have to go.'

'Position?' Macdara said taken aback. ' Don't be so ridiculous. You're family, Fergal, not an employee.' In a last-ditch attempt to persuade him to change his mind, the elderly man stood, feet planted, in front of the door, blocking his exit. He placed a detaining hand on the younger man's arm. 'Reconsider please, Fergal. I know there must be a rational explanation for what happened out in the woods today. Let's sit down together like men, and work it out.'

'Oh, there is an explanation all right.' Fergal's mouth took on a bitter twist. 'But that explanation, rational or irrational, needs to come from Orla, your *real* family. And, while she's about it, you might also ask her what on earth she thought she was doing climbing into my bed stark naked.' He nodded at Anya and Macdara, both of whom looked shell-shocked at this latest disclosure. 'Oh yes, bold as brass, on the night Sister Martha was murdered. This, bear in mind, being the woman who purports to be terrified of me. Strange how she somehow managed to set aside her fears on that night.' He hoisted his rucksack into a more comfortable position, distributing the weight more evenly. 'She'll deny it, of course. And, to be sure, I have no proof. I never kiss and tell. So, it's her word against mine. Again,' Fergal said heavily. His gaze went to Anya. 'And in case you're wondering, no I didn't. For, strange though it may seem, Orla never interested me in that way.' His eyes burned into Anya's. 'There's only ever been one woman for me.' He gave a rueful grin, and looked at Macdara. 'Sorry, Mac. I tried to heed your warning. But love is a funny thing. It's got no ears.' Moving him gently to one side, Fergal left them then, without a backward glance, his back ramrod straight, head proudly erect. Betrayal apparent in every line of his body.

JC was just leaving his office for the night when his phone vibrated. He pressed the message button and grinned at the words scrolling across the screen. *Dark-haired boy 0. Blue-eyed girl 2.*

# Chapter 28

Anya replaced the telephone on its rest.

'That was Bridie,' she told Macdara, who had sat slumped at the kitchen table since Fergal had left more than two hours before. In that brief period of time, his face looked to have collapsed inwards, every line and wrinkle standing out in stark relief as never before. There was a dead look about his eyes, as if all life had left them, as if he were already blind. 'She'll be back in a week, she reckons. Karen has had the baby – Kieran, they've called him – and mother and child are both in good health.'

Macdara nodded. 'It will be good to have her back. Her replacement was nice, but it's not the same.' He looked up at Anya, his face full of misery. 'Bridie will get some shock when she finds out about Fergal. She thought the world of that boy. He was the son she never had, that's what she used to say.'

Macdara hunched his shoulders, bringing them up around his ears. 'The son *I* never had, for that matter. Did you know that, Anya? Fergal was far more of a son to me than Connor ever was. Odd that, isn't it, to have nothing in common with your own child? But it's true nevertheless. I don't pretend to have much insight or to be a deep thinker, but I sometimes think my disappointment with Connor led me to taking a harder line with Nessa.'

Rheumy-eyed, he splayed his hands on the table before him, appearing to examine them in detail, though in truth he was reliving the past. An ironic smile flirted at the corners of his mouth for an instant. 'Kids! Parents have such high expectations. Press this button and they should do this. Press that button and they should do that. As if they come fully programmed with user-friendly instructions. Not so, Anya. What they come with is their own mindset and, more often than not, it's as far removed from yours as an alien's.' He drummed his fingers to underscore the point. 'You know, it shames me to admit it, but I felt not only disappointed but angry too when Connor and his wife couldn't conceive, as if he had failed me on that score too.'

'Failed?' Anya's brow knitted, then cleared. 'You're talking about Lismore.'

'Yes, Lismore. Isn't that what all men want, to see their son follow in their footsteps, to build upon and improve the family business? To carry on the name?' Macdara sighed. 'Pride, you see, but natural all the same, and that's what I wanted too. But Connor had nothing but disdain for Lismore. He wanted a life that was more than shit and shovels – his very words.'

'But then Fergal came along,' Anya smiled.

'Yes, Fergal came along and from day one that boy was mine, even more so when Connor's marriage fell apart a few years in and his wife skipped off with some other fella who knows where.'

'She didn't want the child?' Anya's soft heart smote her. She longed to find Fergal, wrap him in her arms and kiss away the sense of rejection she knew he must have felt and was, no doubt, feeling again at that very point in time.

'Apparently not. I suspect she only went through with the adoption to please Connor. And, who knows, maybe he only went through with it to give me what I wanted. He certainly made no attempt to curtail Fergal's visits to Lismore, and the arrangement worked well for everyone. Until now.' A small groan escaped his lips. 'Dear God, what if he never comes back? I might as well jack it all in. Lismore without Fergal just wouldn't be the same place.'

In an effort to gee him up a bit, Anya deliberately injected a slight note of impatience into her voice. 'Oh stop it, Mac! There's no point wallowing. Fergal is hurt, that's all that's to it. He needs time away from everyone to lick his wounds and who can blame him?' She smiled to take the sting out of her words. 'But, rest assured, he will be back. He loves you far too much not to return.'

He loved her too, she thought, her heart singing with a joy it was difficult, even in this moment of crisis, to contain. 'Mac,' she asked tentatively, unable to prevent herself from pursuing this particular train of thought, 'what did Fergal mean about trying to heed your warning?'

'I warned him off you,' Macdara confessed. 'I was worried you might be hurt again. But Lady Kathleen rather forcefully pointed out the error of my ways and, recently, I was rather hoping you would get together. In fact, the pair of us had high hopes for you both in Dubai.' Macdara looked at her frankly. 'In fact, I'm surprised Lady Kathleen didn't try to help matters along in some way, especially as the Sheikh is an old friend.'

As Macdara continued to talk, the penny dropped for Anya. Mr and Mrs Fitzgerald! The honeymoon suite! In retrospect Lady Kathleen's hallmark was all over it. Anya didn't know whether to laugh or cry, but Macdara was still speaking and so she pushed thoughts of this to one side until later.

'Tell me, Anya,' Macdara said now. 'Do you feel the same way about Fergal?' He held his hand up. 'No. No don't answer that. I can see by your face that you do. Oh, Anya child, I'm sorry for being such an interfering old man. I seem to have made something of a habit of messing up other people's lives. Can you forgive me?'

'There's nothing to forgive, Mac,' Anya said softly. 'How can I blame you for looking out for me? You only did what you thought was best.'

'I hope I haven't spoilt your chances.' Macdara's eyes went to the window, trying to penetrate the dark, trying to divine Fergal's whereabouts. 'I hope he comes back but, even if he does, there's still the question of Orla to be addressed. We still haven't got to the bottom of what happened out in the woods.'

'Oh yes, the question of Orla!' Anya said, an odd tone in her voice that brought Macdara's attention swivelling back to her.

'Anya?'

'Oh look, I hate to point this out to you, Mac, but Fergal is right. She does have questions to answer too.'

Macdara shifted uncomfortably. 'The bed thing, you mean. I confess I find that hard to believe. Orla's a lady. Why would she make herself cheap like that? She only has to snap her fingers, and she could have anyone.'

Anya shrugged. 'She did flirt with him a lot. I witnessed it for myself several times.'

'Maybe you read more into it than was meant,' Macdara suggested hesitantly.

Anya filled in the blanks for herself and shook her head vehemently. 'I don't accept that. Love may be blind, but I'm crystal clear on what I saw.' She cleared her throat. 'And it rankled.'

'It doesn't tally,' Macdara insisted. 'She was genuinely nervous of him because of her unfounded suspicions that he resented her coming back to Lismore. It makes no sense that she would try to seduce him.' His brow cleared. 'Unless it was a foolish attempt to win him over. Silly girl. She could never bear anyone being cross with her. Nancy used to say that Orla lived in a world of love, that she'd be far better off in a convent protected from the harsh realities of the world outside.'

Overwrought from the trials of the day, Macdara's pious construction of events proved too much for Anya. The time had come for some plain speaking. Steeling herself, she took a deep breath. 'Mac, I'm sorry to say this, but you're in real danger of letting the guilt from the past blind you to what's going on in the present. Orla is neither angel nor saint. Like the rest of us, she's flesh and blood and every bit as liable to screw things up.' Macdara started to bristle, but firmly Anya waved him down. 'And regardless of what you might think, I'm not saying this because I'm jealous. I'm saying it because it's the plain unvarnished truth and you need to hear it.' He looked distressed, but she pressed on regardless. The truth was doubtless bitter, but better that than to live in a fool's paradise, Anya told herself. 'A lot of water has run under the bridge since Orla was the little girl you remember,' she said. 'She's a woman now, full-grown, with a woman's faults and failings. And, to be fair to her, no one could be expected to live up to your high hopes and expectations.'

'So,' Macdara accused, when Anya finally took a breather. 'What you're trying to lead up to, and making a very bad fist of, is that you think she lied about the incident with the gun. You think she made it all up, don't you?'

'Well, don't you?' Anya challenged him back.

Macdara shook his head. 'Lied, no! She was upset. Frightened. She may simply have got confused and genuinely thought Fergal was trying to kill her.'

'So upset,' Anya pointed out, 'that's she's out gallivanting with JC somewhere this very evening. When I went up to check on her a while ago, she was on her way down, all dolled up and looking the farthest thing imaginable from someone who, only a few hours ago, supposedly stared death in the face.'

Macdara looked momentarily surprised although, as usual, he went straight on the defence. 'JC is her friend, her very good friend. No doubt the poor child wanted to discuss it with someone who *believed* her, someone who was actually on her side.' His words cut Anya to the bone. 'I thought better of you, Anya, I really did. Why are you stirring things and trying to turn me against my grand-daughter? Have you got an agenda too?'

Anya's eyes filled with tears brought on by a mixture of rage and dismay. 'No, Mac, I don't have an agenda. I *never* had an agenda. If I had, I might well have said yes when you asked me to marry you.' She pressed a hand against her temple, which had begun to throb painfully. 'I cared about you enough then to say no. And I care about you enough now to say, wake up. Something stinks. I'm not entirely sure what. But whatever it is, it's only happened since Orla's arrival.' She nodded to him. 'Goodnight, Mac. I'm going to bed. I suggest you try to get some sleep too. The whys and where-fores of all of this will still be waiting tomorrow.'

Macdara didn't answer, neither did he move. His brain hurt to the point where he felt it might burst. Nothing seemed to make sense any more. His world was all shades of grey, and was getting darker by the moment. Eventually, exhaustion got the better of him and he fell asleep slumped over the table.

Lady Kathleen woke with a jolt, her heart hammering against her chest. There was an air of menace in the room. She'd felt it before, wending its way up along the corridors of Castle Mac Tíre, penetrating the thick stone walls and oozing through keyholes and beneath doorways. An almost tangible presence, thick with evil. Though the fire still burned in the grate, the room felt cold and slightly damp. Shivering, not entirely from cold, she reached over and switched on the bedside lamp, taking comfort as mellow light flooded the room with a blessed sense of normality. Chiding herself for her lurid imagination, she lay on her back and closed her eyes. Castle Mac Tíre was old, older than old, but there were no monsters under the bed and no bogeymen hiding in the wardrobe. Then, just as she was about to switch the light off again, she heard Javier cry out and knew she was fooling herself. There *was* a monster at Castle Mac Tíre. Lady Kathleen thought she even knew his name.

The radio was tuned to Bridie O'Regan's favourite country and western channel. Cradling her newborn baby grandson in her arms, she was swaying gently to a compilation of Crystal Gayle's greatest hits. The baby mewled and Bridie jiggled him, harmonising badly to 'Don't It Make My Brown Eyes Blue'. As a lullaby it proved so effective that she reprised it later whilst putting him to bed. Following the advice of a well known TV doctor, she placed him carefully on his back, pulled the covers up around his shoulders and tucked them into the sides of the cot to prevent him from wiggling down. Sometimes she wondered how her own kids had ever managed to survive without all this expert advice. She chucked the baby under his chin and he beamed up at her. 'Grandma's going to miss you, little man,' she said softly. 'When she goes back to Lismore. It's gonna make my brown eyes blue. Poor old Grandma.' She straightened up, suddenly feeling unaccountably alarmed. The song! There was something about it that had been niggling her ever since she'd heard it on the radio earlier. An association of some sort dangled just out of reach but, the more she tried to remember, the more she drew a blank. Shaking her head, as though to dislodge an irritation, she checked that the baby monitor was working properly, then went downstairs to make a cup of tea.

The answer came to her, floating out of the ether, just as she was drifting off to sleep that night. Jolting upright in the bed, her eyes lit on the luminous statue of the Virgin Mary gleaming an eerie greeny-white on the dressing table opposite. 'Holy God,' Bridie said aloud, as the pieces of the jigsaw she'd been subconsciously working on started to click into place. 'How did I not see it before? It was so obvious with hindsight.' Slightly panicked, she threw back the covers, debating whether to telephone Macdara there and then. But it was past the witching hour, and she needed time to consider how best to broach the subject. She had always been a believer in the old adage, act in haste and repent at leisure. Besides, even if her suspicions proved correct, another few days wasn't likely to make much difference one way or the other. Until then, ignorance was bliss. For Macdara at least.

Anya looked round the coffee shop and spotted Fergal sitting at a table down the far end.

He looked up a little sheepishly as she approached. 'Hi, Anya, thanks for coming. I wasn't sure you would.'

She levered herself into the chair opposite, her heart turning over at the sight of him. He looked gaunt and ill and as if he had barely slept since walking out of Lismore almost a week before.

'I was glad you phoned,' she said, 'considering how you didn't answer any of my calls or texts.' She wondered how much of her heart was showing in her eyes. He wasn't the only one to have barely slept. All she had been able to think of was Fergal. And yet, now that he was here, she didn't quite know what to say or how to act.

'I'm sorry about that,' Fergal dipped his head. 'I guess I was fuming at everyone for taking Orla's word over mine.'

'To be fair,' she pointed out, 'you didn't give us much time to untangle the threads, and even you must admit that arriving hot on Orla's heels with a smoking shotgun in your hands was bound to raise an eyebrow or two.'

A bored-looking waitress stopped by their table and left again with an order for two cappuccinos.

Fergal groaned. 'Yes, I can see that in retrospect. However, the gun was smoking because I'd just let off a couple of rounds at the hound. *Not* at Orla. The first I knew of her presence was when I heard her screaming her head off and then I went racing off to find out what on earth was going on.' Feeling slightly desperate, Fergal reached across the table and grabbed Anya's hand. It felt like an electric shock up her arm. 'It's a total coincidence that she happened to be in the woods at the same time. And that's the God's honest truth. I never tried to kill her. Why would I?'

Reluctantly, Anya withdrew her hand as the waitress returned with the same bored attitude and two steaming cups of coffee to accompany it. When she had bustled off again with an after-thought instruction for them to 'enjoy', Anya leaned forward, voice lowered, because you never knew who might be listening, especially in a small village.

'What would you say if I said I wasn't entirely sure it was a co-incidence? What would you say if I said I thought she might have planned it?'

'I'd say you were crazy,' Fergal said. 'Why on earth would she? That's psychotic behaviour.'

Anya drew a deep breath. 'I agree, but think about it. You mentioned earlier that you were going back out again to look for that stray dog. Correct?'

Fergal nodded. 'So?'

'And Macdara suggested the woods would be a likely place, yes?'

'Sorry, still not getting your drift.'

'And everyone heard him,' Anya continued, willing him to join the dots. 'Everyone! Including Orla. All she had to do then was watch when you left with your shotgun and follow you. As soon as the gun went off, cue hysterical screaming and accusations of attempted murder. Easy.'

Fergal pushed his coffee away untouched. 'No. Not buying it. Why would she go to those lengths to frame me? What has she to gain?'

'Lismore, I'm guessing. What else could it be? With you alien-ated from Macdara, the likelihood is that she'd inherit the estate instead. She is, after all, his blue-eyed girl who can do no wrong.'

'That would never work.' Fergal was sceptical. 'Orla doesn't have the experience to run Lismore. Nor the passion. Haven't you noticed? She rarely even takes her own horse for a ride these days. She's too busy shopping in Dublin.'

'Makes no difference if her intention is to sell it and pocket the proceeds.' Anya sipped at her cappuccino, dabbing some froth from her upper lip. She could see Fergal thinking over what she'd said, forehead puzzling and clearing, puzzling again, trying to cobble it all together in a way that made sense.

'Have you voiced these suspicions to Mac?' he asked at length.

'God, no! Tell him I suspect his long-lost granddaughter is planning to screw him over? Not me. I'm nowhere near brave enough, although I did try to point out that, like the rest of us, Orla has feet of clay.' Her voice caught a little. 'That brought on accusations of stirring, and then he demanded to know what my agenda was.'

'What the hell!' Fergal looked both horrified and angry. 'Jesus, he really is in thrall to her, isn't he? It's like he's under a spell or something.'

'In some ways he is, but it's not a spell, it's a huge burden of guilt. He simply can't get past how he treated her mother, and the knock-on effect upon Sinéad and herself when they were young. Hence, he's over compensating by the bucketload, and is eager to wear the hair shirt.'

'Of course, that's all just conjecture and amateur psychology,' Fergal said. 'There's not one iota of proof.'

'True,' Anya admitted. 'But, think about it, it does make sense.' She grinned a little shamefacedly. '*Cui bono.* That's what they say in those detective films. Who benefits?'

'Do you ever wish you could turn back the clock, Anya?' Fergal asked suddenly. 'When things get too murky and too complicated?'

Anya's eyes were soft. 'All the time.' Her hand crept shyly across the table towards him. 'Come back, Fergal, please. Mac needs you, more even than he realises.' She dipped her head shyly. 'And so do I.'

Fergal leaned down and scooped up his rucksack from off the floor.

'You know, I was hoping you'd say that,' he said. 'In fact, that hope has been the only thing that kept me going over the last few days.'


Lady Kathleen watched Javier carefully when he came in the following morning with her breakfast tray. Though he appeared to be his usual bright, smiling self, she could tell by the residual puffiness round his eyes that he'd been crying.

'A rose,' he pointed to the bud vase he had placed on the tray, alongside her breakfast cereal and coffee. 'I bringed you a rose. It will make you happy.'

Lady Kathleen smiled as he helped her sit up in the bed, though she saw him wince with the effort as he bent over, as if his back was in agony. Carefully, he placed the tray upon her lap, a small moan, quickly suppressed, escaping his lips.

'Thank you, Javier,' she said, and motioned for him to take the chair next to her, not missing the way he sat carefully on the edge of the seat. She sprinkled sugar on her cereal, added milk and, avoiding looking at him directly, she asked the question she been side-stepping for all too long. 'Now, tell me why it is you are intent on making me happy, when you are so clearly unhappy yourself?'

There was silence for a moment, except for the crackling of the dried cereal flakes expanding in the liquid. Then Javier gave a shaky laugh. 'Me? Why am I not happy? I am happy, my lady. Believe me, I am too happy.' He beamed at her, willing her to believe he was in a state of total bliss. Lady Kathleen gave him a searching look.

'Then, my dear, why do I hear you crying some nights? Why do I hear you screaming and why does the sound freeze the blood in my veins?' She didn't miss the look of panic that flashed across his face, the raw fear apparent in his eyes, if only for a fleeting second.

'Dreaming. You must be dreaming, my lady. Why should I cry? Why should I scream?' He looked at her kindly. 'Sometimes people when they are a little bit more old, they are dreaming things. Not good things. Devils.' Javier made horns of his fingers, smiled at her comically. For once, Lady Kathleen refused to be distracted by his clowning. She had started down this path and although it wasn't pleasant, she was determined to pursue it right to the bitter end.

'Javier,' her voice was soft. 'Please stand up.' He did so, looking puzzled and slightly alarmed. 'Now,' she said calmly, 'turn around and take your shirt off.'

'No. Please no, my lady. Do not ask me to do this. I am begging you.' The panic was back in Javier's eyes, and this time it remained staring back at her like a frightened child. He held a hand up to remonstrate, remembered his position of subservience and let it fall away again.

'Javier, turn around and take your shirt off,' Lady Kathleen insisted, hating herself for the pain she was causing him, yet determined to follow through on her suspicions. There was something very, very wrong at Castle Mac Tíre, and she was intent on finding out exactly what it was.

'Please, my lady,' Javier made a frantic last-ditch plea, but Lady Kathleen overruled him.

'*Now*, please, Javier. Thank you,' she said softly, as long years of obedience to authority having rendered him powerless to resist and he started to undo his buttons.

As his shirt slipped from his shoulders to reveal his naked back, Lady Kathleen's hand flew to her throat. Dear Jesus! It was worse than she imagined. Far worse. For his sake, she quelled her first instinct, which was to be sick, and willed the bile back down. She took a deep breath held it for a count of four and released it slowly, a technique she had learned as an actress to help steady any sign of nerves. 'Okay,' she said quietly, when her heart had begun to beat a little less erratically, 'you can put your shirt back on. Then, you and I need to have a little talk.' Appetite completely fled, she moved her breakfast tray over to the far side of the bed, totally uncaring that her coffee slopped over on to her favourite satin counterpane. The stain would never come out. But there were worse things in life, and an example of what could happen, degraded, almost dehumanised, was standing in front of her. Truly, her heart bled for Javier as, riven with humiliation and distress, he adjusted his clothing and slumped into the chair next to her, wincing as he came into contact with its back. Trembling still, he plucked nervously at his fingers, flexing and pulling them, twisting a gold signet ring round and round his little finger.

Lady Kathleen wanted nothing more than to cry for this young man, but she forced herself to be strong.

'I want to know everything,' she said. 'When this abuse started. *Why* it started. I mean it, Javier. You are to tell me everything. You are to hold nothing back.'

'JC …' Javier looked worried, his eyes lifted slightly, then skittered away again as if he was frightened they would give too much away.

'He is not here,' Lady Kathleen said, a note of steel in her voice. 'Which, make no mistake, is just as well for him. Now, my dear, let's hear it from the beginning. I promise you, there is nothing to fear.'

Javier sighed, a heartfelt sigh that seemed to dredge itself all the way up from his toes. He twisted his ring again, round and round, pulled it off, slid it back on again. 'You won't like it, my lady. I think it is not good for you to hear it.'

'I'll be the judge of that,' Lady Kathleen said, firm but kind. 'And I'll even start it off, shall I? Make it easier for you. Once upon a time there were two young lovers, JC and Javier, right?'

Javier's face crumpled in dismay. 'You know this? How do you know this?

Lady Kathleen laughed grimly. 'Javier, my dear, I learned about more things than just acting in Hollywood. I can sniff out a gay man through ten yards of designer quilting and a heavy head cold.' She held her hands up in surrender. 'And I confess, I've pretty much always known of JC's inclinations, though I did a good job of burying my head in the sand and hoping it would just go away. Life, I feel, would have been simpler that way. Perhaps he would have got married. Perhaps there would have been grandchildren – this old castle needs children running about the place to give it life.' Her chin jutted. 'But, JC is what he is, and no amount of wishing otherwise can change that.'

'But you are not disgusted? By JC? By me?' Ashamed, Javier's eyes slid into a corner of the room and stayed there.

Lady Kathleen shrugged. 'Disgusted, no. Love, of whatever kind, is something to be treasured. There is far too little of it in the world, as it is. But that discussion is for another day. What I need now is to hear the whole story, Javier. Start at the beginning. Leave nothing out.'

Javier nodded assent. He took a deep breath and his shoulders straightened slightly, as he decided to put his trust in Lady Kathleen. She had never been anything less than kind to him. She would do nothing to hurt him. Of that he was sure. 'I will tell you all,' he said. 'You are right. JC and me, we, are lovers. And he *does* love me, my lady. Really! He loves me.' Sad, his eyes left the corner and flitted like panicked butterflies looking for a place of safety on which to land. 'But, he hates me too. One day, I am thinking he will kill me.' He struck his breast. 'My fault. It is all my fault. It is because of me that he loses his ranch at the end of the world.'

'Explain,' Lady Kathleen encouraged gently, reaching over and taking his hand to stop the constant fidgeting. 'Explain why you feel it is your fault.'

## Estancia Del Fin Del Mundo

It had been a blisteringly hot day, with the temperatures hovering somewhere in the mid forties, dropping only slightly below with the advent of evening. Not a breath stirred the air. Trees and flowers stood limp and lifeless, as though made of plastic. Water evaporated from the water troughs, almost as soon as they were filled. Even the insects, the flies that normally plagued the horses, biting their necks and sucking their blood, had retired to whatever shade they could find, beating their wings lazily, ineffectually, in a bid to cool the air around them.

JC and Javier had been out on the pampas all day, herding and branding cattle, hard and exhausting work. As the sun slipped its moorings and began to drift westward in the sky, they were only too happy to follow its example, return to the ranch and stable their worn-out *criollos* for the night.

'You will join me for dinner,' JC invited. 'My parents have left for Buenos Aires. I do not expect them home before tomorrow.' He shot Javier a significant look. 'And I have given Maria the evening off. So there will be just us two.'

'You are certain?' Javier looked nervously about. As a lowly ranch hand, he lived in a dormitory with the rest of the men and ate with them in a communal cookhouse. One such as he was never invited into the boss's house.

'Certain,' JC confirmed cheerfully. 'Come.' He too checked to make sure they were not observed, then ushered Javier indoors. They ate steak and drank wine. Too much wine, rich and red as the blood of a martyred saint. The alcohol made them daring, careless. Amorous. When JC rose and beckoned Javier to follow him through to his bedroom, Javier did not object.

'It has been a long day,' JC said. 'A good day. Now all it needs is a perfect ending.'

Javier would as soon have cut out his own heart as deny his friend anything. JC, his elder by only a year, had been his God, his hero, since first he had come to work at the *estancia*, a poverty-stricken twelve-year-old. Over time they had grown closer and closer, until eventually, that closeness had ripened into love. Since then they had sought every opportunity to be together in that way, hungrily grabbing each and every furtive opportunity, knowing that discovery would mean disaster. Homosexuality, though legal in Argentina for close on two hundred years, was still frowned upon in the world of macho ranchers, where drinking and womanising were the order of the day. Anyone caught in the act risked at the very least a severe beating, and at worst, death.

JC undressed first and then watched as, slowly, erotically, Javier removed his own clothing. Despite the best efforts of the overhead fan to cool the air, sweat rolled in glistening rivers down their tanned bodies, pooled on abdominals honed to hard ridges from tough physical labour, rolled down sinewy arms and thighs. Like ill-fated moths drawn inevitably to a flame, they moved towards each other, hands, lips, grasping, greedy, drunk as honeybees on the nectar of forbidden love.

Arriving home unexpectedly, JC's parents discovered them sound asleep, wrapped in each other's arms, intertwined, naked. There could be no mistaking the fact that they were lovers. Enraged, his father had set about the pair of them with his belt, flaying them from blissful sleep to terrified wakefulness.

'Get out of my sight, Juan Carlos,' he roared, lashing the belt buckle-side down across his son's back again and again. 'You are not fit to bear the proud and glorious name of Fernandez de Rosas. I am ashamed of you and you are dead to me. Do you hear? Dead!'

As JC ran, shamed, from the house, his mother stood by and wept helplessly. From the corner of his eye, he saw her hand go up, as if she would call him back. But she did not complete the motion and his banishment was complete.

'That was the last time, JC saw his father,' Javier ended his story. 'That is why the *estancia* passed to his uncle.'

'And that is why JC takes revenge on you,' Lady Kathleen said softly, fitting the pieces together. 'He does to you what was done to him. Only worse.' For JC had branded Javier with the same iron he used to brand cattle and now the skin of the young man's back was blistered and scarred forever, the flesh flayed and torn, but the lettering still decipherable. 'Property of JC'.

'Yes,' Javier said softly. 'And when the pain upon him grows too much to bear, when the memory of his ranch at the end of the world becomes too much to carry on his shoulders, he brands me again. Fresh.' A tear slid down his face. 'That is why I scream, my lady. That is why I cry.' He made a 'that's all' gesture with his hands. 'Now, you know. You know everything.'

'But why, Javier?' Lady Kathleen asked, pity and horror on her face. 'Why do you stay with him? Why do you not go? I will give you the money if that's what's troubling you. I will send you somewhere safe.'

'I love him,' Javier said simply. 'What is my body, when he already has my heart? To live without him is not to live at all.'

'But he is ashamed of your love,' Lady Kathleen pointed out, humbled in the face of such honesty and selflessness. 'He hates that he loves you. He hates what he is.'

'Even so,' Javier said. 'Even so.'

When Javier left, Lady Kathleen replayed his story over and over in her head. She felt heartsick at her grandson's callousness and also culpable too to some degree. She was familiar with JC's ruthless streak; she had witnessed it many times over the years, but had always comforted herself with the notion that it was nothing more than high spirits coupled with a strong personality. Roisin, she recalled not without regret, had timidly raised the odd concern, only to be shouted down by her husband, who revelled in his son's machismo and ability to bend others to his will. And Lady Kathleen, God forgive her, had been complicit in fostering that illusion, assuring her worried daughter that boys would be boys, and it was no big deal. She maintained the fallacy even as he bullied other children unmercifully and rode roughshod over their feelings.

Macdara's little granddaughter, Sinéad, had been particularly susceptible to JC's machinations, yet she hero-worshipped him. Orla, on the other hand, had been less in awe of him, much less inclined to give in to his hectoring. If memory served correctly, she gave as good as she got and whenever the pair met up, sparks flew, with blood spilt on occasion.

So what, Lady Kathleen pondered now, had prompted such a radical change in Orla's feelings? That she was in love with JC was obvious. That he was not in love with her was, in the light of Javier's revelations, also sadly obvious. Plainly he was deliberately leading her on, using her to mask his homosexuality from the eyes of the world. Her recent premonition that someone was going to get badly hurt in that relationship looked more likely than ever to bear fruit. Poor Orla. Like so many girls before her she had been sold the myth that beauty was everything, that the lucky possessor of blond hair and blue eyes was guaranteed the Midas touch. But much of the gold in circulation wasn't real. It was fool's gold. And blue eyes often brought out the green eyes in others. The thought brought Lady Kathleen up short. Her eyes narrowed. There was something about that phrase that set something to tugging at the corner of her mind? She gave herself a little shake. No matter, it would keep.

Lady Kathleen yanked the pillow from behind her head and laid it over her face, wanting to take her pain and hide away from the world. Her chest felt tight, aching. A sob rose, escaped, then gave birth to another. She felt conflicted. Regardless of what he had done, JC was all that remained of her own flesh and blood. He was the last tangible link to her beloved Roisin. And he had been good to her, no doubt about it. He had promised to restore Castle Mac Tíre to its former glory, and was making good on that promise. But that goodness was now tarnished by the suspicion that he was simply feathering his own nest. When she died, Castle Mac Tíre would, after all, be his. For the first time in years, Lady Kathleen found herself wishing she had died in the accident on set in which she had broken her back. Contradiction in terms though it was, life would have been so much simpler.

# Chapter 29

Orla was annoyed, yet not altogether surprised by Fergal's return. He would have been an idiot to have let Lismore slip through his fingers quite so easily, especially as she had no proof that he'd tried to kill her. Which, of course, she didn't, because he hadn't. Nevertheless, she was gratified to sense a new reserve between himself and Macdara, a loosening of the ties that bound. A crack had appeared in their previously impervious relationship, making her slightly more confident that Fergal should not count his horses just yet.

Lismore was still to play for and, at this point in time, Orla held the ace, as her unhappy grandfather had turned in her direction for solace, solace she was only too happy to provide. Accordingly, she upped her role of caring granddaughter to the point, sometimes, where she wished it could all have been for real. Irritatingly, because it was quite unexpected, she often found herself really enjoying Macdara's company, appreciating that slightly wicked sense of humour that was not dissimilar to her own. She began to look forward to walking with him round the estate, listening to him boast of how he'd built it up from virtually nothing to the success it was now. Only when Macdara got on to the subject of her grandmother and, inevitably as night follows day, Sinéad, did the happy house of cards come tumbling down around her ears. It was much too late for bonding, she told herself, and the train of events set in motion several months earlier could not now be derailed.

Orla went to her wardrobe and took out the Cleopatra costume she had hired for the upcoming Egyptian extravaganza at the Hell Fire Club and laid it on the bed. It was lovely, a work of art, a tangle of golden threads skilfully woven together to form a thing of beauty. Tangled threads. Tangled web. There were tangled threads spinning out around her in every direction, some of her making, some not. She sat on the bed, suddenly bone weary. Oh, what a tangled web. Ironically, she wasn't the one doing all the deceiving. She was the biter, bit. Tears came to her eyes. JC!

Anya was working late in the office at Lismore. The time differential between countries sometimes necessitated her working odd hours. She didn't mind and quite enjoyed the solitude, in fact, along with the satisfaction of getting so much more done without the distraction of people coming and going. When the door opened suddenly she looked up in surprise, surprise turning quickly to horror as Clare Keating burst in, slammed the door behind her and pressed her back to it. She held up a warning hand, and put a black-nailed finger to her lips.

'Sssh, there's a good girl.' She grinned as Anya sat rooted to the spot. 'What? Not got a welcome smile for your old mother then, although I see you recognise me.' She grinned wider, revealing teeth that were every bit as neglected as the rest of her person. 'Even though I don't need a mirror to tell me I haven't exactly improved with age.' The grin faded. 'And you, madam, have had no small part to play in that.'

Anya felt as though she might be sick. Her heart pounded so loudly, she was sure it must be audible to the other woman. The pen in her hand trembled and scrawled out of control on the page in front of her. She swallowed rapidly, reminded herself that she was no longer a child at the mercy of anybody, including this woman. Nevertheless old habits die hard, and old fears that have lain dormant for years can suddenly reignite and render one powerless. And so Anya's voice, when she finally found it, came out in a nervous croak. 'How did you get in here? What do you want?'

Clare smirked. 'Jesus, talk about a rabbit in the headlights. Listen, lady, no one keeps me out of anywhere I want to go.' Her eyes hardened and she took a step closer. 'As for what I want? Revenge, that's what I want, you little bitch.' She drew her hand expressively down her filthy clothes and scarecrow figure. 'For this. For all this. For all the shit you put me through with your mealy-mouthed lies.'

'They weren't lies,' Anya said quietly. 'You know that.'

'I know fuck all!' Spittle flew from the other woman's mouth. 'Except that you've been living off the fat of the land for years, spoiled and mollycoddled by all and sundry, especially by that stupid nun, while I've been selling my arse to stay alive.' Her eyes darted slyly around the room. 'Yeah, sweet, very sweet. What you might call a cosy little set-up. I bet you've accumulated a nice little nest-egg for a rainy day.' She hammered against her chest. 'Well, here's the rainy day, come to collect.'

Anya swallowed rapidly. She thought about screaming, except it was difficult enough just to speak, let alone muster up the strength for anything more. She clutched the pen tightly in an effort to still her trembling fingers..

Her voice wavered. 'I think you'd better leave or—'

'Or what?' In two strides Clare Keating was across the room and leaning menacingly over her. 'Before the cavalry ride to your rescue? Before Sister Martha comes galloping in with her lies and accusations?' She tittered, as Anya shrank back. 'Oops, she can't though, can she?' She bent forward, the savage light of triumph in her eyes. 'Cos she's fucking dead! Walked on to a knife, so I heard. Should have watched her step, silly old busybody. That's what happens when you get in the wrong person's way. Like you, Anya.'

A terrible suspicion was growing in Anya's mind, a suspicion almost too awful to contemplate. Her insides were quaking. The pen fell from her suddenly nerveless fingers and rolled off the edge of the desk landing on the floor like a black exclamation mark.

'Did you ...' Anya's voice trailed off, as suspicion turned to horrible certainty.

'Mind your beeswax!' Clare Keating snapped, but there was something about her, a sudden shiftiness, a look in her eye, that pointed to her guilt.

'It was you!' Anya clapped her hand across her mouth, fearful of what she might do. It was too much to take in. Sister Martha. Lovely, kind, gentle Sister Martha, killed in cold blood by her own mother. For what? For showing kindness to a damaged child? Anya let out a long groan, shaking her head as if to dislodge the image.

'No fucking loss. One Holy Mary penguin is the same as another.'

And with Clare's callous words, Anya felt the fear slip from her, to be replaced by a fury such as she had never known. Springing from the chair, fingers locked into claws she launched herself at her mother, knocked her to the floor and straddled her.

'Why?' she screamed, putting her hands around the woman's scrawny neck and squeezing tightly. 'Why?' Gasping, Clare Keating fought to dislodge her, but she was no match for the younger, stronger woman.

'Please,' she gurgled as her throat was compressed, thrashing her head to and fro. 'Anya, you're choking me.' But, buoyed up by the suppressed fury of years, at long last finding an outlet, Anya didn't even hear her. Her entire focus was on destroying this woman who had destroyed not only her childhood, but also Sister Martha, the woman she considered to be her real mother. Just before Clare Keating passed out altogether, strong hands wrapped themselves around Anya's waist and firmly hauled her away.

As if in a dream, she came to herself slowly. The red mist disappeared, her breathing normalised and the adrenalin which had been pumping through her body subsided, leaving her weak and shaky.

'Christ, Anya!' Fergal stood before her, his uncomprehending eyes drifting from her to the woman still on the floor and back again. 'What are you doing? Who is that woman?'

Anya grimaced. 'Not woman. Thing! That, Fergal, that pathetic, murdering piece of scum is my mother!'

'Your mother?' Fergal's face cleared. He spread his hands in bewilderment, stared around at the woman who was showing some signs of recovery. 'But why?'

'She killed Sister Martha,' Anya explained, her face crumpling. He put out his arms and she fell into them, burying her face in his chest and sobbing loudly. 'Call the guards, Fergal,' she begged. 'I want her locked away for the rest of her life.'

Clare Keating had different ideas. Whilst Fergal was busy

comforting Anya, she got silently to her feet. She was bruised and shaken, but not yet ready to go quietly. She dug in her pocket for the same knife with which she had despatched the nun. The movement brought Fergal's head spinning towards her. She pointed the knife at him.

'Shame I can't stick around, gorgeous,' she said. 'Places to go, people to see, you know how it is!'

As Fergal made a move towards her, she waved the knife threateningly. Panicked, Anya caught his arm. 'No, Fergal. Let her go. The guards will catch up with her.'

'I should have used this on you, while I had the chance,' Clare said, lovingly stroking the blade of the knife. 'It would have been poetic justice considering how you and Sister Martha shared so much.' As, incensed, Fergal made another move, Clare shook her head. 'Ah! Ah! Not a good idea. Better a live coward, than a dead hero.'

'He's not a coward,' Anya said bravely. 'You're just not worth bothering with. Besides, like I said, the guards will catch up with you.'

'But perhaps not before I catch up with you.' Clare headed for the door. 'And next time there won't be any pleasant little interludes like this. Next time, Anya, it's strictly business.'

'How did she get in?' Fergal asked, hurrying over to the phone as the door slammed in Clare's wake. 'How come she wasn't noticed by somebody?'

'I don't know,' Anya shook her head. She still looked drained and shocked. The whole experience had left her shaken. 'Smuggled in by Liam, maybe?'

Fergal looked grim. 'He'd bloody better not have.' He tapped out the emergency number into the phone on Anya's desk and waited for the dial tone.

'I hope they get her, I hope she rots in prison. I'd gladly throw away the key myself,' Anya raged. She watched Fergal speak into the phone, but oddly it was Sister Martha's voice she could hear.

*Anya, love, he who seeks vengeance must dig two graves: one for his enemy and one for himself. Let the good Lord take care of all that kind of stuff. Your job is just to live your life as best you can.*

Fergal replaced the receiver and gazed at her perplexed. 'You know, Anya, you're a very odd girl, sometimes. I can't see what on earth you've got to smile about.'

'No, I don't suppose you can.' Anya's smile widened. She went over to the window and gazed up at the night sky, concentrated on finding the very brightest star. 'I heard you,' she mouthed up at it. 'Loud and clear.' She closed her eyes as a deep feeling of peace washed over her and finally washed the past clean away. For the first time in her life, Anya felt truly ready to move on.

Orla emerged from the bathroom and towelled herself dry. Usually, by this time, she would be well into party mode, but tonight she felt flat as a glass of two-day-old champagne. A dull headache throbbed at her temple. Stress induced, she guessed. She toyed with the idea of having a spliff, but she couldn't be arsed going through the pantomime of rolling up.

She threw the towel to the floor and retrieved her underwear from the drawer. Victoria's Secret, bought on a trip with her sugar daddy back in what was beginning to seem like another lifetime. Pure silk. Luxurious. She stepped into the panties, secured the bra in place and went to look in the mirror, examining her body almost dispassionately. She had always been desired by men. Most men, anyway. Until recently, rejection was something that happened only to other women.

A dry smile came to Orla's lips as she recalled how, creased with embarrassment, Macdara had quizzed her regarding Fergal's allegation that she had tried to seduce him. She'd been prepared for that. In the circumstances, it was only to be expected that Fergal was going to sling every piece of mud he could find. But, oh! she'd put in a performance to be proud of: wide-eyed, shocked to the core, distraught that her dear *Grandy* could believe such a vile thing of her. By the time Orla had finished weeping and wailing, Macdara had looked as if he wanted to crawl under the nearest hedge and never come out again. As he slunk away, she was quite sure she heard the gratifying, grating sound of an ever-widening fissure opening up between himself and Fergal. The stupid thing was that she'd only gone to his room to spite Anya, anyway. And she never would have done it if she hadn't believed the other girl to be a spoiled princess. But that was the problem: you couldn't be sure who anyone was these days. It made life damn difficult.

JC was angry. Angry, humiliated, hurt and betrayed by the two people he believed would stand staunchly by his side for all time. He loved his grandmother, but Lady Kathleen had disappointed him by delving into things which were, quite frankly, none of her business. He had left her in her room squawking and clucking like an angry hen, uttering threats and imprecations, and come to clear his head by the tranquil shores of Wishbone Lake. Today the lake was in repose, an unfurled length of satin in variegated shades of blue and grey, a direct contrast to when it had been dragged in the search for the missing Lismore stable lass. Then the waters had been a veritable maelstrom, churned up and heaving, a more accurate depiction of how he himself was feeling at this present moment in time.

A flock of starlings flew overhead, then turned suddenly as with one accord, and darted back whence they came. Would that he could turn back time so easily, undo the one night's work that had led him to this place. JC picked up a stone and skimmed it across the water. One. Two. Three hops before it sank and the ripples marking its passing, spreading radially outwards. A fitting metaphor for actions and consequences. Had he not thrown the stone, there would have been no ripples and the surface of the water would have remained smooth and undisturbed. Had he not fallen in love with Javier, had he not invited him into his room to make love on that fateful night, he would not have disappointed his father. He would not have been banished from his home. Javier, his lover. His unwitting nemesis. He loved him. He hated him. He couldn't live without him. Even now, knowing that Javier had betrayed their secret to Lady Kathleen, JC burned with the need for him, with an unquenchable desire that defied all logic and reason. Yet, he had banished him, and he had hurt him.

Dejected, JC sat on a flat rock by the water's edge. He stared across to where the tower of the Hell Fire Club was visible through a break in a clump of trees on the far side. The one small window stared back blank-eyed and secretive. He intended to knock it all down, eventually. But right now it stood taunting him with its ugliness, mocking his powerlessness to do other than dream of what might have been. Castle Mac Tíre would no longer be his. In the light of what Lady Kathleen termed his shocking behaviour towards Javier, she had decided that upon her death Castle Mac Tíre should be gifted to the State.

JC supposed he should be grateful that she had allowed him to go ahead with the Egyptian Ball that evening, since the tickets had already been sold. After that, she told him, crying as if her heart would break, he must make his own way. Her grief was of little consolation. His ranch was lost to him. Castle Mac Tíre was lost to him. And his only hope of recovering the former now lay with Orla and her ability to bamboozle Macdara into handing over Lismore. For her devotion, at least, he was grateful. A susurration from above told him that the starlings were back. Their massed shadow flitted across his upturned face, then danced away across Wishbone Lake, before breaking into a thousand bird-shaped shards that disappeared into the reeds.

Reminded that time too was on the wing, JC stood up, unaware of Javier watching him from amongst the trees on the far side. JC had ordered him to leave, but Javier had defied him. Lady Kathleen needed him, and JC needed him too. He reached out in spirit to JC, his mouth forming words only his heart could hear. *'Te amo, Juan Carlos Fernadez de Rosas. Te amo.'*

As Orla prepared for the Egyptian ball, her thoughts left Lismore and went in search of JC. He had been so long absent from her life. And then, out of the blue, had come the fateful phonecall that had placed her in the here and now; and now that she was here, everything looked about to go belly-up. Orla had recognised his voice at once, would have recognised it even after a thousand years. All the old feelings had come spilling back as if, like Snow White, they had simply been sleeping. She recalled clearly how her heart had juddered like a wild thing in her chest, how her pulse had quickened to the point where she felt like she might faint, how she stumbled and stammered, quite overcome, till his cool voice admonished her to get a grip. It had never occurred to her to question how he had found her, nor to berate him for the many years of silence. As ever, she remained without question his adoring little slave. She was also at the time up shit creek without a paddle, and therefore more than willing to listen to what he had to say, starting with the story of her grandfather's blindness and how they could turn it to their own advantage.

Orla sprayed a cloud of perfume into the air and, still clad only in her underwear, walked into the mist. Tonight, more than ever, she wanted to look her best. To *be* the best, the most beautiful she had ever been. Beautiful, powerful and liberated. Yes, liberated. No more the slave. The thought was heady, intoxicating, even as knives of torture stabbed at her heart. It all came down to Javier!

She sat at her dressing table and rummaged through her make-up box looking for the eyeliner pen that would give her Cleopatra's kohl-rimmed cat's eyes.

Javier! Property of JC! She had tried to rationalise the branding, kidded herself that JC was different, that he moved on a plane of his own, that he was special, that he had a God-given dispensation to do whatever it was that made him happy. If other people got hurt in the process, then so what! They were just collateral damage. Javier was collateral damage. A servant of no account. Except that he wasn't. He and JC were lovers. Subconsciously she had known that from the first time she saw the young Argentinian at Castle Mac Tíre, and had seen the hunger flare in JC's eyes as they fastened on him, a hunger, conspicuous by its absence in his dealings with her. With the 20:20 vision of hindsight, of course, it all made perfect sense.

She slathered on moisturiser, worked it into her face and throat and waited for it to absorb, then picked up a light foundation and went through the same routine.

How clever JC had been, seducing her only with words, with

Technicolor promises of a happy-ever-after life in his ranch at the end of the world. Dancing the tango under a scraffito sky. Whetting her appetite with the odd fillip, a dry kiss, something more intimate, only if he could not avoid it. Dangling her on a string, keeping her sweet with promises of what would come later, after they were married. Tell me you love me, she'd insisted time after time. Because, in her heart, her stupid, vapid, empty, broken heart, she knew he did not. Because, in her heart, her stupid, vapid, empty, broken heart, she knew that to JC she was never more than the key to Macdara's wealth.

She finished her make-up, paying special attention to her eyes, the windows to the soul. For, tonight, she wanted him to gaze into them and read the truth. That she was finally free of him. The truth about him had finally set her free.

Resolved that things were going to change, that she, most of all, was going to change, and for the better, Orla picked up the gold sunray-pleated tunic of her costume and put it on.

She wound her hair in a skein and twisted it up at the back of her head, securing it with an ornamental comb. She placed a gold and jewelled circlet fashioned to resemble an asp on top, and secured it with a couple of kirby grips. The effect was stunning. Hopefully, unforgettable.

From outside she heard a horse neigh, an engine stutter into life, a voice raised in a snippet of a popular song.

She had been addicted to JC. Now, she was finally clean, and he owned no part of her. She owed him no allegiance. That was reserved for the one person in the world who had never betrayed her; the one person in the world she had betrayed, albeit unwittingly.

Determination blazing in her eyes, she straightened her shoulders and lifted her chin.

'Carry on Cleo,' she said aloud. 'Go kick his asp!'

# Chapter 30

*Dubai*

It was Monique's last night in Dubai. She was all packed up and ready to embark on the new life she had planned for herself. She was going to set up a fancy dress business back in Australia with the money she had managed to save working at the palace. Tarting It Up! it would be called. Monique looked at the discarded French maid's uniform puddled in the corner where she had kicked it earlier. She wouldn't be needing that again. That belonged to a different life now, as did her days as a stripper and worse. Her name too, come to that. After today, she would revert to being Mary-Jane Pearson.

Humming a little tune, she picked up her mobile phone and scrolled through the address book searching for Anya's number. She checked her watch. It was almost midnight in Dubai, which meant it was around eight o'clock in the evening in Ireland. She pressed the green telephone symbol on her mobile phone and waited for the ring tone. 'Hi, Anya,' she said, when the phone was picked up at the other end. 'It's me, Monique. Bet you never expected to hear from me.'

Anya switched off her mobile, though she continued to stare at it disbelievingly. It was lovely to hear from Monique, and thrilling to hear her plans for the business. With her bubbly personality, not to mention her personal experience – the French maid's outfit came to mind – Anya had no doubt Monique would make a success of her new venture. And she wished her all the best. The part of the conversation that perplexed her, the part that had her staring at her phone like it was two pounds of Semtex ready to explode at any second, was the verbal postscript Monique had tacked on to the end of the conversation.

'Oh, by the way, Anya, remember that photograph I showed you, the one with the girl you thought you recognised? Well, I remembered her name afterwards. It was Sinéad.' Having delivered her bombshell and with a cheery 'Keep your pecker up, mate', the born-again Mary-Jane Pearson rang off.

'Jesus!' That was Anya's first reaction. Her second was that she needed to find Fergal urgently.

And together they would need to find Macdara. Anya's heart raced as pennies started dropping into place and the magnitude of the fraud being perpetrated on Macdara began making itself apparent. Poor Macdara, how his heart would break all over again. She felt like the angel of death as she went in search of Fergal.

Truly, it was a bizarre and bewildering evening, Anya thought as she went to look in the stables, where Fergal had headed after the guards had left earlier on. The stables were where he did his thinking, his place of peace. He took comfort in the animals, loved their simplicity, the sense of calm surrounding them. Unlike humans, they were without guile. He felt both humbled and privileged, he said, to be around them. As she crossed the yard, a taxi pulled up and a moment later Orla, dressed as Cleopatra emerged from the house.

'Oh, hi Anya,' she called. 'What do you think of the outfit?' She did a little twirl. 'Do I make a good Cleopatra, or what?'

Anya schooled her face to blankness. 'Cleopatra reputedly had dark hair,' she said. 'And dark eyes. But, apart from that ...'

'Oooh, picky,' Orla grinned. 'Still, I daresay nobody at JC's Egyptian party will be quite so pedantic. Blonde. Brunette. Who cares? It's ancient history.'

'True,' Anya said, biting her lip. 'But history has a way of repeating itself, and people have a way of showing their true colours.' She rolled her eyes, self-deprecatingly. 'Oh, listen to me rattling on. You go and enjoy yourself.' While you can, she added *sotto voce*, as Orla gave her a searching look before clambering into the cab.

\*

'Bye now,' Bridie O'Regan called, climbing into the taxi cab and waving goodbye to her daughter and son-in-law. It was long past the kiddies' bedtime and they were already tucked up for the night. 'Take care of yourselves now, do you hear me?'

As the vehicle drove away, Bridie leaned back against the seat and closed her eyes wearily. For once, she was not looking forward to going back to Lismore. The more she chewed things over, the more her gut instinct told her she was right. The clue was in the song. Don't it make my brown eyes blue. The medicine box Bridie had noticed on Orla's dressing table, but upon which she'd placed no significance at the time, had contained not medicine, but contact lenses. *Blue* contact lenses. And when she had made that connection, other discrepancies began to make themselves apparent. On an individual basis they were all pretty trivial, but when looked at as a whole, and under a different construction, a bigger, more sinister picture emerged. The messy room, for example. On reflection, Orla had been the one who had always been neat and tidy, quite faddy really. She lived her life by the motto that there was a place for everything and everything in its place. And, in Bridie's experience, tidiness was just as much in a person's DNA as blue eyes or brown eyes, a thought which brought her full circle.

The cab drove past a church and Bridie duly made the Sign of the Cross, sending up a prayer as she did so. 'Dear God, let me be wrong,' she implored. 'Don't do this to Mac. He doesn't deserve this, God. The poor man has suffered enough.'

The Egyptian night at the Hell Fire Club was living up to its PR. It promised to be the event, not only of the year but of the decade. A steady stream of chauffeured vehicles drove up, discharged their splendidly clad occupants and drove away again. A young Saudi prince, one of the Hell Fire Club's greatest devotees, arrived by helicopter and since there was no landing pad, suffered the ignominy of shinning down a rope ladder. Really getting into the spirit of things, he had come dressed as Anubis, the dog-headed Egyptian god, which gave rise to much hilarity amongst the onlookers, especially when his loin-cloth, the remainder of his costume, blew up revealing tiny leopardskin briefs. Inside the club was heaving with more Egyptian gods, kings, queens, and even a mummy or two. One had thoughtfully brought along his own sarcophagus and was lugging it about on wheels, getting in everyone's way.

Rivers of champagne flowed as freely as the Nile, and JC had even managed to source roast locusts which were going down a storm amongst the more adventurous of palate. Banqueting tables laden to bursting with platters of exotic foods were lined up along one entire side of the room, flanked by golden flagons of wine and spirits. The guests drank not from glasses, but from jewel-stemmed goblets. Bronzed, half-naked Egyptian slaves, male and female, circulated among the revellers with clear instructions to cater for every requirement, with the emphasis on *every*. The Saudi prince had already disappeared into one of the many private rooms with a posse of dusky young maidens and a large flagon of champagne.

In an ante room for gold members only, a mountain of snowy cocaine was proving something of a draw, as well as bowls of ket and ecstasy. Liam, dressed as a Pharaoh, congratulated himself on pulling all the stops out to put that little lot together. There was nothing more the little bastards could wish for, and he expected to be amply rewarded for his efforts. Moreover, after tonight Liam had decided that he was cutting loose and going out on his own. Fuck the whole lot of them, JC, and the mob at Lismore. Liam was a man of substance now, with bigger fish in his sights than a toffee-nosed Argentinian prick, and a nice hoard in the bank, enough to be getting on with anyway. Added to that, he'd sorted, en route, whatever problems had presented themselves. Like Kitty.

Occasionally, in the early days, Liam had woken in a sweat, his heart pounding, having dreamt that Kitty's body had floated to the surface of Wishbone Lake. But, as time passed and nothing happened, the dreams faded and he grew more confident that he had committed the perfect crime. Now, a gorgeous young female slave sashayed past, reminding him of Anya, the notch on his bedpost that got away. He had fucking Fergal to thank for that. The bastard had taken him to one side recently and warned him that if he so much as caught Liam looking at her, he'd castrate him between two house bricks. Liam winced at the thought and, unconsciously, tightened his thighs. He would have decked him, had Fergal not also made it plain that he knew all about the increasingly large orders he had placed for ketamine but how the contents of their surgery cupboards suggested otherwise.

Fergal's advice had been to hand in his notice and go quietly, for Macdara's sake. Of course, if he preferred, there was also the house brick option. Never mind, there would be many more Anyas, Liam comforted himself, as the pretty little slave sashayed back the way she'd come, batting her kohl-rimmed eyes in his direction. Anyway, as a parting gift, he'd delivered her mother to her earlier, stowing her away in the back of his Land Rover. Shame he hadn't been able round to witness what followed but, by all accounts, there had been a helluva hullabaloo, and the guards had crawled all over Lismore like cockroaches for hours after. They wouldn't find Clare though, at least not alive, if he got to her first. Keating was dangerous to his cause. She was a loose cannon, a liability. And she needed taking out.

His gaze went round the room in search of the little slave again and found her, conveniently parked outside the door to one of the private rooms. Liam smiled. Clare Keating could wait. In the meantime, he intended to take full advantage of JC's hospitality.

Even amongst the gorgeously clad guests, Orla stood out, although her radiance owed as much to her state of mind as to her external appearance. For the first time in her entire life, she felt free, disinclined to allow any man to call the shots in her life, to use her, manipulate her, make her his fall-guy. Those days were over and, broken heart aside, the knowledge was heady stuff. Head held high, as high as that of the queen she represented, Orla surveyed the room looking for JC.

She found him in a corner, chatting to a young man so effeminate-looking that he made even the most girlish woman in the room look butch. Orla's lip curled. Now that she had allowed the scales to fall from her eyes, her gaydar, once so acute she could spot a homosexual from birth, was back in full working order.

She reached out and took a goblet of wine from a passing slave. JC's hand was possessively on the young man's shoulder now. He was insinuating himself into his personal space, bit by bit, and was no doubt charming the pants off him. Orla grinned without humour. He had never been interested in charming the pants off her. It made her sad to think of how she had debased herself, desperately trying and failing to seduce him; how she had inured herself to the look of sheer disgust on his face, not always successfully hidden, whenever she dared to place his hand on her breast or when she kissed him. All that talk of saving sex for marriage. Marriage! The only marriage he was interested in was one of convenience. His intended bride was Lismore and the dowry it could bring, not her. His lover was Javier, but even he couldn't compare with the real love of his life, that blasted ranch in Argentina.

She sipped her wine and smiled absently at a man with the head of a cat. Bastet, she thought he was called. It was to be hoped he didn't run into Anubis. Over in one corner, a couple were dancing, the man guiding his partner through a complicated series of turns and spins. The tango. JC had promised to dance it with her. But it took two to tango, and she was bowing out. Let him be content with the fact that he had already led her a merry dance. Now it was her turn to take the lead.

She trembled slightly at the vow she'd made earlier, the vow to confess all and come clean. Her grandfather was not a bad man, merely a misguided and grief-stricken man. She knew that now. Neither had he been in possession of all the facts. He would forgive her. It would take time. But he would forgive her. A golden thread on her bodice had come loose. She pinched it off carefully. It was time to start unravelling the web.

JC took his leave of the young man and set out to look for Orla, intent on a major charm offensive. She was his last hope, the one straw that might just pull him out of the water, before he went completely under and drowned. He found her, looking incredibly beautiful, draped across a ruby-satin chaise longue. At moments like this, he wished he was other than he was, but life had not played fair in that respect. Women, no matter how stunning or alluring, held no appeal for him sexually and never had. It was his curse, and his strength. But ultimately the rock upon which he perished.

'Hi, darling,' she smiled at him through elongated cat-like eyes as he approached and held out a beckoning hand. 'Come, sit beside me.' Her eyes swept over his gladiator-style costume and a wicked glint came into them. 'Mark Antony, I presume?' Deliberately, she shoved her hand under his leather skirt. Surprise, surprise, he pushed it away. This time, she was prepared for the rejection. This time it didn't hurt quite so much.

'Not now, Orla.' JC tried for jokey, but failed to keep the reproof from his voice. 'This is hardly the time or the place.'

'Really?' Orla said innocently. 'Is that not the purpose of all those private rooms? So lovers can get their kit off?'

'Only the guests,' JC said. 'The host can hardly disappear off to play hanky-panky. Something might come up. Somebody might need me.'

'Have it your way,' Orla said carelessly, and then pointed across at the young man she had seen JC speaking to. 'Perhaps I'll go and chat him up instead. Then again, perhaps not. It's obvious the boy's gay.' She raised an eyebrow. 'Was it obvious to you, JC? I saw you chatting to him earlier. Somehow I can't imagine it was. You Argentinians are so, well, macho, aren't you? So homophobic? I can't imagine you'd have got quite so close to him if you'd guessed he was a shirt-lifter.' The offensive term was designed to wound and she had the dubious satisfaction of seeing him squirm.

'Orla!' he said sharply. 'Whatever's got into you tonight? You're acting very strangely.'

'Competition for you, am I, JC?' She looked at him mock kindly. 'In the acting sense, I mean? You yourself are such a consummate actor.'

Unable to take any more of this bewildering new Orla, JC leapt to his feet. 'I'm sorry, I have to go, darling,' he forced the endearment, though it burned his tongue like acid. 'We'll talk later. Right now I need to have a word with the caterers about something.'

He gestured vaguely round. 'Enjoy yourself. We'll catch up later, okay?'

'Oh, indeed,' Orla smiled sweetly. 'I'll catch you out later. Slip of the tongue, JC,' she said as he turned to look at her. 'Slip of the tongue. Nothing to worry about.'

# Chapter 31

Macdara, alerted by Javier to the fact that Lady Kathleen was most unwell, was visiting her at Castle Mac Tíre. Shocked at her appearance, he was trying to persuade her to let him call a doctor.

'No,' she told him, shaking her head. 'What ails me, my dear, no doctor can cure.'

'Please, Kay,' he begged. Thoroughly distressed, Macdara paced her bedroom like a caged lion. 'Please don't talk like that. There must be something somebody can do.' He came over and dropped to one knee by her bedside, cradled her hands between his own. They felt dry, like rice paper, and as though they might crumble away under the slightest pressure. 'Tell me. Tell me what I can do to help.'

'Nothing.' Lady Kathleen gently withdrew one of her hands, reached over and stroked his face. 'I am beyond saving.' She smiled sadly. 'And almost, if not quite, past caring too.'

'But why?' Macdara moaned. 'Won't you please tell me what's wrong?'

'I am burdened with a secret, Mac,' she confessed. 'But since it is a secret, I cannot share it with anyone else. Not even with you, my best and dearest friend.'

'But, is it so bad?' Macdara asked. 'Perhaps you are getting it out of proportion?'

'Would that it were so,' Lady Kathleen said fervently, tears starting to her eyes. 'It has cost me my grandson. It has cost him Castle Mac Tíre. Those are the proportions, Mac.'

'Dear God.' Macdara pulled himself slowly to his feet and sat in the chair next to her bed. 'What has he done? Can it really be so bad that you are prepared to disinherit him?'

'You know me, Mac. I am an actress, yes, and prone to great dramatic outbursts. But, I swear, in this instance the truth is far stranger than fiction.' The tears – she was surprised she had any left – spilled over and rolled down her face. 'The truth will set you free. That old chestnut. It's not necessarily true, Mac. Sometimes a lie, a falsehood, an omission of the real facts, can be far kinder.'

'Have you ever lied to me to protect me?' Macdara asked softly.

Lady Kathleen bowed her head. 'Yes.' She had lied to him by omission when she had failed to tell him how she loved him, how she had always loved him, how jealous she had been of his and Nancy's happiness. She had lied *because* she loved him.

'Are you trying to protect me from something now?'

Lady Kathleen's mind flashed back to the day of Sister Martha's funeral, and how the sunlight had glinted in Orla's golden hair. Orla's *too* golden to be natural hair. She thought of her and JC trick-acting on the lawn, her sense of foreboding that something was awry. It had taken a while to figure out exactly what was wrong and even when she had done so, the idea sounded so preposterous, so barking-mad crazy, that she had dismissed it assiduously each and every time it reared its nasty head. And yet as an actress she was more than familiar with role play, and she was enough of a woman of the world to know that far more acting happened off the stage than on.

'Kay?' Macdara sounded anxious, watching the array of emotions flit across her face. 'Kay, what aren't you telling me?'

She dithered for a moment, then baulked. No! She couldn't do it to him. Orla, whether the real Orla, or her sister Sinéad masquerading as Orla, had brought back the joy into his life. She had heard him laugh in the past few months far more often than in the many years preceding. This, despite the fact that he was going blind. This, despite the fact that he was going to have to give up his beloved Lismore. She had no idea what Sinéad's motive might be but, whatever it was, her return to Lismore had done her old friend the power of good.

Lady Kathleen bit her lip and smiled through her tears. 'Nothing, Mac,' she said, 'there is nothing to tell.'

Macdara regarded her shrewdly. He knew her well enough not to be entirely convinced, but his main concern just then was to find out what he could do to help her. He saw her shudder and went to close the window Javier had left slightly ajar. Macdara stood for a moment looking out, just about able to make out the distant strains of music coming from JC's Hell Fire Club, although it was more bass than music. Trees, tall like sentinels, obscured the club from view. But every now and then, when the wind blew, they stood at ease, allowing lozenges of orange light to shine through the gaps.

'That is the last event at the Hell Fire Club,' Lady Kathleen spoke to his back. 'Tomorrow JC will go who knows where, and I will make arrangements to have it razed to the ground.'

'But, why?' Macdara asked quizzically, half-turning away to look at her. 'JC invested so much money in it and, by all accounts, it's very successful. Can't you get someone else to run it? It's not like you couldn't use the money.'

'No, I will have it demolished,' Lady Kathleen insisted. 'It is a bad place with an evil history. No good can come of it, though I let myself be persuaded otherwise.' She was tired and the strain showed in her voice. 'Can evil run in a family, Mac? Is it like a gene, do you think, recessive in one generation, dominant in the next?'

Macdara stayed silent for a moment, then he shook his head. 'If you had asked me that a year ago or, possibly, even a few months ago, I might have said it is. But lately I've been thinking that evil is not intrinsic. It's a perception by others, an attribution to an action we dislike or which hurts us in some way, rather than an actual reality. The perpetrator may have an entirely different view of the matter. Who is to say which is correct?'

He, Lady Kathleen guessed, was thinking of Sinéad, whilst she, inevitably, was thinking of her grandson. Macdara's views accorded with her own. It helped. Made her feel less guilty for still loving JC, despite his deplorable treatment of the gentle Javier as well as the more complex Sinéad.

Macdara turned back to the window. The wind had risen and turned marauder. It slashed at the trees like an invading army, scattering the serried ranks so that they fought and thrashed and sprang apart beneath the onslaught. Macdara strained to hear the music, heard instead a faint crackling, popping sound, a sound he had heard once before and which, even now, had the power to lift the hairs on the back of his neck. The lights from the Hell Fire Club were more visible now, orange and red and yellow. Like an optical illusion, they seemed to loom, recede, loom again, then burst into the air in a fountain of burning sparks, shaming the few stars that had ventured out into the night sky.

'Oh, my God!' Macdara blurted, his face ashen as he took in the implication. His heart thudded loud as a drum. He experienced an odd feeling of disassociation from reality suddenly, almost as though he had been transported back in time. Back to the day Nancy had died inside the burning barn.

His voice escalated in horror. 'The club, Kathleen. The Hell Fire Club, it's on fire.'

*Clare was flat out, her arm extended across the table, punctured from her latest shot, a used syringe a short distance away from her outstretched hand. The girl watched carefully for signs of movement, before slowly, carefully, placing one foot and then the other on to the floor. As quietly as humanly possible, she pulled herself into an upright position, using the headboard of the bed for leverage. The floorboards squeaked slightly. Alarmed, she quickly transferred her weight to another, relieved when Clare didn't stir. Her legs felt weak, rubbery, as if the bones inside had been removed, though she had started to practise walking, just a little, whenever she got the chance. Building up her strength. She had no clear plan in mind, no escape strategy mapped out, just a yearning to get away from the room she viewed as a prison and the woman she saw as a jailer. Now that the opportunity had finally arisen, she knew she had to take it.*

*The blood pounding in her veins, so loud she was sure no one could sleep through the noise, she tip toed across the room, picking her steps with care, scarcely daring to breathe. Clare had come back in a towering rage earlier and in her haste to medicate herself with as many drugs as possible, she had grown lax and left the key in the door. Shaking like a leaf, the girl reached out her hand, paused a moment to check on the sleeping woman one last time, then slowly turned the key in the lock. It turned easily, but she was not free yet, not until she had successfully navigated each and every steep, worn step that spiralled down from the old tower. It was pitch dark at the top of the stairs but to search for the light switch was to risk discovery. The only answer was to feel her way, inch by inch, and pray to God she didn't miss and end up breaking her neck.*

*The dark in the tower was unlike any she had known before. Unrelieved black, without even the slightest chink of light, it enshrouded her, making her feel as though she had somehow stumbled into a parallel universe, totally cut off from the rest of the world. There was, however, no option but to go forward, knowing that each and every step was leading her that bit closer to freedom. Step by step, she descended, inch by careful inch; and then finally, just as her nerves could take no more, she was at the bottom and the great wooden door that led to the outside was in front of her, shrunken in its old warped frame, powerless to stop the night from seeping through the edges, from beckoning her onward.*

*As before, the key was in the lock. It turned easily. Once. Twice. Freedom was hers.*

*Almost in a trance, she walked down the outside steps, steadying herself on railings held together by nothing more than habit and rust. The air outside was warm, gloopy as syrup. She drew it in in great gulps, filled her lungs with its sweetness, and slowly looked around, trying to get her bearings, willing herself to remember the layout of the place she had known so well, as a child. Dimly, she registered music playing nearby, people, noise, car doors slamming, laughter grating the silence to shreds. Gingerly she followed the source, careful to stick to the shadows. There was a party under way in the old church adjoining the far side of the tower. She vaguely remembered it in its ruinous state. But now it had been restored, and strangely costumed people, some wearing animal masks, were going in and out. They frightened her. They were so loud. So boisterous. A beautiful girl, dressed all in gold came out and stood at the door. Cleopatra, surveying her kingdom. She shrank further back into the shadows, knowing where she had to go, who she had to see. The game was over. It was time to reveal her hand. She was better now. Not sick. Not a junkie any more.*

*As though with independent memory, her feet led her down a path she thought she knew, past a copse of trees huddling together like leaf-shawled gossips, to the shores of a lake. Her lips curved. Wishbone Lake.*

*Tired suddenly, worried and anxious, assailed by doubts, she paused by the water's edge. Behind, she could hear the tribal thrum, thrum of the bass music rocking its amplifiers. She stood still for a while, so still that a water vole crept curiously out of the reeds and stared at her, before natural wariness reasserted itself and sent it scuttling off again. It was as if the movement of the little creature released her too.*

*Straightening her shoulders, she stared across the water, the doubts replaced by resolve. Then somebody torched the sky.*

The taxi was on the final leg of the journey back to Lismore when the radio crackled into life.

'Will all drivers please note,' came the disembodied voice at the other end, 'there is a massive fire at the Lismore Hell Fire Club. Drivers are advised to take diversionary tactics.'

Bridie jack-knifed in her seat as if she'd been shot. She rapped urgently on the back of the driver's seat. 'I need to go there,' she said, just as a fire engine raced past them, blue lights flashing, siren blaring. 'Please, take me as near as you can. I know the family that owns it. I might be able to do something to help.' Her mind raced, filled with cameos of Macdara, the fire in the barn, Nancy's death. Sinéad! As they approached Lismore, she caught the acrid whiff of smoke, saw the sky over Castle Mac Tíre lit up as though by fireworks, red tongues of flame leaping like demons for the moon.

The cabbie drew to a halt. 'Sorry, love,' he said. 'This is as near as I can go.' He gestured to flashing blue lights in front of them. 'The guards have blocked off the road.'

Bridie waited no longer. She grabbed a ten-euro note and tossed it to him, then she was out of the car and running towards Castle Mac Tíre, traversing fields and ditches, her panic lending her the kind of stamina she had not known for more than thirty years.

*

Anya found Fergal in Glengarriff's stable. The horse had knocked himself again and Fergal was tenderly attending to the injured area. He looked up in surprise as she blocked his light for a moment.

'Anya? What brings you here? I thought you might have made an early night of it after all that business with your mother.'

'Please don't call her that,' Anya said, even in her distressed state unable to stomach so close an association with the woman. She took a deep breath. 'Anyway, believe it or not, she's not the most important thing on my mind right now. We've got far greater things to worry about.'

'Such as?' Fergal wrapped a bandage over the poultice and pinned it securely in place.

'Macdara,' Anya said bluntly. 'And Orla, who isn't Orla at all, but her sister, Sinéad.'

'You're talking in riddles,' Fergal said, gently returning Glengarriff's hoof to the floor and patting his flank gently.

'Just hear me out,' Anya insisted, her face so grave that he immediately fell silent.

'Let me get this straight,' Fergal said, when she told him of her suspicions. 'You're saying Orla and Sinéad are one and the same person, is that right?'

'That's right.' She went and stood at the half-door to the stable, gazing out over it into the night. Fergal came and stood beside her. He could smell her perfume, the same one she'd worn in Dubai. It made his senses reel.

'It's a lot to swallow,' he said, trying hard to keep himself on track and refrain from pulling her into his arms and kissing her till she begged for mercy.

'It is, but it's not impossible,' Anya pointed out, as searingly aware of him as he was of her, yet also greatly comforted by his presence. 'And, after what Monique said, it's got to be more than just a coincidence.'

'But where's the real Orla then?' Fergal frowned into his glass. 'Who's to say she wouldn't just turn up out of the blue and rumble the deception? Bit of a risk for Sinéad.'

322

'Unless Sinéad *knows* her sister won't turn up.' A moth of some sort blundered past. Anya tracked its erratic flight. 'Maybe she's dead. Monique also mentioned a sister who was a serious junkie. She thought she might well be dead by this stage.'

'Which,' Fergal agreed, 'would leave the field clear for Sinéad to engage in the deception. But what I don't get is why she should go to all that trouble. Why didn't she just turn up as herself? It seems downright crazy to go to those lengths.'

'Because Macdara blamed her, remember, for his wife's death. God knows what effect that had on her. I daresay she knew it unlikely she would receive anything like the fanfare her blue-eyed sister could have expected.'

'Then why come back at all?'

'Loneliness, maybe. Who knows? If Orla really is dead, maybe a primeval need to touch base with the only family she has left?' In which case, Anya felt she could really relate to the other girl. Since losing Sister Martha, she had occasionally dabbled with the idea of getting in touch with her mother's family. But fear held her back. Fear of rejection. Fear that she would be a disappointment to them, or they to her.

'It all sounds completely bonkers.' Fergal looked sceptical. 'On the other hand, would a completely sane person pull that stunt about me shooting at her? She might well be insane.'

'My worry is Macdara,' Anya said. 'He'll be devastated.' It was a clear night and the moon shone full on her lovely face, lending a silver cast to her eyes.

'You really love him, don't you?' Fergal said softly. 'He's a lucky man.' He turned and pulled her gently into his arms. Surprised, her head tipped back and he took advantage of the moment to kiss her tenderly on the lips. 'Do you love me as much?'

'Oh yes! Every bit as much. Possibly even a bit more,' Anya said with fervour.

'Then I'm a lucky man too.' Fergal punctuated his words with little kisses. 'The luckiest man in the whole world.'

'Fergal,' Anya extracted herself gently from his grip. 'I need to tell you something.' She hesitated. 'It's about Monique – I saw you

323

with her in Dubai, out in the garden.' Where the moon met water.

'Really? You came to look for me?' Fergal looked pleased first, then worried. 'Oh, you think …? No. Nothing happened, I promise. The truth is I couldn't sleep, knowing you were a mere breath away on the other side of that ridiculous wall of pillows and that I wasn't allowed to reach over and touch you. In the end, I was so frustrated, I went to walk it off.'

'But I saw you in her arms,' Anya insisted.

'For a split second,' Fergal admitted, 'before I realised that opportunistic sex was a poor substitute for the love I felt for you. She wasn't overly happy, as I recall. I think the doorman got lucky though.'

Anya's brow cleared. That went some way towards explaining Monique's strange mood after her claimed one-night-stand with Fergal. Her heart started to sing with pure happiness.

'Are you really saying you loved me back then?'

'Long before that,' Fergal said. 'Virtually from the day you arrived at Lismore, looking all mouse-like and frightened.'

'But Macdara warned you off. He told me.'

'Yes. He was so protective of you, like he wanted to wrap you up in cotton wool and stow you in a glass case away from any harm. I didn't quite know how to approach you. What to make of you.'

'There were reasons for that,' Anya said shyly. 'Reasons I'd rather not go into at the moment.' Not quite able to believe her own daring, she reached out and traced the line of his lips with her fingers. 'One day. One day when the time is right, I'll tell you everything.'

'Fair enough, I won't push you.' Fergal caught her hand and kissed each finger in turn. 'But maybe that time will come sooner than you think.' He held her slightly away from him. 'Anya, did you ever think of getting married? To me, I mean.'

Anya smiled. 'Fergal,' she asked softly. 'Is that a proposal?'

He nodded. 'I suppose it is.'

'Well then the answer is yes. Most definitely yes.' Anya sighed with delight as he pulled her back into his arms and took up where he had left off a moment before. And then all hell broke loose.

'Fire! Fire!' A groom yelled, running out of a nearby stall, mobile phone in hand. 'Over at the Hell Fire Club. The services are calling for volunteers. It's burning out of control.'

Fergal and Anya didn't wait to hear any more.

Orla was steadily getting drunk, fuelling herself on champagne. She glanced at the bottle, green, floral. Perrier-Jouet! It conjured a memory of another lifetime, a balcony in Sydney. Was she really the same girl who had stood there on New Year's Eve gazing out at the fireworks breaking over Sydney Harbour? Odd, she couldn't seem to relate to her at all. That girl seemed strangely innocent now, despite the murkiness of her private life. What she had become since made all of that pale into insignificance. She had become a monster, JC's monster, eaten up with thoughts of revenge. His monster. His puppet. His fool!

Someone made to take the bottle from her. She snarled and they retreated empty-handed. She topped up her glass and drank deeply, her eyes searching for JC amongst the crowd thronging the room. Snatches of conversation came her way, shards of brittle laughter, both fake and drunken. She was reminded of *The Orgy*, Hogarth's painting of a room full of licentious, immoral and vulgar people getting off their faces, more bestial than human. That impression was, of course, strengthened in a more literal sense by the animal masks surrounding her, many of which had long since been abandoned by their owners so that they now stood on various perches around the room, gaping lifelessly through empty eye sockets. Perhaps it was the wine goggles that enabled her to see things more clearly, but suddenly her surroundings seemed to take on a new clarity and Orla could see the club for what it really was, tacky and tawdry, filled with tacky and tawdry people. And suddenly she wanted to cry for something that was lost to her, something that had been stolen from her so long ago she could no longer remember what it was like. Her innocence.

The glass fell from her fingers and shattered on the ground. She drank now directly from the bottle, violently self-medicating. A group of revellers rushed past carrying makeshift torches they'd lit from one of the fire pits. Through a haze Orla watched one slip on a wet pool of spilled alcohol. The torch fell from his hand. Time seemed almost to stop and the bystanders to freeze with the enormity, the inevitability of what was going to happen next.

There was a whoosh of blue and yellow flames. Then a scream.

Fire!

'Has anyone seen Orla?' Frantically, Macdara ran from group to group desperate for news of his granddaughter. Truly, it was a nightmarish scene, a reel from a Wes Craven horror movie. Small groups of fantastically costumed people, some wearing bizarre animal masks, huddled together, eerily lit up against a background of wall-to-wall flame. The smell of burning wood was all pervasive, choking, eye-stinging. The concerted efforts of several teams of firefighters, drawn from near and far, did little to quench the inferno. Instead, it hissed and spat, like an enraged devil, shooting fountains of embers high into the air, feeding off its own rage and momentum.

'Mac! Mac!' Bridie yelled, catching sight of him as he dashed from one group to another. 'Are you all right?' She ran and caught up with him, her hair wild from her flight across the fields, her breath dredged up in hard gasps.

'I'm fine!' Macdara shouted above the noise, his face blackened by soot. 'It's Orla. I can't find her anywhere.'

'I'm sure she's fine.' Bridie waved a hand round to indicate the party-goers. 'She'll be somewhere amongst that lot, you'll see.' Her eyes scanned the crowd. 'Look, there's Anya and Fergal. Maybe they've seen her?'

Hopeful, they strode across, but Anya and Fergal had just arrived on the scene and were looking shell-shocked at the Danteesque blaze unfolding before them.

'Did they get everybody out?' Anya asked, clutching on to Fergal's hand for dear life.

'I think so,' Bridie told them, flinching as there was a loud bang and part of the Hell Fire Club's roof caved in.

'But I can't find Orla,' Macdara said, his face creased with worry.

'I expect she's with those people over there,' Fergal echoed Bridie's words. 'It's complete chaos here. It'll take a while to round up everybody.'

'What started the blaze?' Anya asked.

'Too early to say,' Bridie said. 'But it seems like they had indoor fire pits. That might have been a factor.'

'Jesus.' Fergal shook his head. 'I've never been a big fan of JC, but I wouldn't wish this on my worst enemy. This will ruin him, for sure.'

A sudden collective scream went up, and they saw that the fire had spread to the old disused tower tacked on to the side of the club. Flames were licking up the walls, seeking footholds on the old stones, climbing ever higher. The scream changed to a disbelieving groan as a woman bolted from amongst the crowd and ran up the burning steps leading to the wooden door which had also caught ablaze and was going up like tinder. She seemed to pause for a moment and scan the crowd as though looking for someone. Gold on gold, against the flames, she stood in her ridiculous Cleopatra outfit, one slender hand raised almost in apology or farewell. Then the flames leaped higher and, just like a magician's vanishing act, she was gone.

'Orla!' Macdara's shout knifed from his throat. 'Orla!' His legs buckled and he would have fallen had Fergal and Anya not moved quickly to catch him. 'Orla!' The cry became a sob, a cry of pain, the only sound to be heard now in the dreadful silence that had fallen. Apart from the spiteful chuckle of the all-consuming flames.

JC stood riveted to the spot, staring at the blazing tower, not quite able to believe the evidence of his eyes. How could everything have gone so wrong in such a short space of time? How could he have lost everything?

Liam appeared at his side, cradling an Anubis dog mask abandoned by one of the revellers and to which he had taken a shine.

'Fucking stupid bitch,' he said, following the direction of JC's gaze. 'What the hell did she do that for? What could possibly be so

327

important in that old place it's worth risking your life for?'

JC didn't reply. Instead, shorn of all pride, his dignity no longer a thing of importance, he dropped to his knees, buried his face in his hands and to Liam's disgust wept openly for all to see, like a big girl's blouse to quote one of the vet's favourite phrases.

Head bent, Macdara was sitting on a chair someone had found for him somewhere. His sobs had died away to just the odd hard grunt of pain. One hand lay across his heart, as if to hold it in place. His body heaved and shook. Bridie, Fergal and Anya closed ranks around him, protecting him from the inquisitive stares and sympathetic glances of the onlookers, despite all three also being in a state of deep shock. Little by little, the firefighters were winning the battle and the flames, though far from vanquished, were beginning to lose their teeth.

Gradually there was a susurration among the crowd, a low murmuring like wind hissing through a field of corn, growing and swelling into tones approaching near wonderment. Looking up for the cause, they saw a girl walk towards them, golden hair unbound, loose around her shoulders. She was dressed in a gown of some sort, long and white. It pooled at her bare feet and whispered along the grass behind her. She looked like a ghost. She almost was a ghost.

'Orla?' Macdara staggered to his feet, hands shaking, reaching for her. 'Orla?'

'Hello, Grandy,' she said, just before she collapsed at his feet.

Liam threw the mask into the passenger seat of his car and prepared to climb in after it. Although he'd been drinking heavily right up to the minute the club caught fire, he reckoned the guards would have more on their minds with all the hoo-ha going on around them than chasing after drink-drivers. He was proved wrong about that.

'Mr O'Hanlon?' A guard approached from behind and tapped him on the shoulder. 'Mr Liam O'Hanlon, can I ask you to move away from the vehicle, please?'

Liam swore softly beneath his breath but did as he was told. He turned around, his eyes widening as half a dozen guards moved purposefully in a semi circle towards him.

'Whoa, fellas!' He held his hands up in a faux jocular gesture. 'No need for that. It was just a couple of drinks, that's all. And it's not even as if you caught me in the act. For all you know, I might simply have been intending to have a kip in the car.'

'Liam O'Hanlon,' the first guard spoke again, both face and voice completely devoid of humour. 'I am arresting you on suspicion of attempted murder. You are not obliged to say anything unless you wish to do so, but anything you say may be taken down in writing and may be used in evidence.' Brusquely, he unclipped a set of handcuffs from his belt.

'What is this?' Liam struggled as the guard grabbed his hands and clamped the cuffs over his wrists. 'It's a fucking wind-up, isn't it?' He laughed unconvincingly. 'Come on, which bastard's idea is this of a funny joke?'

'It's no joke, sir,' the guard said, motioning to his colleagues, who duly broke formation, three on either side. Liam gasped as Kitty stepped through the centre gap.

'Hi, Liam,' she said. 'What's the matter? Pretty Kitty got your tongue?'

A Detective Garda was taking a statement from Javier.

'So, let's get this clear, Mr Perez. You were in the vicinity of Wishbone Lake when you saw Liam O'Hanlon wade out and drop Katherine Brennan in the water. Is that correct?'

Javier nodded earnestly. 'Correct, yes. I go there sometimes when I cannot sleep.' He tapped his head. 'When this one has too much busyness going on inside.'

The guard looked grave. 'I see. And, what happened next?'

Javier looked outraged. 'He ran away and left her to drown.'

'At which point you rescued her?'

Javier nodded vigorously. 'At first, I am afraid she is dead.' He smiled widely, and the guard could easily see why the local population, including his own daughter, were completely smitten by the exotic young man. 'But no. She is strong, Kitty. Very strong.'

'And you didn't think to call an ambulance or inform the authorities?' the guard asked, with a sharp look. 'Like *normal* people would have done!'

Javier stared kindly back. 'Of course, but Kitty say no. She was *muy* frightened he would come back and kill her. *Muy, muy* frightened. She wanted to hide, somewhere safe. I took her to Castle Mac Tíre. Plenty of empty rooms there that nobody ever go in.'

'Understandable to a degree, but still very wrong, Mr Perez,' the guard admonished. 'You realise I could charge you with wasting police time, which is a very serious matter? Several hundred man hours were wasted on the search.' He rapped sharply with his pen on the desk. 'And what about Kitty's parents? Did it not, perhaps, occur to you that they might be going through hell, climbing the walls with worry?'

Javier glared, slightly indignant. 'Yes. Yes, I am not stupid, Mr Policeman. But would they not climb more walls if Mr O'Hanlon he come back and … ?' He spread his hands and gave a deep Argentinian shrug.

The guard sighed, knowing this was one argument he had no chance of winning. 'Any idea why he tried to kill her?'

Javier patted his stomach. 'Because of the *chico*. Except there was no *chico*. Kitty, she just wants to get married.' He leaned forward confidentially. 'So she tell him little bit lie.'

Perplexed, the guard shook his head. 'So, she was trying to trick him into marriage, playing the baby card? And he wanted to kill her for that. Seems a bit harsh. My wife did exactly the same thing, but I didn't kill her.'

Javier's eyes slid to the clock on the wall. It was five a.m. and, despite JC's warning for him to stay away, he needed to get back to Castle Mac Tíre by six. After the contretemps with JC, poor Lady Kathleen was barely sleeping at all. He disliked leaving her alone.

'Drugs too,' he said, slightly impatient. 'Mr O'Hanlon, he is stealing drugs from the animal surgery at Lismore. And,' he tacked on, almost as an afterthought, 'he is also knowing who killed that poor nun lady.'

Wearily, the guard picked up his phone and dialled his

subordinate. 'Jim,' he said into the mouthpiece. 'Bring me in a large mug of tea, there's a good lad. It's tough going with Speedy Gonzales here. Plenty of sugar, and strong enough to stand the spoon in.'

# Chapter 32

Orla sat propped up against a mound of pillows in her hospital bed. She looked pale, ethereally pale, and gaunt, the skin of her face stretched across her cheekbones, tissue-paper thin. Her hair was caught back in a loose ponytail and, devoid of make-up, she looked more like a teenage waif than a woman in her twenties.

And yet, the doctors assured a preternaturally anxious Macdara, she was on the mend and was in surprisingly good physical condition, considering her ordeal. Since it was the first day she was deemed well enough to receive visitors for any length of time, Macdara, Bridie, Fergal and Anya all sat grouped around her bed. Macdara and Bridie each held one of her hands in a proprietary way, as though fearful she might vanish.

'Now,' Macdara prompted gently. 'Are you able to tell us what happened? How you came to be here. Why Sinéad was impersonating you? Everything?'

Orla's eyes filled with tears. She blinked them back. 'For me. It was all for me, Grandy.' Her voice was rusty, hoarse-sounding, like it hadn't been used for a very long time. 'I went off the rails, you see.' She nodded, as Macdara looked disbelieving. 'Yes, me, Grandy, your blue-eyed girl. Poor Sinéad, she took it very badly, she felt she had let me down.' She sniffed, closed her eyes, briefly remembering back to that time. 'There was a party, Sinéad's party. I met a boy. He was a junkie. And soon so was I.' The revelation emerged in short staccato bursts. Gently she pulled her hands free from Bridie and Macdara's grip, and held out her forearms to display the old track marks running the length of them.

'As junkies go, I was top of the class. There was nothing I didn't put up my nose, swallow, or stick into my arms. Sinéad got me into rehab several times, taking any job she could to pay for my treatment.' She made a little moue. 'And I mean *any* job.' Macdara looked sick at this revelation. It wasn't necessary for Orla to fill in the gaps. They could all imagine what she meant.

'I didn't make it easy for her, either,' she confessed. 'Junkies don't. In fact, I fought her all the way. Anyone else would just have given up and left me to die in squalor. Had the boot been on the other foot, I might well have done so myself. But Sinéad was better than me.' She held Macdara's gaze. 'She was always better than me. Stronger. Fearless. I depended on her far more than she ever depended on me. When Mother died, it was Sinéad who held us together. In truth, I feel like I'm the one who betrayed her.' She fell silent for a moment, unable to continue. Emotion, raw and painful, thickened the air in the room, as everyone felt the full impact of her words.

Macdara, more than anyone, felt sick to the pit of his stomach, shamed, guilt-ridden. He steeled himself to hear it all. He neither deserved, or wished to be spared any part of it. He captured her hand again. 'Go on,' he said softly. 'I'm listening now.'

Orla nodded, a faraway look in her eyes. 'She was at the end of her tether when JC phoned out of nowhere with a plan that would benefit them both. She was ecstatic to hear from him.' She smiled tremulously. 'She loved him, you know. From the time she was a child. There was nothing she wouldn't have done for him.' She caught Macdara's eye again. 'Including carry the blame for his psychotic behaviour.'

'Such as?' Macdara felt his skin beginning to prickle with foreboding.

'Loppy-Lou, Grandy. JC drowned her.'

'And, and the fire in the barn?' He found himself focusing intently on her lips, dreading her next words, instinct telling him what they would be.

'JC too. Then he put the matches in her hand and told her to give them to you.'

'Oh, Jesus!' Macdara's stomach flip-flopped. He felt like he might throw up. 'But why did she never say anything?' Distressed and feeling guilty too, Bridie shot him a look of profound sympathy.

Orla shrugged, as if it was obvious. 'I told you, because she loved him. More than loved him. She was obsessed with him. Honestly, Grandy, Sinéad would have faced a firing squad for him and carried his deepest, dirtiest secrets to her grave.' She bit her lip so hard that what little colour there was there blanched to white. 'And, in case you're wondering why I never said anything, it's because I never knew. I only found out the day before the fire.'

'Why then, I wonder,' Bridie mused. 'Why tell after all those years?'

'He broke her heart,' Orla said. 'Smashed it to smithereens.' Her mouth wobbled and her glance went to the window as she struggled to compose herself.

'She thought they would get married, that he would whisk her off to Argentina to his ranch at the end of the world. But of course he was simply using her to get his hands on Lismore. His plan was to sell it and buy back the ranch.' Her brow furrowed. 'But not for Sinéad. For Javier and himself. They're lovers. Did you know that?'

Fergal gave a long slow whistle through his teeth. 'It's all starting to make sense. But what I don't understand, Orla, is why she kept you concealed. She must have known Macdara would move heaven and earth to get you the help you needed.'

Orla shot an apologetic look at Macdara. 'Sorry, Grandy, but she felt like you'd really let us down in the past, and let Mother down too. How on earth were you going to react if a junkie turned up on your doorstep? If the plan to get Lismore was to work, her only hope was to masquerade as me.' She smiled sadly. 'She was pretty good at it too, you must admit. She had already gone blonde and adding the blue contact lenses pretty much took care of things appearance-wise. So many years had passed since you last saw us, she didn't think you'd look that closely. If anything, she figured out it would be the little things that would seal the deal: calling you Grandy, my special name for you; wearing my bracelet with the VIP charm on it. Reminding you, Bridie, of the pink scrambled eggs. Poor Sinéad, she used to be so jealous of those pink eggs.'

Bridie dabbed at her eyes, looking thoroughly ashamed. 'God help me, what a monster I was, making flesh of one and fowl of the other, and you both only innocent children. I could kick myself now. I could kick myself all the way to eternity and back.'

'No, all the guilt is mine,' Macdara said with feeling. All those years, I turned Sinéad into a pariah, a scapegoat. And look what came of it,' he said bitterly. 'A whole raft of tragedy was set in motion through my bullheadedness. Nancy was right. Sinéad was just an innocent child. I should have known better.' His mouth twisted. 'No wonder she wanted to extort her revenge. Who wouldn't?'

'Let yourself down from the cross, Mac,' Fergal said softly. 'How were you to know that she was protecting JC?'

Macdara was unconvinced. To his way of thinking he deserved nothing less than crucifixion, nails through his hands and feet, a crown of thorns, the lot.

'I'm surprised JC didn't object to her bringing you to Ireland,' Anya said. 'Was that not a complication too far? All that ducking and diving and risking discovery?' A thought struck her. 'All those shopping trips to Dublin? She was really visiting you, wasn't she?'

'Yes,' Orla admitted. 'Although once or twice she really did go to make it look authentic. And got some very nice shoes, as I recall.' She gave a wan smile. 'As for JC, of course he wasn't happy. But Sinéad refused to leave me behind. She insisted he find some-where safe for me, somewhere she could keep a close eye on me.' Orla's glance went back to the window, although everyone had the impression she was looking inward. 'Sinéad was such a dreamer, an incurable romantic. She spent her life in search of the happy ending.' She rolled her eyes. 'Eventually, she hoped to take me to Argentina to live with her and JC. I can't imagine that went down too well with him. He could never stand me and the feeling was mutual. Regardless, it was Sinéad's way or the highway.'

'And so JC came up with the idea of keeping you in the old, disused tower,' Anya said. 'With my mother as your nurse.'

'Not a great idea.' Orla gave her an apologetic look. 'She was an even worse junkie than me. I was on a strict regime of methadone devised by a doctor back in Oz, but after a while Clare used my supply to supplement her own habit. I ended up going cold turkey, which wasn't pleasant, although it turned out to be a good thing in the long run.'

'I can't imagine how awful it was for you.' Anya's heart ached for her, as she thought of what the other young woman must have gone through. 'My mother was an evil woman. I'm glad she's dead.'

And truly Anya was glad. She hadn't, as once she'd vowed, shed even a single tear for Clare. When the firemen had unexpectedly pulled not one, but two bodies from the ruins of the tower, Clare's and Sinéad's, Anya had felt nothing other than stark relief and the sense of a huge burden being lifted from her shoulders.

She had dreamed of Sister Martha that night. They were walking together round a small park near the convent. The dream was in black and white with accents of colour, a red rose, a green bench, the tail end of a shimmering rainbow. The nun led her over to the bench and pointed to a small plaque that had been nailed on the toprail. The inscription was very small and Anya had to lean closer and squint to read it: *Forgiveness is the fragrance that the violet sheds on the heel that has crushed it.*

Anya had woken up then, though the vividness of the dream lingered for a long while afterwards. She recognised the quotation as one of Mark Twain's, a favourite author of both hers and Sister Martha's. She also recognised the significance of the dream. Sister Martha had forgiven her mother and she was asking Anya to do the same. And, maybe, one day she would. One day. But not yet. However, the tightness in Anya's chest at the mere thought of Clare had already started to ease just a little, and the red-hot hatred was beginning to lose something of its blistering edge. There was still a long way to go, but it was a start.

Exhausted, Orla lay back against the pillows and closed her eyes, just as a nurse stuck her head round the door.

'Okay, that's enough,' the nurse said briskly, her look bouncing from the patient to the gaggle of visitors gathered round her bed. 'You can come and visit her again tomorrow. In the meantime, the poor child needs to catch up on her beauty sleep.' She clapped her hands smartly together like a school teacher. 'Come along now. Chop! Chop! Some of us haven't got all day, even if you have.'

No one objected. The nurse was right. Orla looked totally drained. One by one, they said their goodbyes and filed out.

Macdara lingered behind just long enough to drop a kiss on his beloved granddaughter's forehead. 'I love you, sweetheart,' he whispered. 'And I'm heartsick I had your sister all wrong. I'd give anything to turn back time and start all over again.' It was the old lament, uttered by virtually everybody on the planet at one time or another. A lament as useless now as always.

Orla's eyes fluttered briefly open. 'I love you too, Grandy,' she said. 'It's good to be home.'

# Epilogue – One Year On

## Argentina

Astride his horse, JC sat staring down at his beloved Estancia Del Fin Del Mundo. There were no tourists today, no barbecue singeing the air, just an air of desertion about the place and a sign, *Se Vende*. Dust devils whirled round the yard, whipped up by the first eddies of the Santa Rosa wind. The air was hot, dry. It scratched at his throat and made his eyes water. Or so he excused the sudden moistness that made it difficult to see. He blinked rapidly. A bird flew overhead, a vulture, surprisingly graceful in flight for such an ugly, cumbersome-looking creature. He shaded his eyes and watched it flap and swoop away, soaring high on the wind, high on the scent of carrion, some poor dead creature.

'Might as well come and eat me,' JC yelled after it, suddenly furious. 'Me, the late Juan Carlos Fernandez de Rosas.' His gaze turned once more to the 'for sale' sign nailed to a post outside the ranch. His shout turned to a whisper. 'I am dead too.' He bent his head and wept.

Javier spotted him from a long way away, a lonely figure hunched low over his horse's neck on the brow of Colina De Diablos, Devil's Hill. Hesitant, he reined in for a moment, then with a sudden look of determination, spurred his mount to a gallop. Hearing the muffled pounding of the horse's hooves on the hard-baked sand, JC spun round. Javier slowed his horse first to a walk, then to a complete halt. Their eyes met, black on black, unfathomable pools across the distance in between.

JC spoke first, his voice grating. He jerked his head towards the ranch. 'All this I lost,' he said, 'because of you.' His chin came up, a flash of the old arrogance in the lift. 'And you, my friend? What did you lose?'

Slowly, Javier placed his hand across his chest. 'My heart. My reason. My dignity. Myself.' He smiled gently. 'My world. You!' He nudged his horse and moved forward till the two men were within touching distance. 'I am your property, JC,' he said. 'You cannot leave me behind.'

JC looked away for the moment. He could see the vulture circling in the distance, its talons splayed, readying itself to pounce, enacting the age old circle of life and death.

Thinner, more drawn, older than Javier remembered, JC brought his gaze back.

'No, my friend,' he said, choking a little on the emotion of the moment. 'You are not my property. You *are* me. I *am* you. Apart, we are nothing.'

'Then come,' Javier said. He wheeled his horse about. 'We have plans to make.'

JC looked at him curiously. 'Plans?'

Javier grinned. '*Si*. You want your ranch back, don't you?'

## Lismore Estate

Macdara knelt at a recently dug flower-strewn grave, his hands clasped in prayer. The skeletal remains of autumn leaves swirled round him dislodged from their perches by a biting December wind. His hands had lost all sense of feeling and turned white in stark contrast to the fretwork of corded blue veins on the backs. He barely noticed. His focus was reserved for the temporary headstone, a simple wooden cross, bearing the words 'Nessa Rafferty nee Fitzgerald. R.I.P'.

It had taken a while, but he had finally managed to bring his daughter home. Back to Lismore. Back to where she belonged.

The grave to her right, also a carpet of flowers, was graced with a similar cross and plaque. 'Sinéad Rafferty, R.I.P. Youngest granddaughter of Macdara Fitzgerald'.

On a slight incline, a short distance away, Anya rose slowly to her feet. She placed a kiss on her fingertips and touched them to the Celtic Cross monument on Sister Martha's grave. 'I love you, Sister Martha,' she said softly. 'Rest in peace.'

She walked away to join Macdara, never once looking in the direction of her mother's grave, isolated and neglected, half-hidden amid a snarl of bushes. *Forgiveness is the fragrance the violet sheds on the heel that has crushed it.* Maybe, when the season of violets came round again, she would go to visit the grave. But, for the moment, only the weeds held sway.

*Kinsale – Co. Cork, Ireland*

Arm in arm, Macdara and Orla walked along the beautiful harbour in Kinsale. The sun was just setting, drawn slowly down, down into the net of the Atlantic Ocean. Small yachts, their white sails dip-dyed to peach by the dying rays, nosed lazily towards the shore. Seagulls, reluctant to bid goodbye to such a glorious day, quibbled and squawked at each other from the top of lamp-posts, eyes glittering, hard, like amber.

'Okay, Grandy?' Orla asked, as they came to a stop and looked out across the silvering expanse of water.

'More okay than I ever believed possible,' Macdara sighed, drawing her tight into his side. 'Although, I don't deserve it.'

'Sinéad wouldn't agree,' Orla said softly, instinctively guessing the route down which his thoughts were veering. 'She loved you, you know. She was just very mixed up. I do know that she'd want you to move on.'

A seabird screeched as it flew past, its shadow falling on his face. 'If only I could go back. Everything would be so different.'

Two little girls skipped past, their father and mother following behind, high-pitched childish voices rhyming some nonsense or other. Inevitably, Macdara dug out a recurring scene from his own memory, the better to torture himself with: Orla and Sinéad, dancing up the avenue at Lismore as kiddies. 'Follow the yellow brick road. Hurry up, Grandy, don't let the Wicked Witch of the West catch you.' Little did they know it wasn't wicked witches they had to worry about, but their own grandfather, thought Macdara gloomily.

'Stop!' Orla warned him, so attuned to his emotions that she could almost tell, frame by frame, what was going on in his head. 'I miss her too every day, but you can't go back, Grandy. And thinking like that is of no use to anyone. Not to you. Not to Sinéad. Not to anybody.'

A bell tinkled in the rigging of a yacht moored close by, the *Happy Ever After*. Orla pointed to it. 'Look at that, Grandy, and memorise it, because that's what we're going to be. Isn't it?' she demanded seriously, then crossed her eyes and pulled a silly face to lighten the atmosphere. 'That's what Mother would have wanted, and Sinéad. We owe it to them.' They fell silent for a moment, each exploring a different memory.

Then Macdara spoke. 'You have a wise head on young shoulders, Orla. You're right, of course. We do owe it to them.'

'Starting right now?' Orla insisted. 'This very moment?'

'This very moment,' Macdara promised. And indeed they were well on their way, he reflected, as they moved off, arm in arm again. Things had panned out far better than he'd any right to expect.

Fergal, ably assisted by his beautiful new bride, Anya, was now in complete charge of Lismore and was busy taking the estate to a whole new level. Macdara had moved to Kinsale, a lovely medieval town in County Cork, where Nancy and he had honeymooned as starry-eyed newly-weds.

In fact, he had bought the actual B&B they had stayed in, with its incredible unspoilt views out over the Atlantic, as well as the wonderful memories that nothing could tarnish. It was a family house now though, no longer a business. A new home and a fresh beginning, for him, for Orla, and for his dearest friend, Lady Kathleen, who had chosen to throw in her lot with him, and who was now in much better health as she revelled in her celebrity status amongst the locals.

Since Cork and Tipperary were neighbouring counties, they were also close enough to visit Lismore on a regular basis and to receive visits in return.

Macdara's eyesight was no better, but it was no worse either. And best of all, Orla was growing stronger by the day and was learning to put the past behind her, though sometimes still she cried in the night. That she had chosen to come and live with him caused Macdara's cup to runneth over.

Orla pulled him to a sudden stop, her nose going up in the air, sniffing appreciatively. 'Yum! Smell that, Grandy. Fish and chips. Let's bring some back for Lady Kay.'

Sublimely grateful for the small things in life and for the fresh start he'd been given, Macdara followed her happily into the shop.

*Ascot, England*

'Yay! Come on! Come on, Glengarriff!' Anya yelled, a rolled-up race programme waving in one hand, the other determined to hold on to her ridiculous hat, which the wind was equally determined to wrench from her. 'Oh, my God, I can't look. I can't look.' She shielded her eyes as Minstrel Boy drew abreast of Lismore's favourite. Then she risked a peek through one eye, and that was half-closed. 'Yes! Yes! Yes!' The programme waved madly again, then fell away dejected as the other horse edged slightly ahead. And then, just as Anya was giving up all hope and was gearing up to plaster on her 'well-second-place-isn't-too-bad' smile, a final, miraculous push from Shaymus, Glengarriff's jockey, sent him galloping clear past the post into first place.

To be accurate, only a nose past. Sufficient, however, to net him the Ascot Gold Cup. Sufficient also to beat the Queen's own runner, Minstrel Boy.

'I can't believe it! I can't believe it!' Anya did a little dance on the spot, then threw her arms around her husband, kissing him over and over again. 'Oh, Fergal, wait till Mac hears this,' she shouted joyously, allowing him, at last, to come up for air. She rummaged in her handbag for her phone. 'I'll phone him now.'

'No need,' Fergal said, laughing at her exuberance. 'Don't you know he'll have been glued to the TV?' He looped his arm through her elbow. 'Come on, Mrs Fitzgerald, you and I need to pay a visit to the winner's enclosure. There's a jockey to congratulate.'

'And a horse to praise,' Anya said, giving up on her hat and letting the wind snatch it from her to go bowling with. 'Oh, who would have thought Glengarriff would do it, especially after his injury last year?'

'Me.' Fergal blew along the tips of his fingers in a gesture of self-congratulation. 'I always knew he had it in him.'

Anya smiled at Fergal adoringly. She quite simply couldn't help herself. Fact! She did adore him. Had anyone asked, she would have told them quite categorically that, thanks to Fergal Fitzgerald, she was the happiest woman in the world. The universe! The cosmos!

'Kitty is going to be so proud too,' she said. 'After what Liam did to her, I seriously thought she'd never trust any man again.'

'Yes, she is. But Shaymus is as different to O'Hanlon as sheepshit is to gold,' Fergal said scathingly. 'There isn't a bad bone in the whole of his body. More importantly, he's a damn good jockey and he rides for us!' Fergal squeezed Anya close. 'You know, this has got to rank as the happiest day of my life.'

'The happiest day? Really?' Anya pretended pique. 'And there was I thinking that might have been our wedding day. Or, maybe the day you discovered we were expecting our own little addition to the Lismore stable.'

'Oh, next to those, of course.' He chuckled. 'Okay, I'll rephrase it. This has got to rank as *one* of the happiest days of my life.'

'That's better,' Anya chirped, following him into the enclosure where Kitty was alternating between smothering both her jockey boyfriend and Glengarriff in kisses.

'Anya! Fergal!' Her eyes were shining. 'Wasn't Shaymus great? Wasn't he fantastic?'

'Great!' Fergal said, just as Anya said, 'Fantastic!'

'He really brought out the best in Glengarriff, didn't he?'

'He did, right enough. Well done, Shaymus.' Fergal gave the young jockey a friendly puck on the arm and walked over to Glengarriff, who was panting and steaming, but looking extremely proud of himself.

'Well done, boy,' Fergal said, patting him on the side of the neck. 'I always knew you had it in you.' He blinked a sudden moistness away from his eyes. 'The first of many, eh?'

*

That night, Anya lay in bed, listening to the even breathing of her husband. This time, there was no wall of pillows marching down the centre of the bed, no obstacle to keep them apart, no misunderstandings, no secrets. She placed her hand upon her stomach, hoping to detect the first small flutter , the new life growing inside her that might never have happened had Fergal not been so understanding.

It caused her both embarrassment and pain to remember the first time Fergal had attempted to make love to her. It had been nothing less than a disaster and would have put most men off for life. Although the logical part of her knew he was nothing like Fat Ted, nothing remotely like the disgusting scum who had abused her as a child, the emotionally scarred part of Anya found it difficult to differentiate. And so, when they moved past the kissing and cuddling stage and Fergal's hand had moved downward, she fought him like a tiger, hissing and spitting, fingers clawed ready to scratch his eyes out.

Bemused by her transition from lover to raging virago, Fergal restrained her gently, held her securely, comfortingly, soothed her, kissed her tears away till they were no more than the odd hiccough against his chest. He was patient, willing to wait for however long it took his beautiful wife to lay her demons to rest.

And, gradually, the protective walls erected round Anya's past came down, brick by brick, felled not by brute force and bullying, but by a process of trust and kindness. And, most of all, by love.

Anya turned on her side and slipped an arm around his waist, tuning into the comforting rhythm of his heartbeat.

'Bye-bye, White Rabbit,' she whispered drowsily into the darkness. 'Alice doesn't live here any more.'